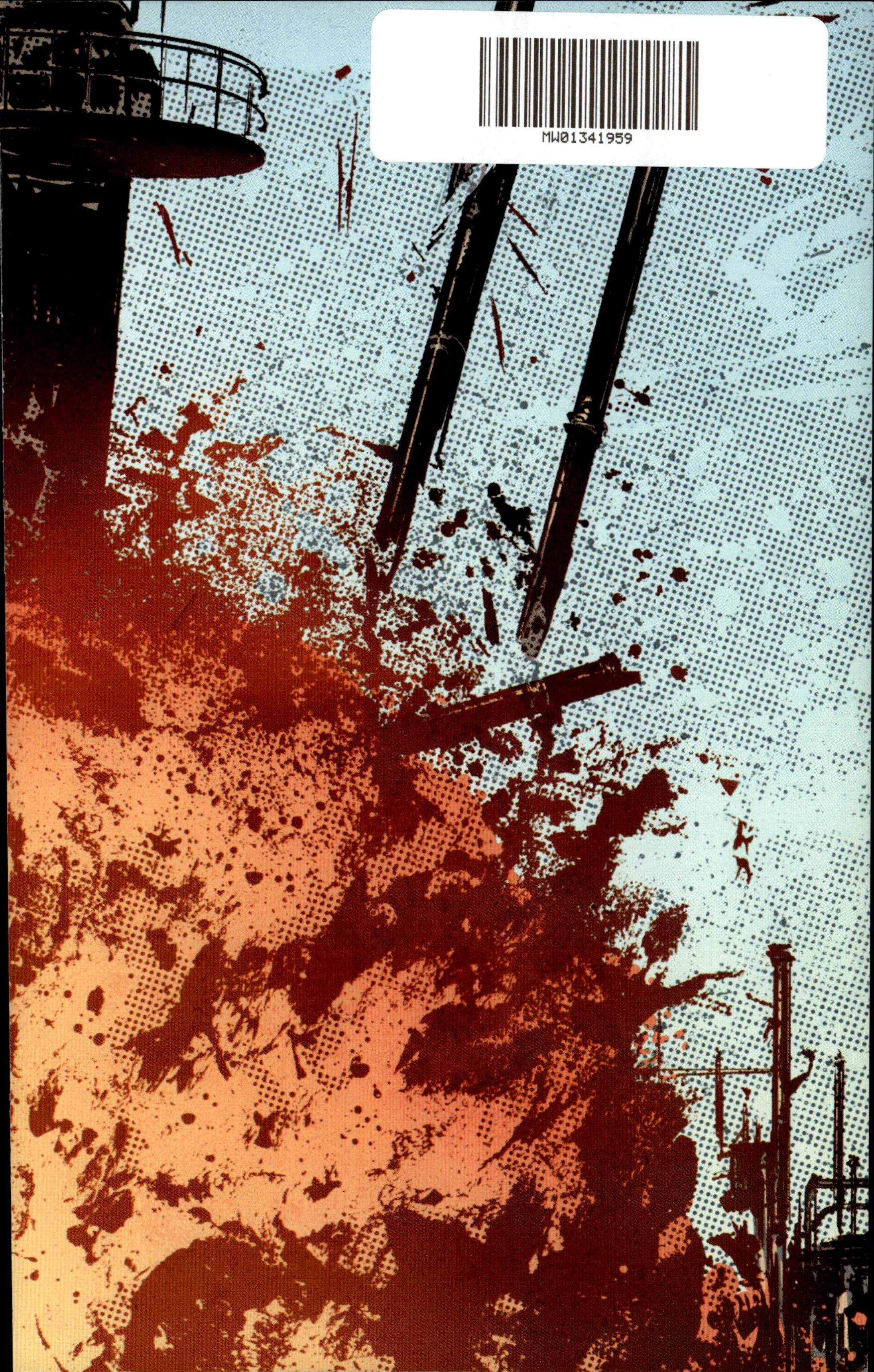

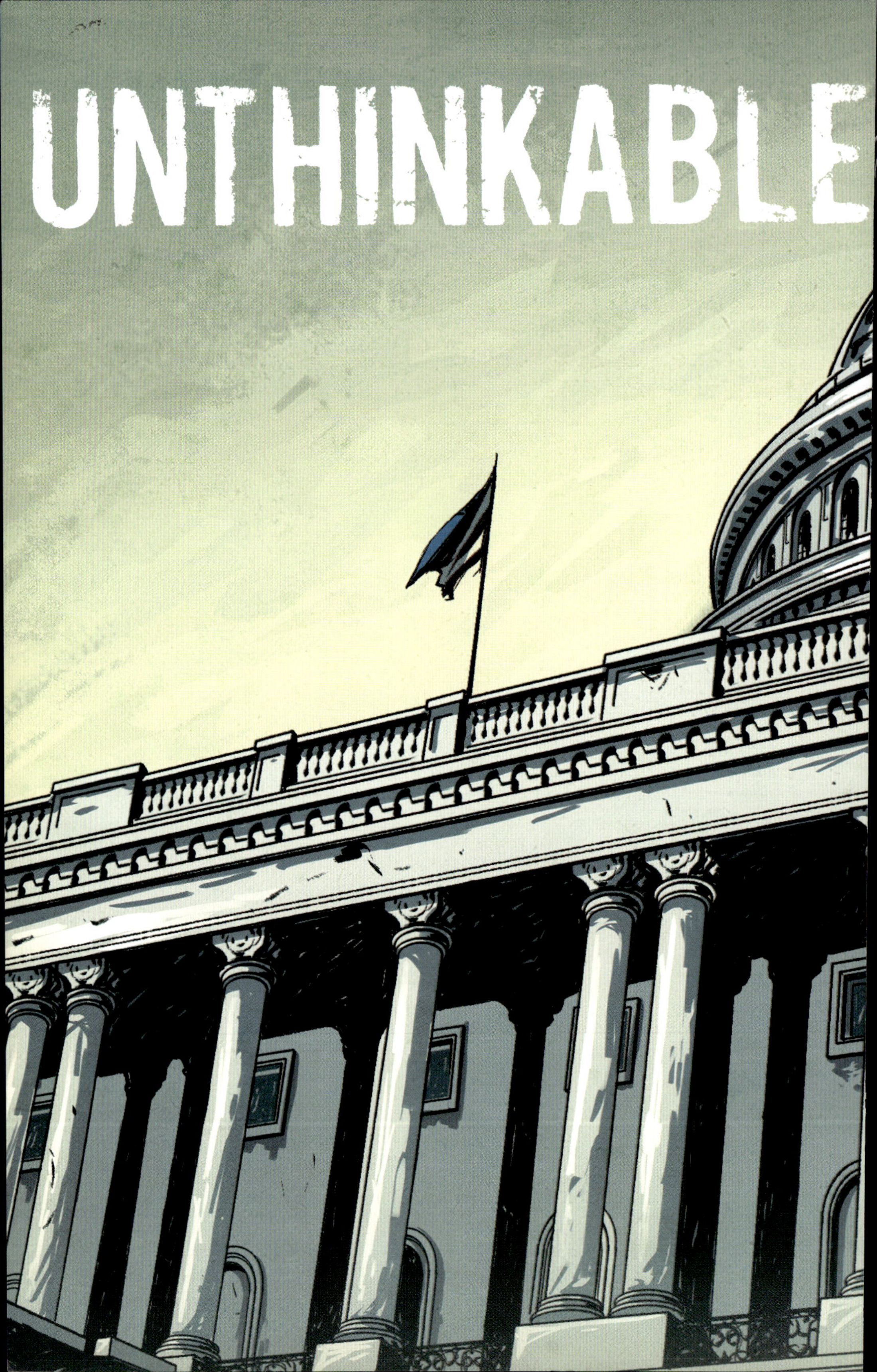
UNTHINKABLE

ADAM FORTIER
vice president,
publishing

CHIP MOSHER
marketing director

MATT GAGNON
managing editor

FIRST EDITION: OCTOBER 2009

10 9 8 7 6 5 4 3 2 1

PRINTED IN KOREA

UNTHINKABLE — October 2009 published by BOOM! Studios. Unthinkable is Copyright Mark Sable and Boom Entertainment Inc. BOOM! Studios™ and the BOOM! logo are trademarks of Boom Entertainment, Inc., registered in various countries and categories. All rights reserved. The characters and events depicted herein are fictional. Any similarity to actual persons, demons, anti-Christs, aliens, vampires, face-suckers or political figures whether living, dead or undead, or to any actual or supernatural events is coincidental and unintentional. So don't come whining to us.

Office of publication: 6310 San Vicente Blvd, Ste 404, Los Angeles, CA 90048-5457.

CREATED AND WRITTEN BY:
MARK SABLE

ARTIST:
JULIAN TOTINO TEDESCO

COLORIST:
JUAN MANUEL TUMBURÚS

LETTERER:
ED DUKESHIRE

MANAGING EDITOR:
MATT GAGNON

EDITOR-IN-CHIEF:
MARK WAID

COVERS BY:
PAUL AZACETA
COLORS/ **NICK FILARDI**

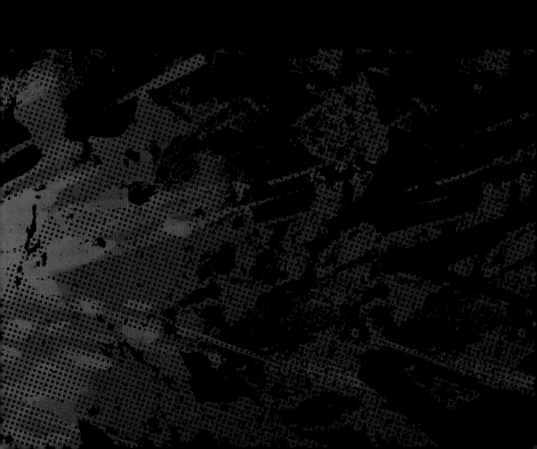

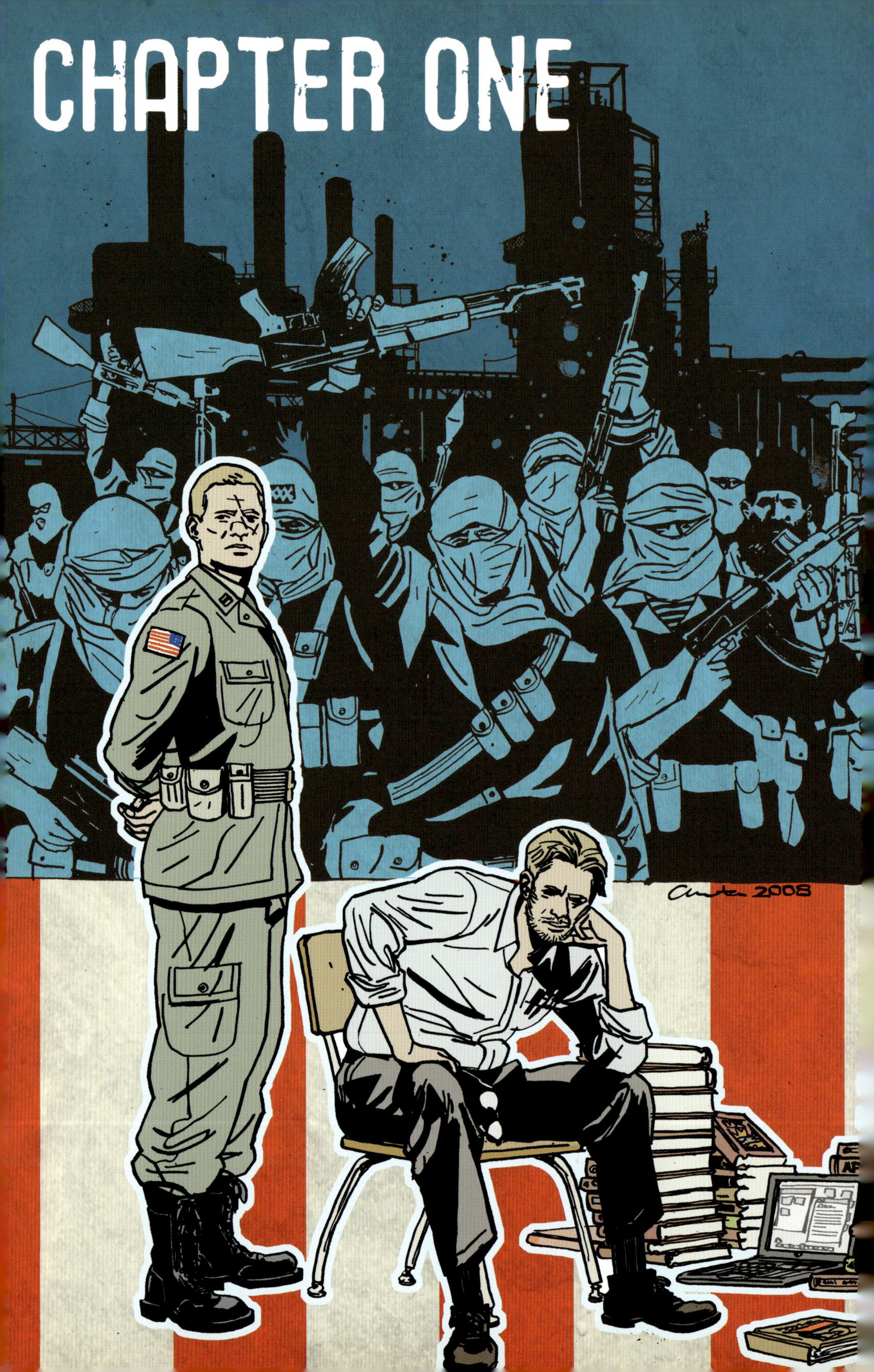
CHAPTER ONE

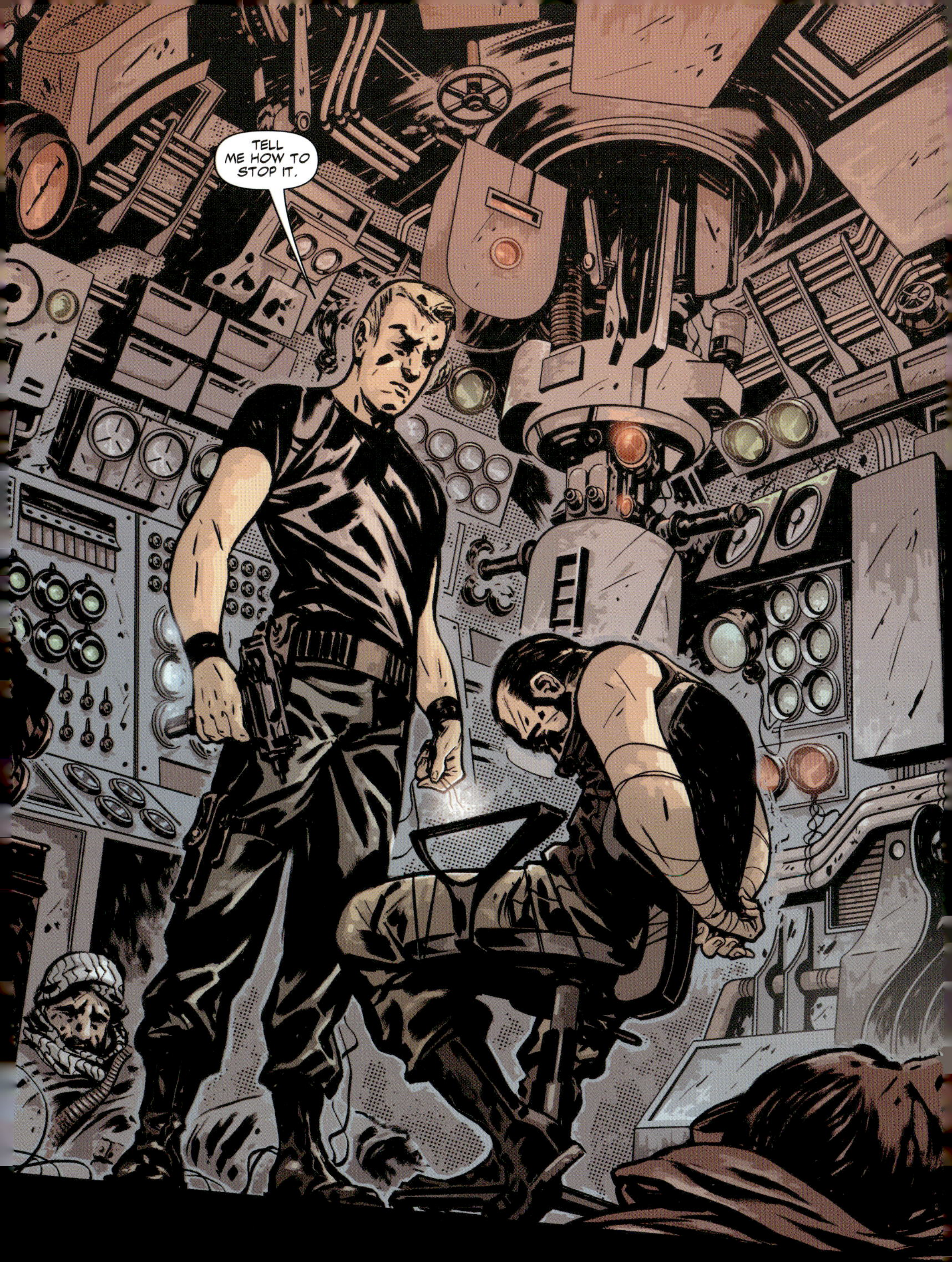
TELL ME HOW TO STOP IT.

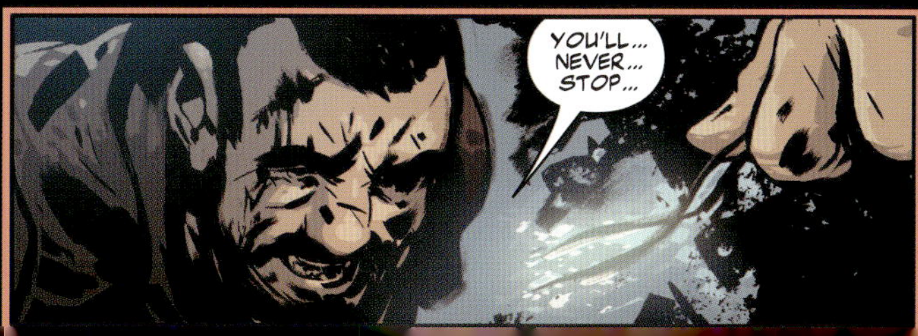
YOU'LL... NEVER... STOP...

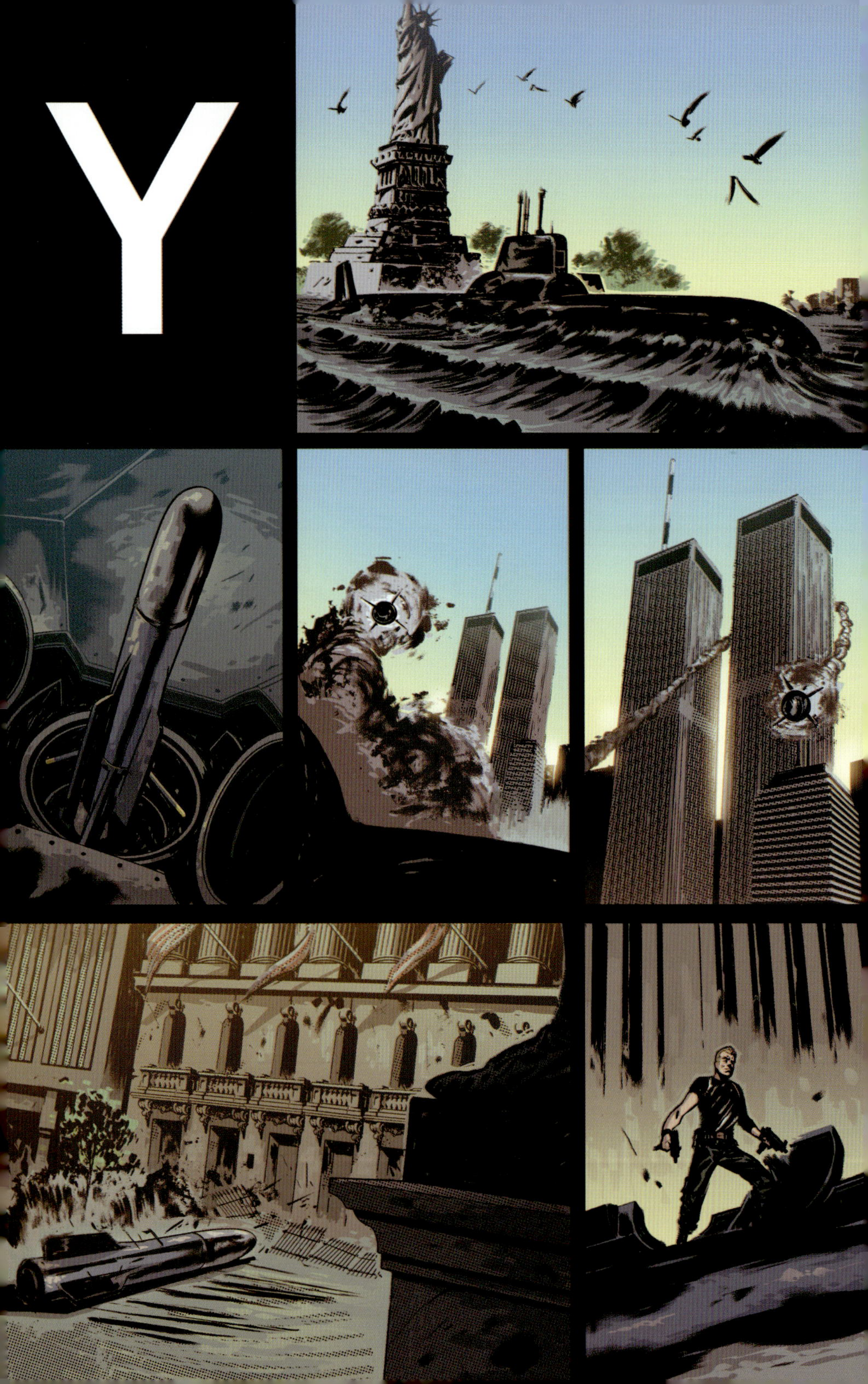
Y

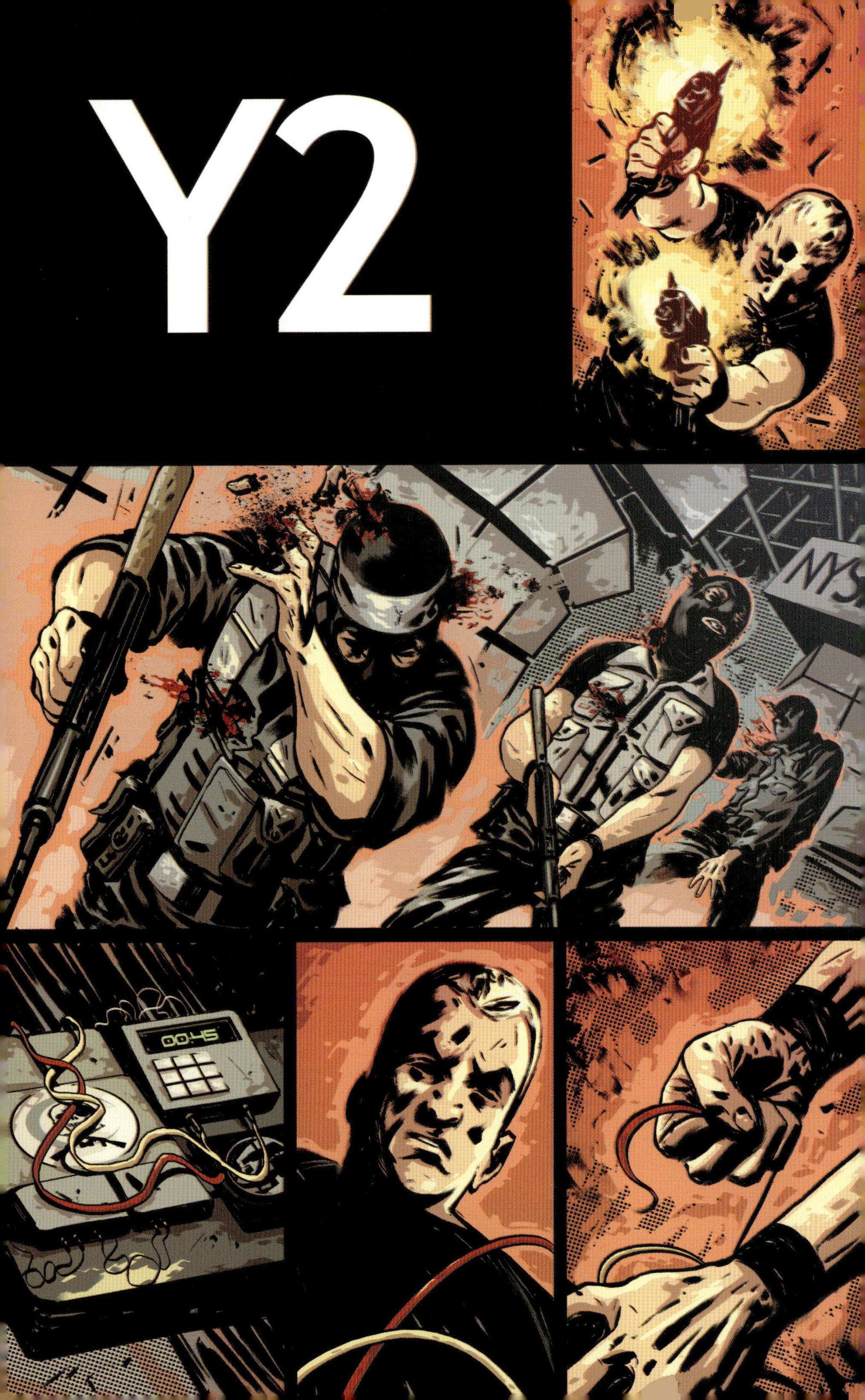
Y2
NYS
00:45

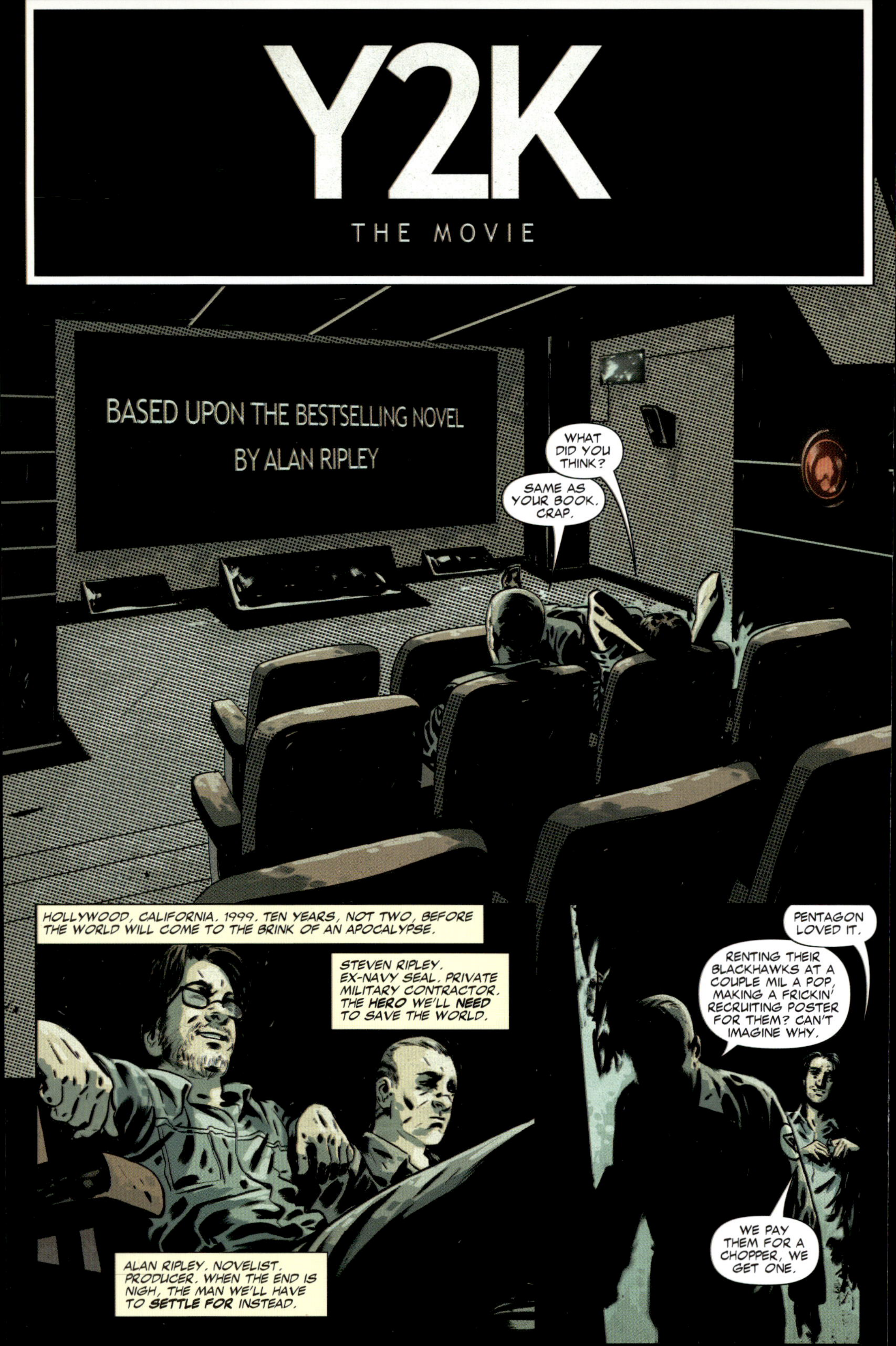
Y2K
THE MOVIE
BASED UPON THE BESTSELLING NOVEL BY ALAN RIPLEY
WHAT DID YOU THINK?
SAME AS YOUR BOOK. CRAP.
HOLLYWOOD, CALIFORNIA. 1999. TEN YEARS, NOT TWO, BEFORE THE WORLD WILL COME TO THE BRINK OF AN APOCALYPSE.
STEVEN RIPLEY. EX-NAVY SEAL. PRIVATE MILITARY CONTRACTOR. THE HERO WE'LL NEED TO SAVE THE WORLD.
ALAN RIPLEY. NOVELIST. PRODUCER. WHEN THE END IS NIGH, THE MAN WE'LL HAVE TO SETTLE FOR INSTEAD.
PENTAGON LOVED IT.
RENTING THEIR BLACKHAWKS AT A COUPLE MIL A POP, MAKING A FRICKIN' RECRUITING POSTER FOR THEM? CAN'T IMAGINE WHY.
WE PAY THEM FOR A CHOPPER, WE GET ONE.

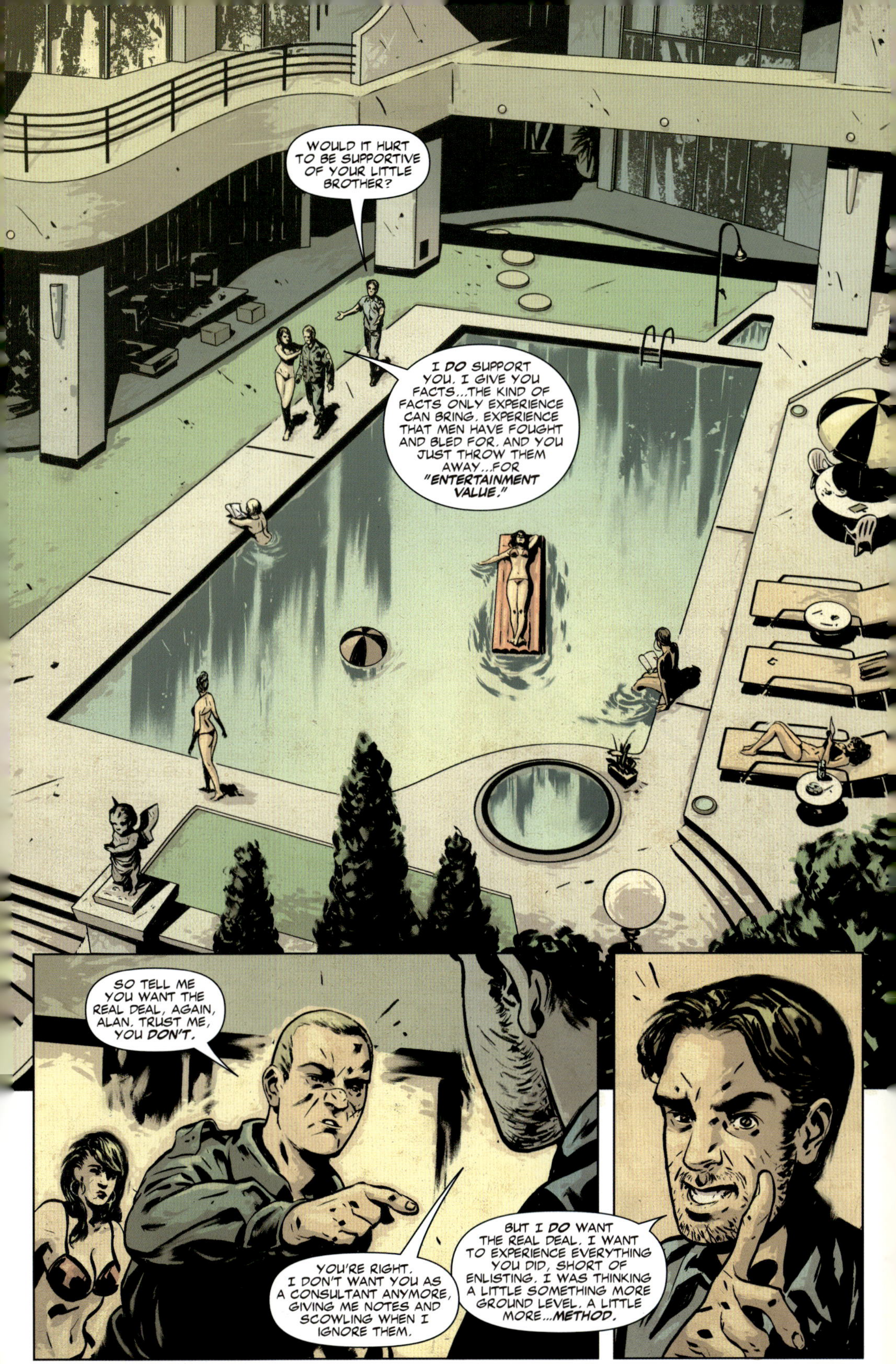
WOULD IT HURT TO BE SUPPORTIVE OF YOUR LITTLE BROTHER?
I ***DO*** SUPPORT YOU. I GIVE YOU FACTS...THE KIND OF FACTS ONLY EXPERIENCE CAN BRING. EXPERIENCE THAT MEN HAVE FOUGHT AND BLED FOR. AND YOU JUST THROW THEM AWAY...FOR ***"ENTERTAINMENT VALUE."***
SO TELL ME YOU WANT THE REAL DEAL, AGAIN, ALAN. TRUST ME, YOU ***DON'T.***
YOU'RE RIGHT. I DON'T WANT YOU AS A CONSULTANT ANYMORE, GIVING ME NOTES AND SCOWLING WHEN I IGNORE THEM.
BUT I ***DO*** WANT THE REAL DEAL. I WANT TO EXPERIENCE EVERYTHING YOU DID, SHORT OF ENLISTING. I WAS THINKING A LITTLE SOMETHING MORE GROUND LEVEL. A LITTLE MORE...***METHOD.***

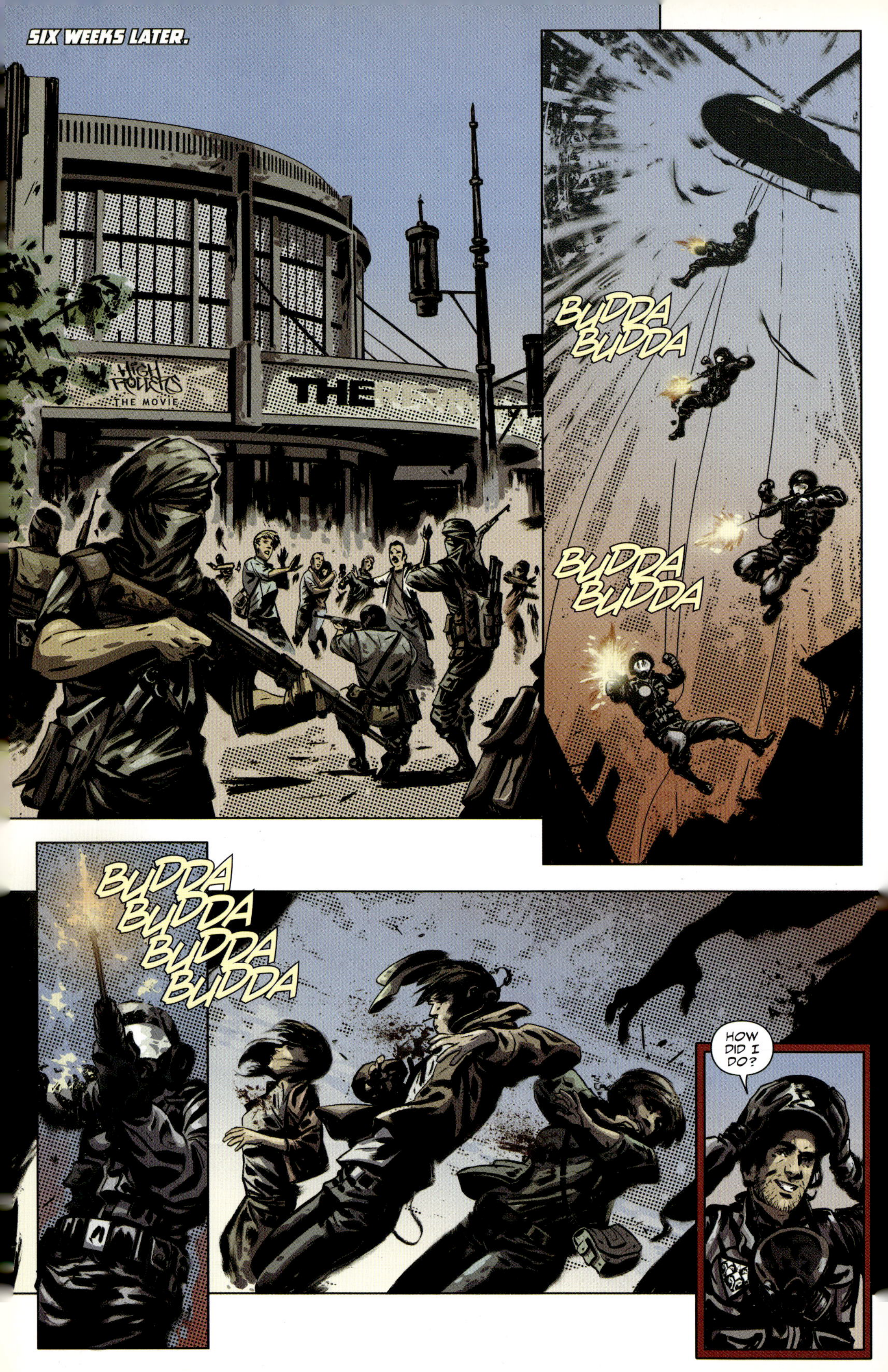
SIX WEEKS LATER.
THE MOVIE
THE
BUDDA BUDDA
BUDDA BUDDA
BUDDA BUDDA BUDDA BUDDA
HOW DID I DO?

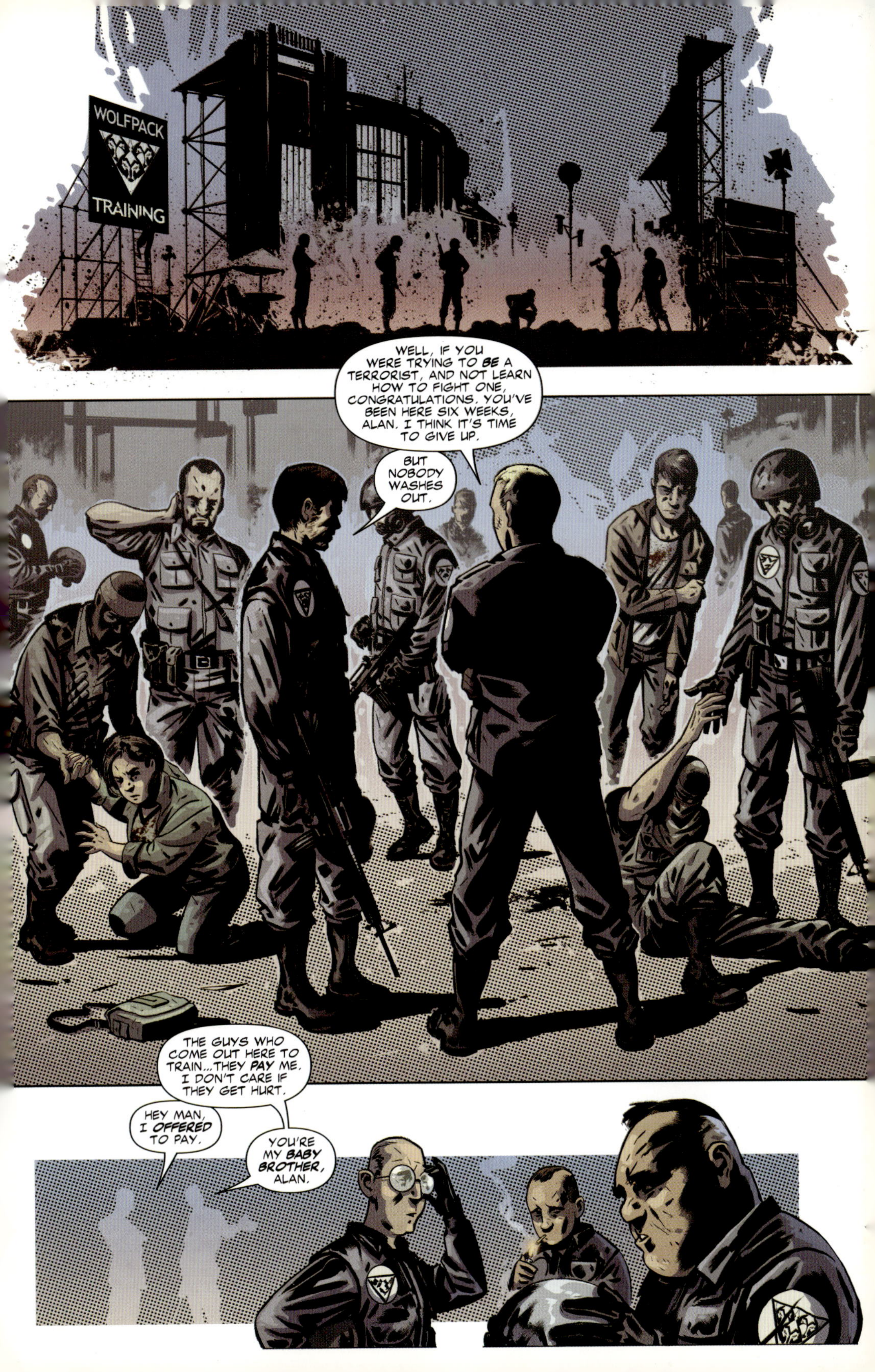
WOLFPACK
TRAINING
WELL, IF YOU WERE TRYING TO BE A TERRORIST, AND NOT LEARN HOW TO FIGHT ONE, CONGRATULATIONS. YOU'VE BEEN HERE SIX WEEKS, ALAN. I THINK IT'S TIME TO GIVE UP.
BUT NOBODY WASHES OUT.
THE GUYS WHO COME OUT HERE TO TRAIN... THEY PAY ME. I DON'T CARE IF THEY GET HURT.
HEY MAN, I OFFERED TO PAY.
YOU'RE MY BABY BROTHER, ALAN.

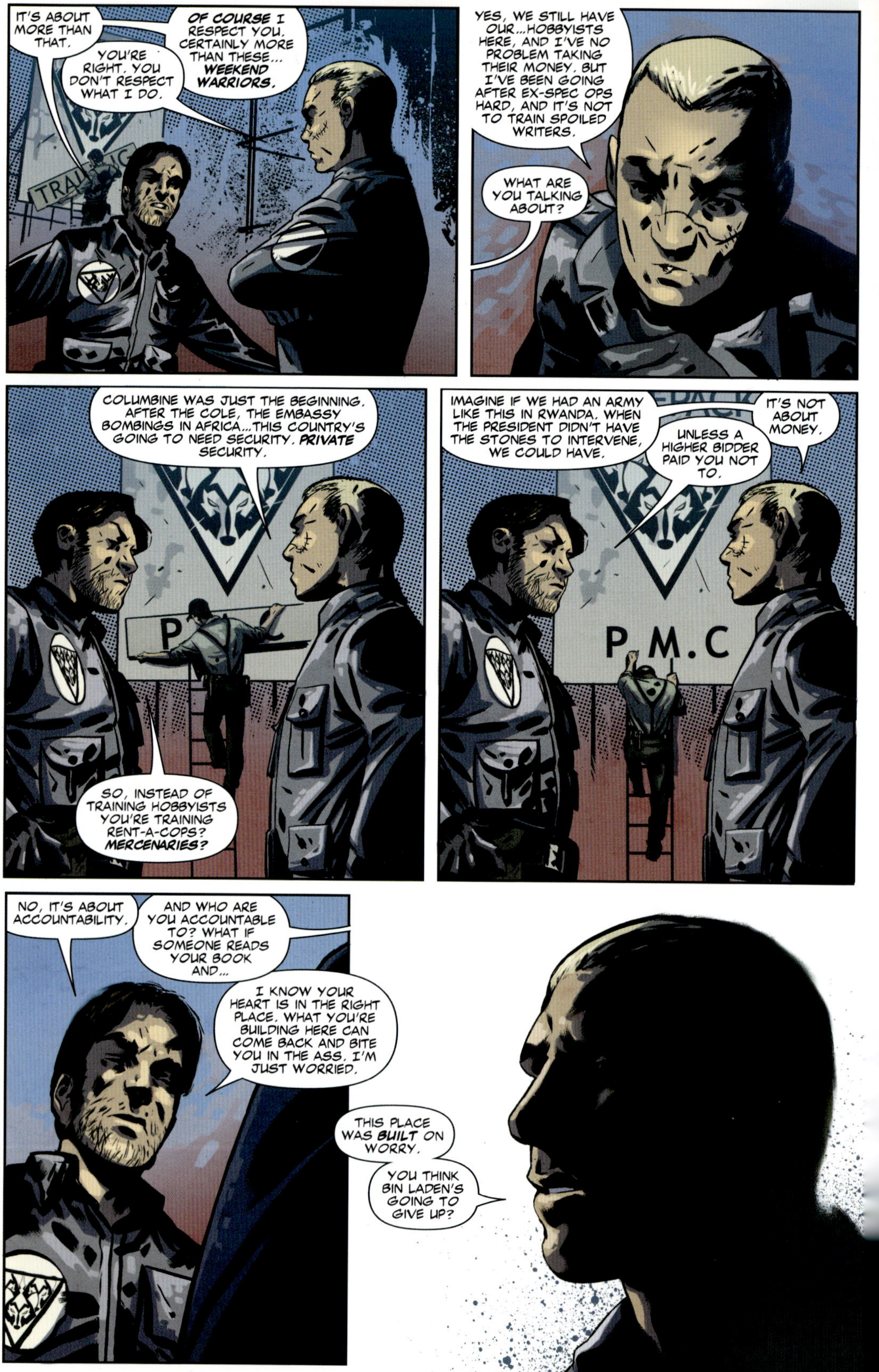
IT'S ABOUT MORE THAN THAT.
OF COURSE I RESPECT YOU. CERTAINLY MORE THAN THESE... WEEKEND WARRIORS.
YOU'RE RIGHT. YOU DON'T RESPECT WHAT I DO.
YES, WE STILL HAVE OUR...HOBBYISTS HERE, AND I'VE NO PROBLEM TAKING THEIR MONEY. BUT I'VE BEEN GOING AFTER EX-SPEC OPS HARD, AND IT'S NOT TO TRAIN SPOILED WRITERS.
WHAT ARE YOU TALKING ABOUT?
COLUMBINE WAS JUST THE BEGINNING. AFTER THE COLE, THE EMBASSY BOMBINGS IN AFRICA...THIS COUNTRY'S GOING TO NEED SECURITY. PRIVATE SECURITY.
SO, INSTEAD OF TRAINING HOBBYISTS YOU'RE TRAINING RENT-A-COPS? MERCENARIES?
IMAGINE IF WE HAD AN ARMY LIKE THIS IN RWANDA. WHEN THE PRESIDENT DIDN'T HAVE THE STONES TO INTERVENE, WE COULD HAVE.
UNLESS A HIGHER BIDDER PAID YOU NOT TO.
IT'S NOT ABOUT MONEY.
P.M.C
NO, IT'S ABOUT ACCOUNTABILITY.
AND WHO ARE YOU ACCOUNTABLE TO? WHAT IF SOMEONE READS YOUR BOOK AND...
I KNOW YOUR HEART IS IN THE RIGHT PLACE. WHAT YOU'RE BUILDING HERE CAN COME BACK AND BITE YOU IN THE ASS. I'M JUST WORRIED.
THIS PLACE WAS BUILT ON WORRY.
YOU THINK BIN LADEN'S GOING TO GIVE UP?

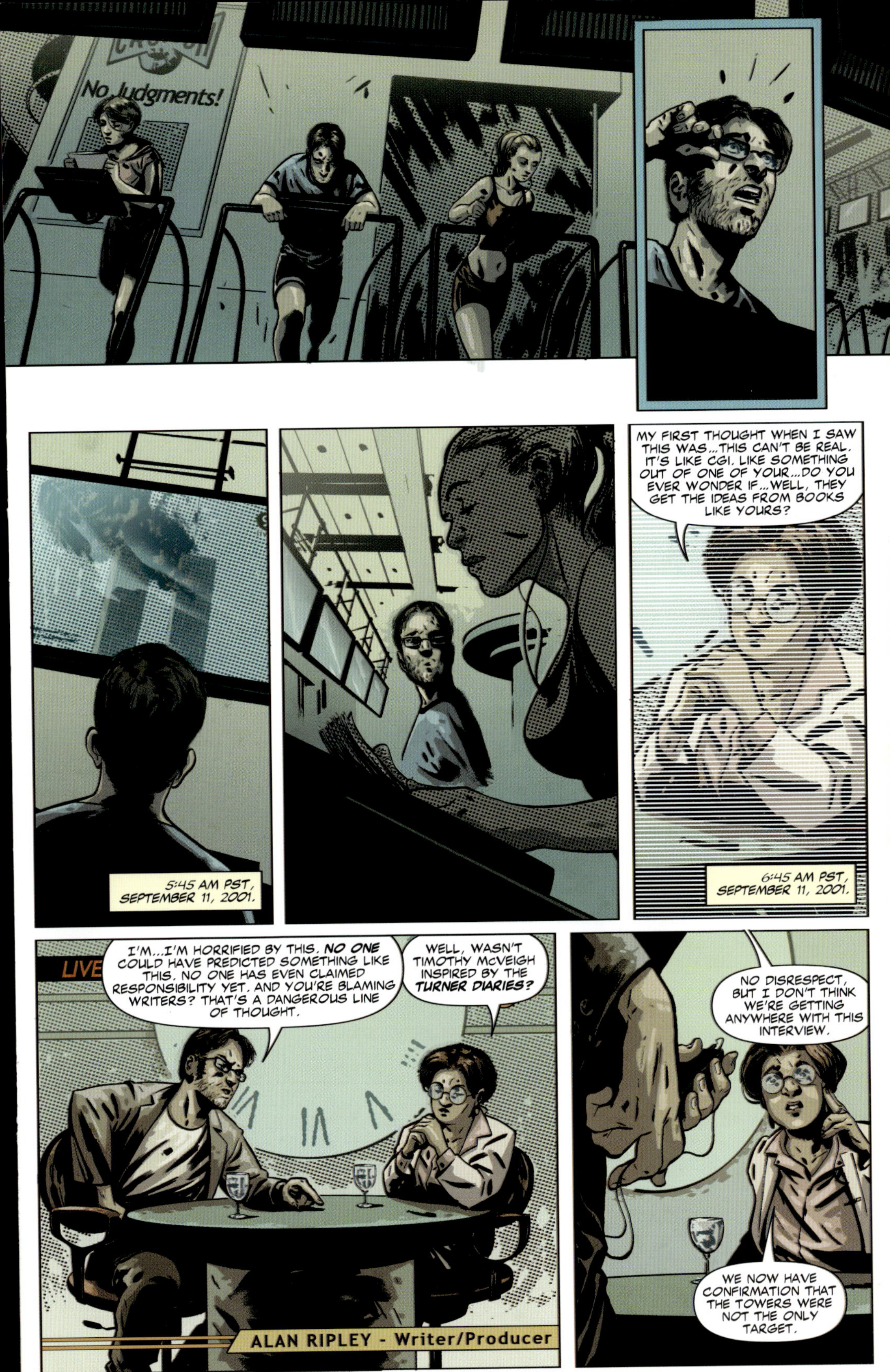
No Judgments!
MY FIRST THOUGHT WHEN I SAW THIS WAS... THIS CAN'T BE REAL. IT'S LIKE CGI. LIKE SOMETHING OUT OF ONE OF YOUR... DO YOU EVER WONDER IF... WELL, THEY GET THE IDEAS FROM BOOKS LIKE YOURS?
5:45 AM PST, SEPTEMBER 11, 2001.
6:45 AM PST, SEPTEMBER 11, 2001.
LIVE
I'M... I'M HORRIFIED BY THIS. NO ONE COULD HAVE PREDICTED SOMETHING LIKE THIS. NO ONE HAS EVEN CLAIMED RESPONSIBILITY YET. AND YOU'RE BLAMING WRITERS? THAT'S A DANGEROUS LINE OF THOUGHT.
WELL, WASN'T TIMOTHY McVEIGH INSPIRED BY THE TURNER DIARIES?
ALAN RIPLEY - Writer/Producer
NO DISRESPECT, BUT I DON'T THINK WE'RE GETTING ANYWHERE WITH THIS INTERVIEW.
WE NOW HAVE CONFIRMATION THAT THE TOWERS WERE NOT THE ONLY TARGET.

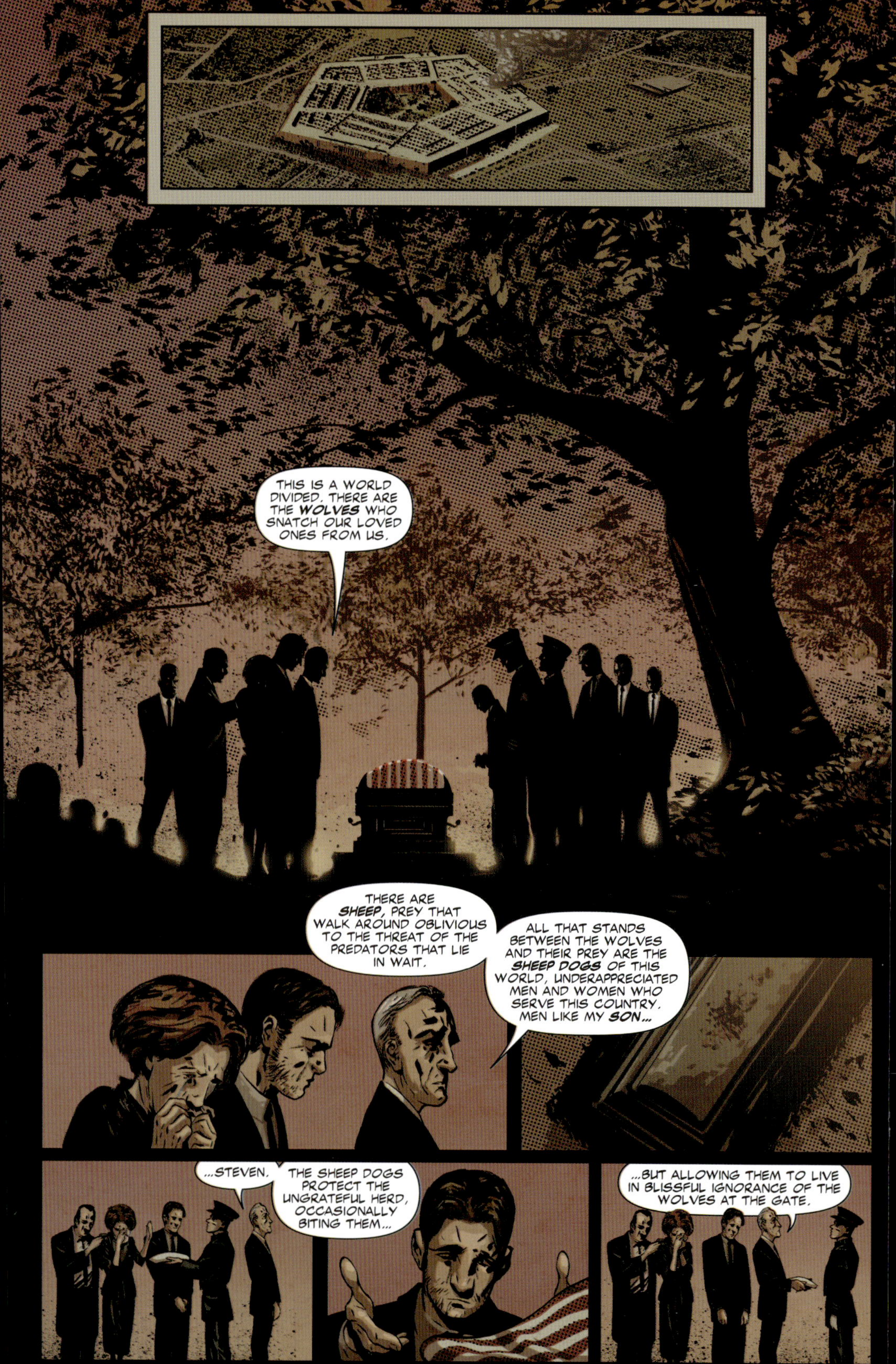
THIS IS A WORLD DIVIDED. THERE ARE THE WOLVES WHO SNATCH OUR LOVED ONES FROM US.
THERE ARE SHEEP, PREY THAT WALK AROUND OBLIVIOUS TO THE THREAT OF THE PREDATORS THAT LIE IN WAIT.
ALL THAT STANDS BETWEEN THE WOLVES AND THEIR PREY ARE THE SHEEP DOGS OF THIS WORLD, UNDERAPPRECIATED MEN AND WOMEN WHO SERVE THIS COUNTRY. MEN LIKE MY SON...
...STEVEN.
THE SHEEP DOGS PROTECT THE UNGRATEFUL HERD, OCCASIONALLY BITING THEM...
...BUT ALLOWING THEM TO LIVE IN BLISSFUL IGNORANCE OF THE WOLVES AT THE GATE.

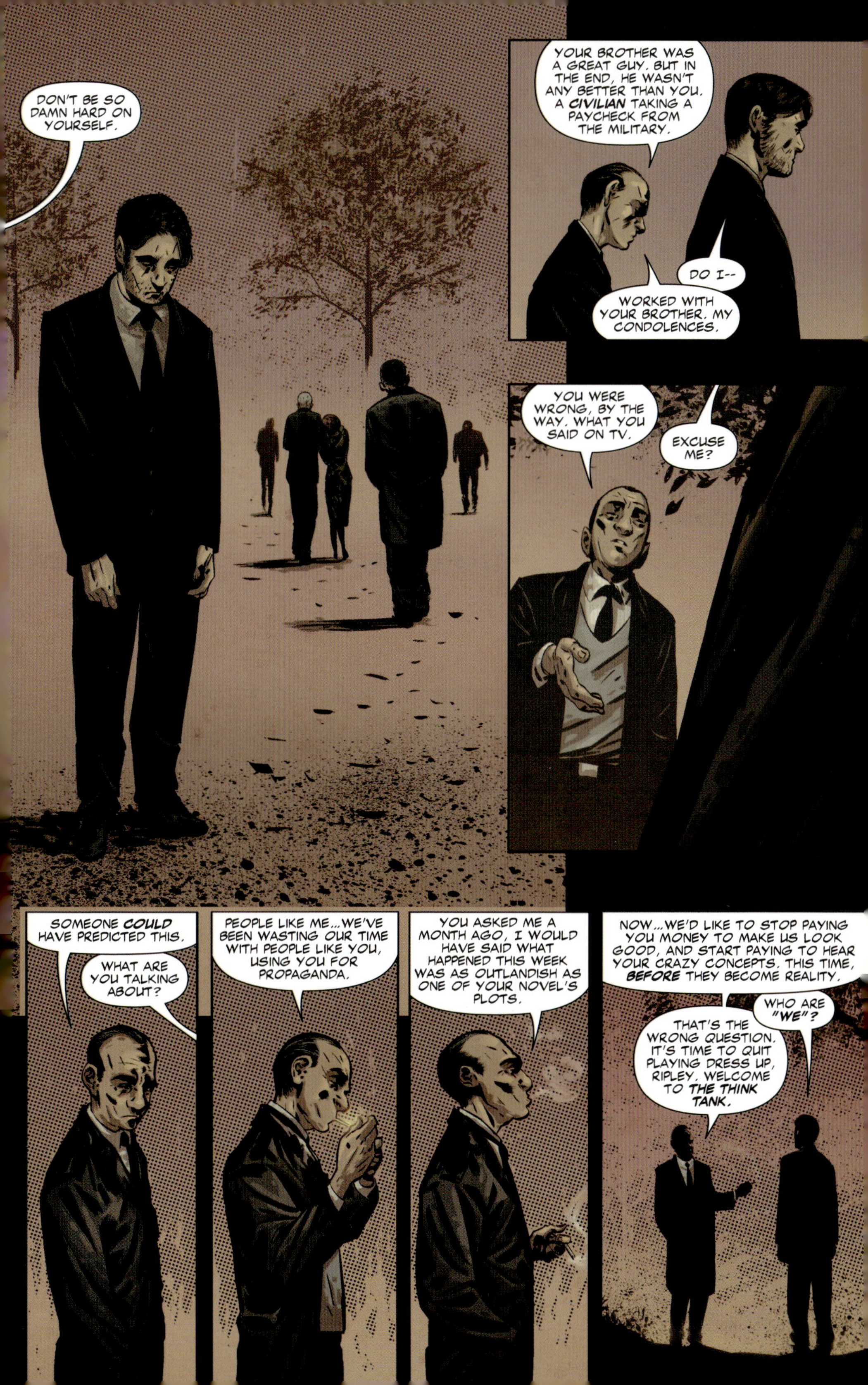
DON'T BE SO DAMN HARD ON YOURSELF.
YOUR BROTHER WAS A GREAT GUY. BUT IN THE END, HE WASN'T ANY BETTER THAN YOU. A CIVILIAN TAKING A PAYCHECK FROM THE MILITARY.
DO I--
WORKED WITH YOUR BROTHER. MY CONDOLENCES.
YOU WERE WRONG, BY THE WAY. WHAT YOU SAID ON TV.
EXCUSE ME?
SOMEONE COULD HAVE PREDICTED THIS.
WHAT ARE YOU TALKING ABOUT?
PEOPLE LIKE ME...WE'VE BEEN WASTING OUR TIME WITH PEOPLE LIKE YOU, USING YOU FOR PROPAGANDA.
YOU ASKED ME A MONTH AGO, I WOULD HAVE SAID WHAT HAPPENED THIS WEEK WAS AS OUTLANDISH AS ONE OF YOUR NOVEL'S PLOTS.
NOW...WE'D LIKE TO STOP PAYING YOU MONEY TO MAKE US LOOK GOOD, AND START PAYING TO HEAR YOUR CRAZY CONCEPTS. THIS TIME, BEFORE THEY BECOME REALITY.
WHO ARE "WE"?
THAT'S THE WRONG QUESTION. IT'S TIME TO QUIT PLAYING DRESS UP, RIPLEY. WELCOME TO THE THINK TANK.

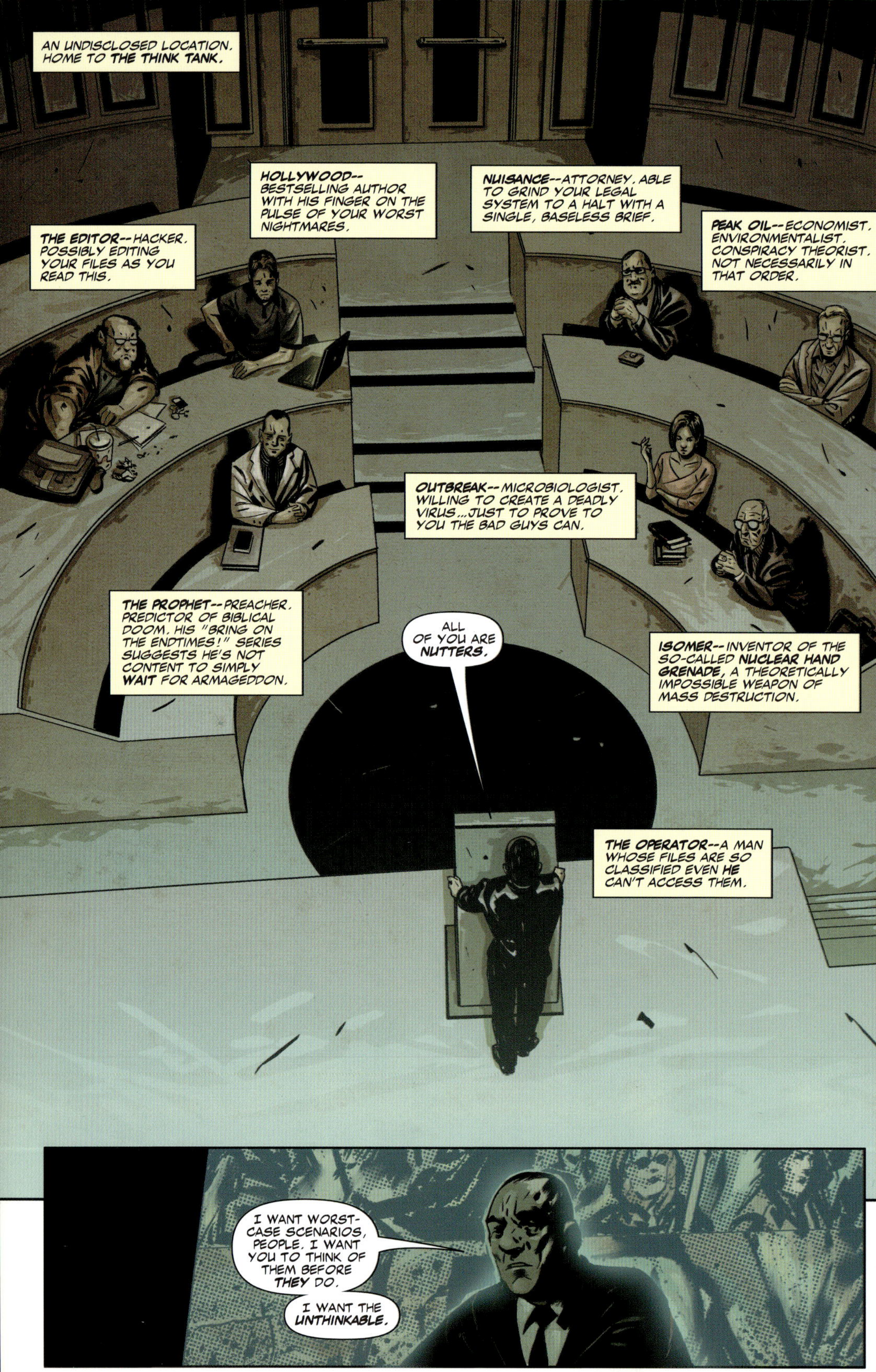
AN UNDISCLOSED LOCATION. HOME TO THE THINK TANK.
THE EDITOR--HACKER. POSSIBLY EDITING YOUR FILES AS YOU READ THIS.
HOLLYWOOD--BESTSELLING AUTHOR WITH HIS FINGER ON THE PULSE OF YOUR WORST NIGHTMARES.
NUISANCE--ATTORNEY. ABLE TO GRIND YOUR LEGAL SYSTEM TO A HALT WITH A SINGLE, BASELESS BRIEF.
PEAK OIL--ECONOMIST. ENVIRONMENTALIST. CONSPIRACY THEORIST. NOT NECESSARILY IN THAT ORDER.
OUTBREAK--MICROBIOLOGIST. WILLING TO CREATE A DEADLY VIRUS...JUST TO PROVE TO YOU THE BAD GUYS CAN.
THE PROPHET--PREACHER. PREDICTOR OF BIBLICAL DOOM. HIS "BRING ON THE ENDTIMES!" SERIES SUGGESTS HE'S NOT CONTENT TO SIMPLY WAIT FOR ARMAGEDDON.
ALL OF YOU ARE NUTTERS.
ISOMER--INVENTOR OF THE SO-CALLED NUCLEAR HAND GRENADE, A THEORETICALLY IMPOSSIBLE WEAPON OF MASS DESTRUCTION.
THE OPERATOR--A MAN WHOSE FILES ARE SO CLASSIFIED EVEN HE CAN'T ACCESS THEM.
I WANT WORST-CASE SCENARIOS, PEOPLE. I WANT YOU TO THINK OF THEM BEFORE THEY DO.
I WANT THE UNTHINKABLE.

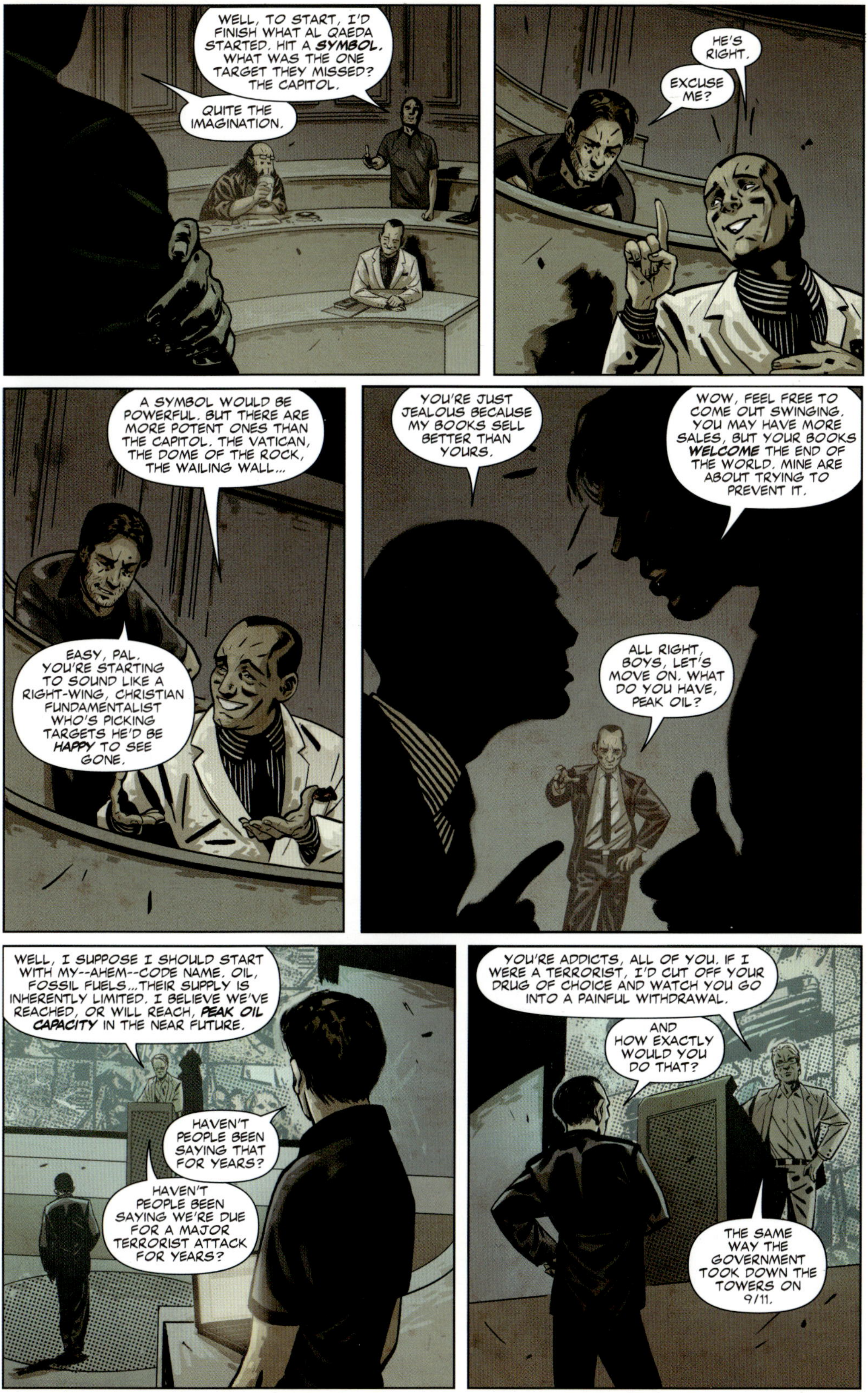
WELL, TO START, I'D FINISH WHAT AL QAEDA STARTED. HIT A **SYMBOL.** WHAT WAS THE ONE TARGET THEY MISSED? THE CAPITOL.
QUITE THE IMAGINATION.
HE'S RIGHT.
EXCUSE ME?
A SYMBOL WOULD BE POWERFUL. BUT THERE ARE MORE POTENT ONES THAN THE CAPITOL. THE VATICAN, THE DOME OF THE ROCK, THE WAILING WALL...
EASY, PAL. YOU'RE STARTING TO SOUND LIKE A RIGHT-WING, CHRISTIAN FUNDAMENTALIST WHO'S PICKING TARGETS HE'D BE **HAPPY** TO SEE GONE.
YOU'RE JUST JEALOUS BECAUSE MY BOOKS SELL BETTER THAN YOURS.
WOW, FEEL FREE TO COME OUT SWINGING. YOU MAY HAVE MORE SALES, BUT YOUR BOOKS **WELCOME** THE END OF THE WORLD. MINE ARE ABOUT TRYING TO PREVENT IT.
ALL RIGHT, BOYS, LET'S MOVE ON. WHAT DO YOU HAVE, PEAK OIL?
WELL, I SUPPOSE I SHOULD START WITH MY--AHEM--CODE NAME. OIL, FOSSIL FUELS...THEIR SUPPLY IS INHERENTLY LIMITED. I BELIEVE WE'VE REACHED, OR WILL REACH, **PEAK OIL CAPACITY** IN THE NEAR FUTURE.
HAVEN'T PEOPLE BEEN SAYING THAT FOR YEARS?
HAVEN'T PEOPLE BEEN SAYING WE'RE DUE FOR A MAJOR TERRORIST ATTACK FOR YEARS?
YOU'RE ADDICTS, ALL OF YOU. IF I WERE A TERRORIST, I'D CUT OFF YOUR DRUG OF CHOICE AND WATCH YOU GO INTO A PAINFUL WITHDRAWAL.
AND HOW EXACTLY WOULD YOU DO THAT?
THE SAME WAY THE GOVERNMENT TOOK DOWN THE TOWERS ON 9/11.

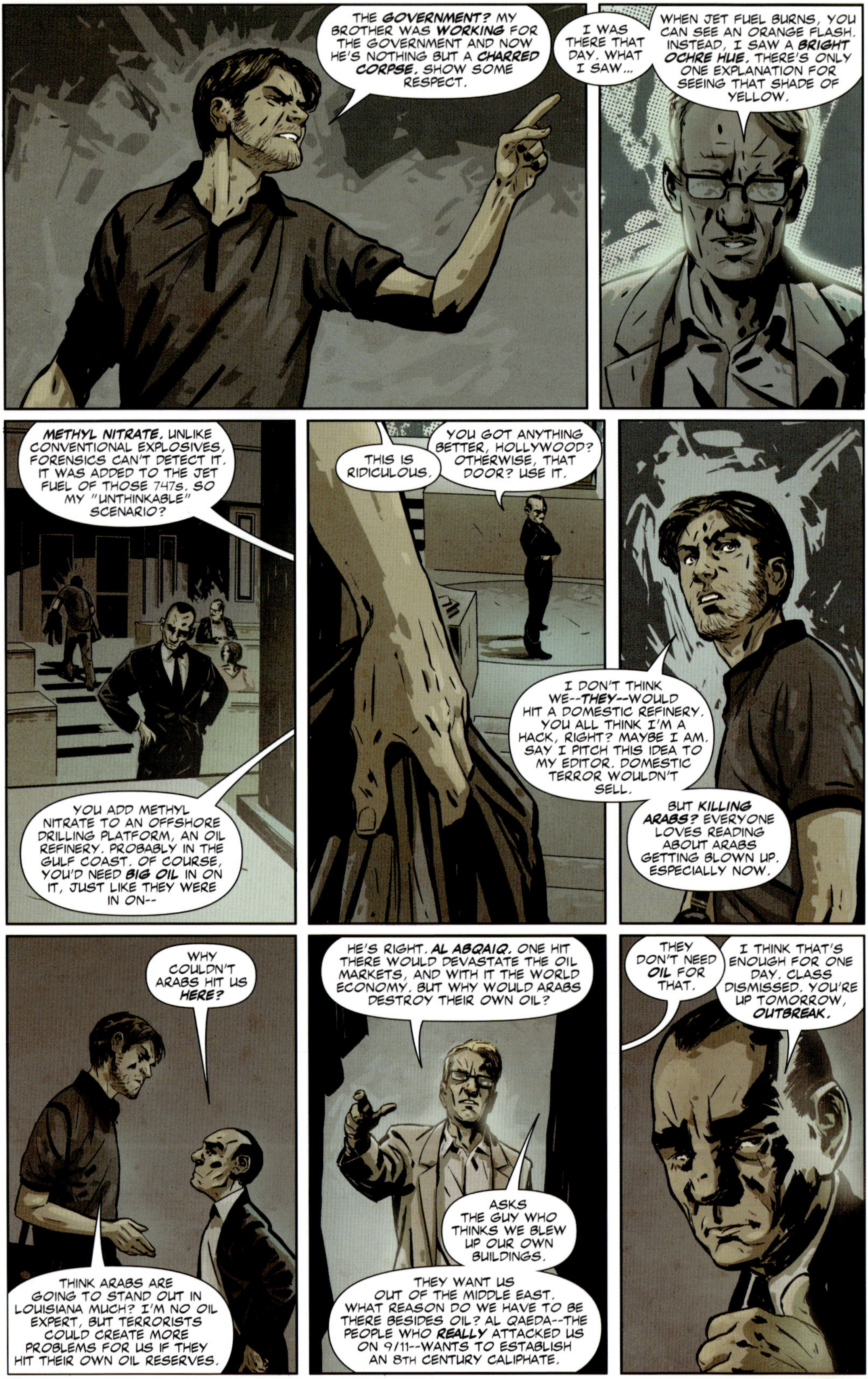
THE GOVERNMENT? MY BROTHER WAS WORKING FOR THE GOVERNMENT AND NOW HE'S NOTHING BUT A CHARRED CORPSE. SHOW SOME RESPECT.
I WAS THERE THAT DAY. WHAT I SAW...
WHEN JET FUEL BURNS, YOU CAN SEE AN ORANGE FLASH. INSTEAD, I SAW A BRIGHT OCHRE HUE. THERE'S ONLY ONE EXPLANATION FOR SEEING THAT SHADE OF YELLOW.
METHYL NITRATE. UNLIKE CONVENTIONAL EXPLOSIVES, FORENSICS CAN'T DETECT IT. IT WAS ADDED TO THE JET FUEL OF THOSE 747S. SO MY "UNTHINKABLE" SCENARIO?
YOU ADD METHYL NITRATE TO AN OFFSHORE DRILLING PLATFORM, AN OIL REFINERY. PROBABLY IN THE GULF COAST. OF COURSE, YOU'D NEED BIG OIL IN ON IT, JUST LIKE THEY WERE IN ON--
THIS IS RIDICULOUS.
YOU GOT ANYTHING BETTER, HOLLYWOOD? OTHERWISE, THAT DOOR? USE IT.
I DON'T THINK WE--THEY--WOULD HIT A DOMESTIC REFINERY. YOU ALL THINK I'M A HACK, RIGHT? MAYBE I AM. SAY I PITCH THIS IDEA TO MY EDITOR. DOMESTIC TERROR WOULDN'T SELL.
BUT KILLING ARABS? EVERYONE LOVES READING ABOUT ARABS GETTING BLOWN UP. ESPECIALLY NOW.
WHY COULDN'T ARABS HIT US HERE?
THINK ARABS ARE GOING TO STAND OUT IN LOUISIANA MUCH? I'M NO OIL EXPERT, BUT TERRORISTS COULD CREATE MORE PROBLEMS FOR US IF THEY HIT THEIR OWN OIL RESERVES.
HE'S RIGHT. AL ABQAIQ. ONE HIT THERE WOULD DEVASTATE THE OIL MARKETS, AND WITH IT THE WORLD ECONOMY. BUT WHY WOULD ARABS DESTROY THEIR OWN OIL?
ASKS THE GUY WHO THINKS WE BLEW UP OUR OWN BUILDINGS.
THEY WANT US OUT OF THE MIDDLE EAST. WHAT REASON DO WE HAVE TO BE THERE BESIDES OIL? AL QAEDA--THE PEOPLE WHO REALLY ATTACKED US ON 9/11--WANTS TO ESTABLISH AN 8TH CENTURY CALIPHATE.
THEY DON'T NEED OIL FOR THAT.
I THINK THAT'S ENOUGH FOR ONE DAY. CLASS DISMISSED. YOU'RE UP TOMORROW, OUTBREAK.

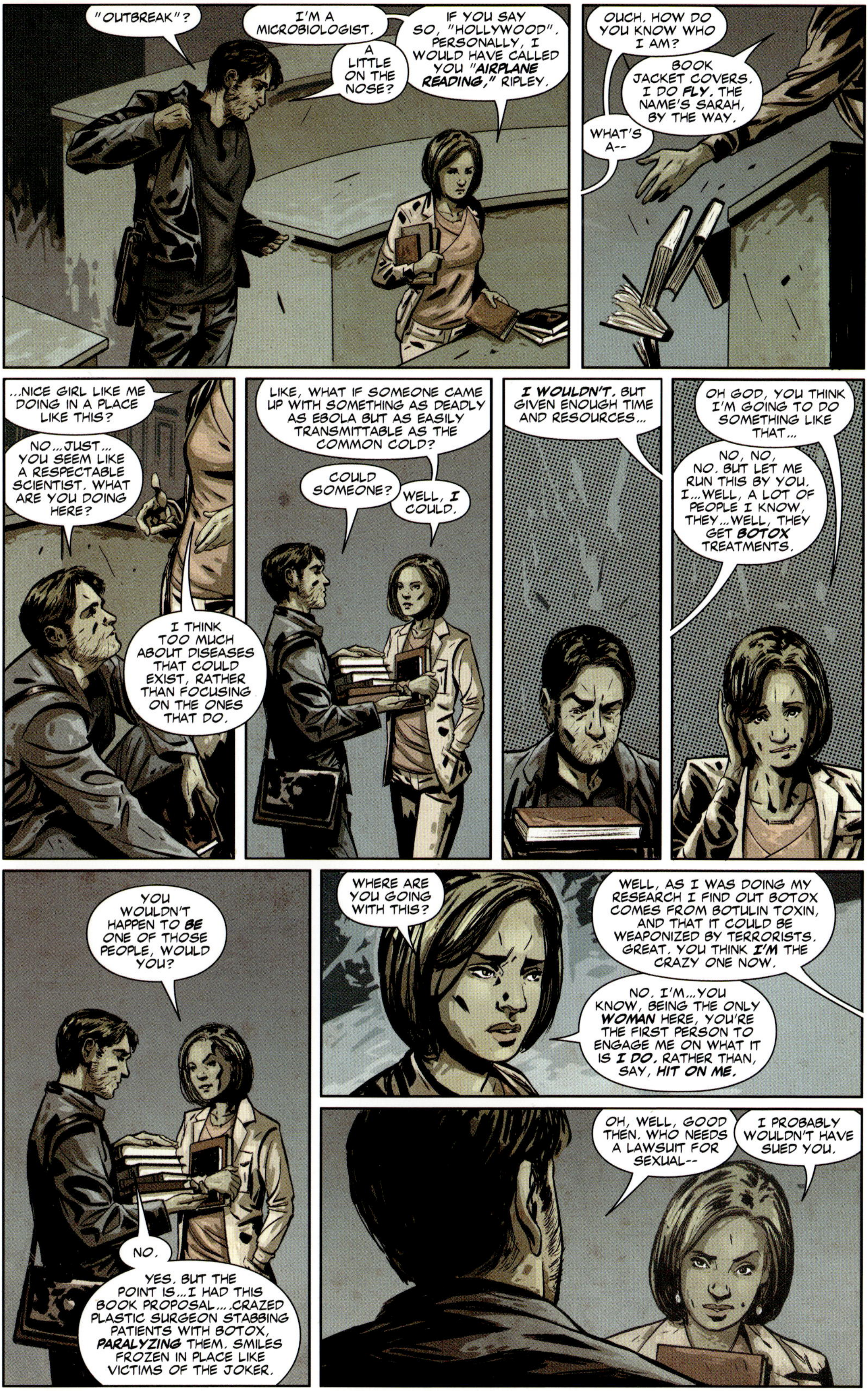
"OUTBREAK"?
I'M A MICROBIOLOGIST.
A LITTLE ON THE NOSE?
IF YOU SAY SO, "HOLLYWOOD". PERSONALLY, I WOULD HAVE CALLED YOU "AIRPLANE READING," RIPLEY.
OUCH. HOW DO YOU KNOW WHO I AM?
BOOK JACKET COVERS. I DO FLY. THE NAME'S SARAH, BY THE WAY.
WHAT'S A--
...NICE GIRL LIKE ME DOING IN A PLACE LIKE THIS?
NO...JUST... YOU SEEM LIKE A RESPECTABLE SCIENTIST. WHAT ARE YOU DOING HERE?
I THINK TOO MUCH ABOUT DISEASES THAT COULD EXIST, RATHER THAN FOCUSING ON THE ONES THAT DO.
LIKE, WHAT IF SOMEONE CAME UP WITH SOMETHING AS DEADLY AS EBOLA BUT AS EASILY TRANSMITTABLE AS THE COMMON COLD?
COULD SOMEONE?
WELL, I COULD.
I WOULDN'T. BUT GIVEN ENOUGH TIME AND RESOURCES...
OH GOD, YOU THINK I'M GOING TO DO SOMETHING LIKE THAT...
NO, NO, NO. BUT LET ME RUN THIS BY YOU. I...WELL, A LOT OF PEOPLE I KNOW, THEY...WELL, THEY GET BOTOX TREATMENTS.
YOU WOULDN'T HAPPEN TO BE ONE OF THOSE PEOPLE, WOULD YOU?
NO.
YES. BUT THE POINT IS...I HAD THIS BOOK PROPOSAL....CRAZED PLASTIC SURGEON STABBING PATIENTS WITH BOTOX, PARALYZING THEM. SMILES FROZEN IN PLACE LIKE VICTIMS OF THE JOKER.
WHERE ARE YOU GOING WITH THIS?
WELL, AS I WAS DOING MY RESEARCH I FIND OUT BOTOX COMES FROM BOTULIN TOXIN, AND THAT IT COULD BE WEAPONIZED BY TERRORISTS. GREAT. YOU THINK I'M THE CRAZY ONE NOW.
NO. I'M...YOU KNOW, BEING THE ONLY WOMAN HERE, YOU'RE THE FIRST PERSON TO ENGAGE ME ON WHAT IT IS I DO. RATHER THAN, SAY, HIT ON ME.
OH, WELL, GOOD THEN. WHO NEEDS A LAWSUIT FOR SEXUAL--
I PROBABLY WOULDN'T HAVE SUED YOU.

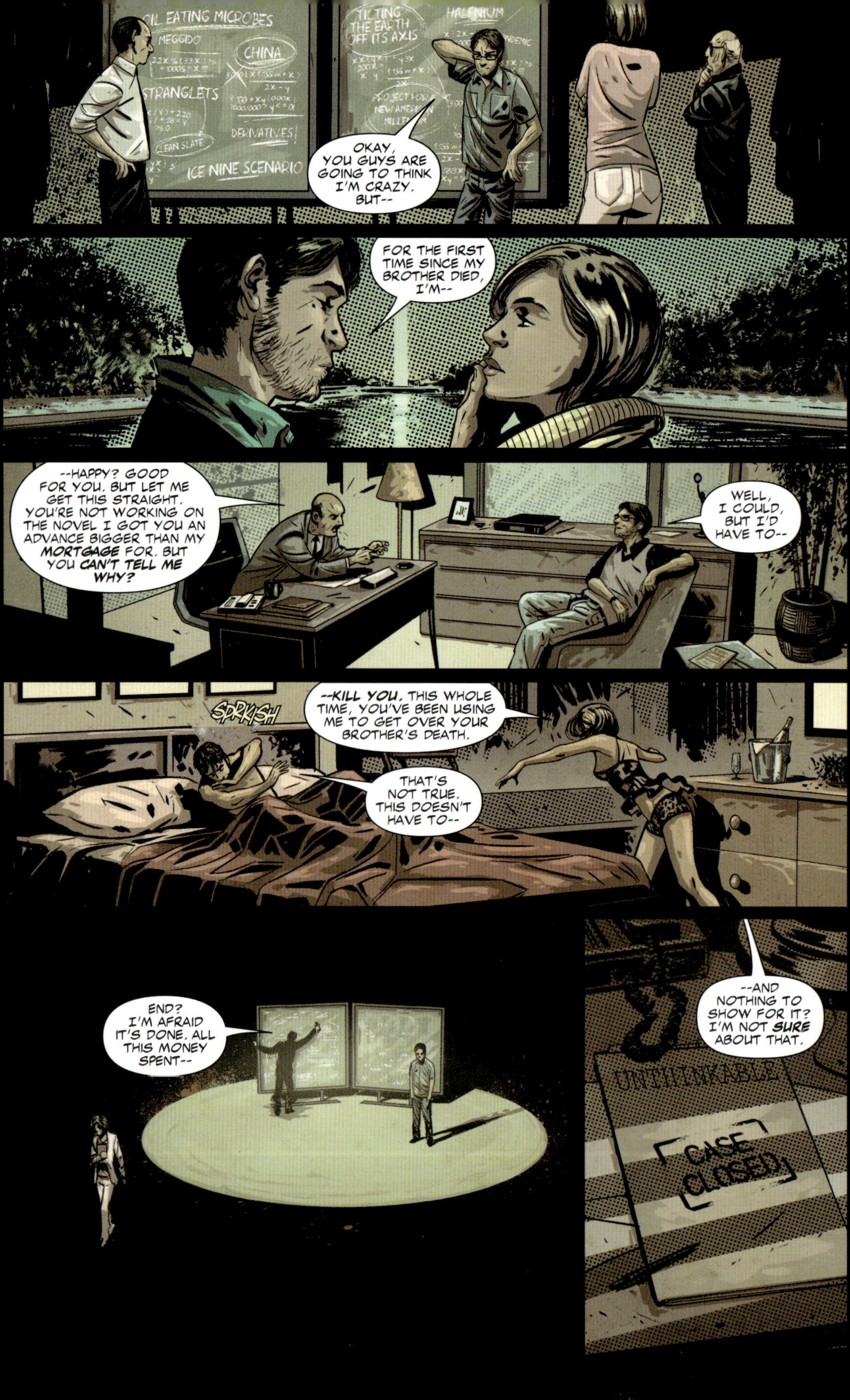
OIL EATING MICROBES
MEGGIDO
CHINA
STRANGLETS
CLEAN SLATE
DERIVATIVES!
ICE NINE SCENARIO
TILTING THE EARTH OFF ITS AXIS
HALENIUM
OKAY, YOU GUYS ARE GOING TO THINK I'M CRAZY, BUT--
FOR THE FIRST TIME SINCE MY BROTHER DIED, I'M--
--HAPPY? GOOD FOR YOU. BUT LET ME GET THIS STRAIGHT. YOU'RE NOT WORKING ON THE NOVEL I GOT YOU AN ADVANCE BIGGER THAN MY **MORTGAGE** FOR, BUT YOU **CAN'T TELL ME WHY?**
WELL, I COULD, BUT I'D HAVE TO--
SPRKISH
--KILL YOU. THIS WHOLE TIME, YOU'VE BEEN USING ME TO GET OVER YOUR BROTHER'S DEATH.
THAT'S NOT TRUE. THIS DOESN'T HAVE TO--
END? I'M AFRAID IT'S DONE. ALL THIS MONEY SPENT--
--AND NOTHING TO SHOW FOR IT? I'M NOT **SURE** ABOUT THAT.
UNTHINKABLE
CASE CLOSED

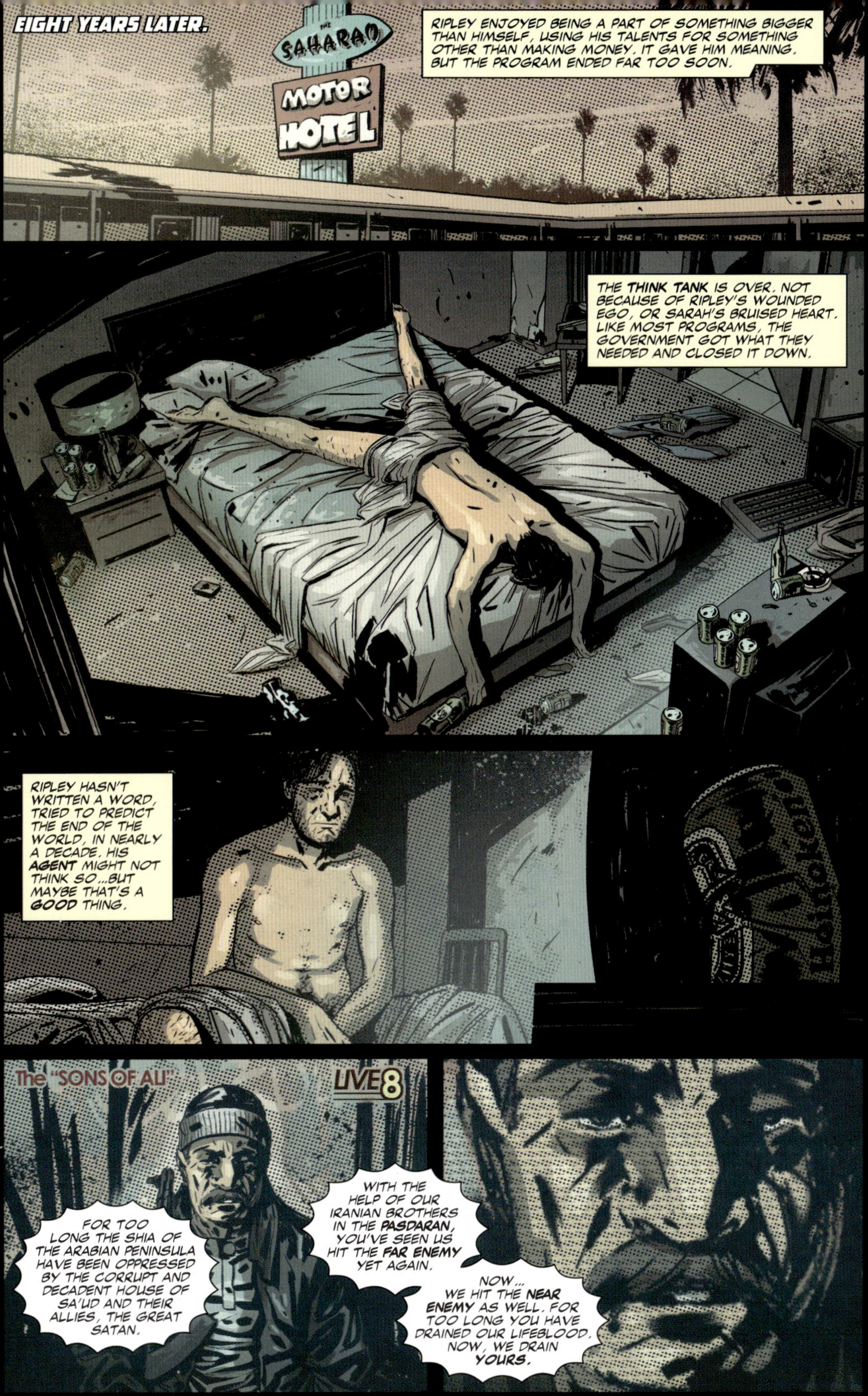
EIGHT YEARS LATER.
THE SAHARAO MOTOR HOTEL
RIPLEY ENJOYED BEING A PART OF SOMETHING BIGGER THAN HIMSELF, USING HIS TALENTS FOR SOMETHING OTHER THAN MAKING MONEY. IT GAVE HIM MEANING. BUT THE PROGRAM ENDED FAR TOO SOON.
THE THINK TANK IS OVER. NOT BECAUSE OF RIPLEY'S WOUNDED EGO, OR SARAH'S BRUISED HEART. LIKE MOST PROGRAMS, THE GOVERNMENT GOT WHAT THEY NEEDED AND CLOSED IT DOWN.
RIPLEY HASN'T WRITTEN A WORD, TRIED TO PREDICT THE END OF THE WORLD, IN NEARLY A DECADE. HIS AGENT MIGHT NOT THINK SO...BUT MAYBE THAT'S A GOOD THING.
The "SONS OF ALI"
LIVE 8
FOR TOO LONG THE SHIA OF THE ARABIAN PENINSULA HAVE BEEN OPPRESSED BY THE CORRUPT AND DECADENT HOUSE OF SA'UD AND THEIR ALLIES, THE GREAT SATAN.
WITH THE HELP OF OUR IRANIAN BROTHERS IN THE PASDARAN, YOU'VE SEEN US HIT THE FAR ENEMY YET AGAIN.
NOW... WE HIT THE NEAR ENEMY AS WELL. FOR TOO LONG YOU HAVE DRAINED OUR LIFEBLOOD. NOW, WE DRAIN YOURS.

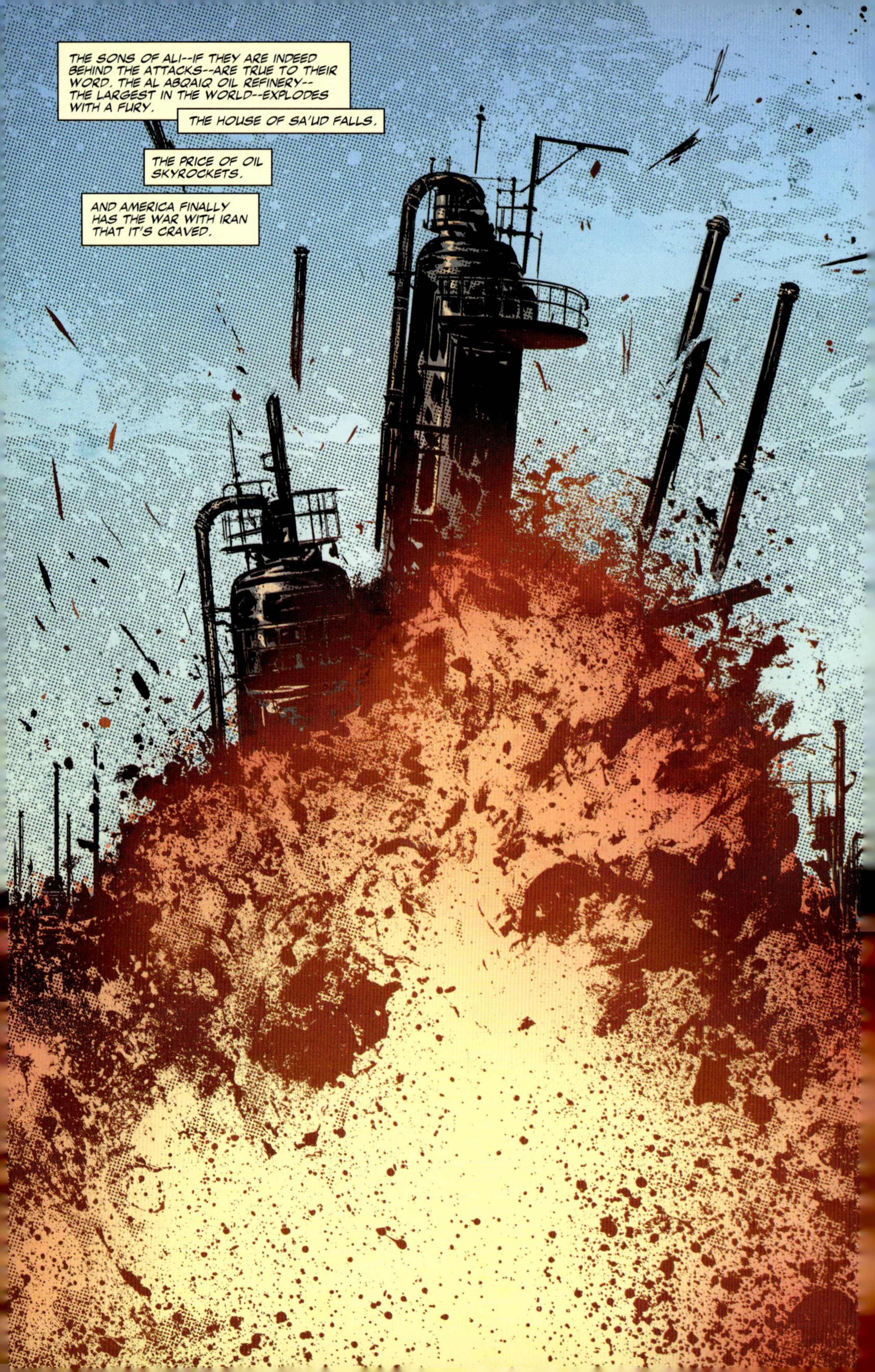
THE SONS OF ALI--IF THEY ARE INDEED BEHIND THE ATTACKS--ARE TRUE TO THEIR WORD. THE AL ABQAIQ OIL REFINERY-- THE LARGEST IN THE WORLD--EXPLODES WITH A FURY.
THE HOUSE OF SA'UD FALLS.
THE PRICE OF OIL SKYROCKETS.
AND AMERICA FINALLY HAS THE WAR WITH IRAN THAT IT'S CRAVED.

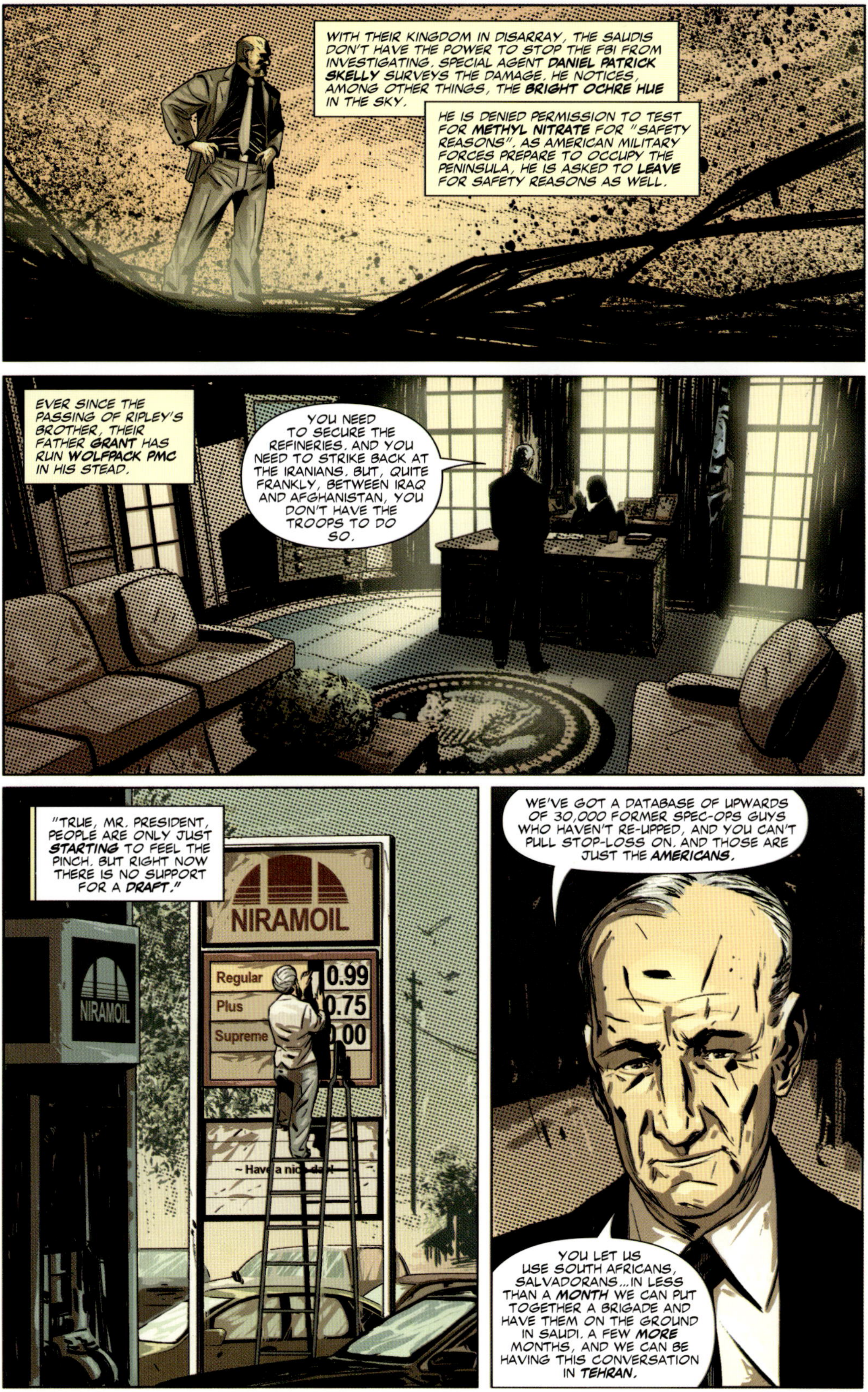

WITH THEIR KINGDOM IN DISARRAY, THE SAUDIS DON'T HAVE THE POWER TO STOP THE FBI FROM INVESTIGATING. SPECIAL AGENT **DANIEL PATRICK SKELLY** SURVEYS THE DAMAGE. HE NOTICES, AMONG OTHER THINGS, THE **BRIGHT OCHRE HUE** IN THE SKY.
HE IS DENIED PERMISSION TO TEST FOR **METHYL NITRATE** FOR "SAFETY REASONS". AS AMERICAN MILITARY FORCES PREPARE TO OCCUPY THE PENINSULA, HE IS ASKED TO **LEAVE** FOR SAFETY REASONS AS WELL.
EVER SINCE THE PASSING OF RIPLEY'S BROTHER, THEIR FATHER **GRANT** HAS RUN **WOLFPACK PMC** IN HIS STEAD.
YOU NEED TO SECURE THE REFINERIES, AND YOU NEED TO STRIKE BACK AT THE IRANIANS. BUT, QUITE FRANKLY, BETWEEN IRAQ AND AFGHANISTAN, YOU DON'T HAVE THE TROOPS TO DO SO.
"TRUE, MR. PRESIDENT, PEOPLE ARE ONLY JUST **STARTING** TO FEEL THE PINCH. BUT RIGHT NOW THERE IS NO SUPPORT FOR A **DRAFT**."
NIRAMOIL
Regular 0.99
Plus 0.75
Supreme
NIRAMOIL
WE'VE GOT A DATABASE OF UPWARDS OF 30,000 FORMER SPEC-OPS GUYS WHO HAVEN'T RE-UPPED, AND YOU CAN'T PULL STOP-LOSS ON. AND THOSE ARE JUST THE **AMERICANS**.
YOU LET US USE SOUTH AFRICANS, SALVADORANS...IN LESS THAN A **MONTH** WE CAN PUT TOGETHER A BRIGADE AND HAVE THEM ON THE GROUND IN SAUDI. A FEW **MORE** MONTHS, AND WE CAN BE HAVING THIS CONVERSATION IN **TEHRAN**.

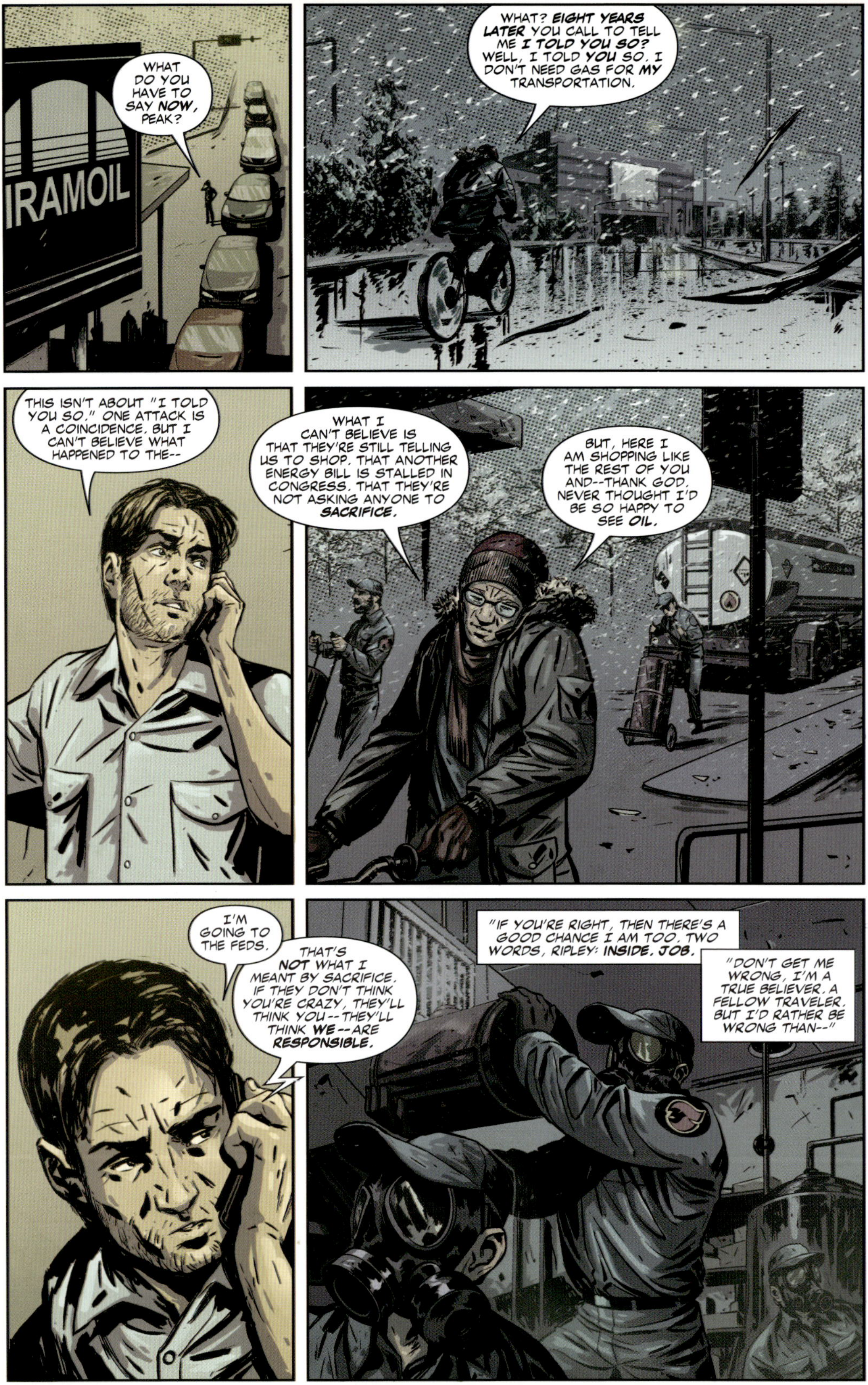
IRAMOIL
WHAT DO YOU HAVE TO SAY NOW, PEAK?
WHAT? EIGHT YEARS LATER YOU CALL TO TELL ME I TOLD YOU SO? WELL, I TOLD YOU SO. I DON'T NEED GAS FOR MY TRANSPORTATION.
THIS ISN'T ABOUT "I TOLD YOU SO." ONE ATTACK IS A COINCIDENCE, BUT I CAN'T BELIEVE WHAT HAPPENED TO THE--
WHAT I CAN'T BELIEVE IS THAT THEY'RE STILL TELLING US TO SHOP. THAT ANOTHER ENERGY BILL IS STALLED IN CONGRESS. THAT THEY'RE NOT ASKING ANYONE TO SACRIFICE.
BUT, HERE I AM SHOPPING LIKE THE REST OF YOU AND--THANK GOD. NEVER THOUGHT I'D BE SO HAPPY TO SEE OIL.
I'M GOING TO THE FEDS.
THAT'S NOT WHAT I MEANT BY SACRIFICE. IF THEY DON'T THINK YOU'RE CRAZY, THEY'LL THINK YOU--THEY'LL THINK WE--ARE RESPONSIBLE.
"IF YOU'RE RIGHT, THEN THERE'S A GOOD CHANCE I AM TOO. TWO WORDS, RIPLEY: INSIDE. JOB.
"DON'T GET ME WRONG, I'M A TRUE BELIEVER. A FELLOW TRAVELER. BUT I'D RATHER BE WRONG THAN--"

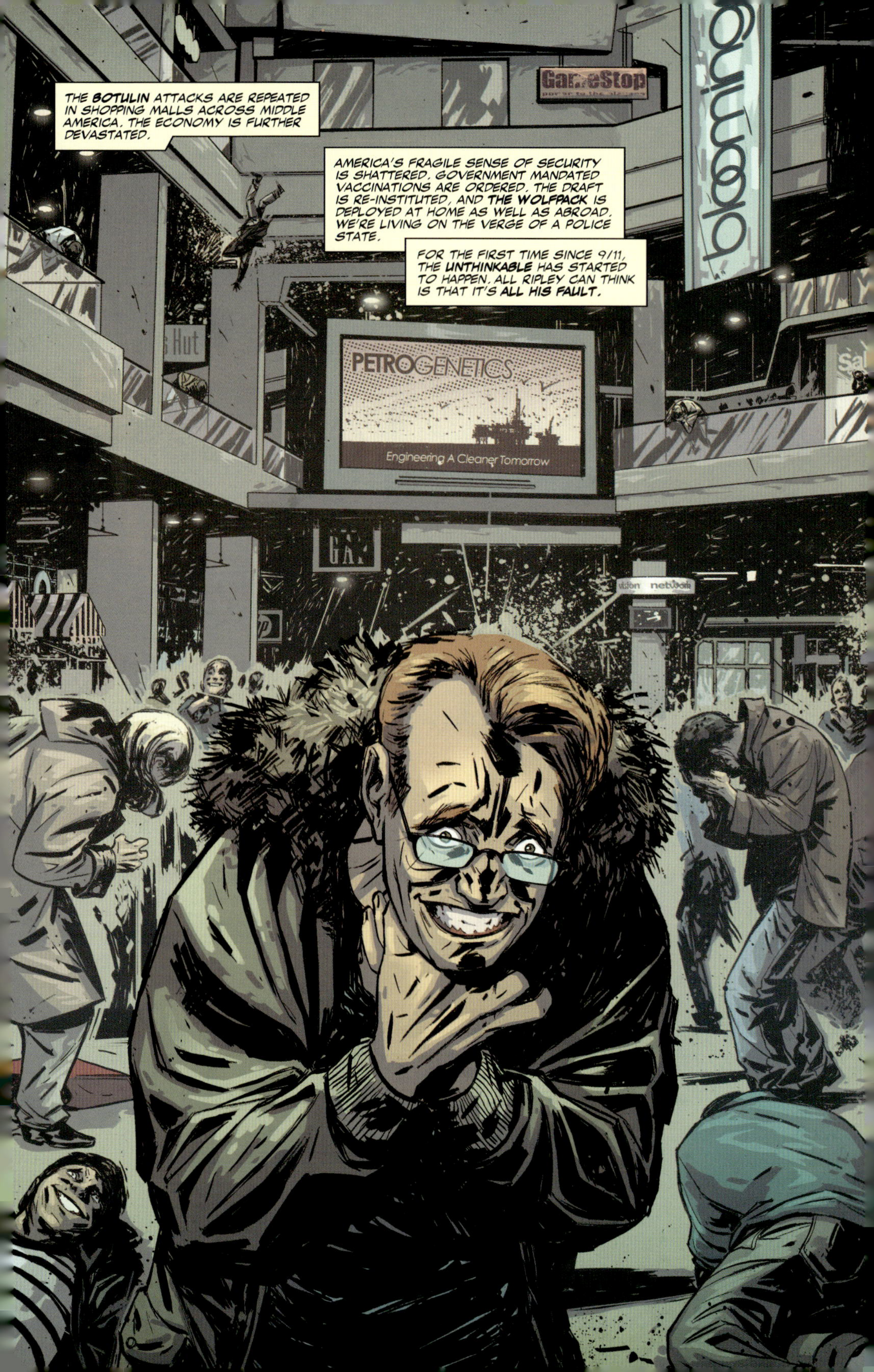
THE **BOTULIN** ATTACKS ARE REPEATED IN SHOPPING MALLS ACROSS MIDDLE AMERICA. THE ECONOMY IS FURTHER DEVASTATED.
AMERICA'S FRAGILE SENSE OF SECURITY IS SHATTERED. GOVERNMENT MANDATED VACCINATIONS ARE ORDERED. THE DRAFT IS RE-INSTITUTED, AND **THE WOLFPACK** IS DEPLOYED AT HOME AS WELL AS ABROAD. WE'RE LIVING ON THE VERGE OF A POLICE STATE.
FOR THE FIRST TIME SINCE 9/11, THE **UNTHINKABLE** HAS STARTED TO HAPPEN. ALL RIPLEY CAN THINK IS THAT IT'S **ALL HIS FAULT.**
GameStop
PETROGENETICS
Engineering A Cleaner Tomorrow
GAP

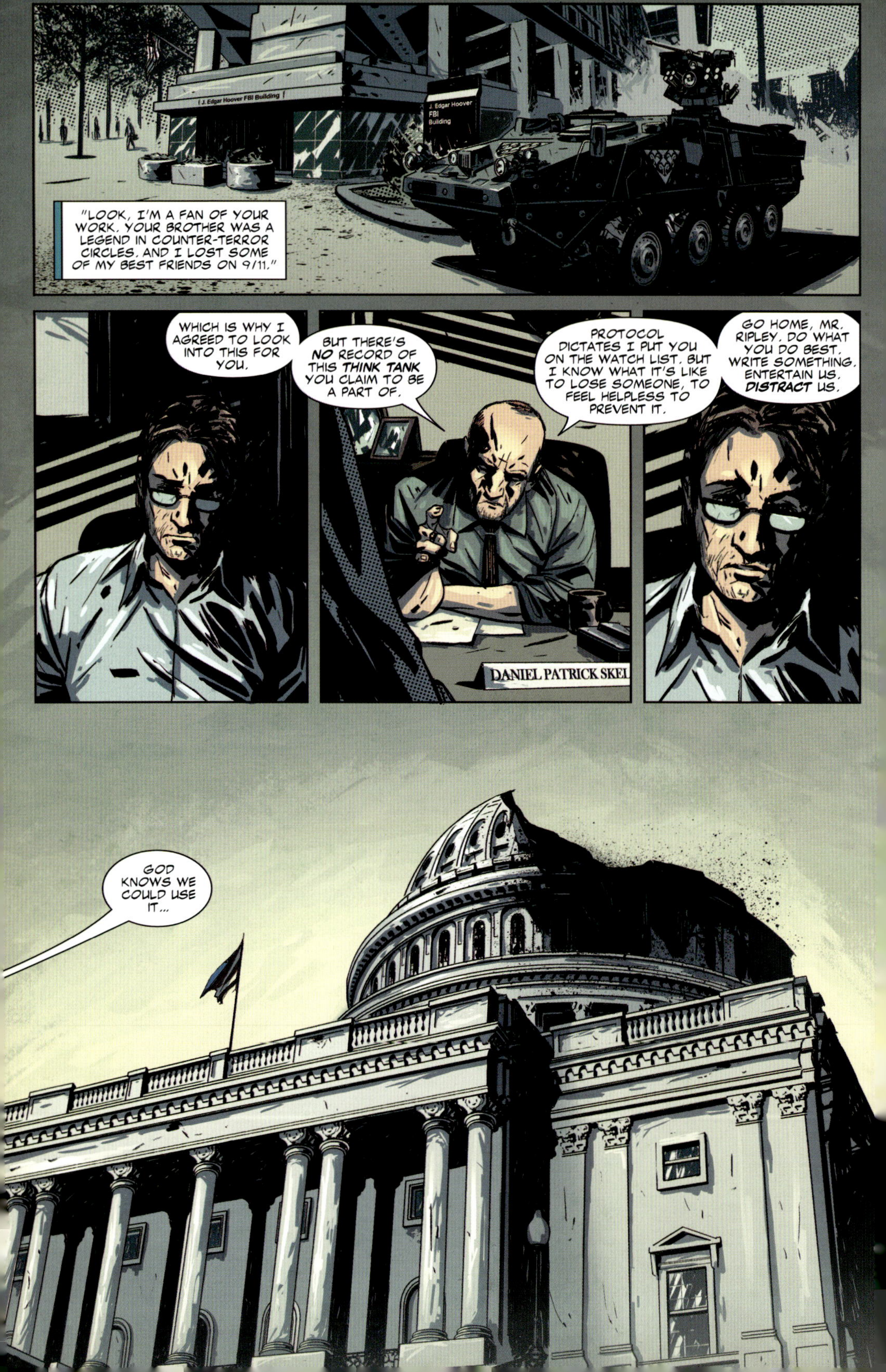
J. Edgar Hoover FBI Building
J. Edgar Hoover FBI Building
"LOOK, I'M A FAN OF YOUR WORK. YOUR BROTHER WAS A LEGEND IN COUNTER-TERROR CIRCLES. AND I LOST SOME OF MY BEST FRIENDS ON 9/11."
WHICH IS WHY I AGREED TO LOOK INTO THIS FOR YOU.
BUT THERE'S ***NO*** RECORD OF THIS ***THINK TANK*** YOU CLAIM TO BE A PART OF.
PROTOCOL DICTATES I PUT YOU ON THE WATCH LIST. BUT I KNOW WHAT IT'S LIKE TO LOSE SOMEONE, TO FEEL HELPLESS TO PREVENT IT.
DANIEL PATRICK SKEI
GO HOME, MR. RIPLEY. DO WHAT YOU DO BEST. WRITE SOMETHING. ENTERTAIN US. ***DISTRACT*** US.
GOD KNOWS WE COULD USE IT...

CHAPTER TWO

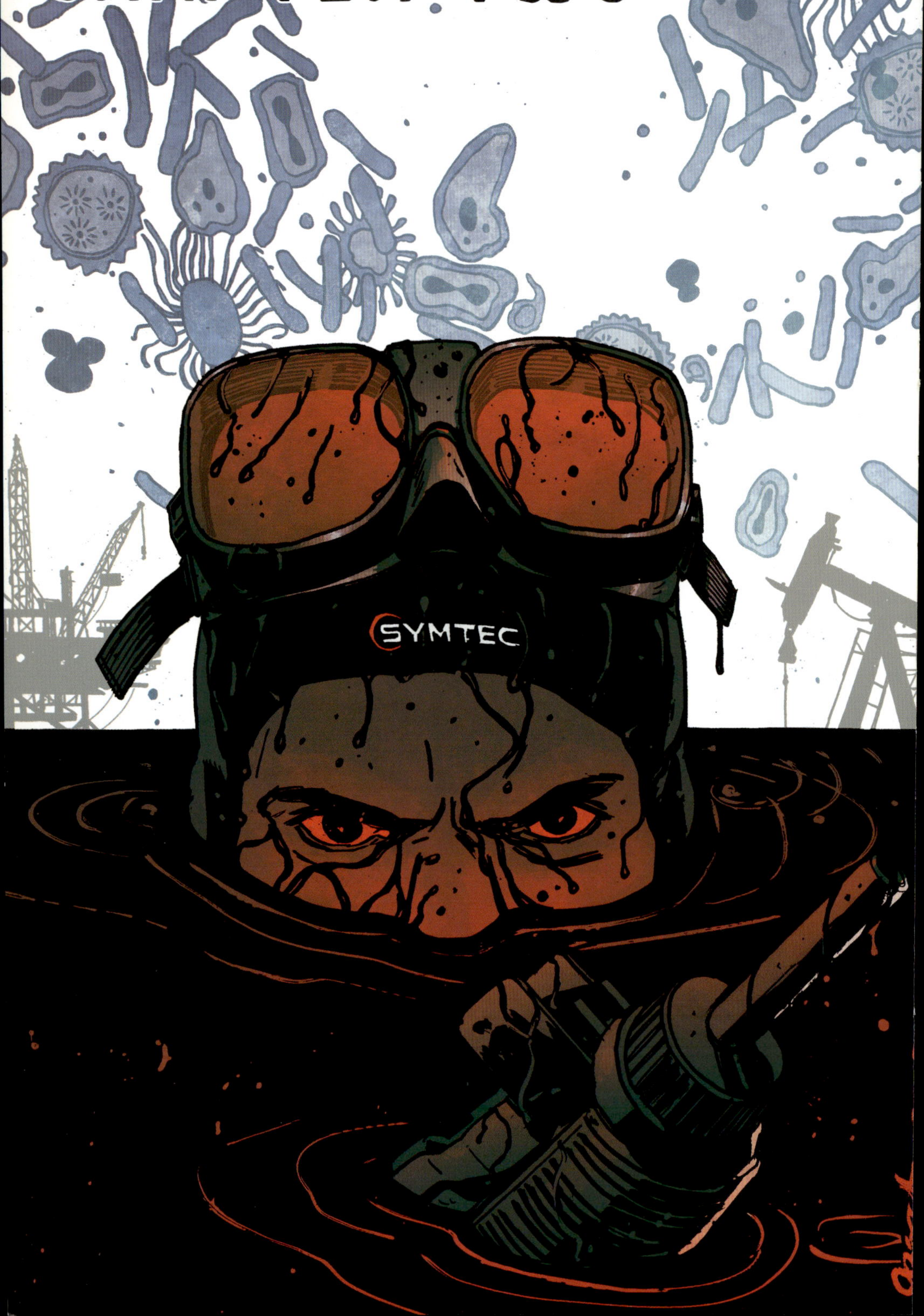
SYMTEC

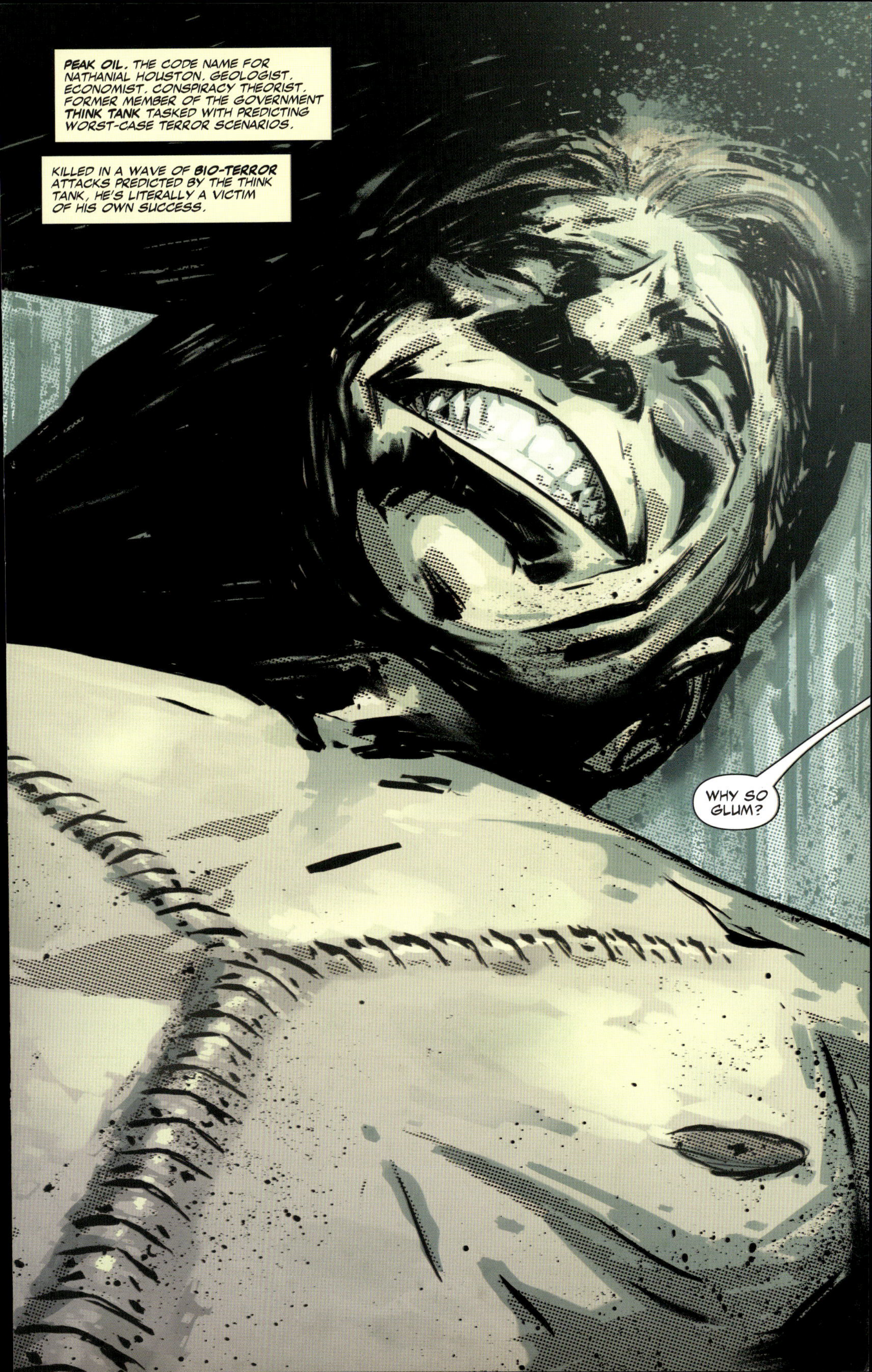
PEAK OIL. THE CODE NAME FOR NATHANIAL HOUSTON. GEOLOGIST. ECONOMIST. CONSPIRACY THEORIST. FORMER MEMBER OF THE GOVERNMENT THINK TANK TASKED WITH PREDICTING WORST-CASE TERROR SCENARIOS.
KILLED IN A WAVE OF BIO-TERROR ATTACKS PREDICTED BY THE THINK TANK, HE'S LITERALLY A VICTIM OF HIS OWN SUCCESS.
WHY SO GLUM?

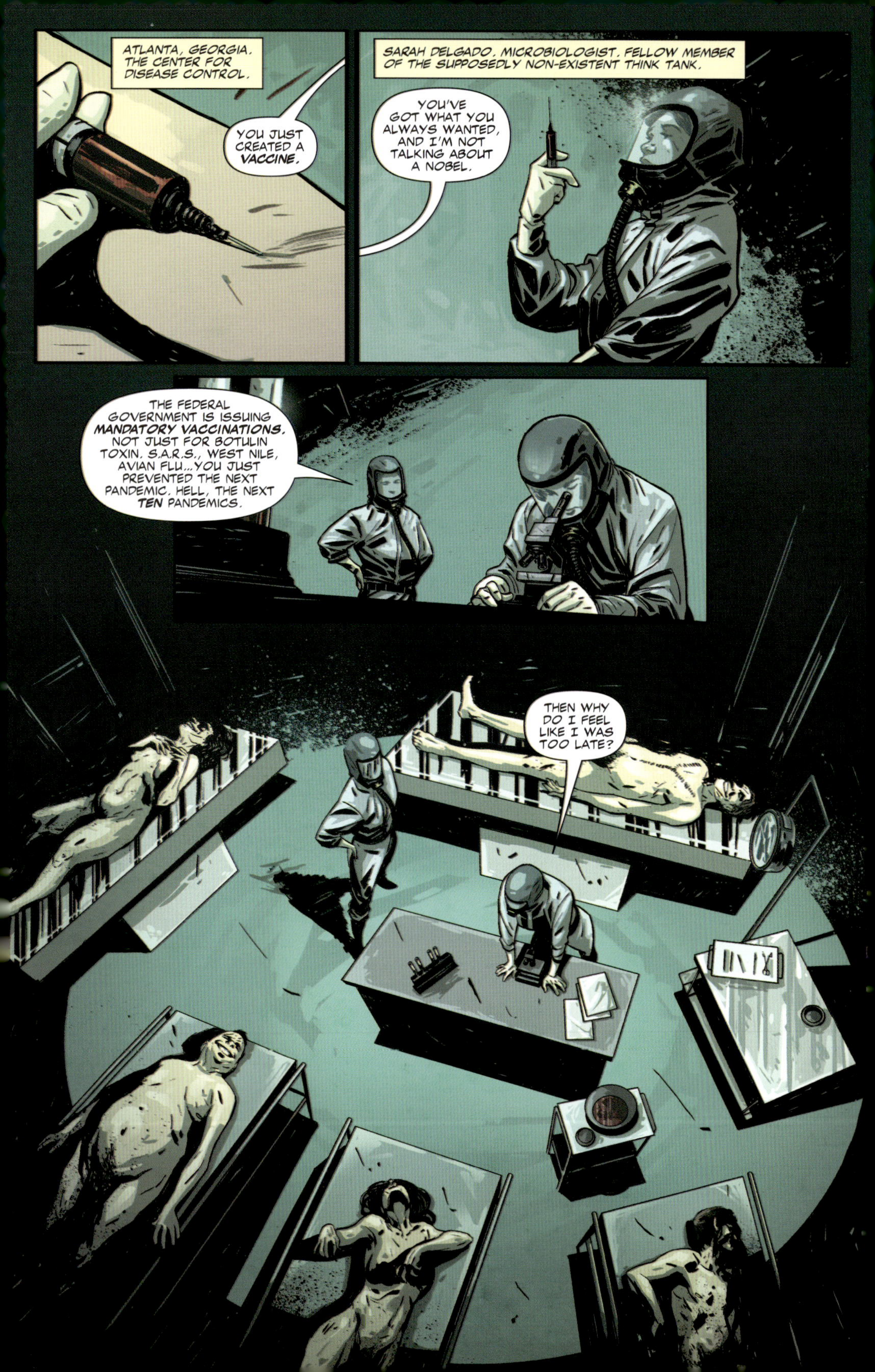
ATLANTA, GEORGIA. THE CENTER FOR DISEASE CONTROL.
YOU JUST CREATED A VACCINE.
SARAH DELGADO. MICROBIOLOGIST. FELLOW MEMBER OF THE SUPPOSEDLY NON-EXISTENT THINK TANK.
YOU'VE GOT WHAT YOU ALWAYS WANTED, AND I'M NOT TALKING ABOUT A NOBEL.
THE FEDERAL GOVERNMENT IS ISSUING MANDATORY VACCINATIONS. NOT JUST FOR BOTULIN TOXIN. S.A.R.S., WEST NILE, AVIAN FLU...YOU JUST PREVENTED THE NEXT PANDEMIC. HELL, THE NEXT TEN PANDEMICS.
THEN WHY DO I FEEL LIKE I WAS TOO LATE?

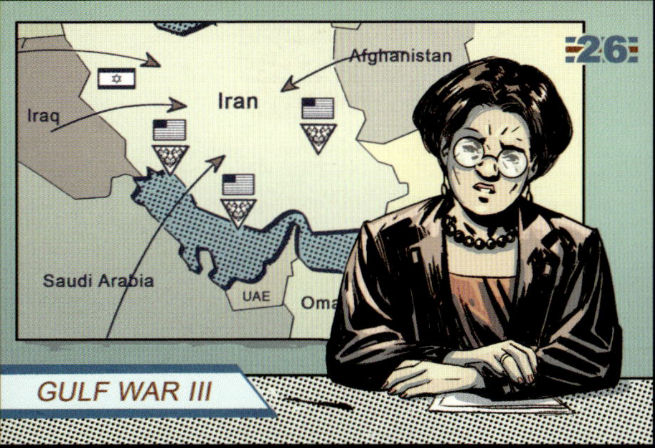
:26:
Afghanistan
Iran
Iraq
Saudi Arabia
UAE
Oma
GULF WAR III

THE ATTACKS ON THE SAUDI OIL FIELDS WERE OFFICIALLY LINKED TO THE IRANIAN REVOLUTIONARY GUARDS.

DESPITE EVIDENCE POINTING TO THE CONTRARY, HEZBOLLAH DENIED RESPONSIBILITY FOR THE BOTULIN ATTACKS AS WELL AS THE DESTRUCTION OF THE U.S. CAPITOL.

NEVERTHELESS, ONCE WE RESPONDED WITH FORCE, THEY VOWED TO STRIKE ON AMERICAN AND ISRAELI TARGETS WORLDWIDE UNTIL WE WITHDREW FROM THE MIDDLE EAST ENTIRELY.

REELING FROM AN ECONOMIC DOWNTURN WITH OIL SUPPLIES DWINDLING, HEZBOLLAH'S "RETALIATORY" ATTACKS WERE ALL THAT WAS NEEDED FOR SUPPORT FOR A DRAFT.

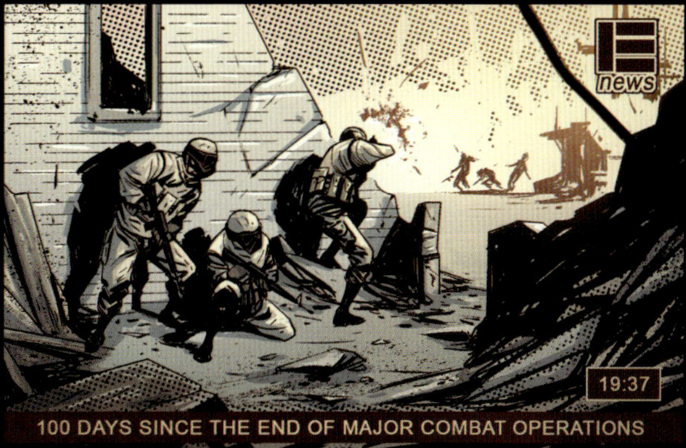
news
19:37
100 DAYS SINCE THE END OF MAJOR COMBAT OPERATIONS

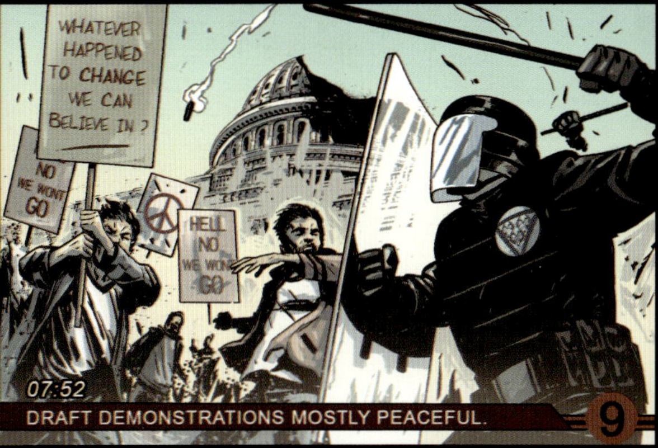
WHATEVER HAPPENED TO CHANGE WE CAN BELIEVE IN ?
NO WE WON'T GO
HELL NO WE WON'T GO
07:52
DRAFT DEMONSTRATIONS MOSTLY PEACEFUL.
9

YOUTUBE VIDEO OF A PREDATOR DRONE FIRING ON THE CAPITOL DOME WAS THE ONLY EVIDENCE FOR AN ALTERNATIVE THEORY.

OFFICIALLY DISMISSED AS A HOAX, MILITARY SOURCES SPEAKING ON BACKGROUND ADMITTED IT WAS POSSIBLE HOSTILE GROUPS HAD RECOVERED A DOWNED DRONE.

CHINA AND RUSSIA CONDEMNED THE ATTACKS BOTH ON AND BY THE U.S, BUT WERE MORE STRIDENT IN THEIR OPPOSITION TO THE LATTER. WHILE THEY INSTITUTED SAFEGUARDS AGAINST A PANDEMIC, THEY REFUSED AMERICAN OFFERS TO SHARE THEIR VACCINES.

THEY WERE MORE INTERESTED IN WHAT REMAINED OF OUR OIL.

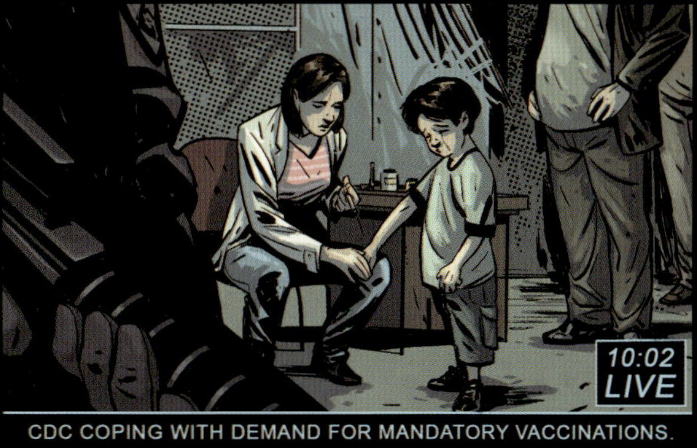
10:02
LIVE
CDC COPING WITH DEMAND FOR MANDATORY VACCINATIONS.

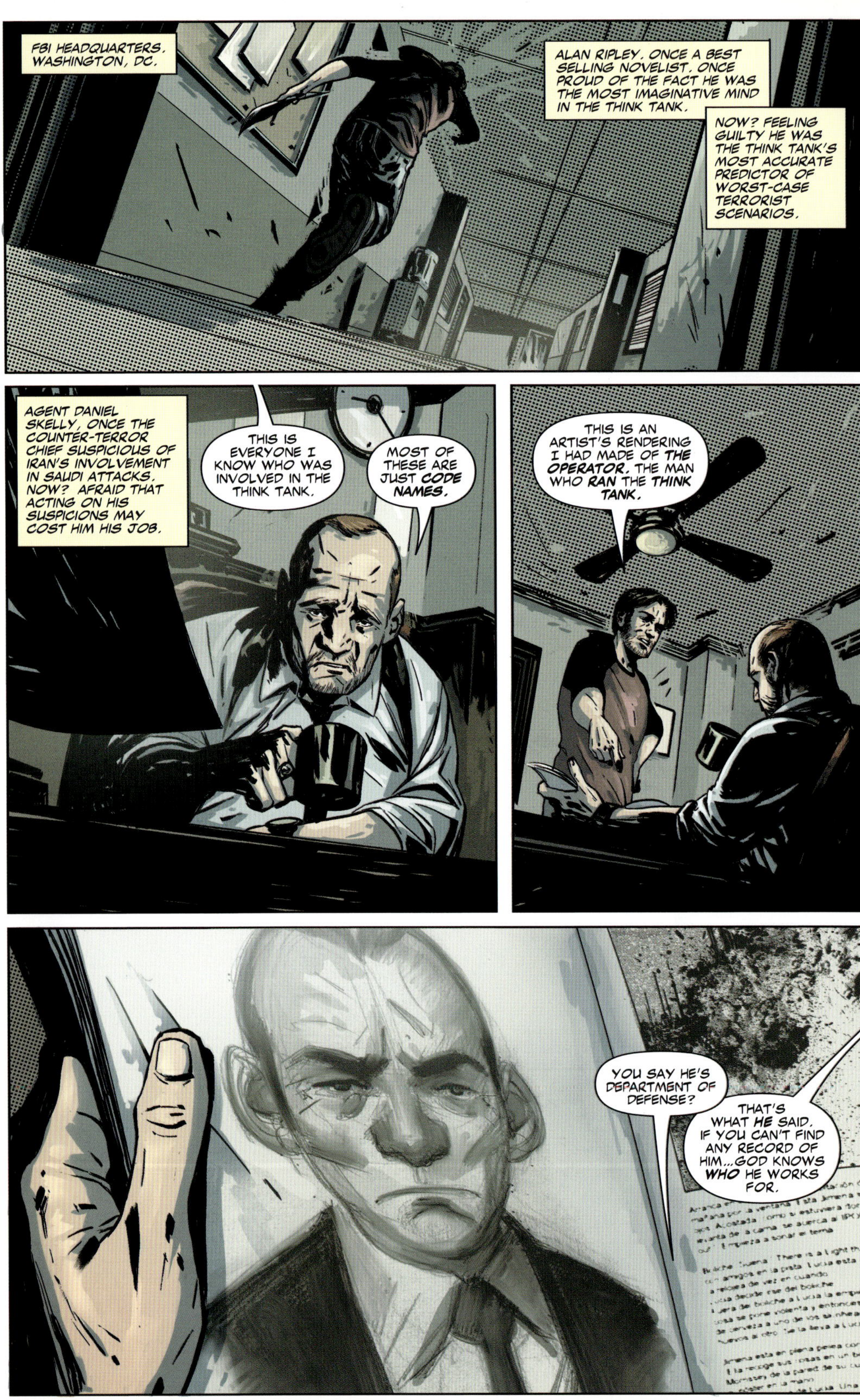
FBI HEADQUARTERS, WASHINGTON, DC.
ALAN RIPLEY. ONCE A BEST SELLING NOVELIST. ONCE PROUD OF THE FACT HE WAS THE MOST IMAGINATIVE MIND IN THE THINK TANK.
NOW? FEELING GUILTY HE WAS THE THINK TANK'S MOST ACCURATE PREDICTOR OF WORST-CASE TERRORIST SCENARIOS.
AGENT DANIEL SKELLY, ONCE THE COUNTER-TERROR CHIEF SUSPICIOUS OF IRAN'S INVOLVEMENT IN SAUDI ATTACKS. NOW? AFRAID THAT ACTING ON HIS SUSPICIONS MAY COST HIM HIS JOB.
THIS IS EVERYONE I KNOW WHO WAS INVOLVED IN THE THINK TANK.
MOST OF THESE ARE JUST **CODE NAMES.**
THIS IS AN ARTIST'S RENDERING I HAD MADE OF **THE OPERATOR.** THE MAN WHO **RAN** THE **THINK TANK.**
YOU SAY HE'S DEPARTMENT OF DEFENSE?
THAT'S WHAT **HE** SAID. IF YOU CAN'T FIND ANY RECORD OF HIM...GOD KNOWS **WHO** HE WORKS FOR.

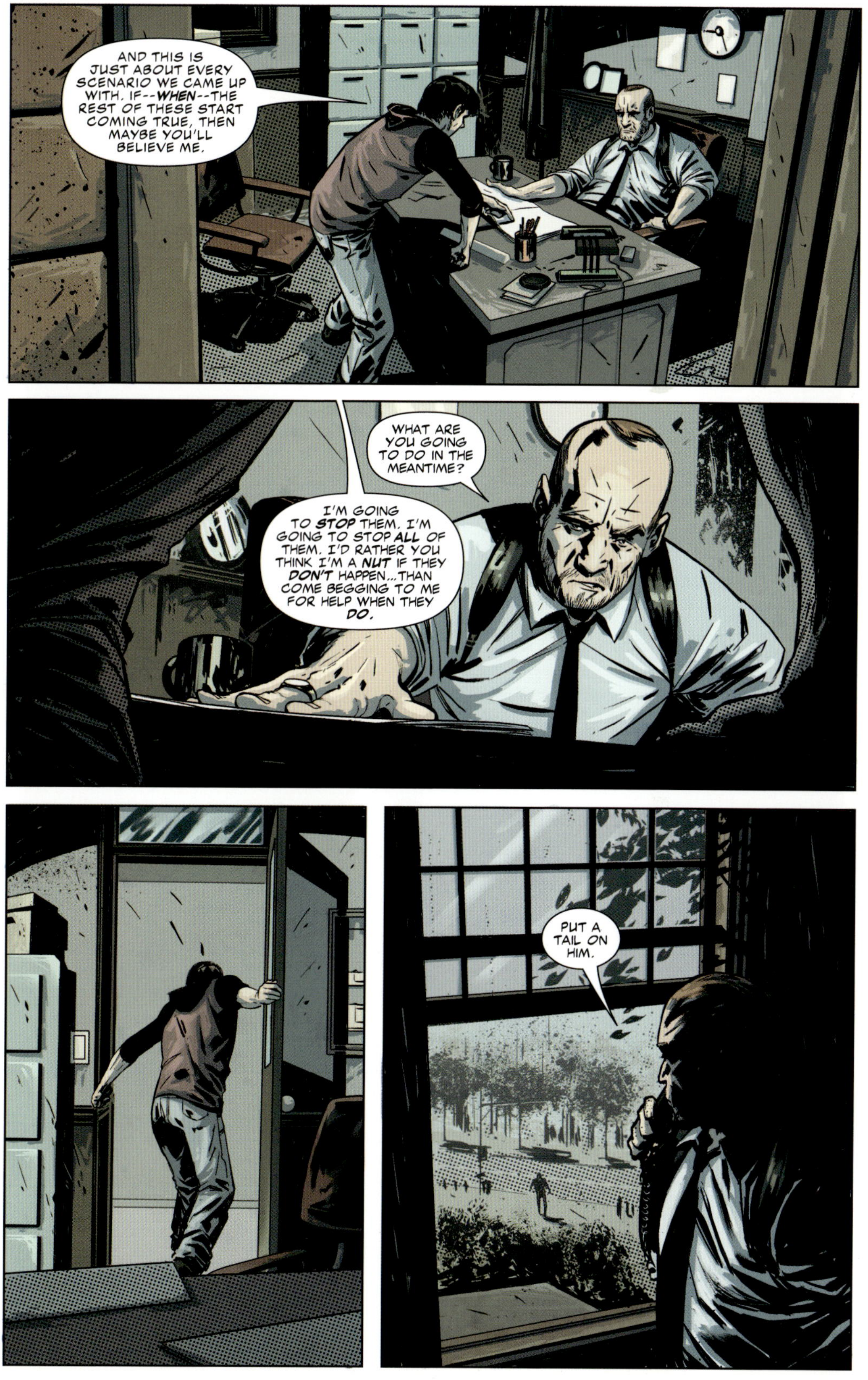
AND THIS IS JUST ABOUT EVERY SCENARIO WE CAME UP WITH. IF--WHEN--THE REST OF THESE START COMING TRUE, THEN MAYBE YOU'LL BELIEVE ME.
WHAT ARE YOU GOING TO DO IN THE MEANTIME?
I'M GOING TO STOP THEM. I'M GOING TO STOP ALL OF THEM. I'D RATHER YOU THINK I'M A NUT IF THEY DON'T HAPPEN...THAN COME BEGGING TO ME FOR HELP WHEN THEY DO.
PUT A TAIL ON HIM.

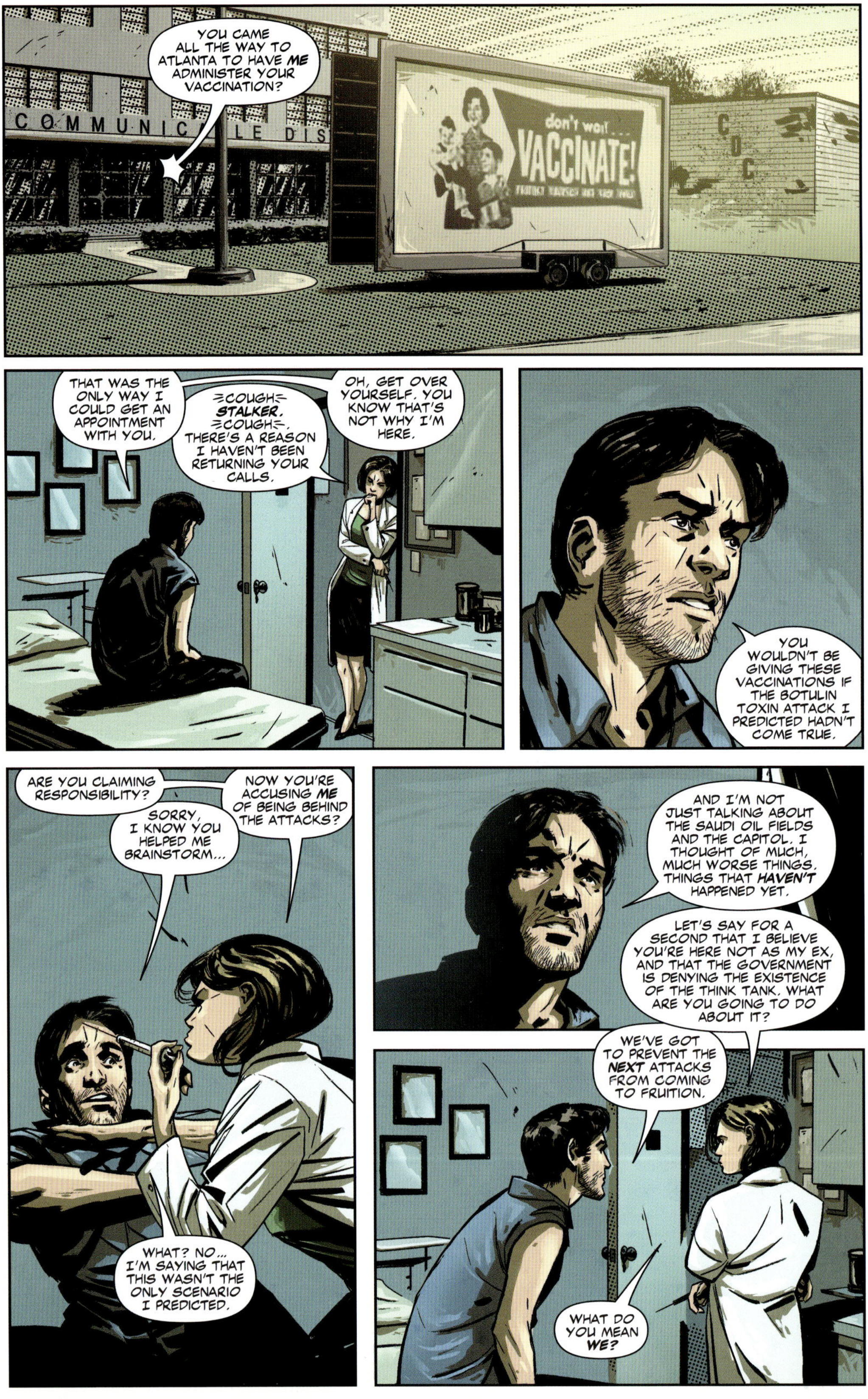
YOU CAME ALL THE WAY TO ATLANTA TO HAVE ME ADMINISTER YOUR VACCINATION?
COMMUNIC LE DIS
don't wait... VACCINATE!
C D C
THAT WAS THE ONLY WAY I COULD GET AN APPOINTMENT WITH YOU.
COUGH STALKER. COUGH. THERE'S A REASON I HAVEN'T BEEN RETURNING YOUR CALLS.
OH, GET OVER YOURSELF. YOU KNOW THAT'S NOT WHY I'M HERE.
YOU WOULDN'T BE GIVING THESE VACCINATIONS IF THE BOTULIN TOXIN ATTACK I PREDICTED HADN'T COME TRUE.
ARE YOU CLAIMING RESPONSIBILITY?
NOW YOU'RE ACCUSING ME OF BEING BEHIND THE ATTACKS?
SORRY, I KNOW YOU HELPED ME BRAINSTORM...
WHAT? NO... I'M SAYING THAT THIS WASN'T THE ONLY SCENARIO I PREDICTED.
AND I'M NOT JUST TALKING ABOUT THE SAUDI OIL FIELDS AND THE CAPITOL. I THOUGHT OF MUCH, MUCH WORSE THINGS. THINGS THAT HAVEN'T HAPPENED YET.
LET'S SAY FOR A SECOND THAT I BELIEVE YOU'RE HERE NOT AS MY EX, AND THAT THE GOVERNMENT IS DENYING THE EXISTENCE OF THE THINK TANK. WHAT ARE YOU GOING TO DO ABOUT IT?
WE'VE GOT TO PREVENT THE NEXT ATTACKS FROM COMING TO FRUITION.
WHAT DO YOU MEAN WE?

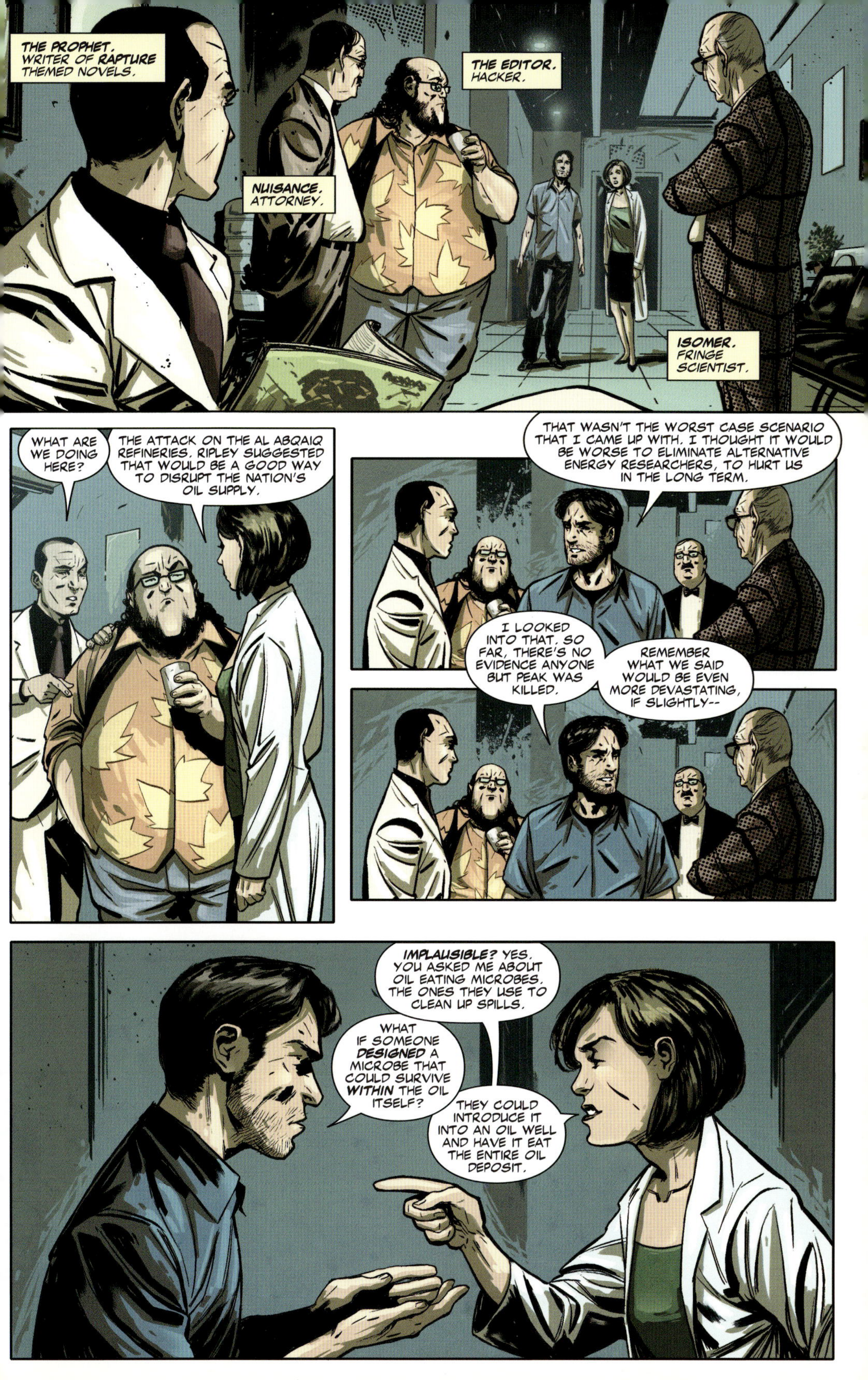
THE PROPHET. WRITER OF RAPTURE THEMED NOVELS.
NUISANCE. ATTORNEY.
THE EDITOR. HACKER.
ISOMER. FRINGE SCIENTIST.
WHAT ARE WE DOING HERE?
THE ATTACK ON THE AL ABQAIQ REFINERIES, RIPLEY SUGGESTED THAT WOULD BE A GOOD WAY TO DISRUPT THE NATION'S OIL SUPPLY.
THAT WASN'T THE WORST CASE SCENARIO THAT I CAME UP WITH. I THOUGHT IT WOULD BE WORSE TO ELIMINATE ALTERNATIVE ENERGY RESEARCHERS, TO HURT US IN THE LONG TERM.
I LOOKED INTO THAT. SO FAR, THERE'S NO EVIDENCE ANYONE BUT PEAK WAS KILLED.
REMEMBER WHAT WE SAID WOULD BE EVEN MORE DEVASTATING, IF SLIGHTLY--
IMPLAUSIBLE? YES. YOU ASKED ME ABOUT OIL EATING MICROBES, THE ONES THEY USE TO CLEAN UP SPILLS.
WHAT IF SOMEONE DESIGNED A MICROBE THAT COULD SURVIVE WITHIN THE OIL ITSELF?
THEY COULD INTRODUCE IT INTO AN OIL WELL AND HAVE IT EAT THE ENTIRE OIL DEPOSIT.

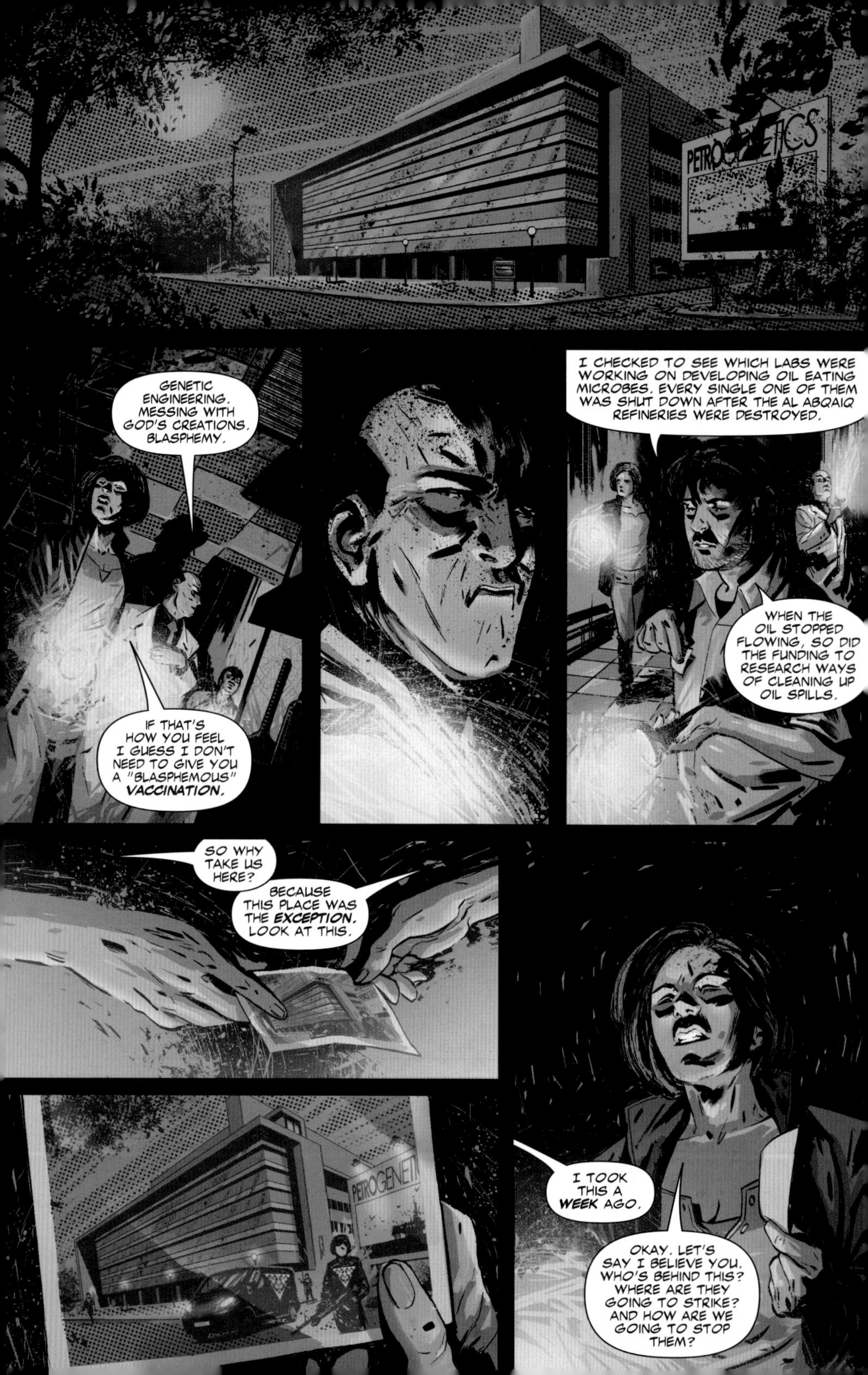
PETROGENETICS
GENETIC ENGINEERING. MESSING WITH GOD'S CREATIONS. BLASPHEMY.
IF THAT'S HOW YOU FEEL I GUESS I DON'T NEED TO GIVE YOU A "BLASPHEMOUS" **VACCINATION.**
I CHECKED TO SEE WHICH LABS WERE WORKING ON DEVELOPING OIL EATING MICROBES. EVERY SINGLE ONE OF THEM WAS SHUT DOWN AFTER THE AL ABQAIQ REFINERIES WERE DESTROYED.
WHEN THE OIL STOPPED FLOWING, SO DID THE FUNDING TO RESEARCH WAYS OF CLEANING UP OIL SPILLS.
SO WHY TAKE US HERE?
BECAUSE THIS PLACE WAS THE **EXCEPTION.** LOOK AT THIS.
PETROGENETI
I TOOK THIS A **WEEK** AGO.
OKAY. LET'S SAY I BELIEVE YOU. WHO'S BEHIND THIS? WHERE ARE THEY GOING TO STRIKE? AND HOW ARE WE GOING TO STOP THEM?

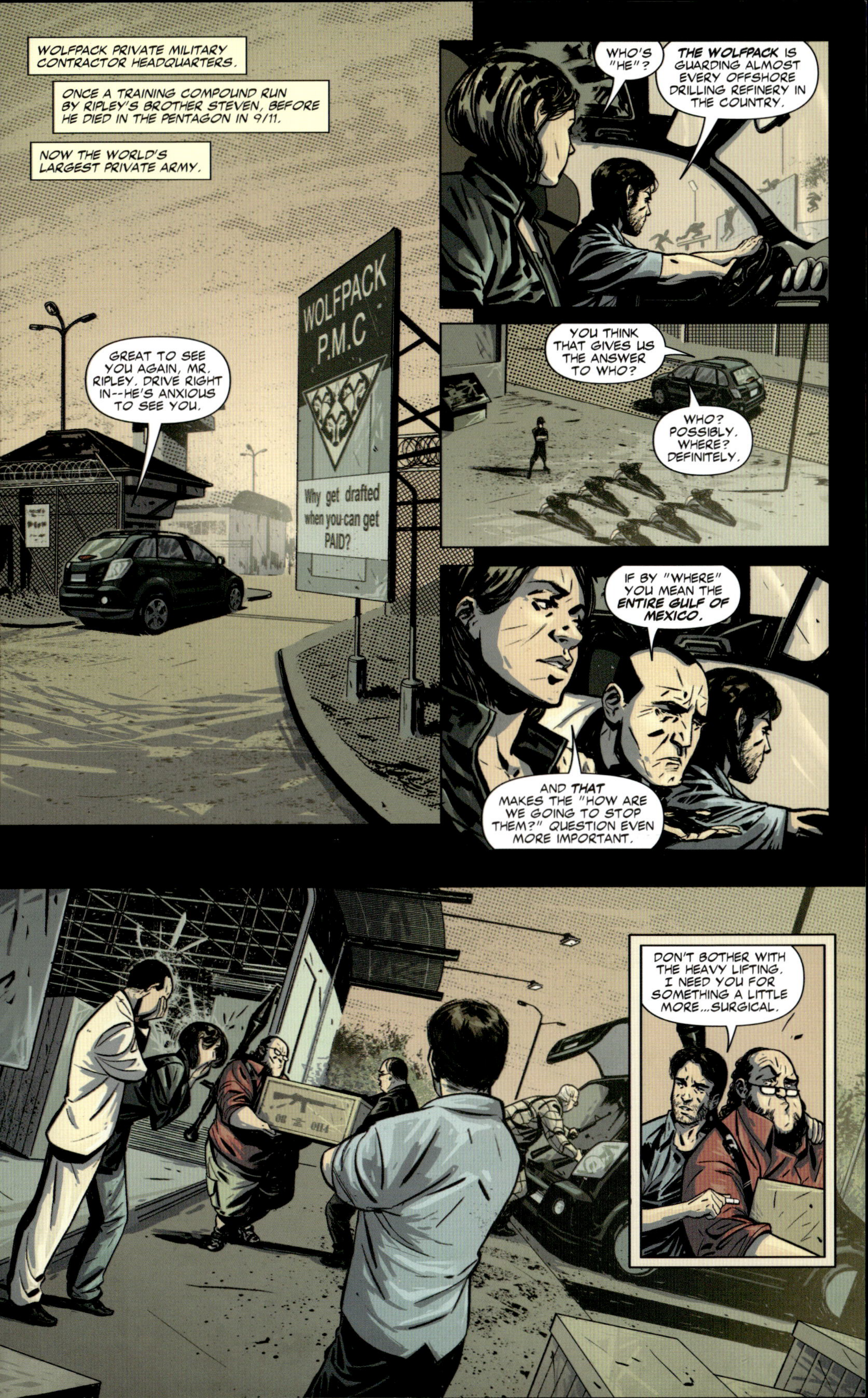
WOLFPACK PRIVATE MILITARY CONTRACTOR HEADQUARTERS.
ONCE A TRAINING COMPOUND RUN BY RIPLEY'S BROTHER STEVEN, BEFORE HE DIED IN THE PENTAGON IN 9/11.
NOW THE WORLD'S LARGEST PRIVATE ARMY.
WOLFPACK P.M.C
Why get drafted when you can get PAID?
GREAT TO SEE YOU AGAIN, MR. RIPLEY. DRIVE RIGHT IN--HE'S ANXIOUS TO SEE YOU.
WHO'S "HE"?
THE WOLFPACK IS GUARDING ALMOST EVERY OFFSHORE DRILLING REFINERY IN THE COUNTRY.
YOU THINK THAT GIVES US THE ANSWER TO WHO?
WHO? POSSIBLY. WHERE? DEFINITELY.
IF BY "WHERE" YOU MEAN THE ENTIRE GULF OF MEXICO.
AND THAT MAKES THE "HOW ARE WE GOING TO STOP THEM?" QUESTION EVEN MORE IMPORTANT.
DON'T BOTHER WITH THE HEAVY LIFTING. I NEED YOU FOR SOMETHING A LITTLE MORE...SURGICAL.

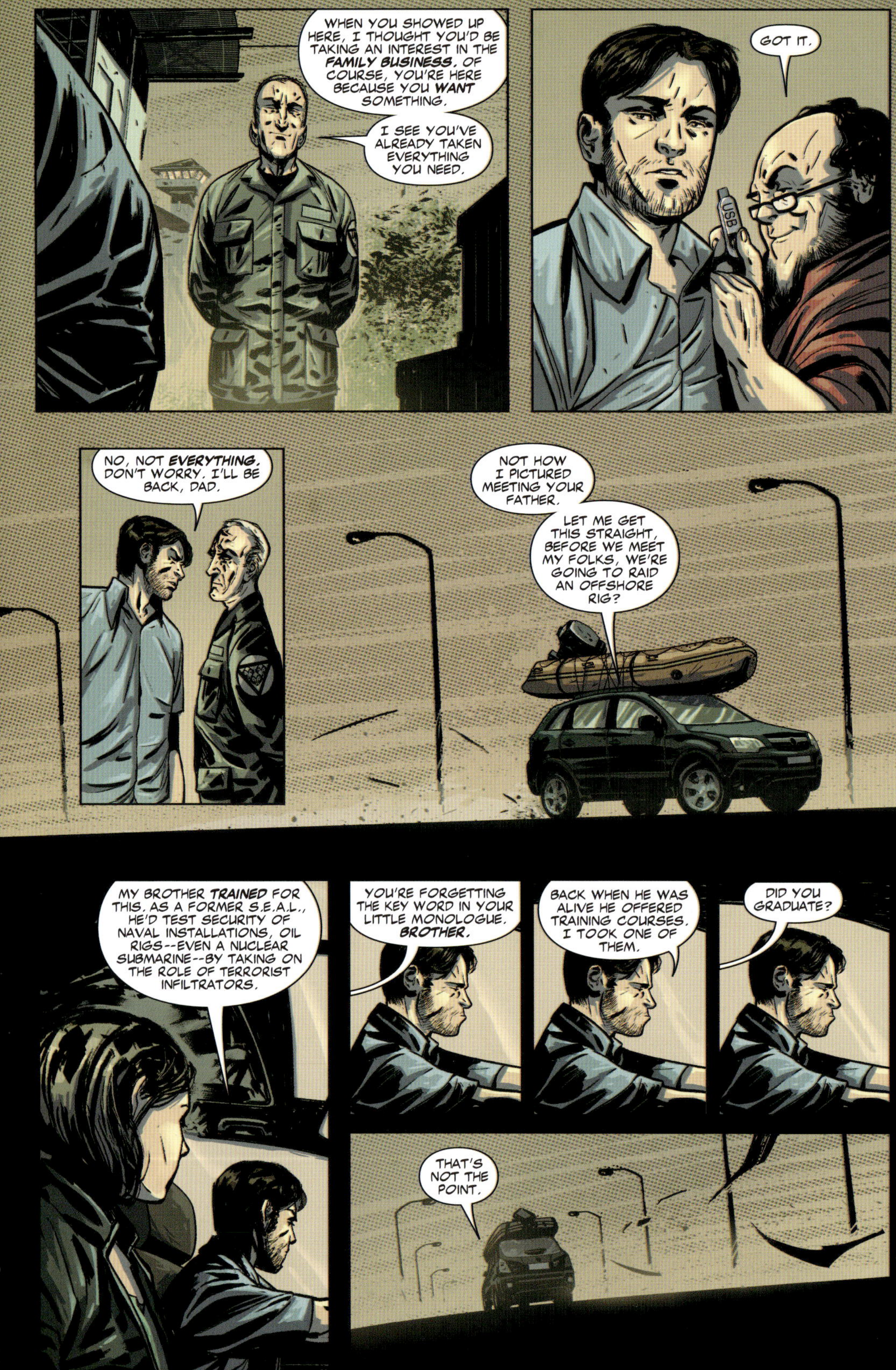
WHEN YOU SHOWED UP HERE, I THOUGHT YOU'D BE TAKING AN INTEREST IN THE FAMILY BUSINESS. OF COURSE, YOU'RE HERE BECAUSE YOU WANT SOMETHING.
I SEE YOU'VE ALREADY TAKEN EVERYTHING YOU NEED.
GOT IT.
USB
NO, NOT EVERYTHING. DON'T WORRY. I'LL BE BACK, DAD.
NOT HOW I PICTURED MEETING YOUR FATHER.
LET ME GET THIS STRAIGHT, BEFORE WE MEET MY FOLKS, WE'RE GOING TO RAID AN OFFSHORE RIG?
MY BROTHER TRAINED FOR THIS. AS A FORMER S.E.A.L., HE'D TEST SECURITY OF NAVAL INSTALLATIONS, OIL RIGS--EVEN A NUCLEAR SUBMARINE--BY TAKING ON THE ROLE OF TERRORIST INFILTRATORS.
YOU'RE FORGETTING THE KEY WORD IN YOUR LITTLE MONOLOGUE. BROTHER.
BACK WHEN HE WAS ALIVE HE OFFERED TRAINING COURSES. I TOOK ONE OF THEM.
DID YOU GRADUATE?
THAT'S NOT THE POINT.

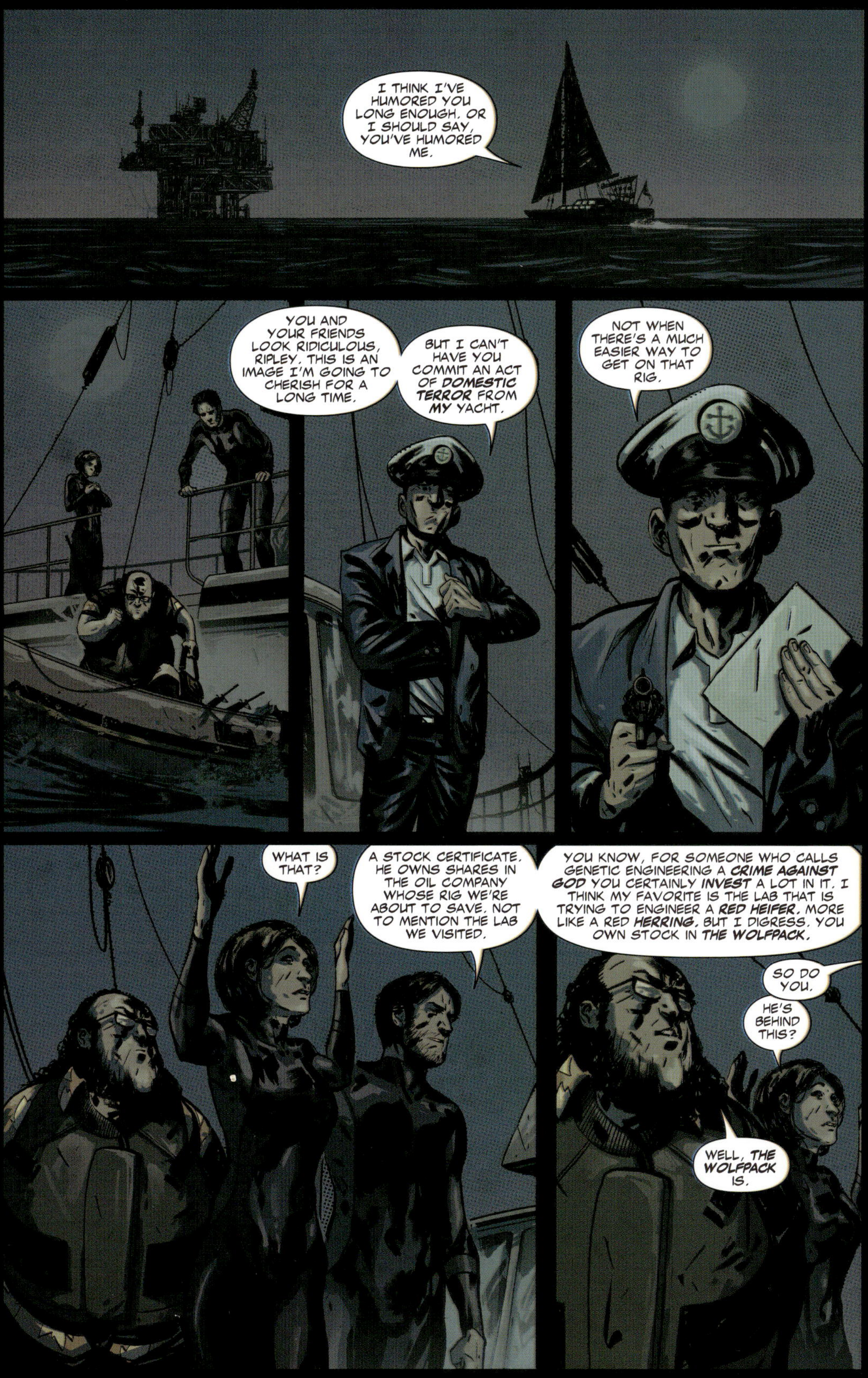
I THINK I'VE HUMORED YOU LONG ENOUGH. OR I SHOULD SAY, YOU'VE HUMORED ME.
YOU AND YOUR FRIENDS LOOK RIDICULOUS, RIPLEY. THIS IS AN IMAGE I'M GOING TO CHERISH FOR A LONG TIME.
BUT I CAN'T HAVE YOU COMMIT AN ACT OF **DOMESTIC TERROR** FROM **MY** YACHT.
NOT WHEN THERE'S A MUCH EASIER WAY TO GET ON THAT RIG.
WHAT IS THAT?
A STOCK CERTIFICATE. HE OWNS SHARES IN THE OIL COMPANY WHOSE RIG WE'RE ABOUT TO SAVE. NOT TO MENTION THE LAB WE VISITED.
YOU KNOW, FOR SOMEONE WHO CALLS GENETIC ENGINEERING A **CRIME AGAINST GOD** YOU CERTAINLY **INVEST** A LOT IN IT. I THINK MY FAVORITE IS THE LAB THAT IS TRYING TO ENGINEER A **RED HEIFER.** MORE LIKE A RED **HERRING.** BUT I DIGRESS. YOU OWN STOCK IN **THE WOLFPACK.**
SO DO YOU.
HE'S BEHIND THIS?
WELL, **THE WOLFPACK** IS.

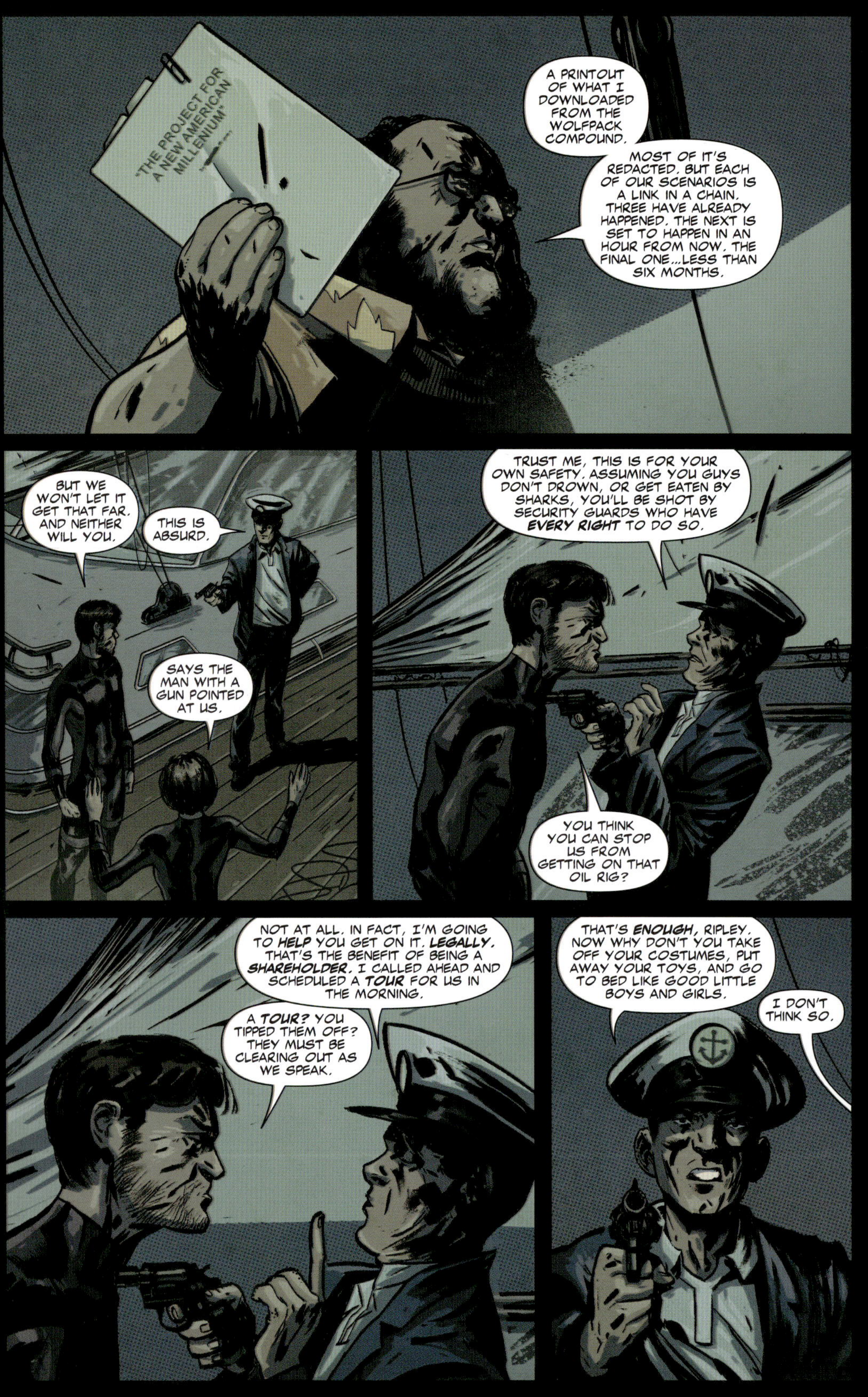

"THE PROJECT FOR A NEW AMERICAN MILLENIUM"
A PRINTOUT OF WHAT I DOWNLOADED FROM THE WOLFPACK COMPOUND.
MOST OF IT'S REDACTED. BUT EACH OF OUR SCENARIOS IS A LINK IN A CHAIN. THREE HAVE ALREADY HAPPENED. THE NEXT IS SET TO HAPPEN IN AN HOUR FROM NOW. THE FINAL ONE...LESS THAN SIX MONTHS.
BUT WE WON'T LET IT GET THAT FAR. AND NEITHER WILL YOU.
THIS IS ABSURD.
SAYS THE MAN WITH A GUN POINTED AT US.
TRUST ME, THIS IS FOR YOUR OWN SAFETY. ASSUMING YOU GUYS DON'T DROWN, OR GET EATEN BY SHARKS, YOU'LL BE SHOT BY SECURITY GUARDS WHO HAVE **EVERY RIGHT** TO DO SO.
YOU THINK YOU CAN STOP US FROM GETTING ON THAT OIL RIG?
NOT AT ALL. IN FACT, I'M GOING TO **HELP** YOU GET ON IT. **LEGALLY.** THAT'S THE BENEFIT OF BEING A **SHAREHOLDER.** I CALLED AHEAD AND SCHEDULED A **TOUR** FOR US IN THE MORNING.
A **TOUR?** YOU TIPPED THEM OFF? THEY MUST BE CLEARING OUT AS WE SPEAK.
THAT'S **ENOUGH,** RIPLEY. NOW WHY DON'T YOU TAKE OFF YOUR COSTUMES, PUT AWAY YOUR TOYS, AND GO TO BED LIKE GOOD LITTLE BOYS AND GIRLS.
I DON'T THINK SO.

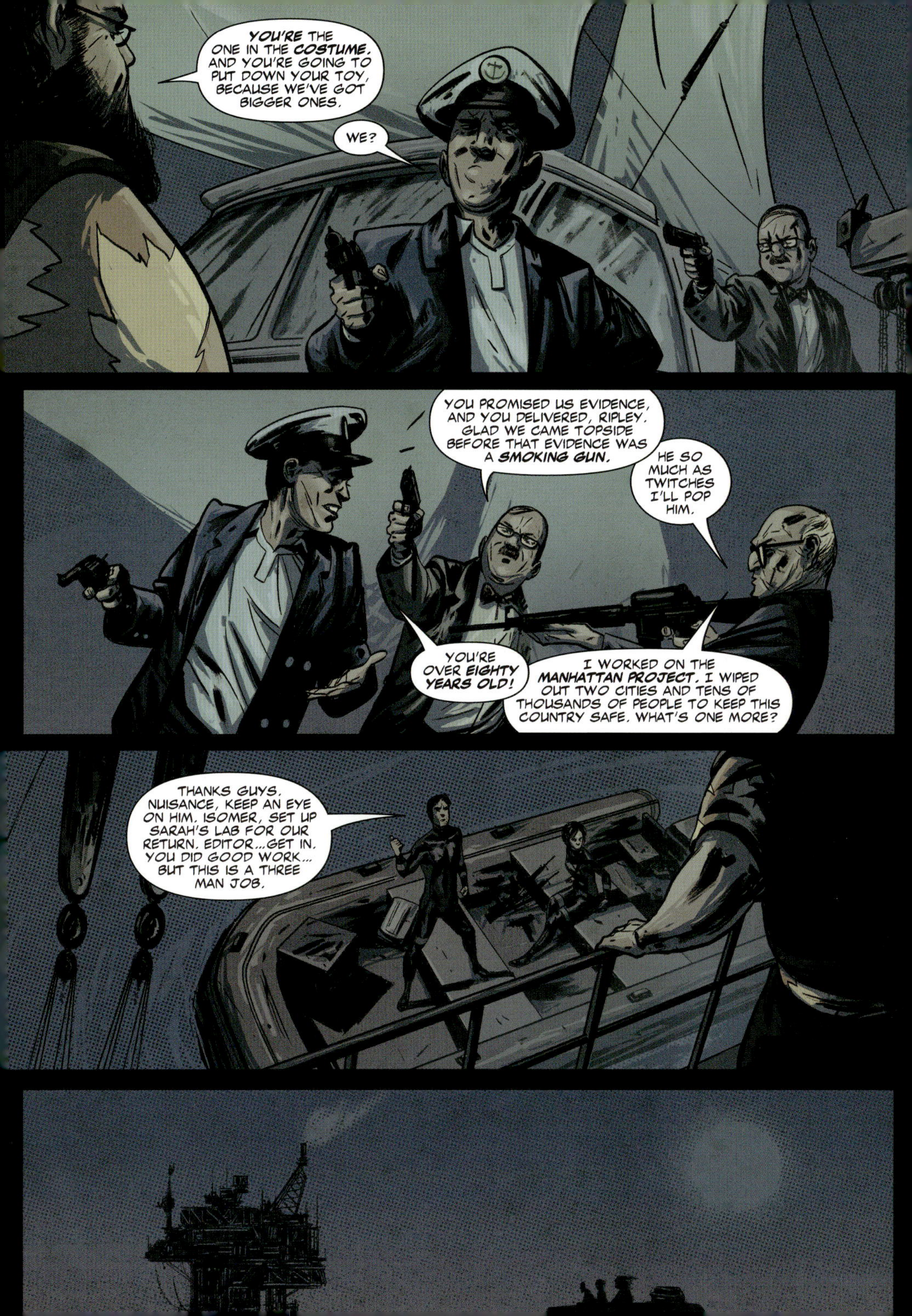
YOU'RE THE ONE IN THE COSTUME, AND YOU'RE GOING TO PUT DOWN YOUR TOY, BECAUSE WE'VE GOT BIGGER ONES.
WE?
YOU PROMISED US EVIDENCE, AND YOU DELIVERED, RIPLEY. GLAD WE CAME TOPSIDE BEFORE THAT EVIDENCE WAS A SMOKING GUN.
HE SO MUCH AS TWITCHES I'LL POP HIM.
YOU'RE OVER EIGHTY YEARS OLD!
I WORKED ON THE MANHATTAN PROJECT. I WIPED OUT TWO CITIES AND TENS OF THOUSANDS OF PEOPLE TO KEEP THIS COUNTRY SAFE. WHAT'S ONE MORE?
THANKS GUYS. NUISANCE, KEEP AN EYE ON HIM. ISOMER, SET UP SARAH'S LAB FOR OUR RETURN. EDITOR...GET IN. YOU DID GOOD WORK... BUT THIS IS A THREE MAN JOB.

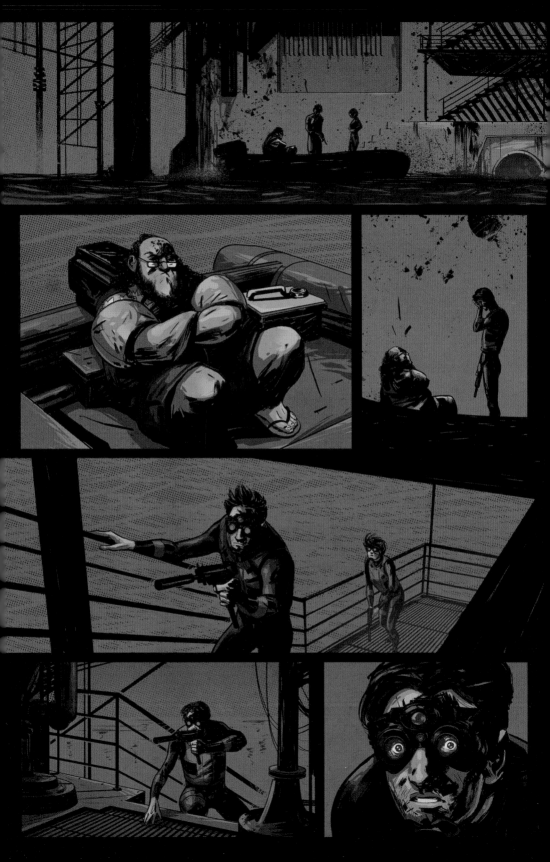

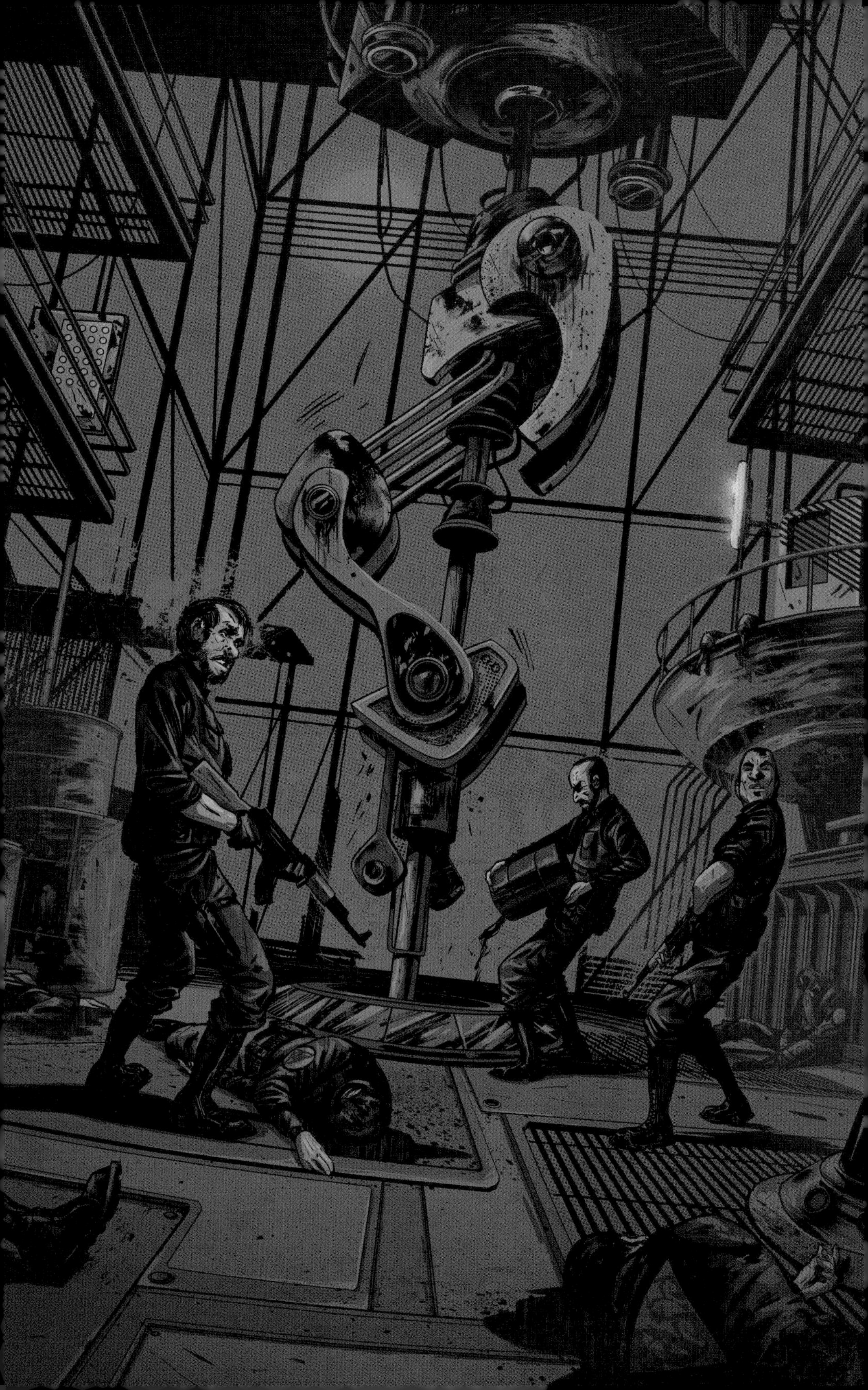

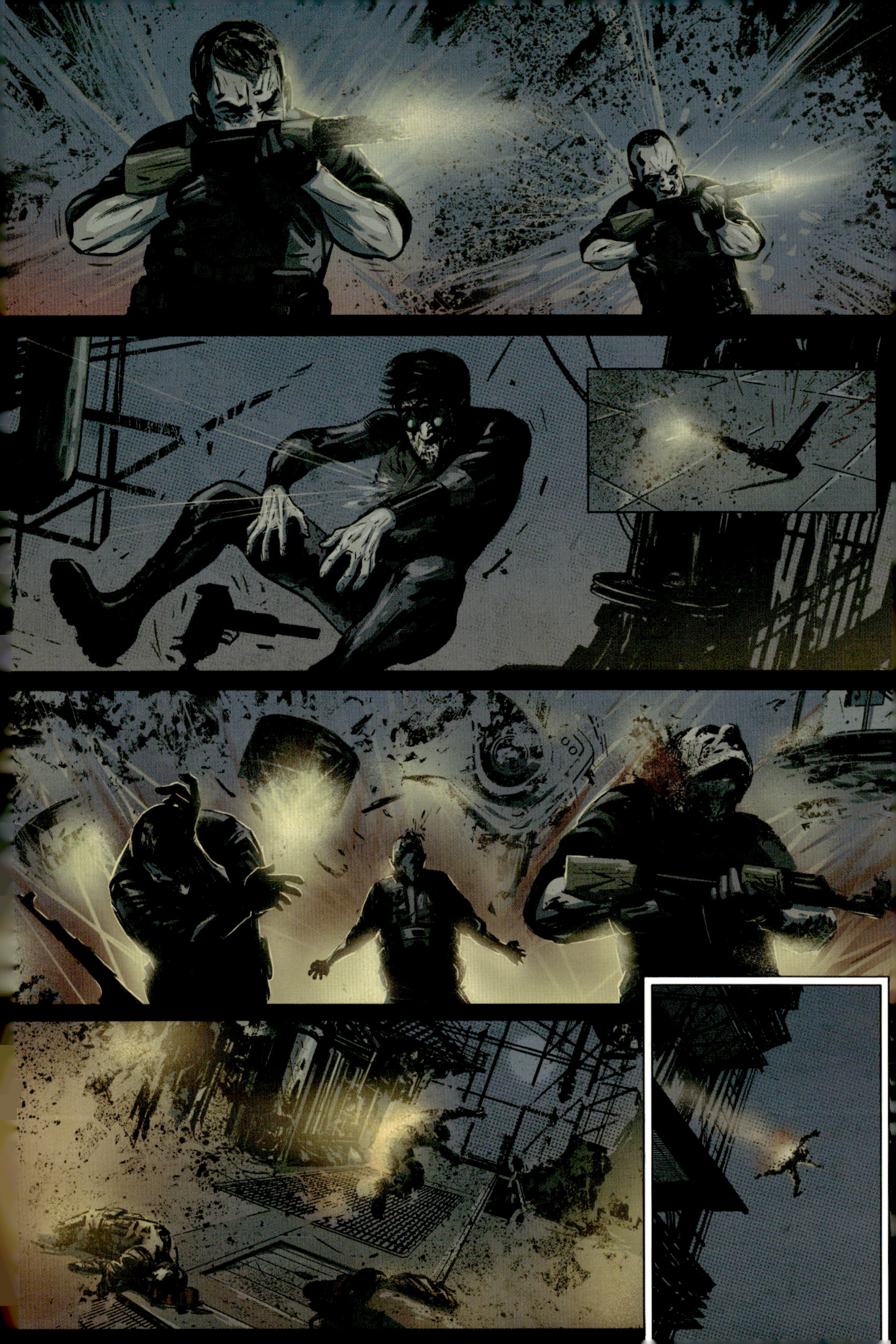

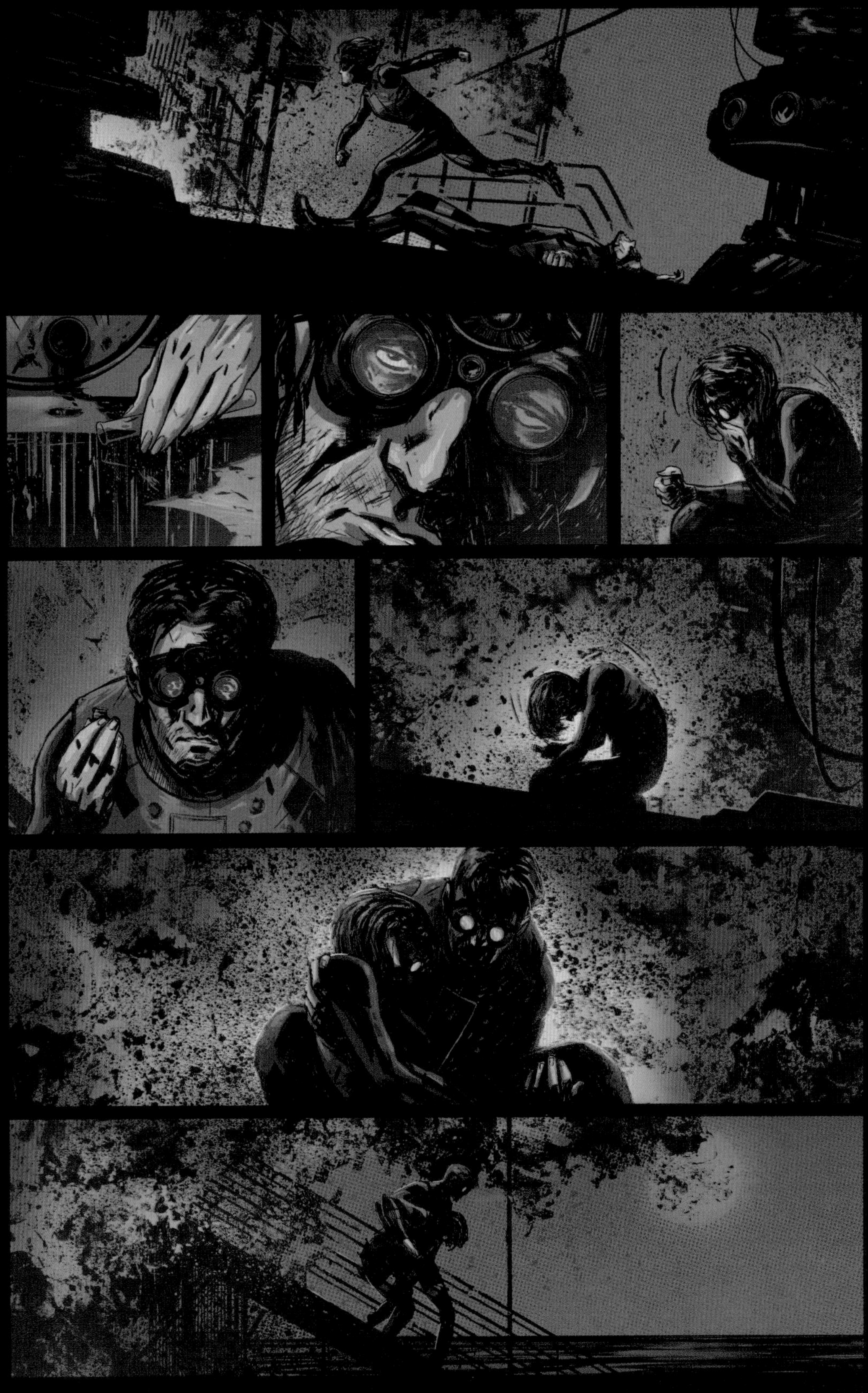

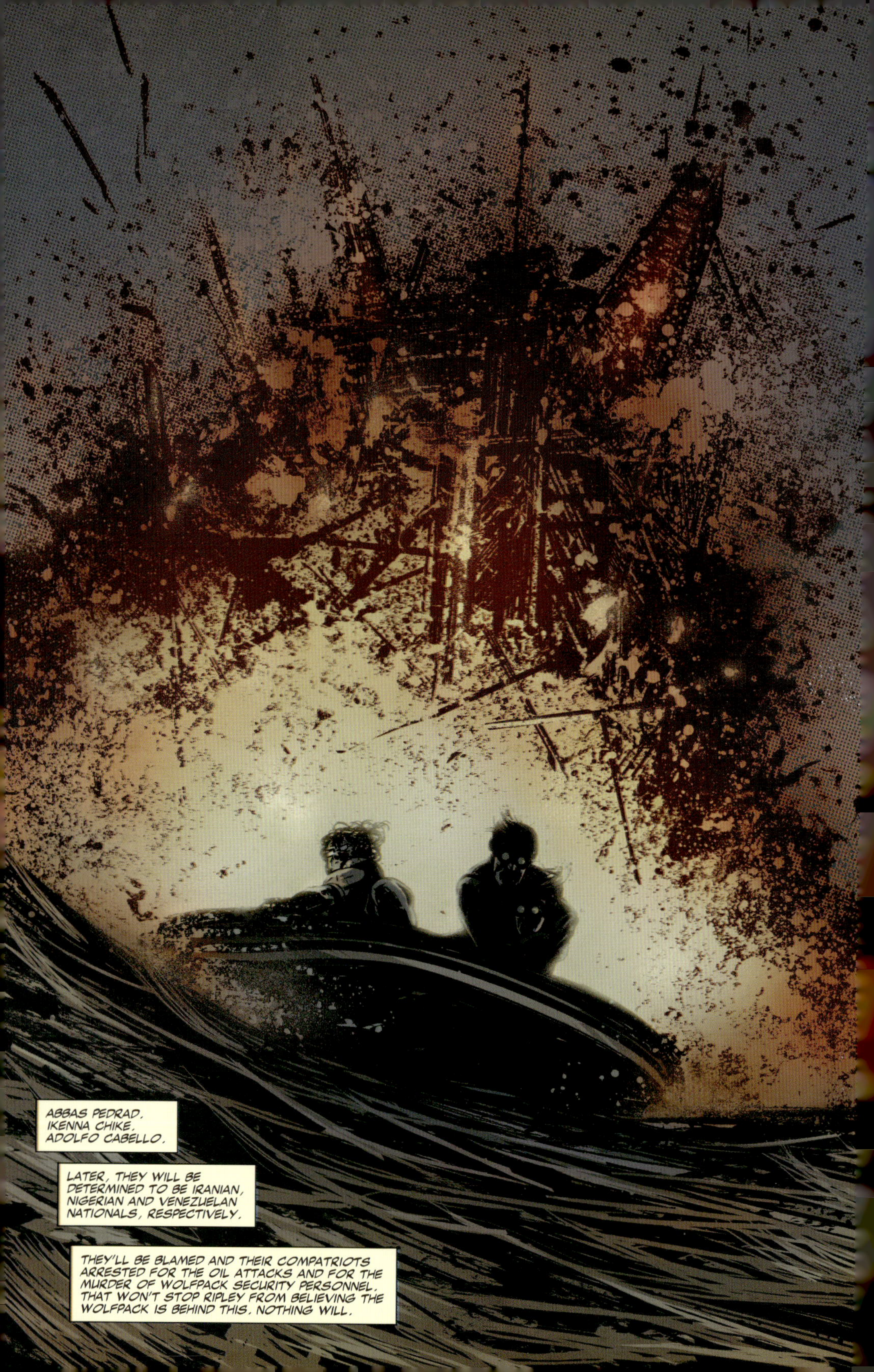
ABBAS PEDRAD.
IKENNA CHIKE.
ADOLFO CABELLO.
LATER, THEY WILL BE DETERMINED TO BE IRANIAN, NIGERIAN AND VENEZUELAN NATIONALS, RESPECTIVELY.
THEY'LL BE BLAMED AND THEIR COMPATRIOTS ARRESTED FOR THE OIL ATTACKS AND FOR THE MURDER OF WOLFPACK SECURITY PERSONNEL. THAT WON'T STOP RIPLEY FROM BELIEVING THE WOLFPACK IS BEHIND THIS. NOTHING WILL.

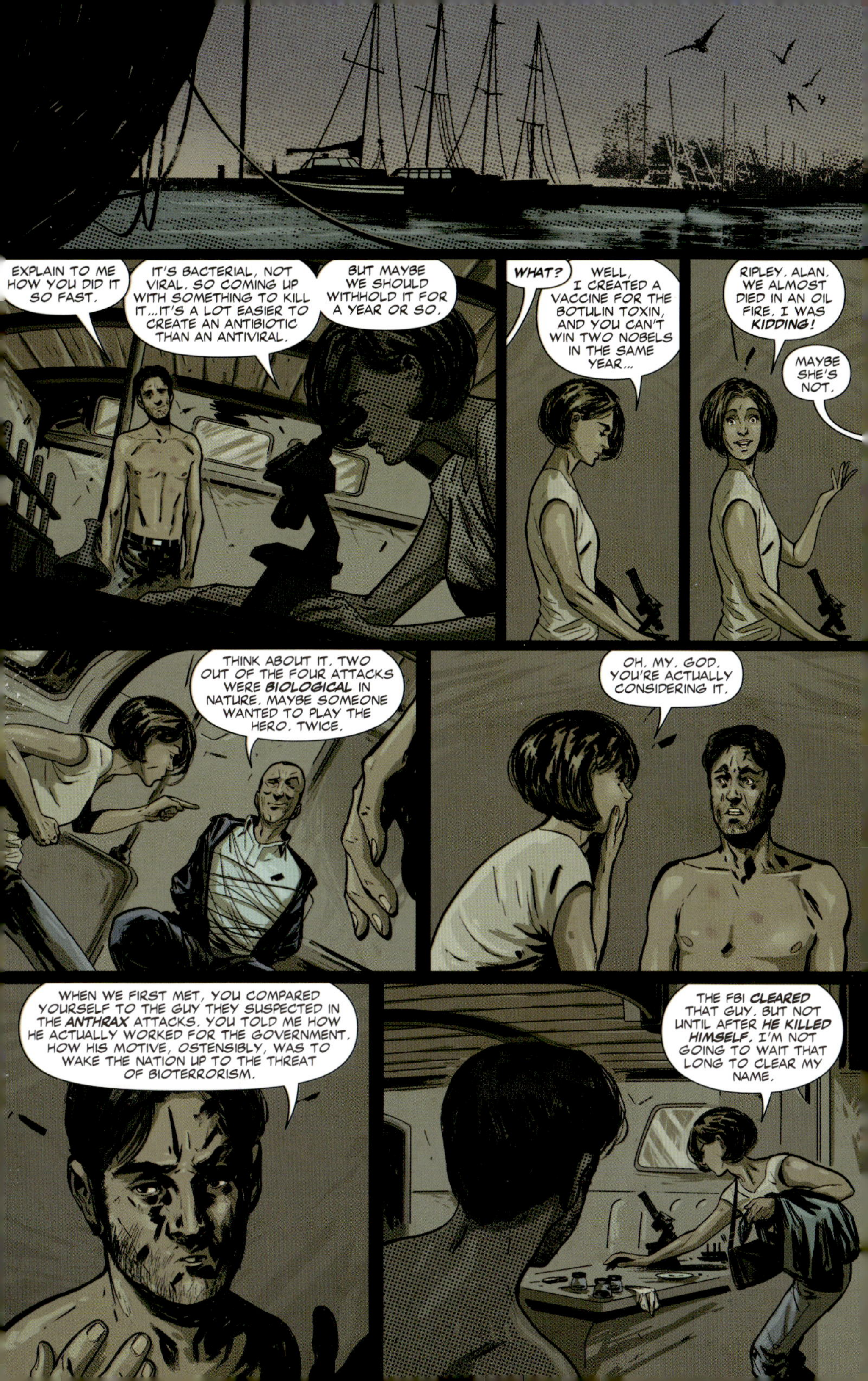

EXPLAIN TO ME HOW YOU DID IT SO FAST.
IT'S BACTERIAL, NOT VIRAL. SO COMING UP WITH SOMETHING TO KILL IT...IT'S A LOT EASIER TO CREATE AN ANTIBIOTIC THAN AN ANTIVIRAL.
BUT MAYBE WE SHOULD WITHHOLD IT FOR A YEAR OR SO.
WHAT?
WELL, I CREATED A VACCINE FOR THE BOTULIN TOXIN, AND YOU CAN'T WIN TWO NOBELS IN THE SAME YEAR...
RIPLEY. ALAN. WE ALMOST DIED IN AN OIL FIRE. I WAS KIDDING!
MAYBE SHE'S NOT.
THINK ABOUT IT. TWO OUT OF THE FOUR ATTACKS WERE BIOLOGICAL IN NATURE. MAYBE SOMEONE WANTED TO PLAY THE HERO. TWICE.
OH. MY. GOD. YOU'RE ACTUALLY CONSIDERING IT.
WHEN WE FIRST MET, YOU COMPARED YOURSELF TO THE GUY THEY SUSPECTED IN THE ANTHRAX ATTACKS. YOU TOLD ME HOW HE ACTUALLY WORKED FOR THE GOVERNMENT. HOW HIS MOTIVE, OSTENSIBLY, WAS TO WAKE THE NATION UP TO THE THREAT OF BIOTERRORISM.
THE FBI CLEARED THAT GUY. BUT NOT UNTIL AFTER HE KILLED HIMSELF. I'M NOT GOING TO WAIT THAT LONG TO CLEAR MY NAME.

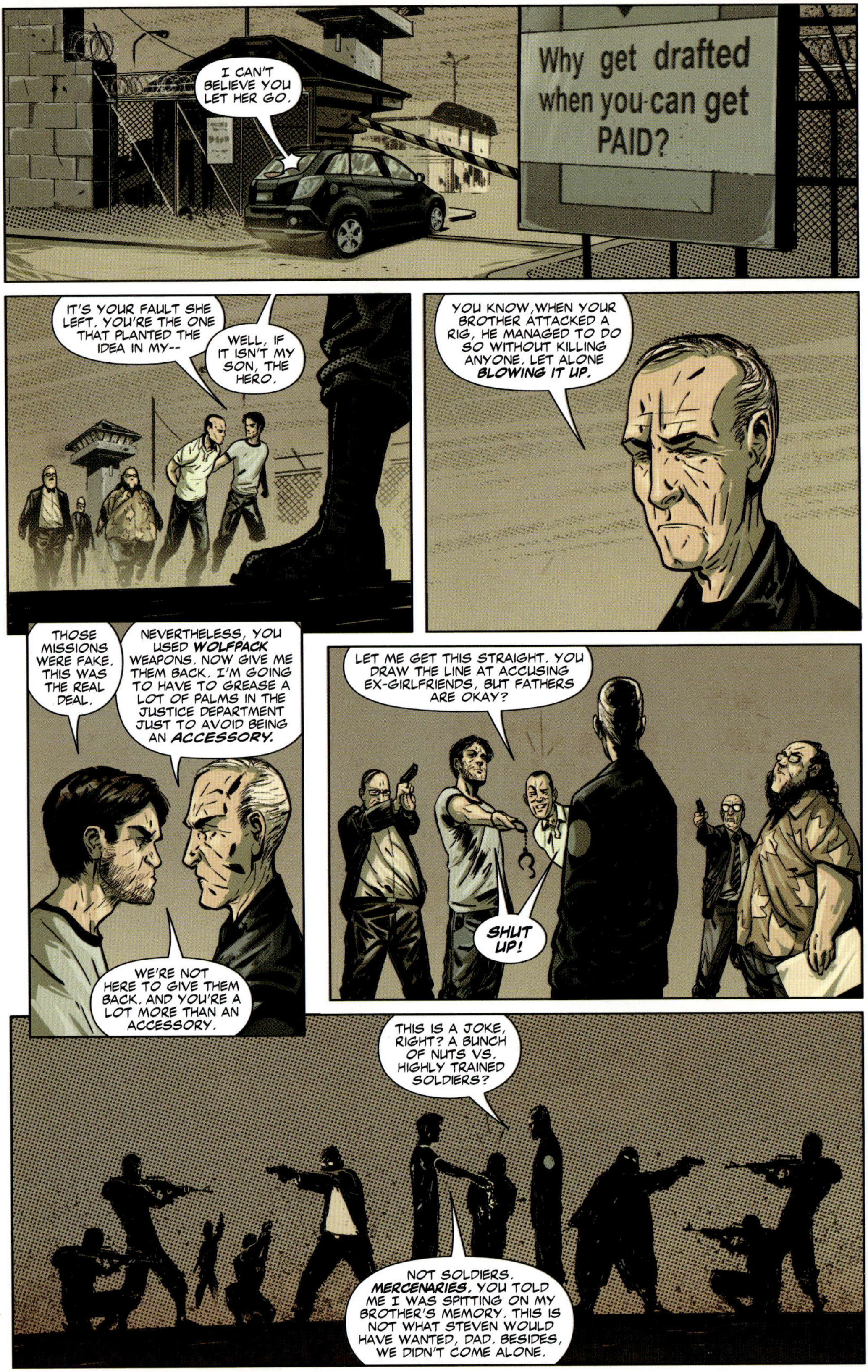
I CAN'T BELIEVE YOU LET HER GO.
Why get drafted when you can get PAID?
IT'S YOUR FAULT SHE LEFT. YOU'RE THE ONE THAT PLANTED THE IDEA IN MY--
WELL, IF IT ISN'T MY SON, THE HERO.
YOU KNOW, WHEN YOUR BROTHER ATTACKED A RIG, HE MANAGED TO DO SO WITHOUT KILLING ANYONE. LET ALONE BLOWING IT UP.
THOSE MISSIONS WERE FAKE. THIS WAS THE REAL DEAL.
NEVERTHELESS, YOU USED WOLFPACK WEAPONS. NOW GIVE ME THEM BACK. I'M GOING TO HAVE TO GREASE A LOT OF PALMS IN THE JUSTICE DEPARTMENT JUST TO AVOID BEING AN ACCESSORY.
WE'RE NOT HERE TO GIVE THEM BACK. AND YOU'RE A LOT MORE THAN AN ACCESSORY.
LET ME GET THIS STRAIGHT. YOU DRAW THE LINE AT ACCUSING EX-GIRLFRIENDS, BUT FATHERS ARE OKAY?
SHUT UP!
THIS IS A JOKE, RIGHT? A BUNCH OF NUTS VS. HIGHLY TRAINED SOLDIERS?
NOT SOLDIERS. MERCENARIES. YOU TOLD ME I WAS SPITTING ON MY BROTHER'S MEMORY. THIS IS NOT WHAT STEVEN WOULD HAVE WANTED, DAD. BESIDES, WE DIDN'T COME ALONE.

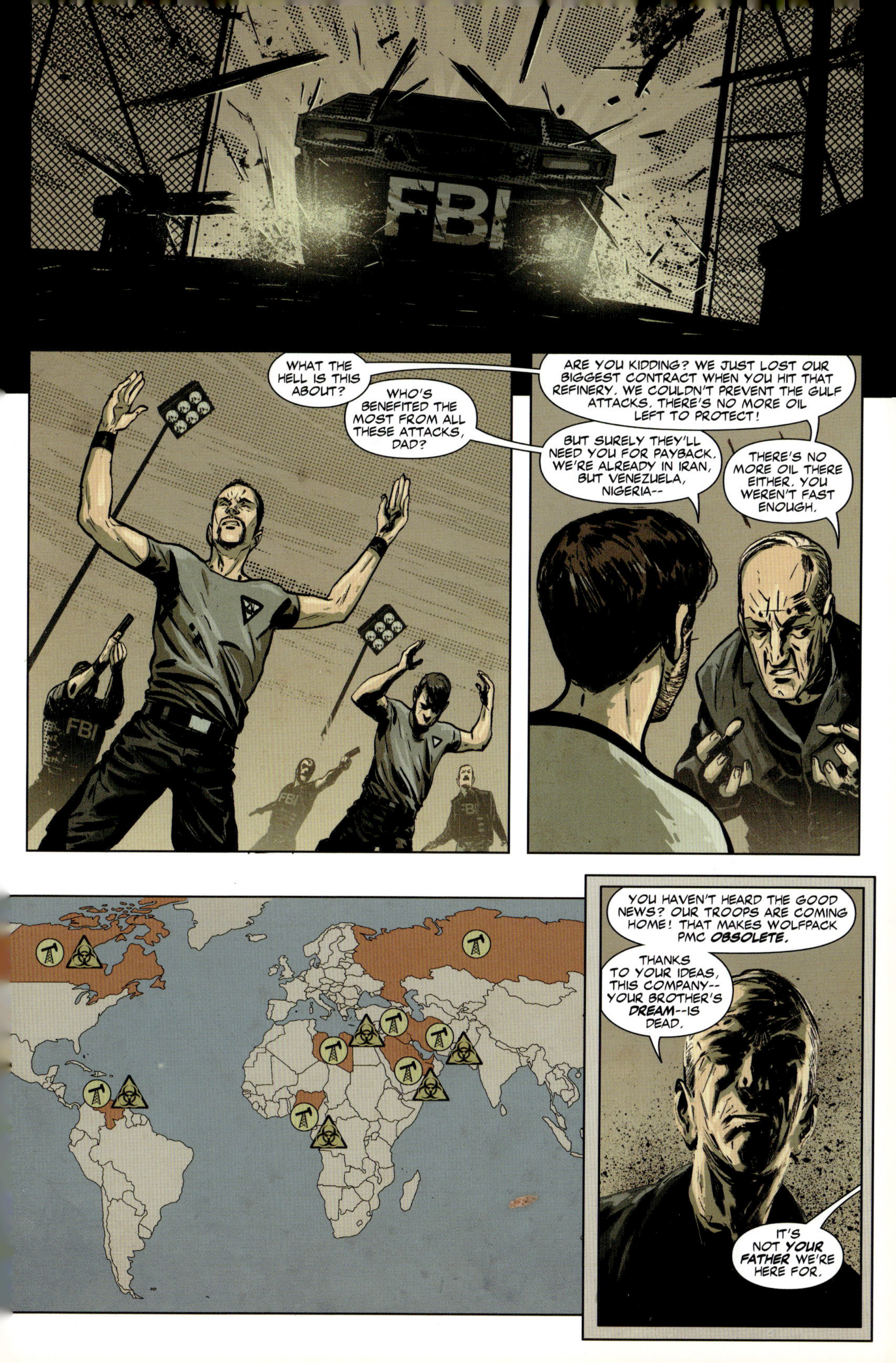
FBI
WHAT THE HELL IS THIS ABOUT?
WHO'S BENEFITED THE MOST FROM ALL THESE ATTACKS, DAD?
ARE YOU KIDDING? WE JUST LOST OUR BIGGEST CONTRACT WHEN YOU HIT THAT REFINERY. WE COULDN'T PREVENT THE GULF ATTACKS. THERE'S NO MORE OIL LEFT TO PROTECT!
BUT SURELY THEY'LL NEED YOU FOR PAYBACK. WE'RE ALREADY IN IRAN, BUT VENEZUELA, NIGERIA--
THERE'S NO MORE OIL THERE EITHER. YOU WEREN'T FAST ENOUGH.
YOU HAVEN'T HEARD THE GOOD NEWS? OUR TROOPS ARE COMING HOME! THAT MAKES WOLFPACK PMC **OBSOLETE.**
THANKS TO YOUR IDEAS, THIS COMPANY-- YOUR BROTHER'S **DREAM**--IS DEAD.
IT'S NOT **YOUR FATHER** WE'RE HERE FOR.

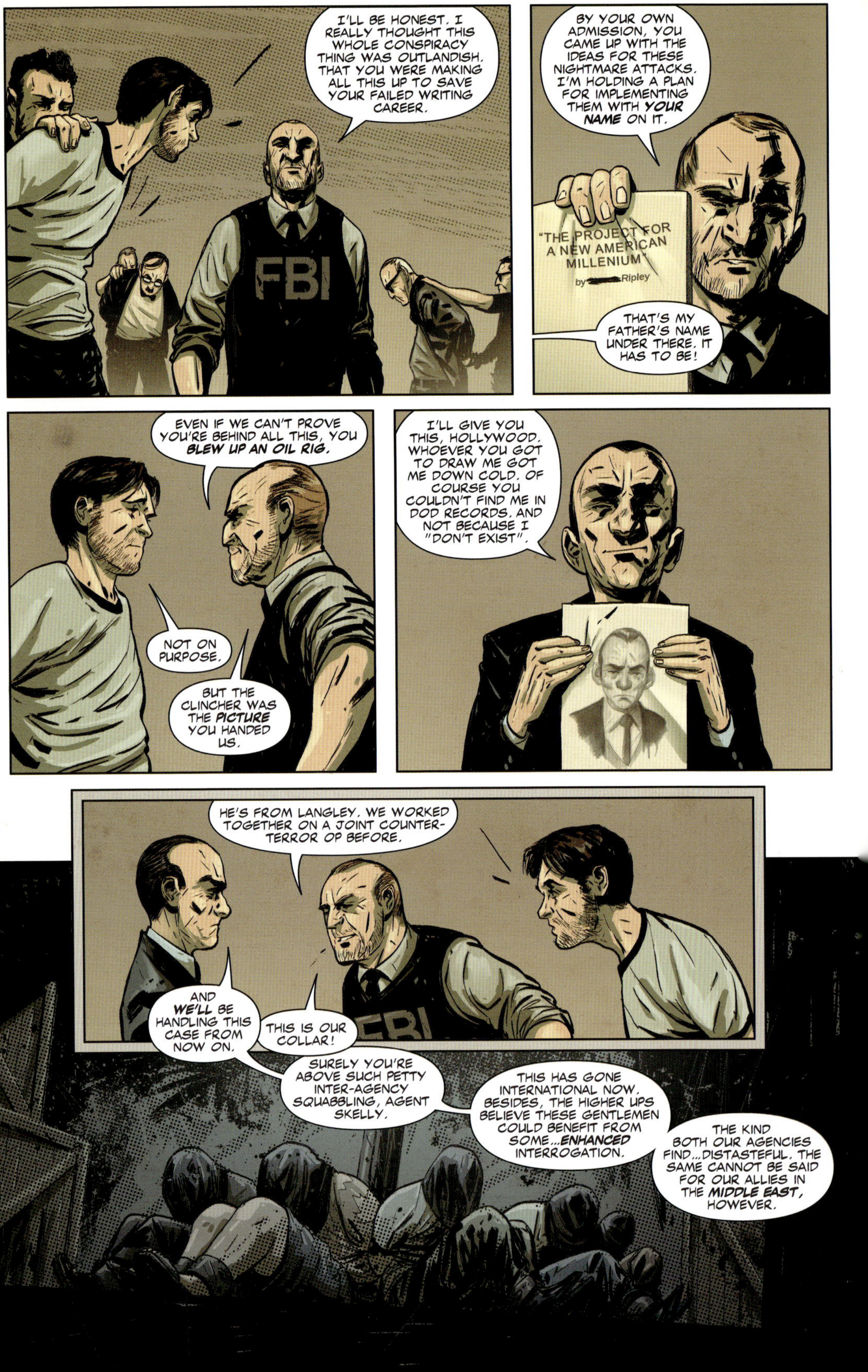
I'LL BE HONEST. I REALLY THOUGHT THIS WHOLE CONSPIRACY THING WAS OUTLANDISH. THAT YOU WERE MAKING ALL THIS UP TO SAVE YOUR FAILED WRITING CAREER.
FBI
BY YOUR OWN ADMISSION, YOU CAME UP WITH THE IDEAS FOR THESE NIGHTMARE ATTACKS. I'M HOLDING A PLAN FOR IMPLEMENTING THEM WITH YOUR NAME ON IT.
"THE PROJECT FOR A NEW AMERICAN MILLENIUM"
by [redacted] Ripley
THAT'S MY FATHER'S NAME UNDER THERE. IT HAS TO BE!
EVEN IF WE CAN'T PROVE YOU'RE BEHIND ALL THIS, YOU BLEW UP AN OIL RIG.
NOT ON PURPOSE.
BUT THE CLINCHER WAS THE PICTURE YOU HANDED US.
I'LL GIVE YOU THIS, HOLLYWOOD. WHOEVER YOU GOT TO DRAW ME GOT ME DOWN COLD. OF COURSE YOU COULDN'T FIND ME IN DOD RECORDS. AND NOT BECAUSE I "DON'T EXIST".
HE'S FROM LANGLEY. WE WORKED TOGETHER ON A JOINT COUNTER-TERROR OP BEFORE.
AND WE'LL BE HANDLING THIS CASE FROM NOW ON.
THIS IS OUR COLLAR!
SURELY YOU'RE ABOVE SUCH PETTY INTER-AGENCY SQUABBLING, AGENT SKELLY.
THIS HAS GONE INTERNATIONAL NOW. BESIDES, THE HIGHER UPS BELIEVE THESE GENTLEMEN COULD BENEFIT FROM SOME...ENHANCED INTERROGATION.
THE KIND BOTH OUR AGENCIES FIND...DISTASTEFUL. THE SAME CANNOT BE SAID FOR OUR ALLIES IN THE MIDDLE EAST, HOWEVER.

CHAPTER THREE

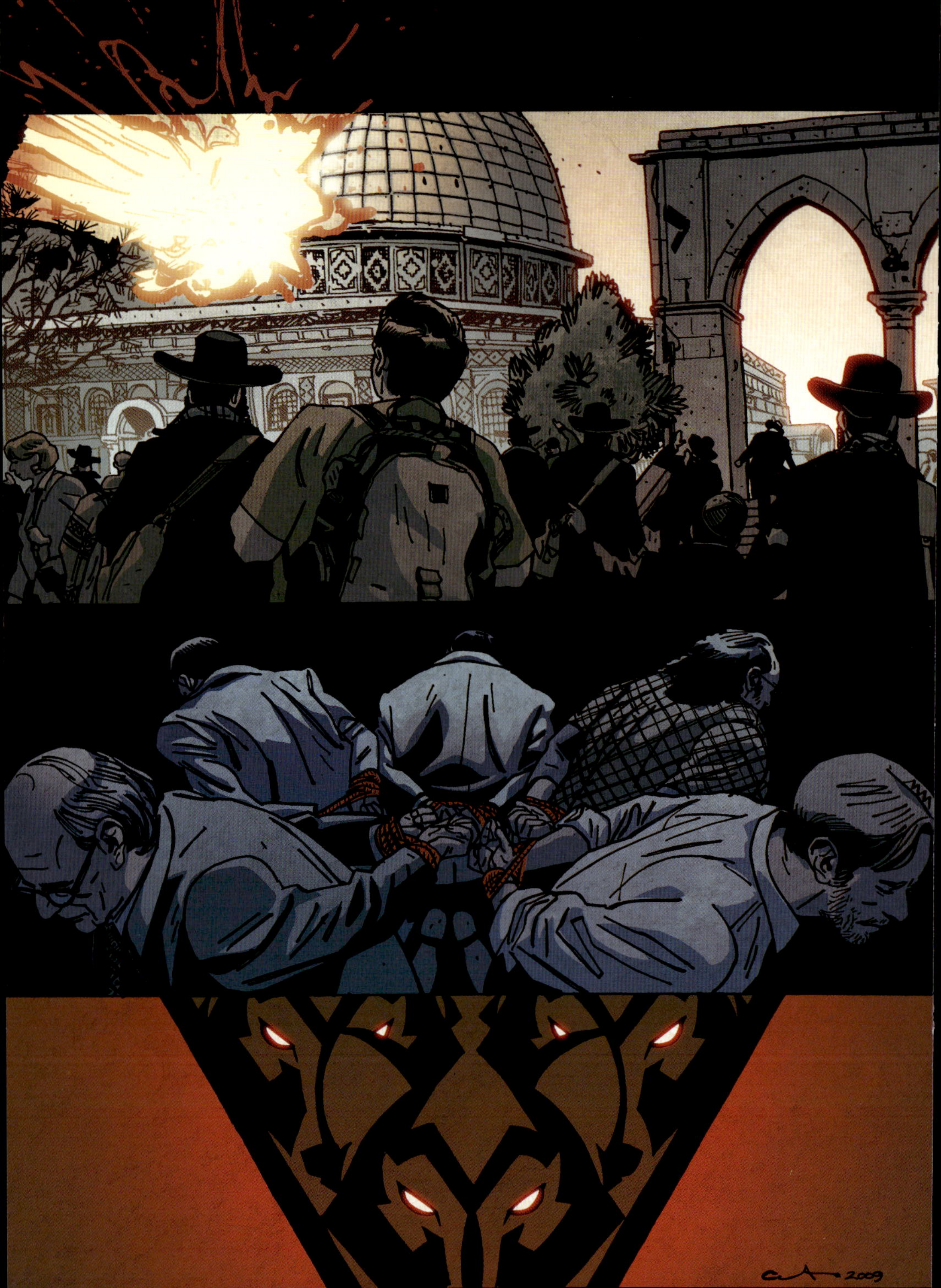

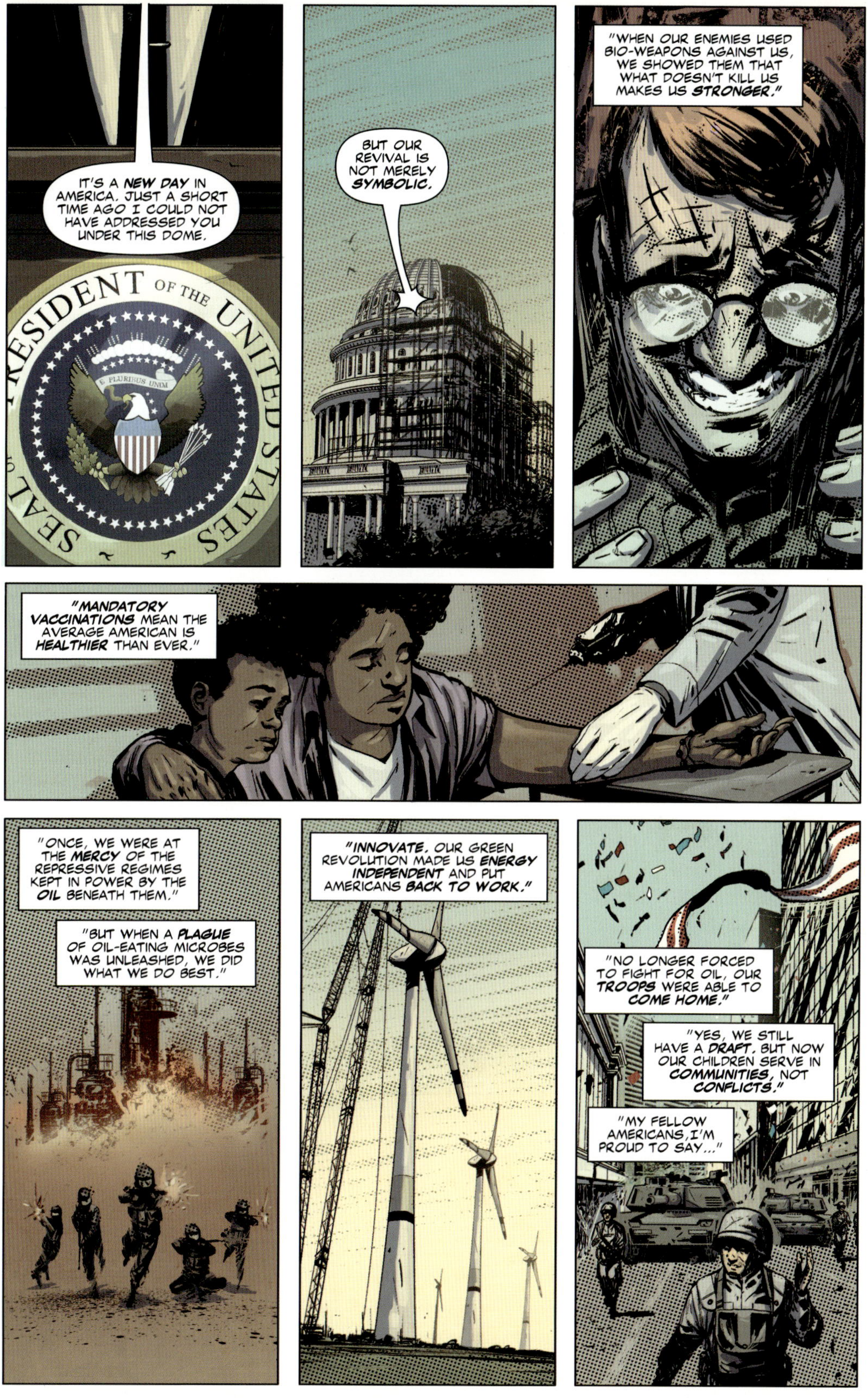

IT'S A NEW DAY IN AMERICA. JUST A SHORT TIME AGO I COULD NOT HAVE ADDRESSED YOU UNDER THIS DOME.
PRESIDENT OF THE UNITED STATES
SEAL OF
E PLURIBUS UNUM
BUT OUR REVIVAL IS NOT MERELY SYMBOLIC.
"WHEN OUR ENEMIES USED BIO-WEAPONS AGAINST US, WE SHOWED THEM THAT WHAT DOESN'T KILL US MAKES US STRONGER."
"MANDATORY VACCINATIONS MEAN THE AVERAGE AMERICAN IS HEALTHIER THAN EVER."
"ONCE, WE WERE AT THE MERCY OF THE REPRESSIVE REGIMES KEPT IN POWER BY THE OIL BENEATH THEM."
"BUT WHEN A PLAGUE OF OIL-EATING MICROBES WAS UNLEASHED, WE DID WHAT WE DO BEST."
"INNOVATE. OUR GREEN REVOLUTION MADE US ENERGY INDEPENDENT AND PUT AMERICANS BACK TO WORK."
"NO LONGER FORCED TO FIGHT FOR OIL, OUR TROOPS WERE ABLE TO COME HOME."
"YES, WE STILL HAVE A DRAFT, BUT NOW OUR CHILDREN SERVE IN COMMUNITIES, NOT CONFLICTS."
"MY FELLOW AMERICANS, I'M PROUD TO SAY..."

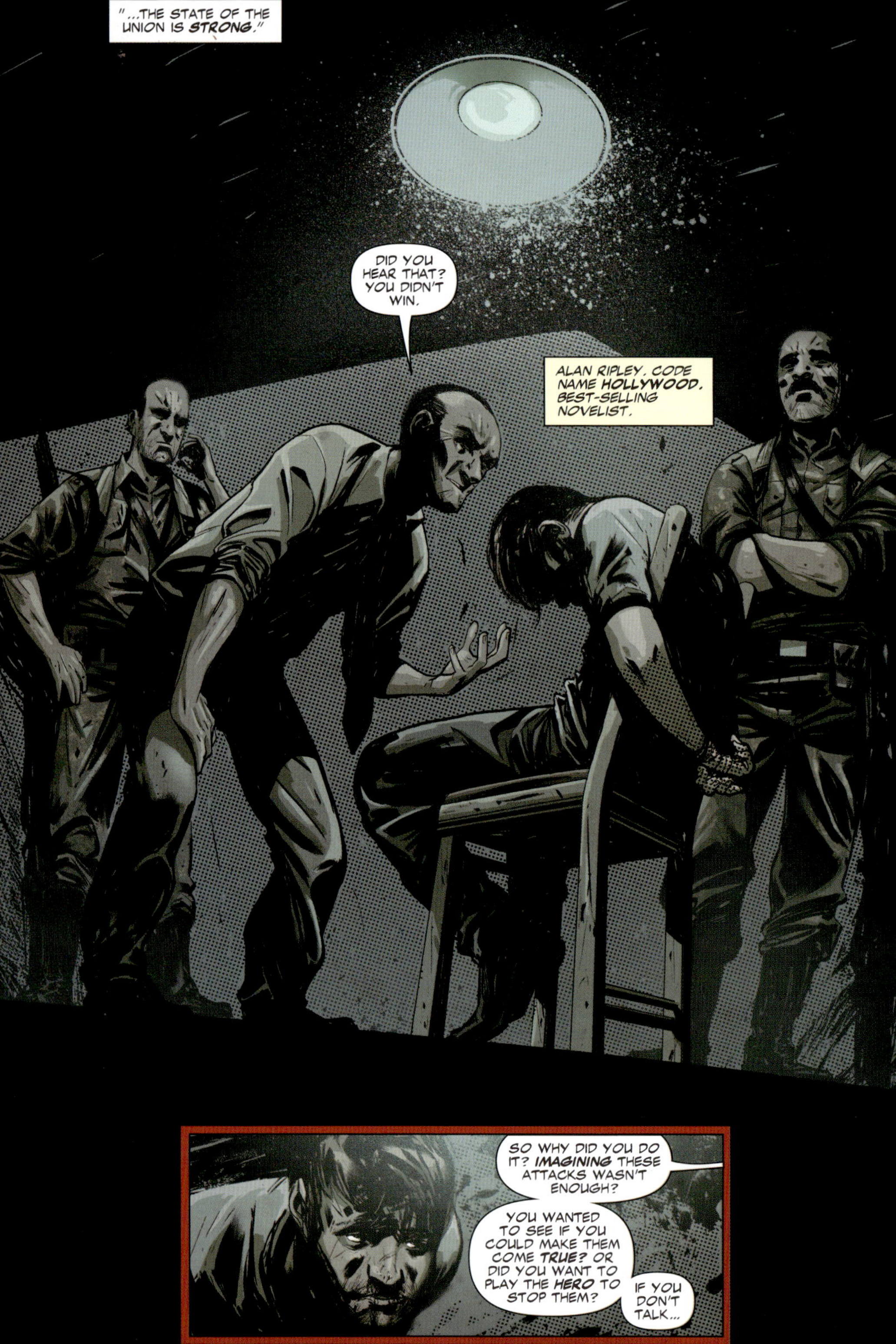
"...THE STATE OF THE UNION IS STRONG."
DID YOU HEAR THAT? YOU DIDN'T WIN.
ALAN RIPLEY. CODE NAME HOLLYWOOD. BEST-SELLING NOVELIST.
SO WHY DID YOU DO IT? IMAGINING THESE ATTACKS WASN'T ENOUGH?
YOU WANTED TO SEE IF YOU COULD MAKE THEM COME TRUE? OR DID YOU WANT TO PLAY THE HERO TO STOP THEM?
IF YOU DON'T TALK...

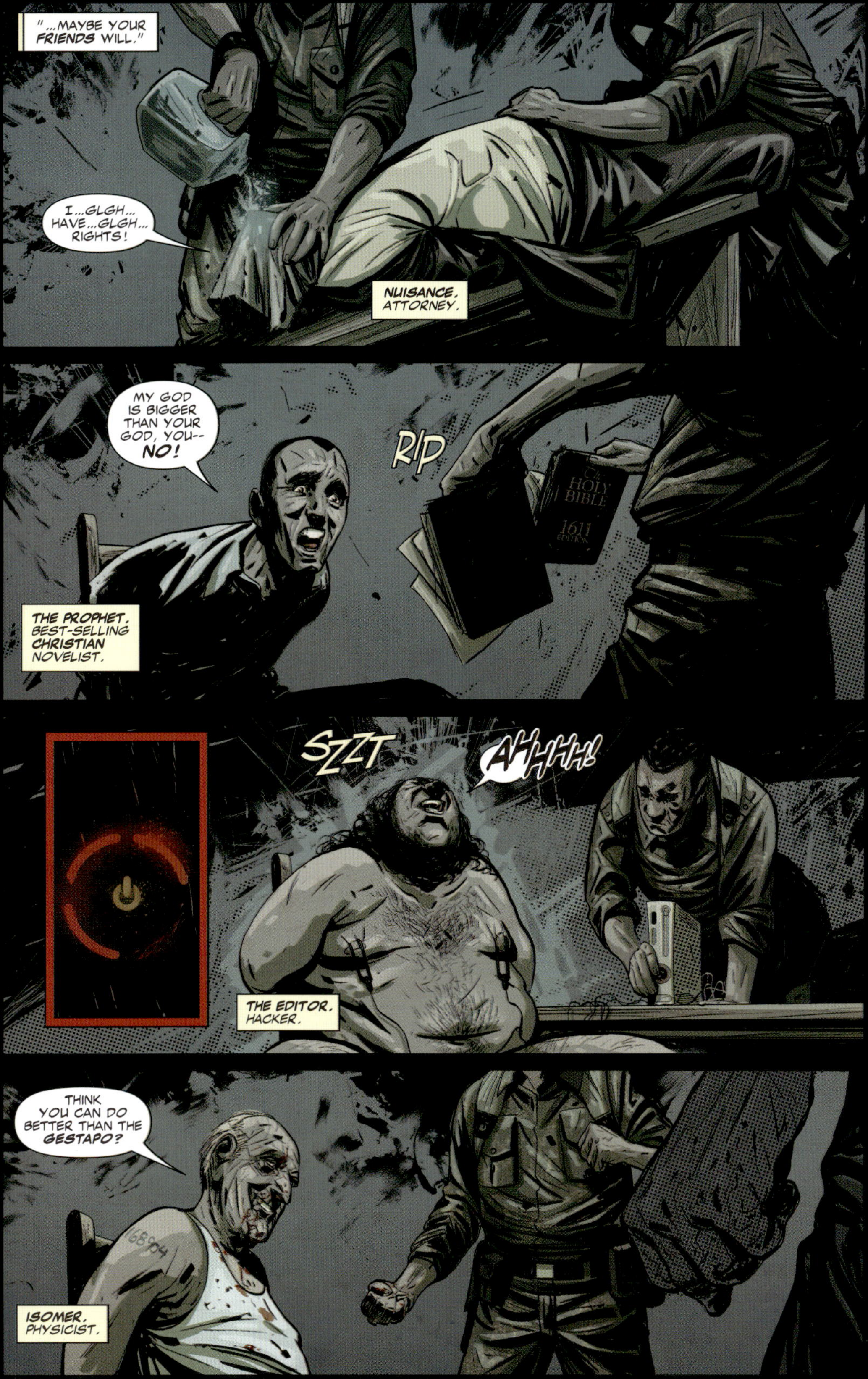
"...MAYBE YOUR FRIENDS WILL."
I...GLGH... HAVE...GLGH... RIGHTS!
NUISANCE. ATTORNEY.
MY GOD IS BIGGER THAN YOUR GOD, YOU-- NO!
RIP
HOLY BIBLE
1611 EDITION
THE PROPHET. BEST-SELLING CHRISTIAN NOVELIST.
SZZT
AHHHH!
THE EDITOR. HACKER.
THINK YOU CAN DO BETTER THAN THE GESTAPO?
168904
ISOMER. PHYSICIST.

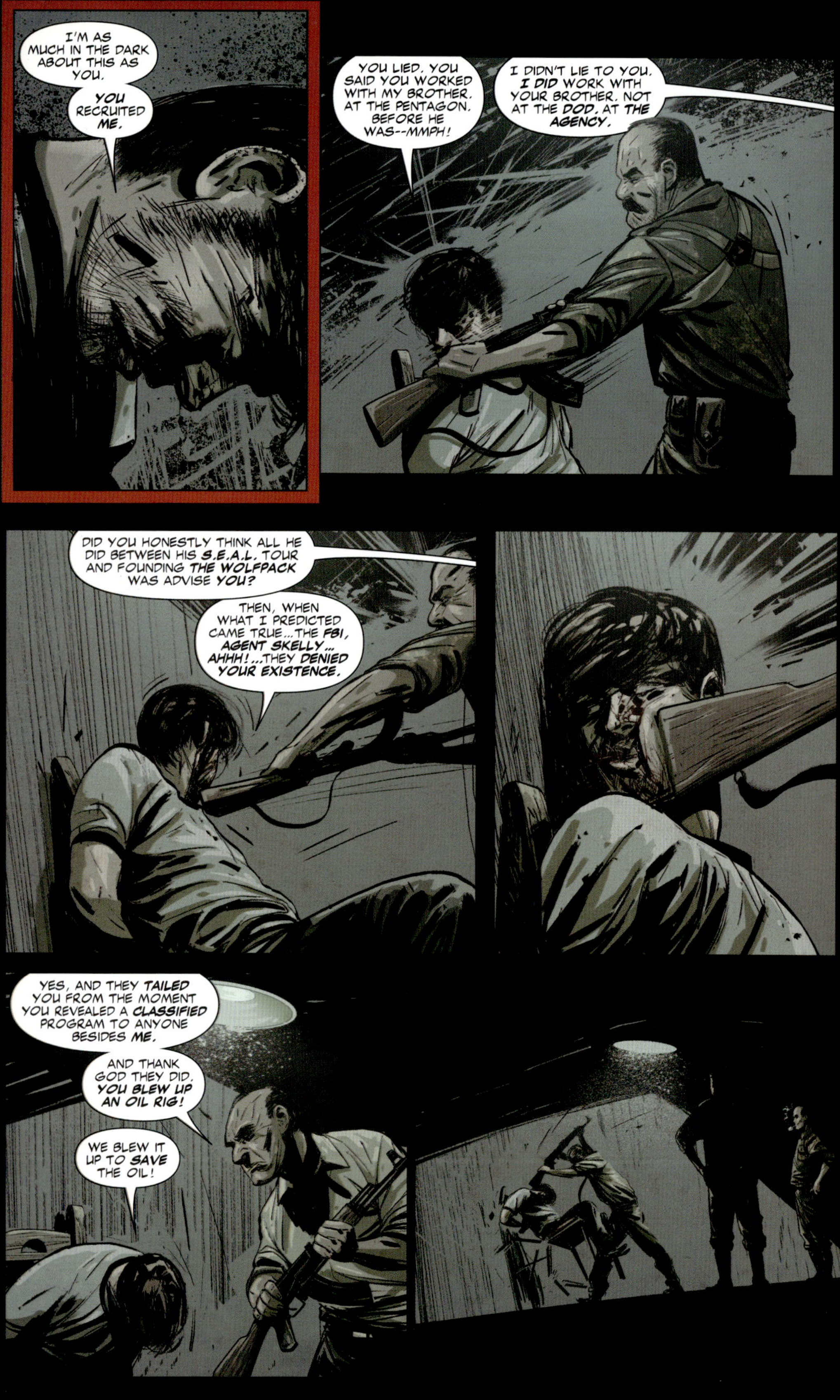
I'M AS MUCH IN THE DARK ABOUT THIS AS YOU.
YOU RECRUITED ME.
YOU LIED. YOU SAID YOU WORKED WITH MY BROTHER. AT THE PENTAGON. BEFORE HE WAS--MMPH!
I DIDN'T LIE TO YOU. I DID WORK WITH YOUR BROTHER. NOT AT THE DOD. AT THE AGENCY.
DID YOU HONESTLY THINK ALL HE DID BETWEEN HIS S.E.A.L. TOUR AND FOUNDING THE WOLFPACK WAS ADVISE YOU?
THEN, WHEN WHAT I PREDICTED CAME TRUE...THE FBI, AGENT SKELLY... AHHH!...THEY DENIED YOUR EXISTENCE.
YES, AND THEY TAILED YOU FROM THE MOMENT YOU REVEALED A CLASSIFIED PROGRAM TO ANYONE BESIDES ME.
AND THANK GOD THEY DID. YOU BLEW UP AN OIL RIG!
WE BLEW IT UP TO SAVE THE OIL!

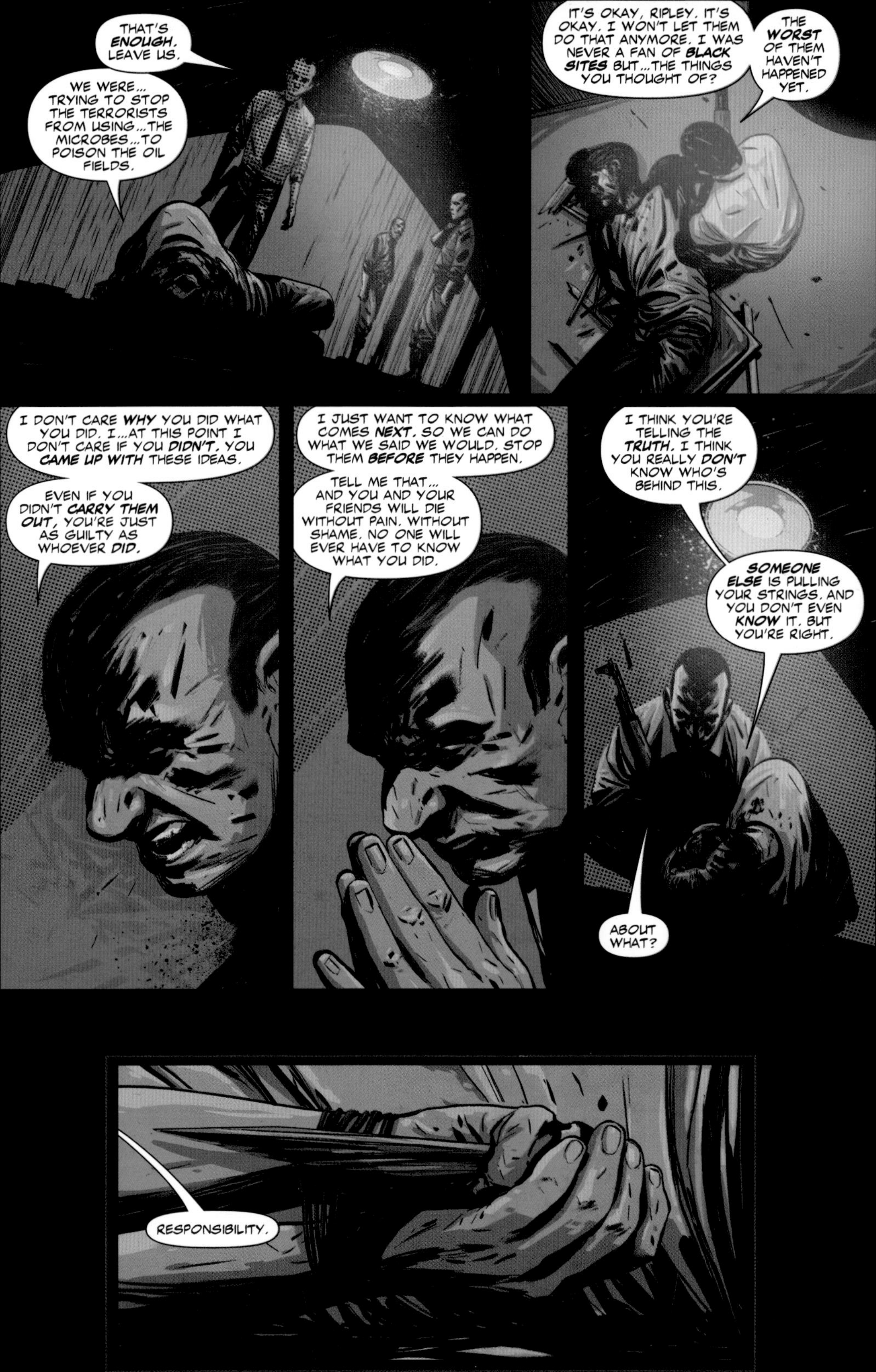
THAT'S ENOUGH. LEAVE US.
WE WERE... TRYING TO STOP THE TERRORISTS FROM USING...THE MICROBES...TO POISON THE OIL FIELDS.
IT'S OKAY, RIPLEY. IT'S OKAY. I WON'T LET THEM DO THAT ANYMORE. I WAS NEVER A FAN OF BLACK SITES BUT...THE THINGS YOU THOUGHT OF?
THE WORST OF THEM HAVEN'T HAPPENED YET.
I DON'T CARE WHY YOU DID WHAT YOU DID. I...AT THIS POINT I DON'T CARE IF YOU DIDN'T. YOU CAME UP WITH THESE IDEAS.
EVEN IF YOU DIDN'T CARRY THEM OUT, YOU'RE JUST AS GUILTY AS WHOEVER DID.
I JUST WANT TO KNOW WHAT COMES NEXT. SO WE CAN DO WHAT WE SAID WE WOULD. STOP THEM BEFORE THEY HAPPEN.
TELL ME THAT... AND YOU AND YOUR FRIENDS WILL DIE WITHOUT PAIN. WITHOUT SHAME. NO ONE WILL EVER HAVE TO KNOW WHAT YOU DID.
I THINK YOU'RE TELLING THE TRUTH. I THINK YOU REALLY DON'T KNOW WHO'S BEHIND THIS.
SOMEONE ELSE IS PULLING YOUR STRINGS, AND YOU DON'T EVEN KNOW IT. BUT YOU'RE RIGHT.
ABOUT WHAT?
RESPONSIBILITY.

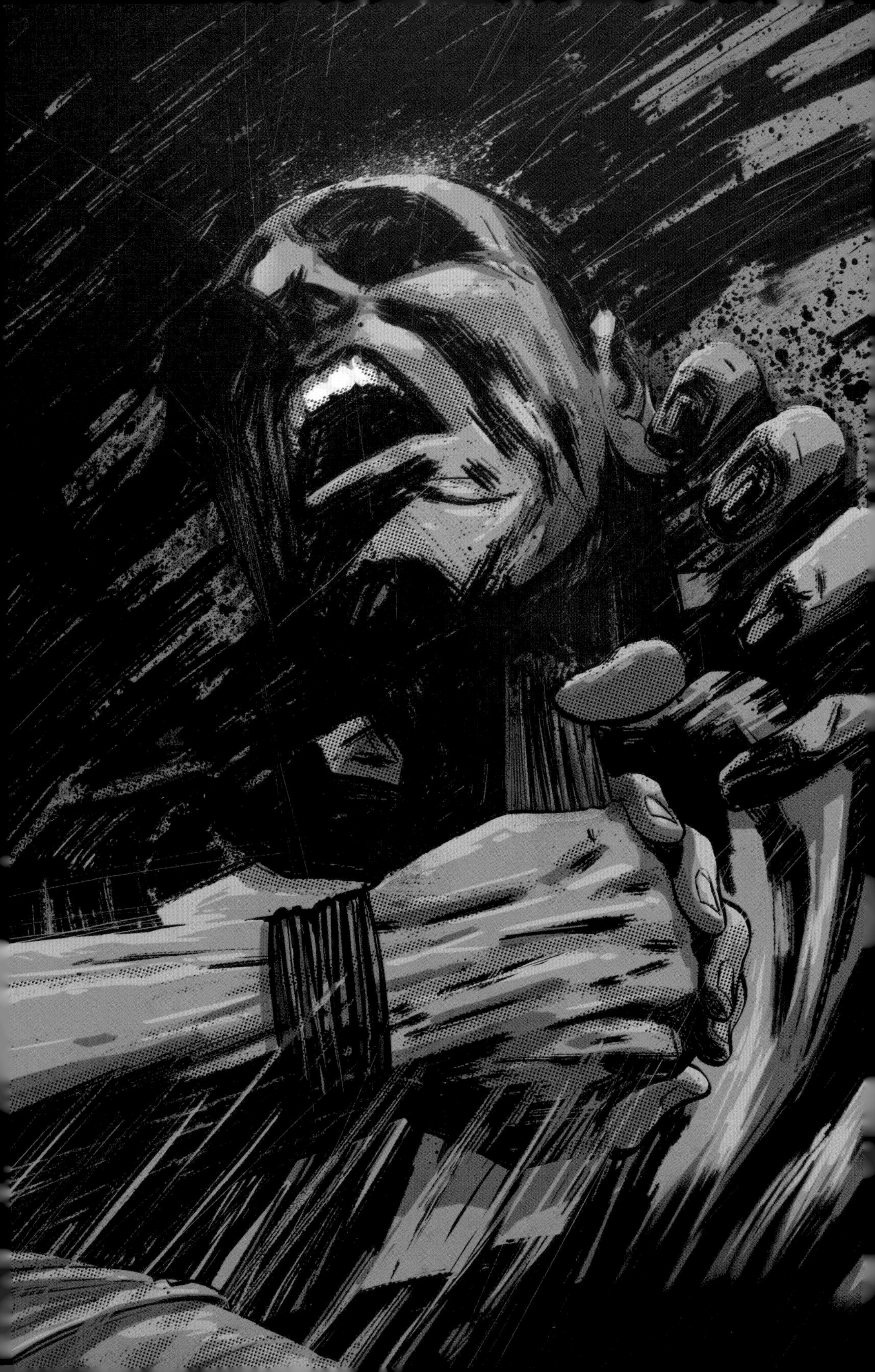

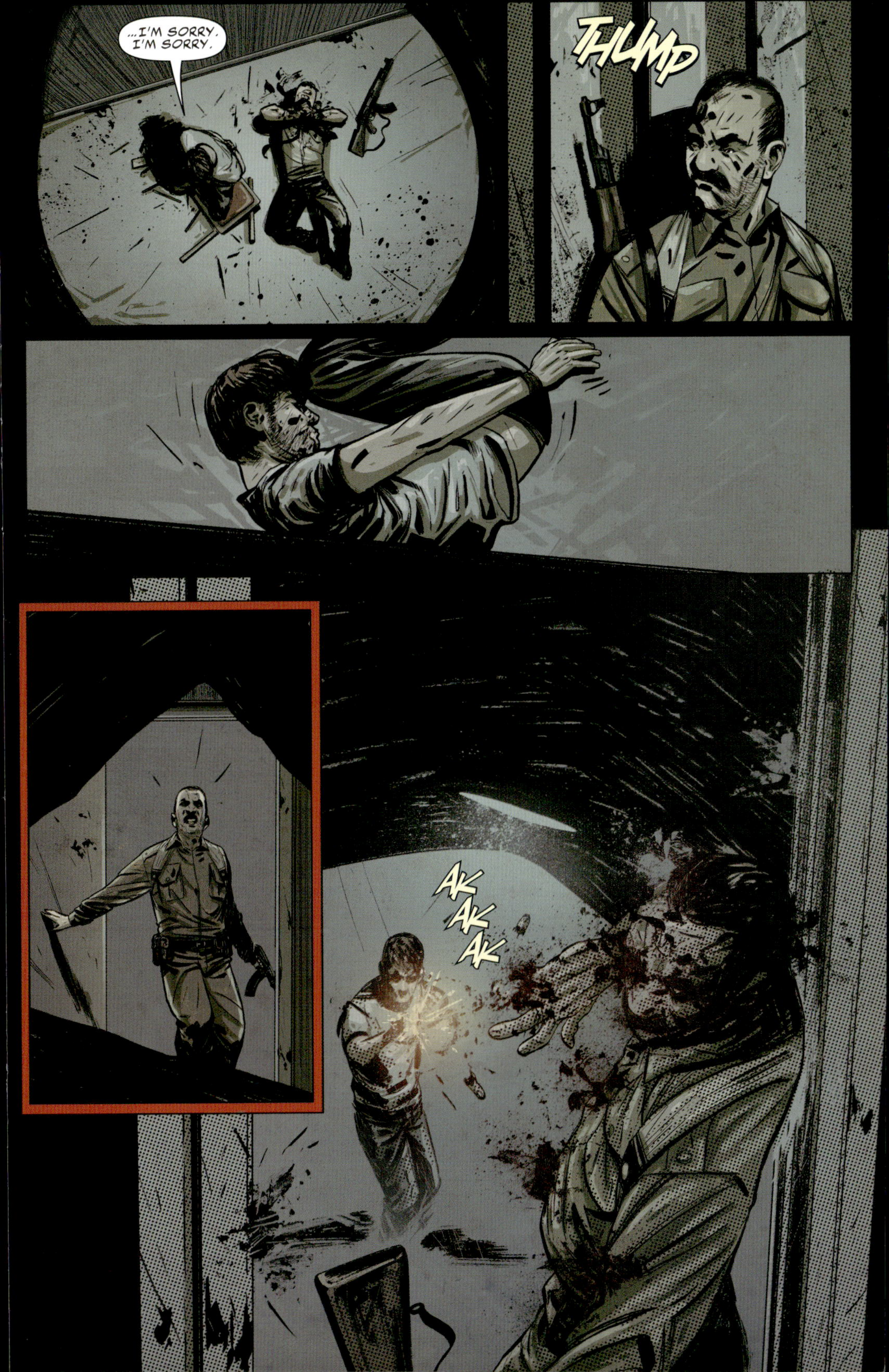
...I'M SORRY. I'M SORRY.
THUMP
AK AK AK

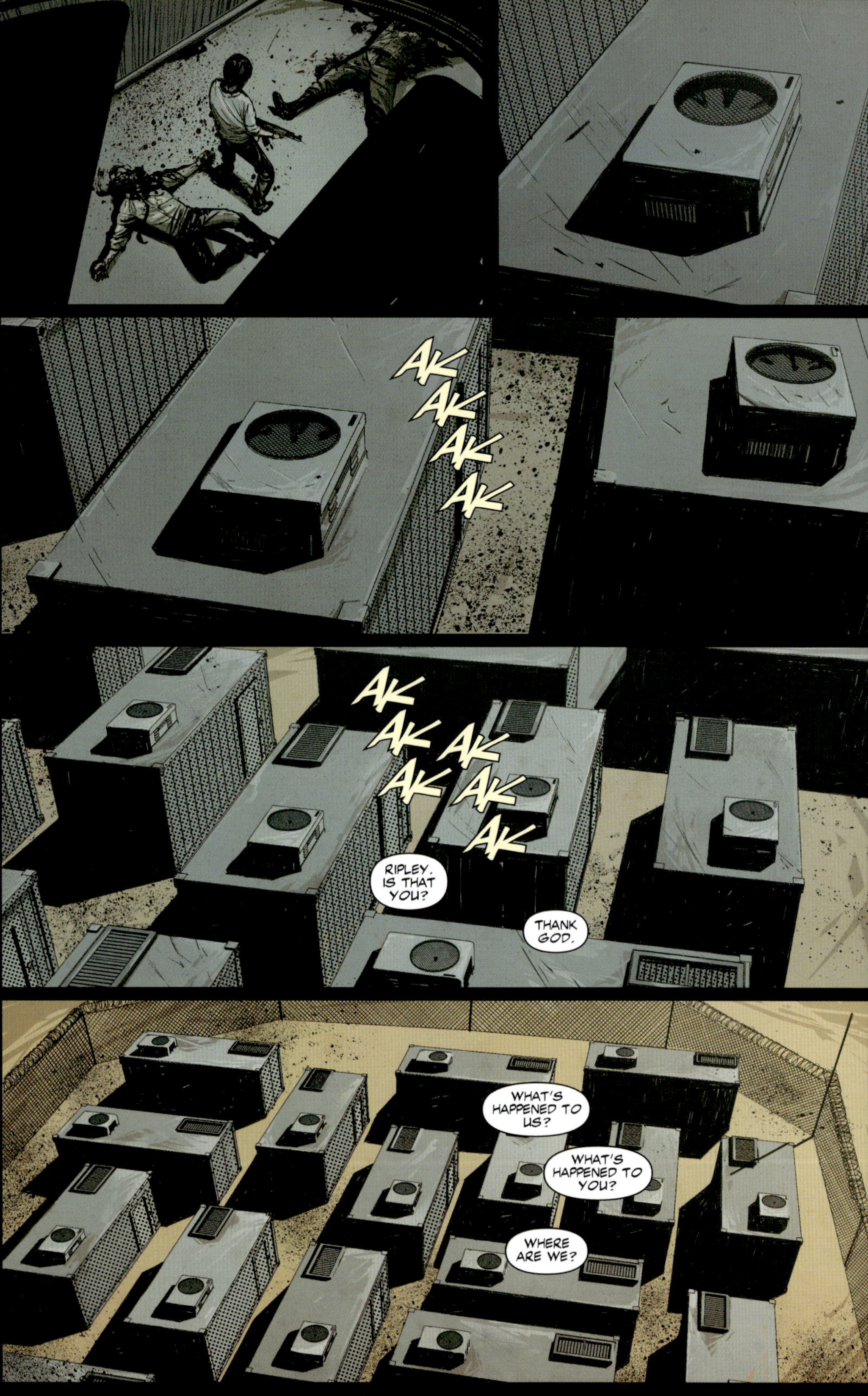
AK
AK
AK
AK
AK
AK AK
AK AK
AK
RIPLEY, IS THAT YOU?
THANK GOD.
WHAT'S HAPPENED TO US?
WHAT'S HAPPENED TO YOU?
WHERE ARE WE?

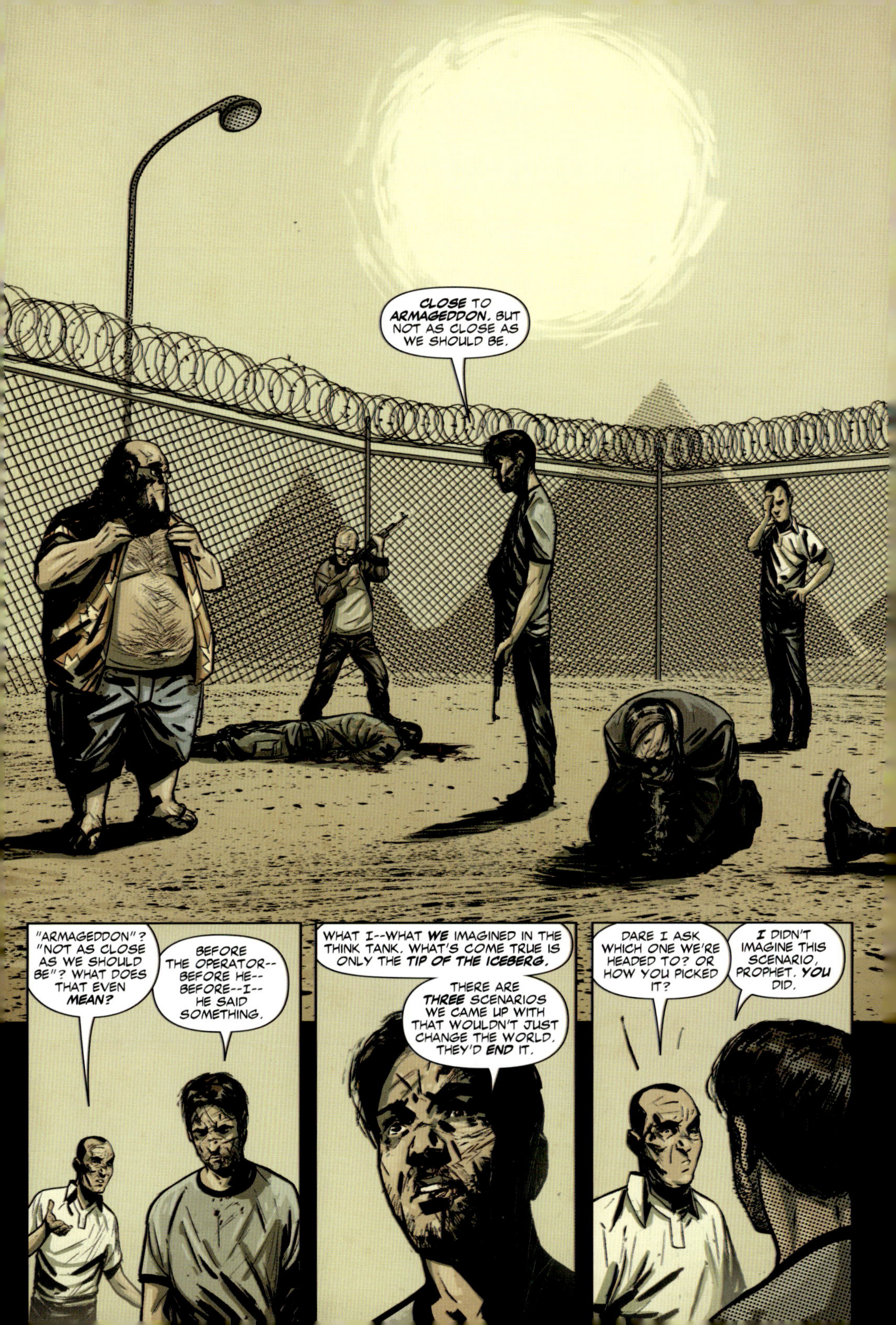
CLOSE TO ARMAGEDDON. BUT NOT AS CLOSE AS WE SHOULD BE.
"ARMAGEDDON"? "NOT AS CLOSE AS WE SHOULD BE"? WHAT DOES THAT EVEN MEAN?
BEFORE THE OPERATOR-- BEFORE HE-- BEFORE--I-- HE SAID SOMETHING.
WHAT I--WHAT WE IMAGINED IN THE THINK TANK. WHAT'S COME TRUE IS ONLY THE TIP OF THE ICEBERG.
THERE ARE THREE SCENARIOS WE CAME UP WITH THAT WOULDN'T JUST CHANGE THE WORLD. THEY'D END IT.
DARE I ASK WHICH ONE WE'RE HEADED TO? OR HOW YOU PICKED IT?
I DIDN'T IMAGINE THIS SCENARIO, PROPHET. YOU DID.

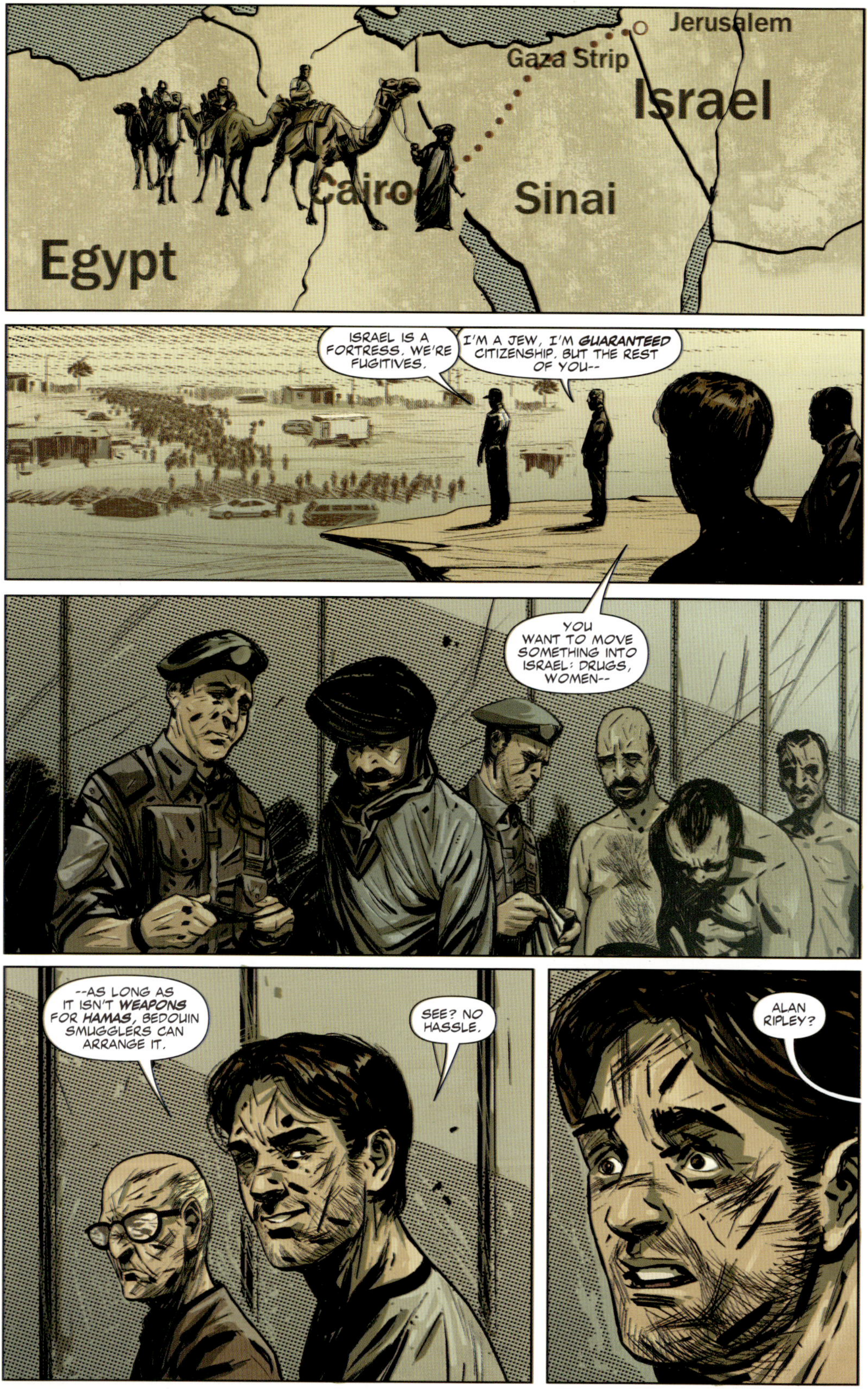
Jerusalem
Gaza Strip
Israel
Cairo
Sinai
Egypt
ISRAEL IS A FORTRESS. WE'RE FUGITIVES.
I'M A JEW, I'M GUARANTEED CITIZENSHIP. BUT THE REST OF YOU--
YOU WANT TO MOVE SOMETHING INTO ISRAEL: DRUGS, WOMEN--
--AS LONG AS IT ISN'T WEAPONS FOR HAMAS, BEDOUIN SMUGGLERS CAN ARRANGE IT.
SEE? NO HASSLE.
ALAN RIPLEY?

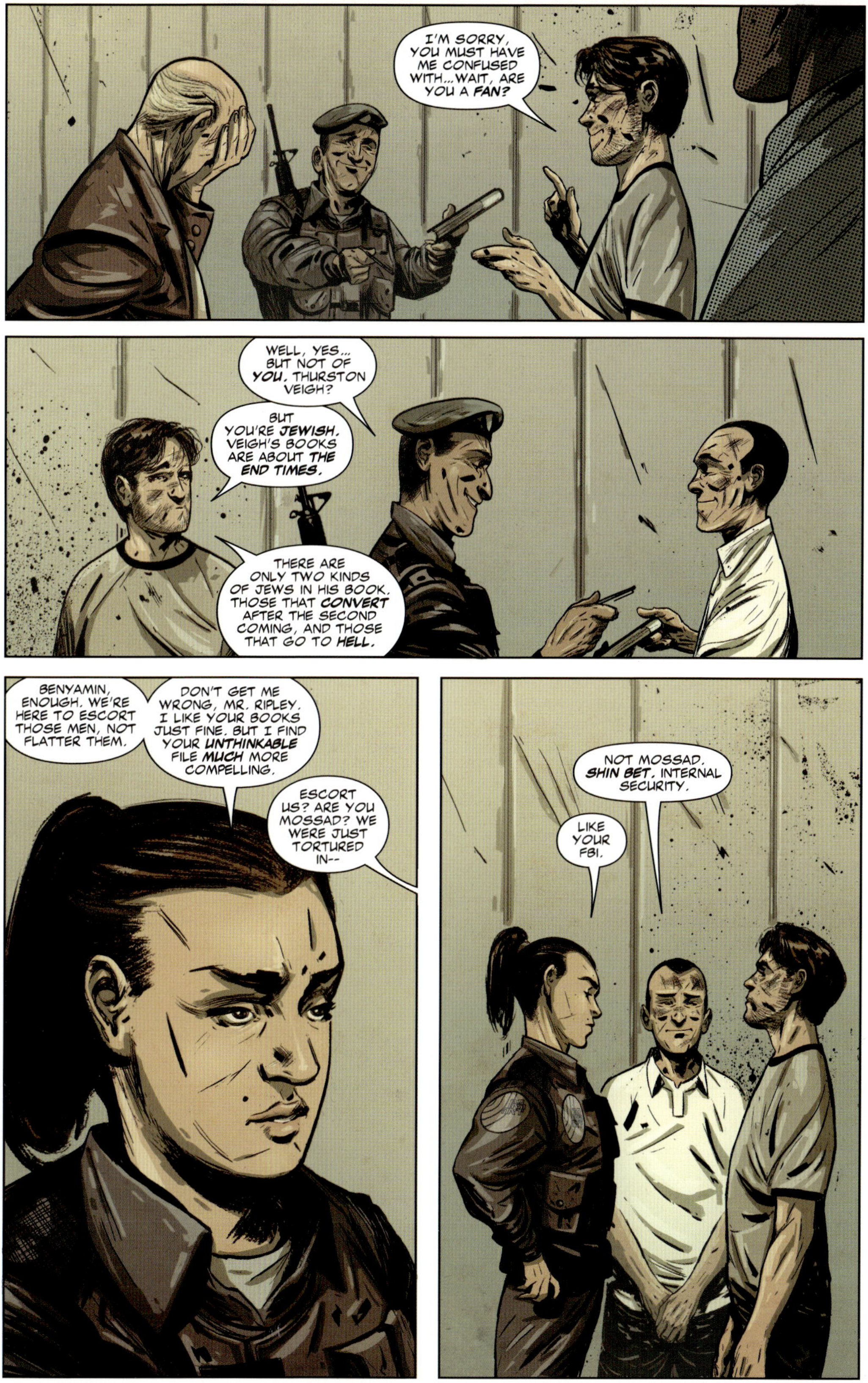
I'M SORRY, YOU MUST HAVE ME CONFUSED WITH... WAIT, ARE YOU A FAN?
WELL, YES... BUT NOT OF YOU. THURSTON VEIGH?
BUT YOU'RE JEWISH. VEIGH'S BOOKS ARE ABOUT THE END TIMES.
THERE ARE ONLY TWO KINDS OF JEWS IN HIS BOOK. THOSE THAT CONVERT AFTER THE SECOND COMING, AND THOSE THAT GO TO HELL.
BENYAMIN, ENOUGH. WE'RE HERE TO ESCORT THOSE MEN, NOT FLATTER THEM.
DON'T GET ME WRONG, MR. RIPLEY. I LIKE YOUR BOOKS JUST FINE. BUT I FIND YOUR UNTHINKABLE FILE MUCH MORE COMPELLING.
ESCORT US? ARE YOU MOSSAD? WE WERE JUST TORTURED IN--
NOT MOSSAD. SHIN BET. INTERNAL SECURITY.
LIKE YOUR FBI.

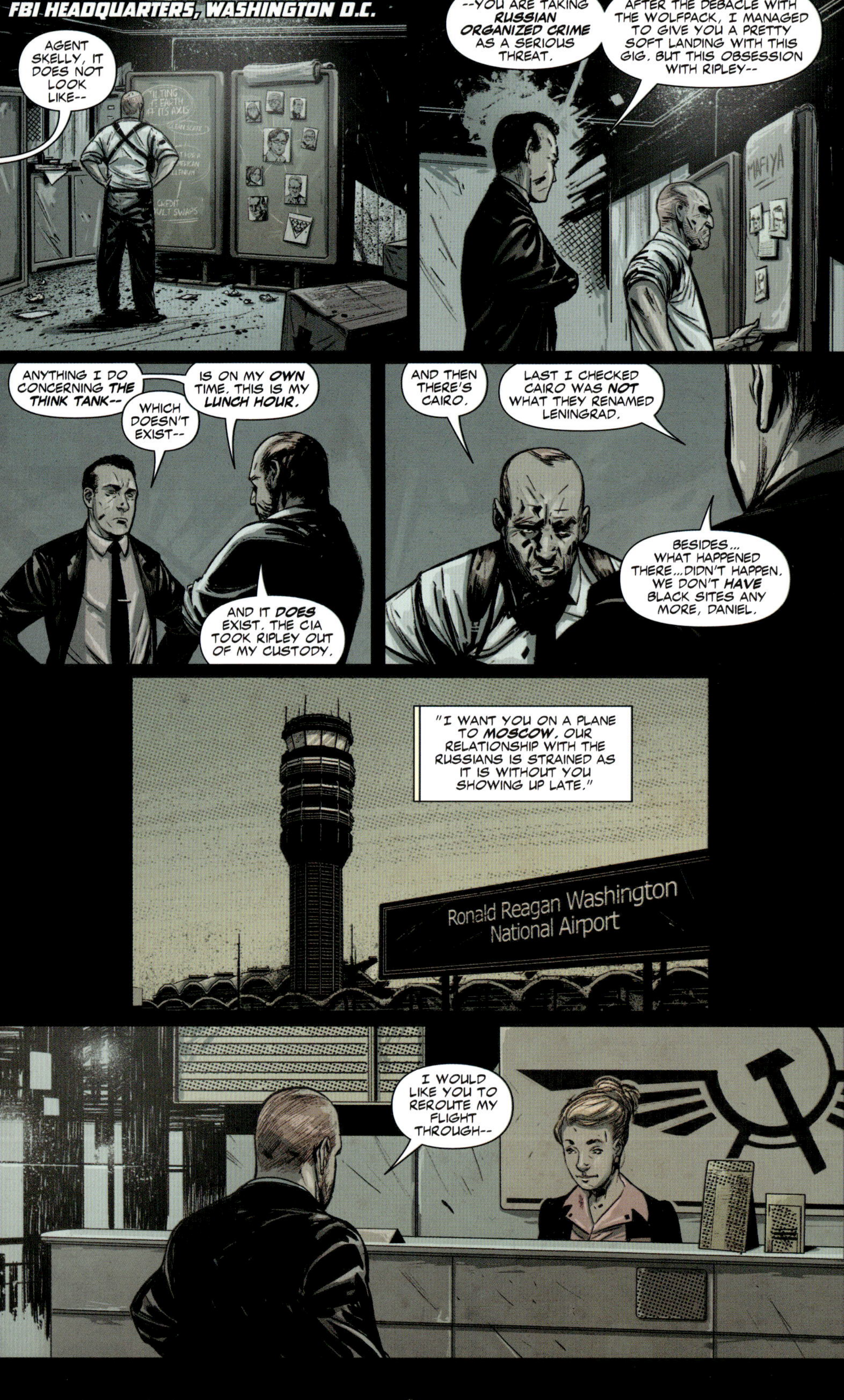
FBI HEADQUARTERS, WASHINGTON D.C.
AGENT SKELLY, IT DOES NOT LOOK LIKE--
--YOU ARE TAKING RUSSIAN ORGANIZED CRIME AS A SERIOUS THREAT.
AFTER THE DEBACLE WITH THE WOLFPACK, I MANAGED TO GIVE YOU A PRETTY SOFT LANDING WITH THIS GIG. BUT THIS OBSESSION WITH RIPLEY--
MAFIYA
ANYTHING I DO CONCERNING THE THINK TANK--
WHICH DOESN'T EXIST--
IS ON MY OWN TIME. THIS IS MY LUNCH HOUR.
AND IT DOES EXIST. THE CIA TOOK RIPLEY OUT OF MY CUSTODY.
AND THEN THERE'S CAIRO.
LAST I CHECKED CAIRO WAS NOT WHAT THEY RENAMED LENINGRAD.
BESIDES... WHAT HAPPENED THERE...DIDN'T HAPPEN. WE DON'T HAVE BLACK SITES ANY MORE, DANIEL.
"I WANT YOU ON A PLANE TO MOSCOW. OUR RELATIONSHIP WITH THE RUSSIANS IS STRAINED AS IT IS WITHOUT YOU SHOWING UP LATE."
Ronald Reagan Washington National Airport
I WOULD LIKE YOU TO REROUTE MY FLIGHT THROUGH--

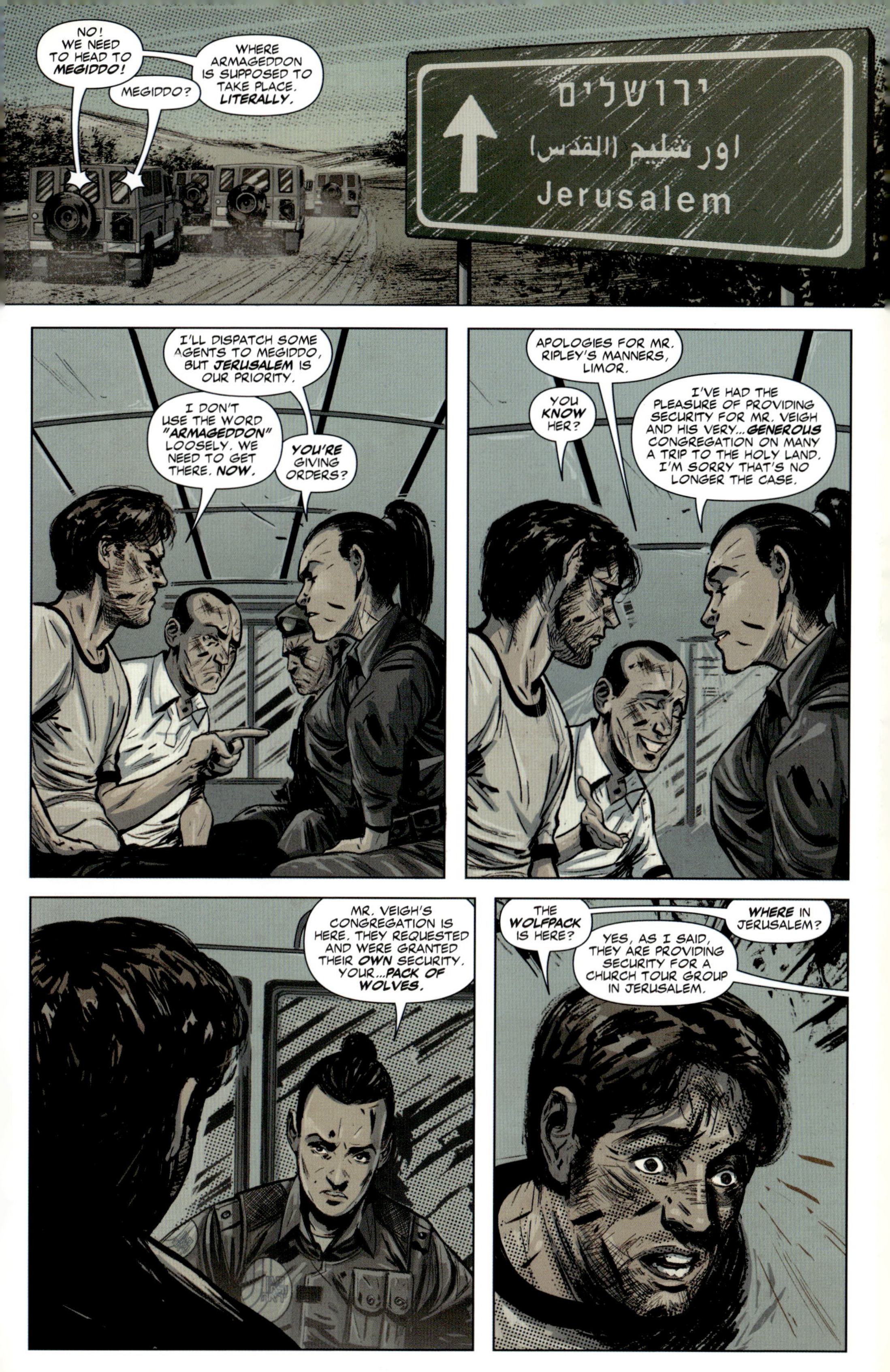

NO! WE NEED TO HEAD TO MEGIDDO!
MEGIDDO?
WHERE ARMAGEDDON IS SUPPOSED TO TAKE PLACE. LITERALLY.
ירושלים
اورشليم (القدس)
Jerusalem
I'LL DISPATCH SOME AGENTS TO MEGIDDO, BUT JERUSALEM IS OUR PRIORITY.
I DON'T USE THE WORD "ARMAGEDDON" LOOSELY. WE NEED TO GET THERE. NOW.
YOU'RE GIVING ORDERS?
APOLOGIES FOR MR. RIPLEY'S MANNERS, LIMOR.
YOU KNOW HER?
I'VE HAD THE PLEASURE OF PROVIDING SECURITY FOR MR. VEIGH AND HIS VERY... GENEROUS CONGREGATION ON MANY A TRIP TO THE HOLY LAND. I'M SORRY THAT'S NO LONGER THE CASE.
MR. VEIGH'S CONGREGATION IS HERE. THEY REQUESTED AND WERE GRANTED THEIR OWN SECURITY. YOUR... PACK OF WOLVES.
THE WOLFPACK IS HERE?
YES, AS I SAID, THEY ARE PROVIDING SECURITY FOR A CHURCH TOUR GROUP IN JERUSALEM.
WHERE IN JERUSALEM?

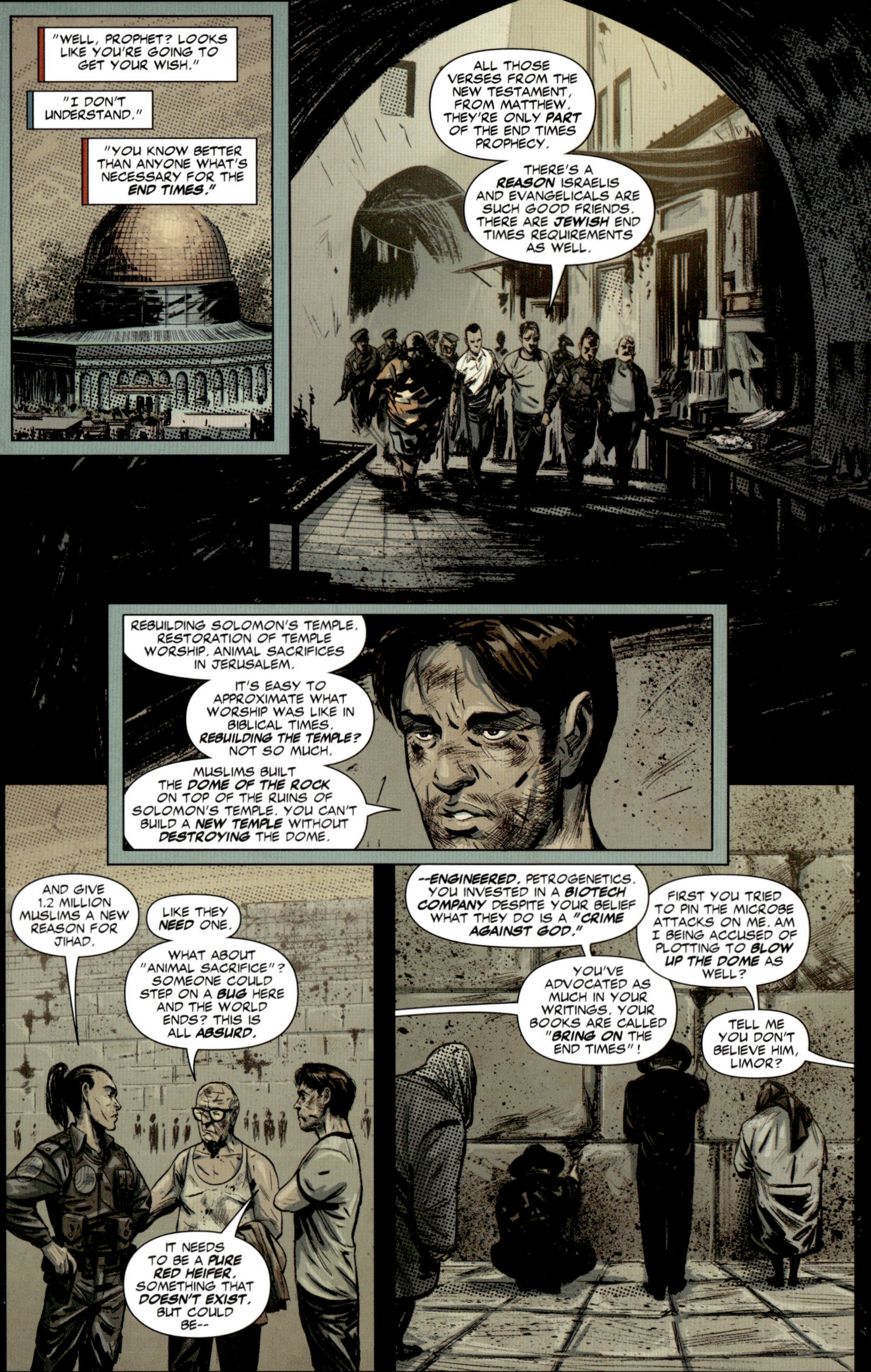
"WELL, PROPHET? LOOKS LIKE YOU'RE GOING TO GET YOUR WISH."
"I DON'T UNDERSTAND."
"YOU KNOW BETTER THAN ANYONE WHAT'S NECESSARY FOR THE END TIMES."
ALL THOSE VERSES FROM THE NEW TESTAMENT, FROM MATTHEW, THEY'RE ONLY PART OF THE END TIMES PROPHECY.
THERE'S A REASON ISRAELIS AND EVANGELICALS ARE SUCH GOOD FRIENDS. THERE ARE JEWISH END TIMES REQUIREMENTS AS WELL.
REBUILDING SOLOMON'S TEMPLE. RESTORATION OF TEMPLE WORSHIP. ANIMAL SACRIFICES IN JERUSALEM.
IT'S EASY TO APPROXIMATE WHAT WORSHIP WAS LIKE IN BIBLICAL TIMES. REBUILDING THE TEMPLE? NOT SO MUCH.
MUSLIMS BUILT THE DOME OF THE ROCK ON TOP OF THE RUINS OF SOLOMON'S TEMPLE. YOU CAN'T BUILD A NEW TEMPLE WITHOUT DESTROYING THE DOME.
AND GIVE 1.2 MILLION MUSLIMS A NEW REASON FOR JIHAD.
LIKE THEY NEED ONE.
WHAT ABOUT "ANIMAL SACRIFICE"? SOMEONE COULD STEP ON A BUG HERE AND THE WORLD ENDS? THIS IS ALL ABSURD.
IT NEEDS TO BE A PURE RED HEIFER. SOMETHING THAT DOESN'T EXIST. BUT COULD BE--
--ENGINEERED. PETROGENETICS. YOU INVESTED IN A BIOTECH COMPANY DESPITE YOUR BELIEF WHAT THEY DO IS A "CRIME AGAINST GOD."
YOU'VE ADVOCATED AS MUCH IN YOUR WRITINGS. YOUR BOOKS ARE CALLED "BRING ON THE END TIMES"!
FIRST YOU TRIED TO PIN THE MICROBE ATTACKS ON ME. AM I BEING ACCUSED OF PLOTTING TO BLOW UP THE DOME AS WELL?
TELL ME YOU DON'T BELIEVE HIM, LIMOR?

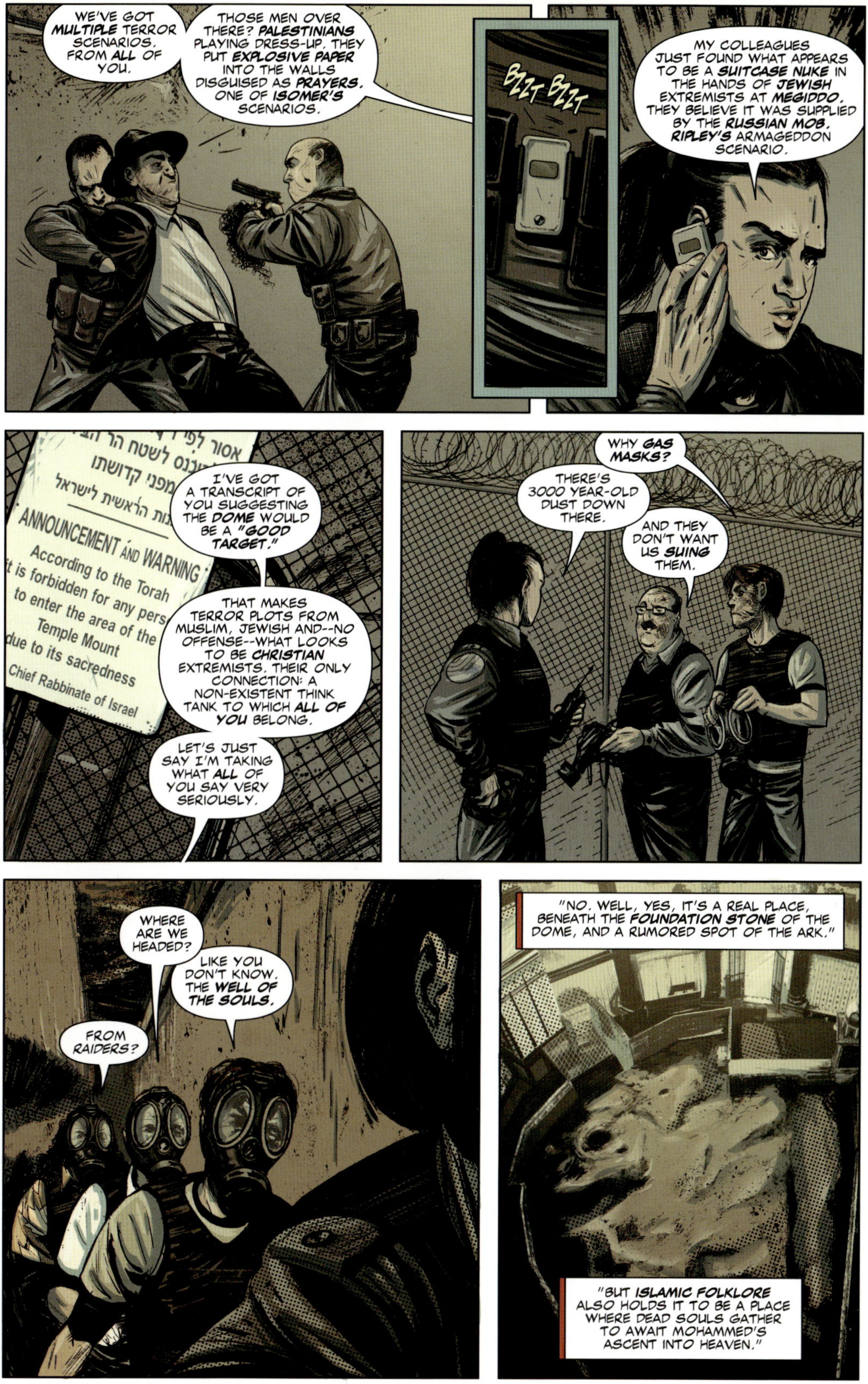
WE'VE GOT MULTIPLE TERROR SCENARIOS. FROM ALL OF YOU.
THOSE MEN OVER THERE? PALESTINIANS PLAYING DRESS-UP. THEY PUT EXPLOSIVE PAPER INTO THE WALLS DISGUISED AS PRAYERS. ONE OF ISOMER'S SCENARIOS.
BZZT BZZT
MY COLLEAGUES JUST FOUND WHAT APPEARS TO BE A SUITCASE NUKE IN THE HANDS OF JEWISH EXTREMISTS AT MEGIDDO. THEY BELIEVE IT WAS SUPPLIED BY THE RUSSIAN MOB. RIPLEY'S ARMAGEDDON SCENARIO.
ANNOUNCEMENT AND WARNING
According to the Torah
it is forbidden for any pers
to enter the area of the
Temple Mount
due to its sacredness
Chief Rabbinate of Israel
I'VE GOT A TRANSCRIPT OF YOU SUGGESTING THE DOME WOULD BE A "GOOD TARGET."
THAT MAKES TERROR PLOTS FROM MUSLIM, JEWISH AND--NO OFFENSE--WHAT LOOKS TO BE CHRISTIAN EXTREMISTS. THEIR ONLY CONNECTION: A NON-EXISTENT THINK TANK TO WHICH ALL OF YOU BELONG.
LET'S JUST SAY I'M TAKING WHAT ALL OF YOU SAY VERY SERIOUSLY.
WHY GAS MASKS?
THERE'S 3000 YEAR-OLD DUST DOWN THERE.
AND THEY DON'T WANT US SUING THEM.
WHERE ARE WE HEADED?
LIKE YOU DON'T KNOW. THE WELL OF THE SOULS.
FROM RAIDERS?
"NO. WELL, YES, IT'S A REAL PLACE, BENEATH THE FOUNDATION STONE OF THE DOME, AND A RUMORED SPOT OF THE ARK."
"BUT ISLAMIC FOLKLORE ALSO HOLDS IT TO BE A PLACE WHERE DEAD SOULS GATHER TO AWAIT MOHAMMED'S ASCENT INTO HEAVEN."

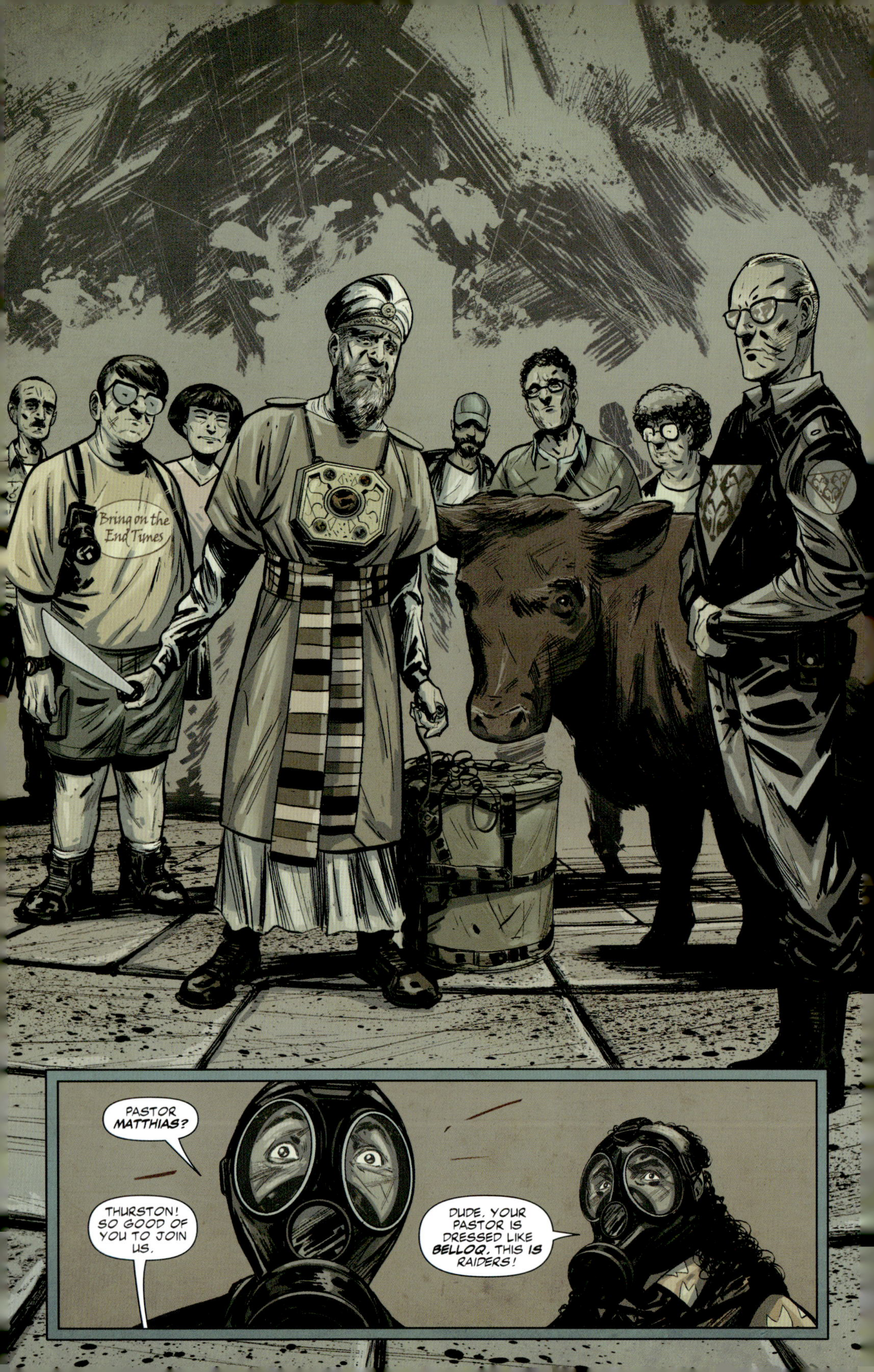
Bring on the End Times
PASTOR MATTHIAS?
THURSTON! SO GOOD OF YOU TO JOIN US.
DUDE. YOUR PASTOR IS DRESSED LIKE BELLOQ. THIS IS RAIDERS!

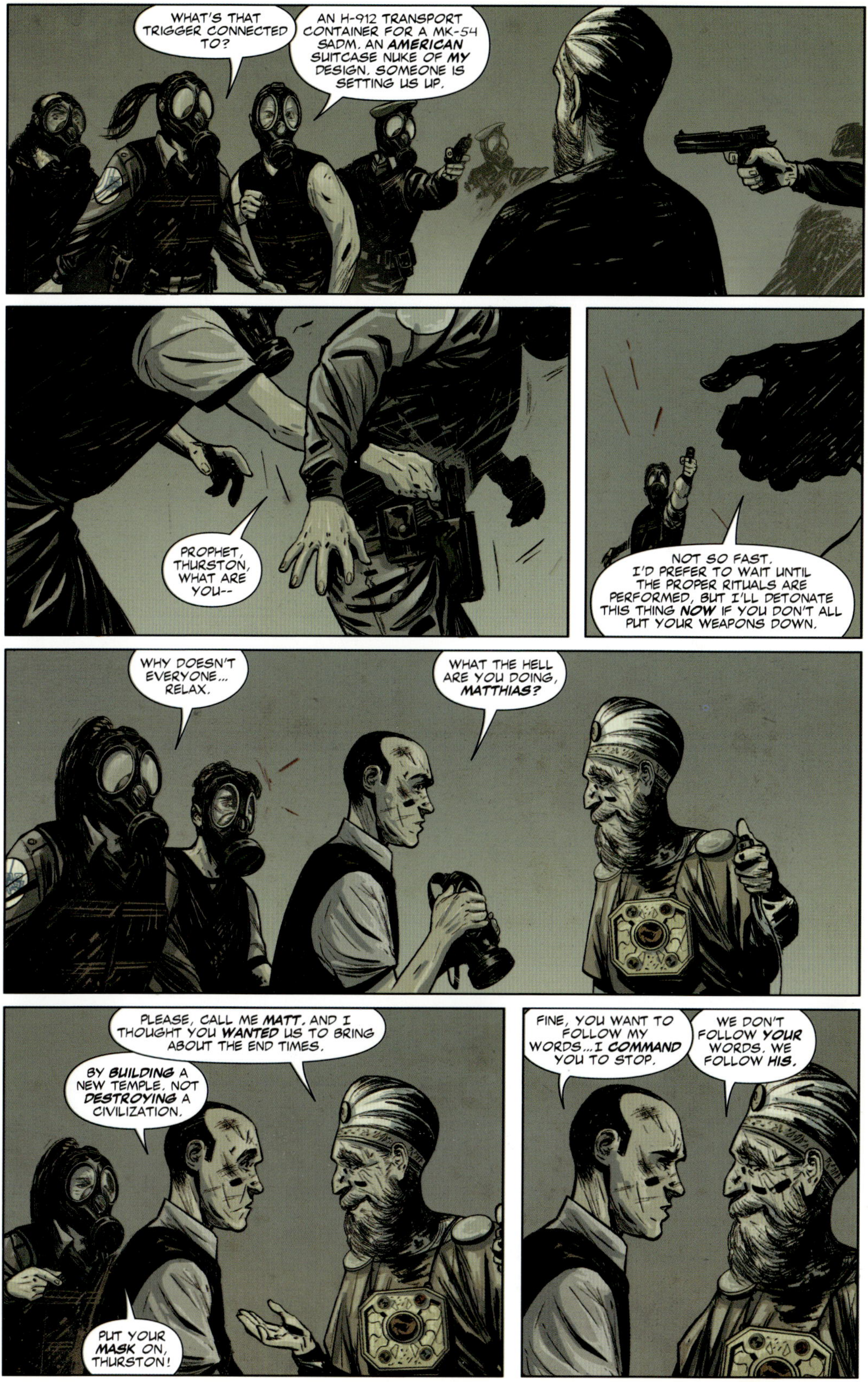
WHAT'S THAT TRIGGER CONNECTED TO?
AN H-912 TRANSPORT CONTAINER FOR A MK-54 SADM. AN AMERICAN SUITCASE NUKE OF MY DESIGN. SOMEONE IS SETTING US UP.
PROPHET, THURSTON, WHAT ARE YOU--
NOT SO FAST. I'D PREFER TO WAIT UNTIL THE PROPER RITUALS ARE PERFORMED, BUT I'LL DETONATE THIS THING NOW IF YOU DON'T ALL PUT YOUR WEAPONS DOWN.
WHY DOESN'T EVERYONE... RELAX.
WHAT THE HELL ARE YOU DOING, MATTHIAS?
PLEASE, CALL ME MATT. AND I THOUGHT YOU WANTED US TO BRING ABOUT THE END TIMES.
BY BUILDING A NEW TEMPLE. NOT DESTROYING A CIVILIZATION.
PUT YOUR MASK ON, THURSTON!
FINE, YOU WANT TO FOLLOW MY WORDS... I COMMAND YOU TO STOP.
WE DON'T FOLLOW YOUR WORDS. WE FOLLOW HIS.

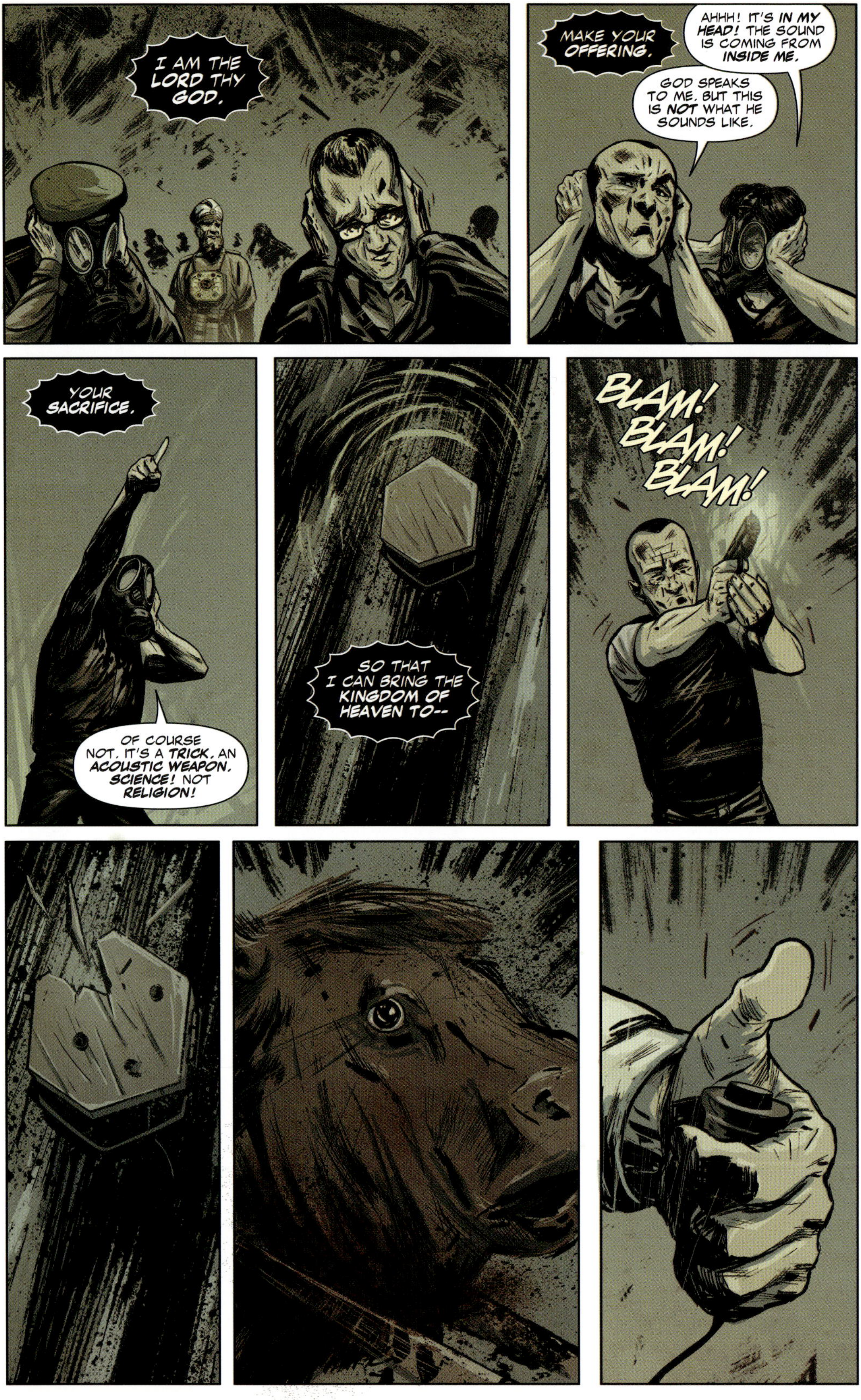
I AM THE LORD THY GOD.
MAKE YOUR OFFERING.
AHHH! IT'S IN MY HEAD! THE SOUND IS COMING FROM INSIDE ME.
GOD SPEAKS TO ME. BUT THIS IS NOT WHAT HE SOUNDS LIKE.
YOUR SACRIFICE.
OF COURSE NOT. IT'S A TRICK. AN ACOUSTIC WEAPON. SCIENCE! NOT RELIGION!
SO THAT I CAN BRING THE KINGDOM OF HEAVEN TO--
BLAM! BLAM! BLAM!

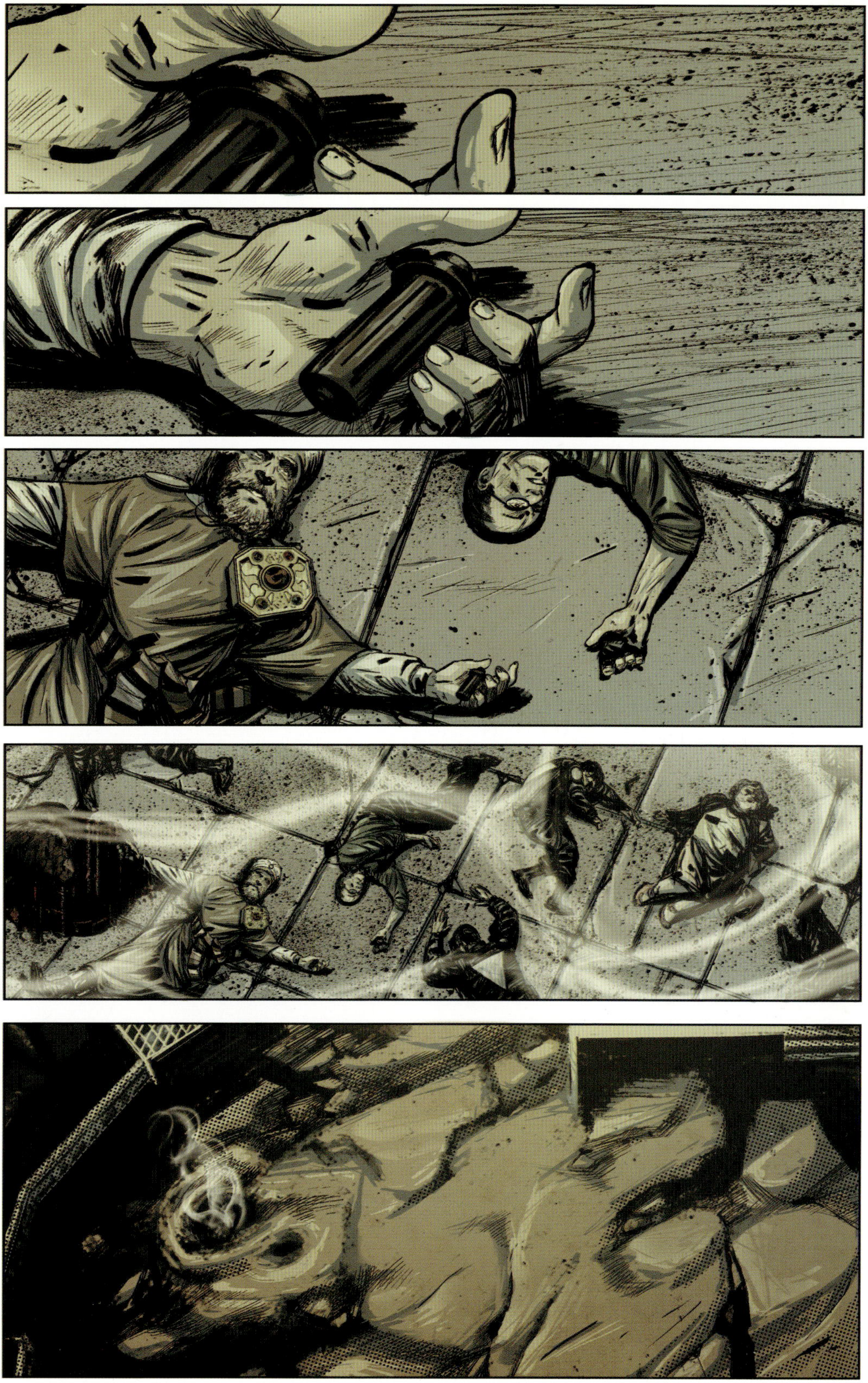

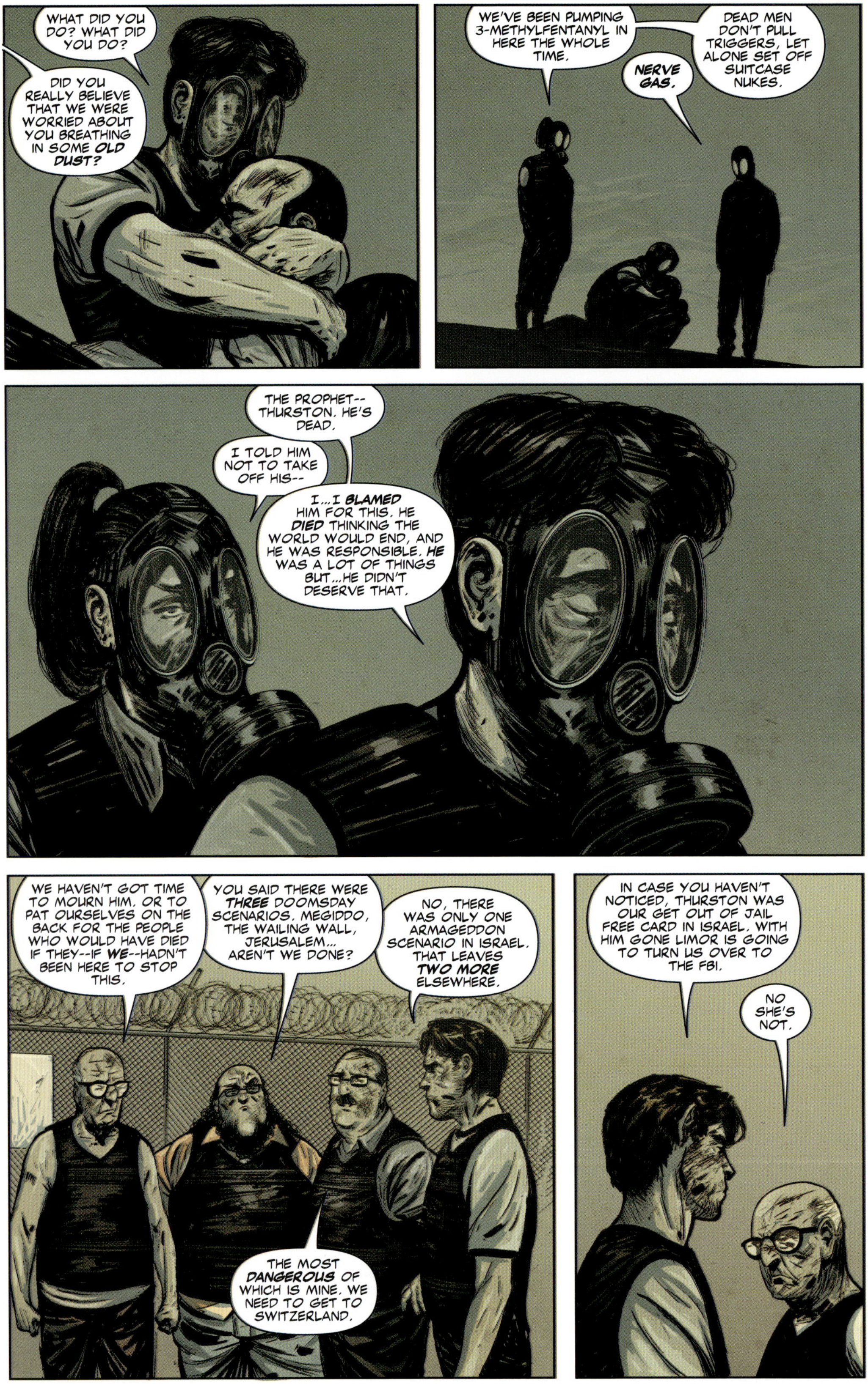
WHAT DID YOU DO? WHAT DID YOU DO?
DID YOU REALLY BELIEVE THAT WE WERE WORRIED ABOUT YOU BREATHING IN SOME OLD DUST?
WE'VE BEEN PUMPING 3-METHYLFENTANYL IN HERE THE WHOLE TIME.
NERVE GAS.
DEAD MEN DON'T PULL TRIGGERS, LET ALONE SET OFF SUITCASE NUKES.
THE PROPHET-- THURSTON. HE'S DEAD.
I TOLD HIM NOT TO TAKE OFF HIS--
I...I BLAMED HIM FOR THIS. HE DIED THINKING THE WORLD WOULD END, AND HE WAS RESPONSIBLE. HE WAS A LOT OF THINGS BUT...HE DIDN'T DESERVE THAT.
WE HAVEN'T GOT TIME TO MOURN HIM. OR TO PAT OURSELVES ON THE BACK FOR THE PEOPLE WHO WOULD HAVE DIED IF THEY--IF WE--HADN'T BEEN HERE TO STOP THIS.
YOU SAID THERE WERE THREE DOOMSDAY SCENARIOS. MEGIDDO, THE WAILING WALL, JERUSALEM... AREN'T WE DONE?
NO, THERE WAS ONLY ONE ARMAGEDDON SCENARIO IN ISRAEL. THAT LEAVES TWO MORE ELSEWHERE.
THE MOST DANGEROUS OF WHICH IS MINE. WE NEED TO GET TO SWITZERLAND.
IN CASE YOU HAVEN'T NOTICED, THURSTON WAS OUR GET OUT OF JAIL FREE CARD IN ISRAEL. WITH HIM GONE LIMOR IS GOING TO TURN US OVER TO THE FBI.
NO SHE'S NOT.

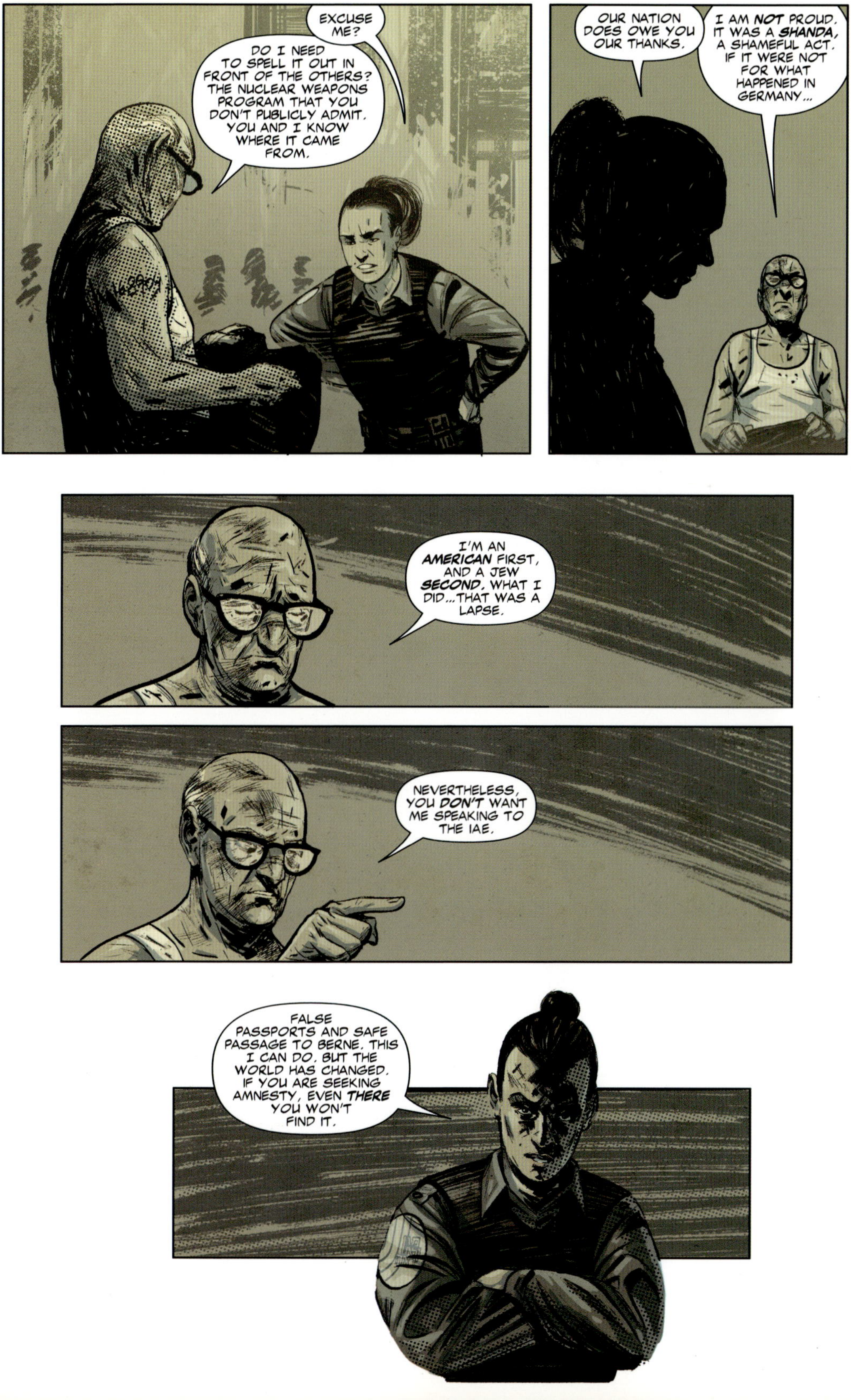
DO I NEED TO SPELL IT OUT IN FRONT OF THE OTHERS? THE NUCLEAR WEAPONS PROGRAM THAT YOU DON'T PUBLICLY ADMIT. YOU AND I KNOW WHERE IT CAME FROM.
EXCUSE ME?
OUR NATION DOES OWE YOU OUR THANKS.
I AM **NOT** PROUD. IT WAS A ***SHANDA***, A SHAMEFUL ACT. IF IT WERE NOT FOR WHAT HAPPENED IN GERMANY...
I'M AN **AMERICAN** FIRST, AND A JEW **SECOND**. WHAT I DID...THAT WAS A LAPSE.
NEVERTHELESS, YOU ***DON'T*** WANT ME SPEAKING TO THE IAE.
FALSE PASSPORTS AND SAFE PASSAGE TO BERNE. THIS I CAN DO. BUT THE WORLD HAS CHANGED. IF YOU ARE SEEKING AMNESTY, EVEN ***THERE*** YOU WON'T FIND IT.

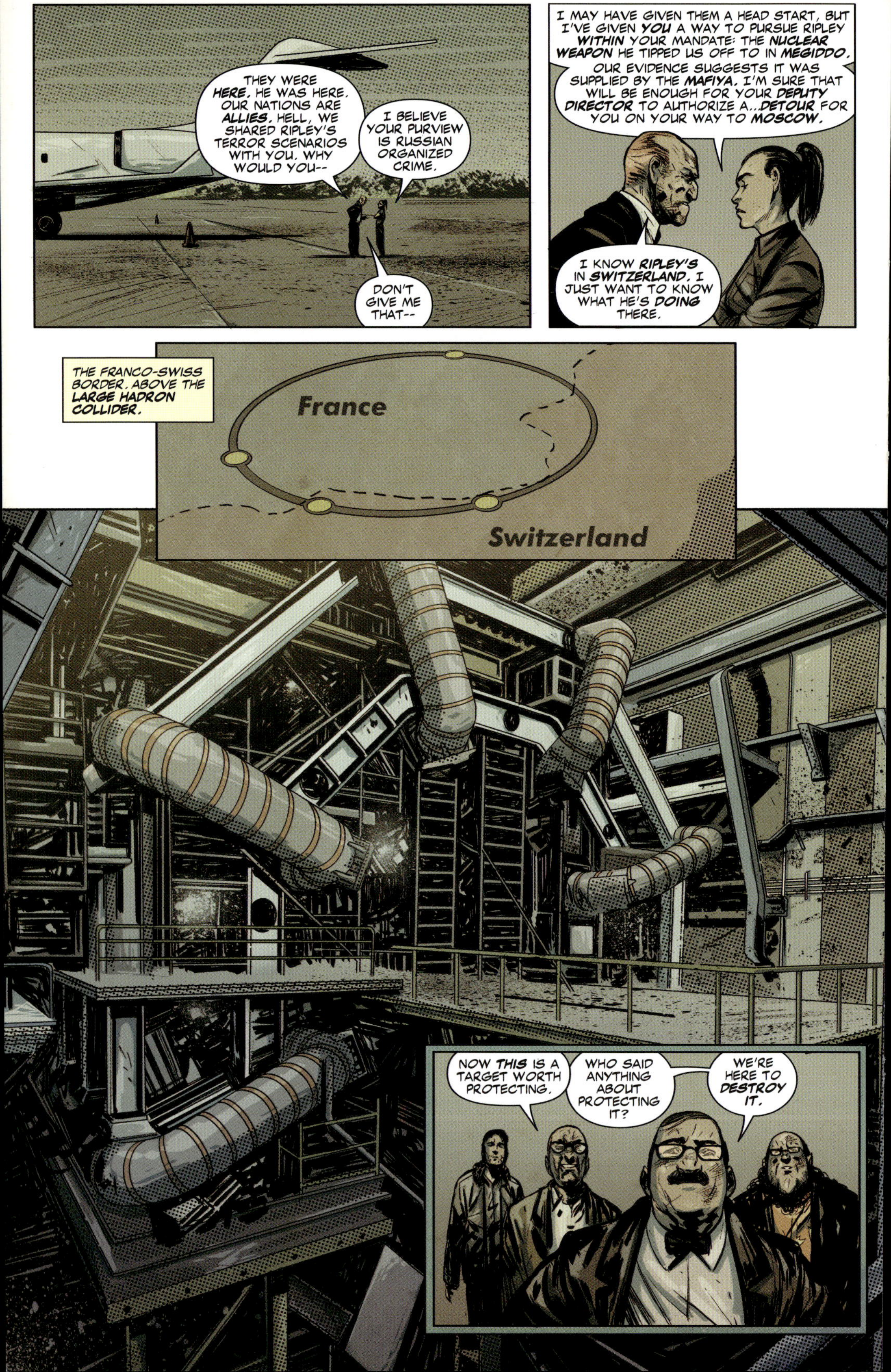
THEY WERE HERE. HE WAS HERE. OUR NATIONS ARE ALLIES. HELL, WE SHARED RIPLEY'S TERROR SCENARIOS WITH YOU. WHY WOULD YOU--
I BELIEVE YOUR PURVIEW IS RUSSIAN ORGANIZED CRIME.
DON'T GIVE ME THAT--
I MAY HAVE GIVEN THEM A HEAD START, BUT I'VE GIVEN YOU A WAY TO PURSUE RIPLEY WITHIN YOUR MANDATE: THE NUCLEAR WEAPON HE TIPPED US OFF TO IN MEGIDDO.
OUR EVIDENCE SUGGESTS IT WAS SUPPLIED BY THE MAFIYA. I'M SURE THAT WILL BE ENOUGH FOR YOUR DEPUTY DIRECTOR TO AUTHORIZE A...DETOUR FOR YOU ON YOUR WAY TO MOSCOW.
I KNOW RIPLEY'S IN SWITZERLAND. I JUST WANT TO KNOW WHAT HE'S DOING THERE.
THE FRANCO-SWISS BORDER. ABOVE THE LARGE HADRON COLLIDER.
France
Switzerland
NOW THIS IS A TARGET WORTH PROTECTING.
WHO SAID ANYTHING ABOUT PROTECTING IT?
WE'RE HERE TO DESTROY IT.

CHAPTER FOUR

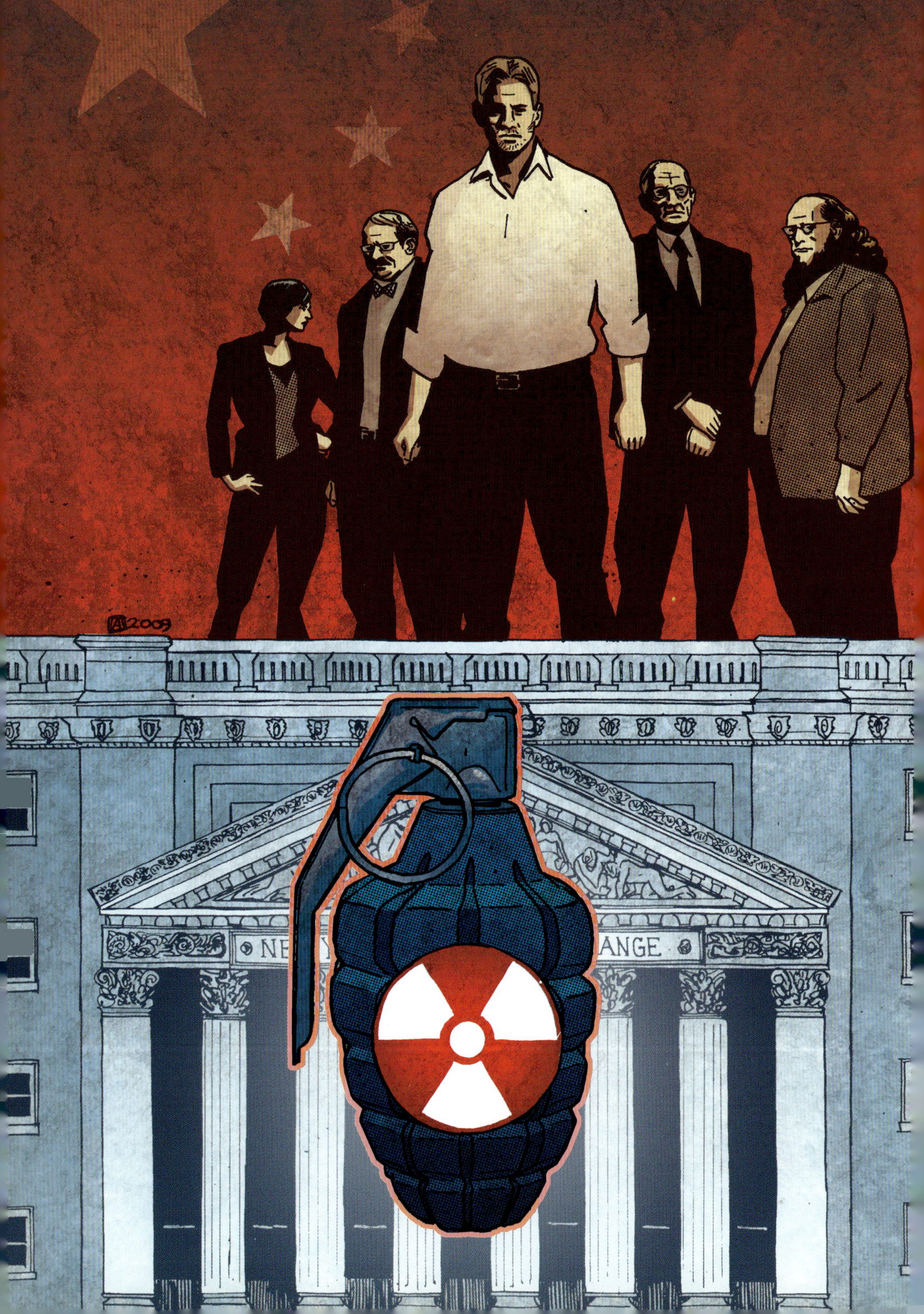

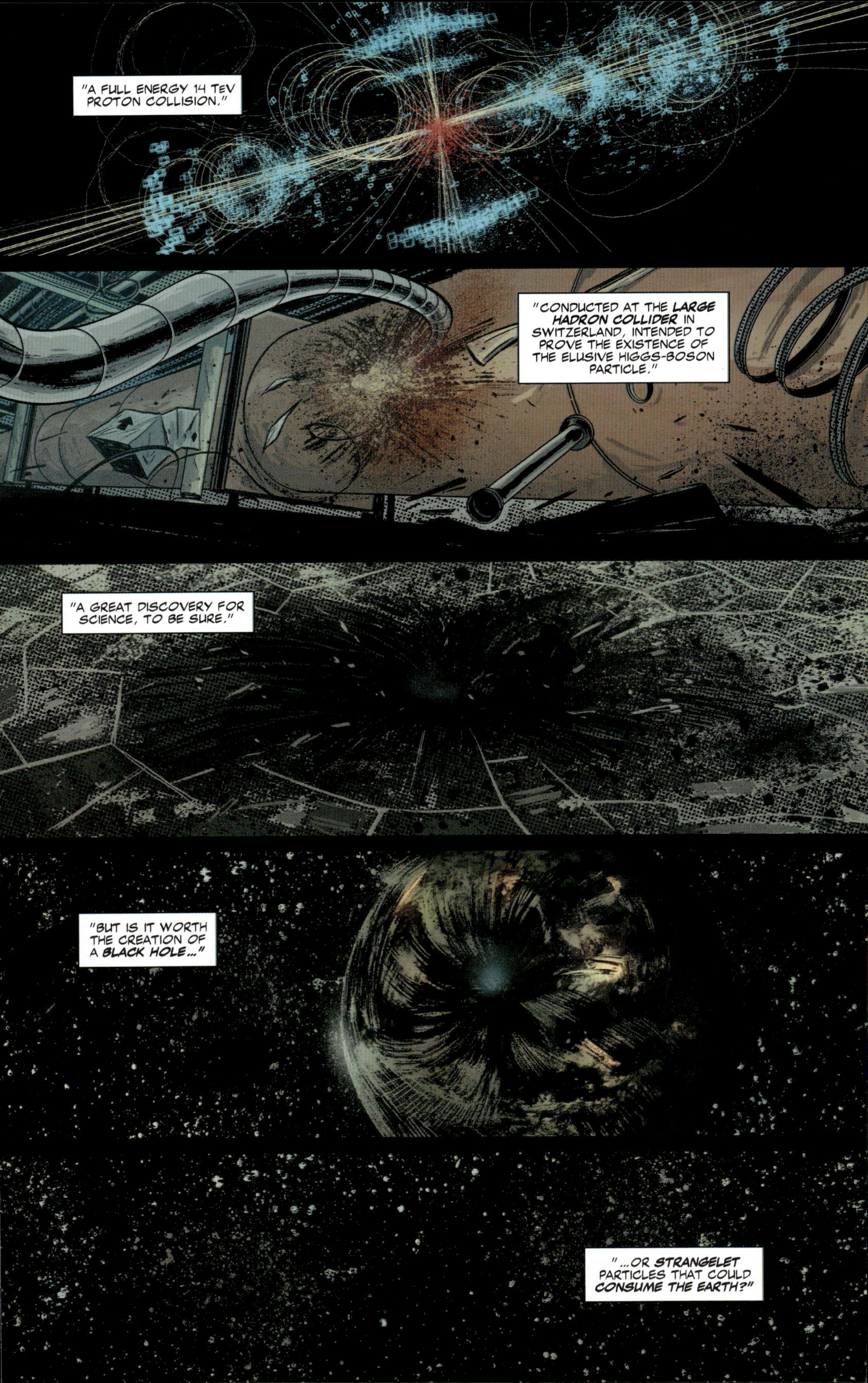
"A FULL ENERGY 14 TEV PROTON COLLISION."
"CONDUCTED AT THE LARGE HADRON COLLIDER IN SWITZERLAND, INTENDED TO PROVE THE EXISTENCE OF THE ELUSIVE HIGGS-BOSON PARTICLE."
"A GREAT DISCOVERY FOR SCIENCE, TO BE SURE."
"BUT IS IT WORTH THE CREATION OF A BLACK HOLE..."
"...OR STRANGELET PARTICLES THAT COULD CONSUME THE EARTH?"

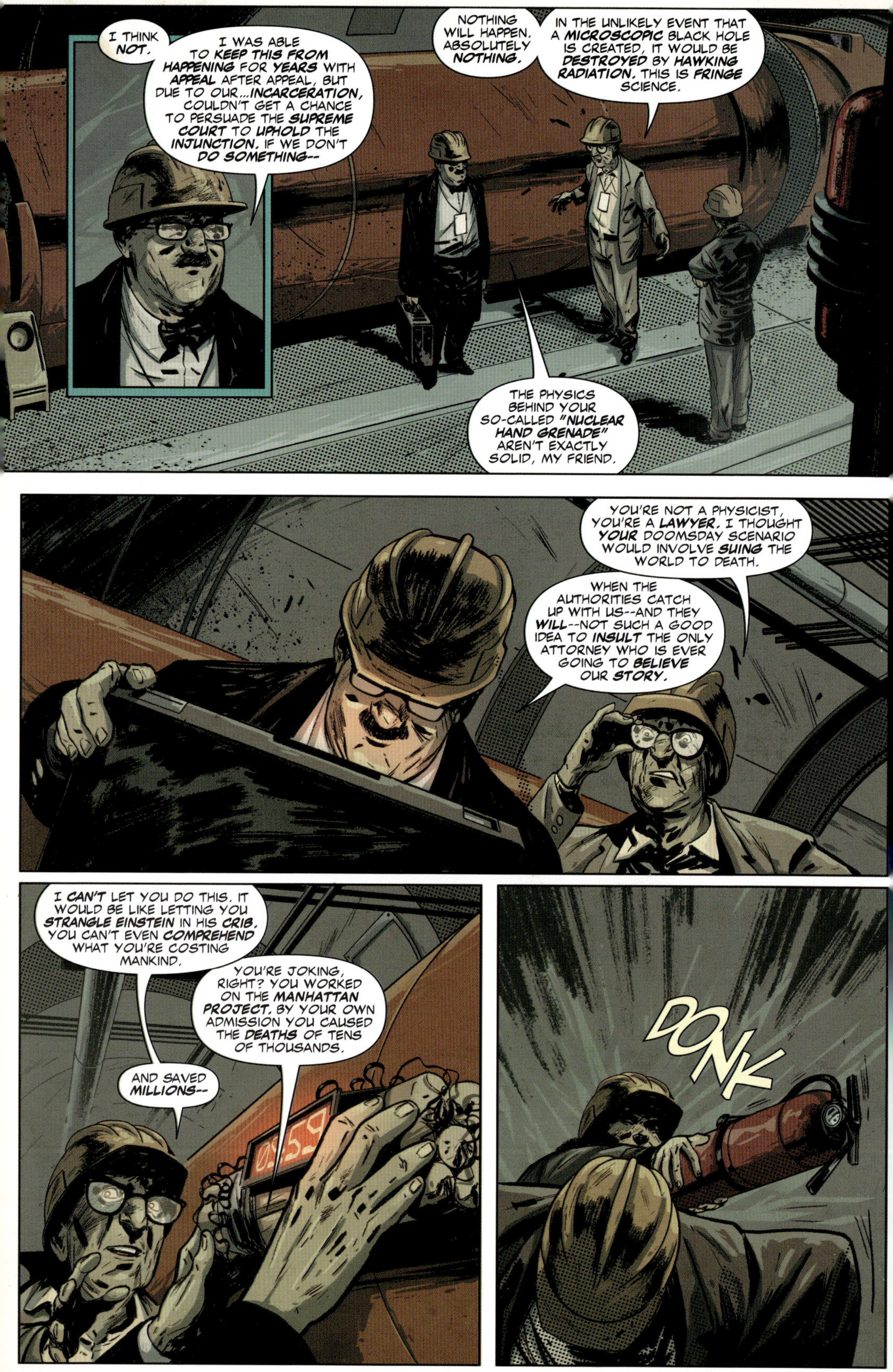
I THINK NOT.
I WAS ABLE TO KEEP THIS FROM HAPPENING FOR YEARS WITH APPEAL AFTER APPEAL, BUT DUE TO OUR...INCARCERATION, COULDN'T GET A CHANCE TO PERSUADE THE SUPREME COURT TO UPHOLD THE INJUNCTION. IF WE DON'T DO SOMETHING--
NOTHING WILL HAPPEN. ABSOLUTELY NOTHING.
IN THE UNLIKELY EVENT THAT A MICROSCOPIC BLACK HOLE IS CREATED, IT WOULD BE DESTROYED BY HAWKING RADIATION. THIS IS FRINGE SCIENCE.
THE PHYSICS BEHIND YOUR SO-CALLED "NUCLEAR HAND GRENADE" AREN'T EXACTLY SOLID, MY FRIEND.
YOU'RE NOT A PHYSICIST, YOU'RE A LAWYER. I THOUGHT YOUR DOOMSDAY SCENARIO WOULD INVOLVE SUING THE WORLD TO DEATH.
WHEN THE AUTHORITIES CATCH UP WITH US--AND THEY WILL--NOT SUCH A GOOD IDEA TO INSULT THE ONLY ATTORNEY WHO IS EVER GOING TO BELIEVE OUR STORY.
I CAN'T LET YOU DO THIS. IT WOULD BE LIKE LETTING YOU STRANGLE EINSTEIN IN HIS CRIB. YOU CAN'T EVEN COMPREHEND WHAT YOU'RE COSTING MANKIND.
YOU'RE JOKING, RIGHT? YOU WORKED ON THE MANHATTAN PROJECT. BY YOUR OWN ADMISSION YOU CAUSED THE DEATHS OF TENS OF THOUSANDS.
AND SAVED MILLIONS--
DONK

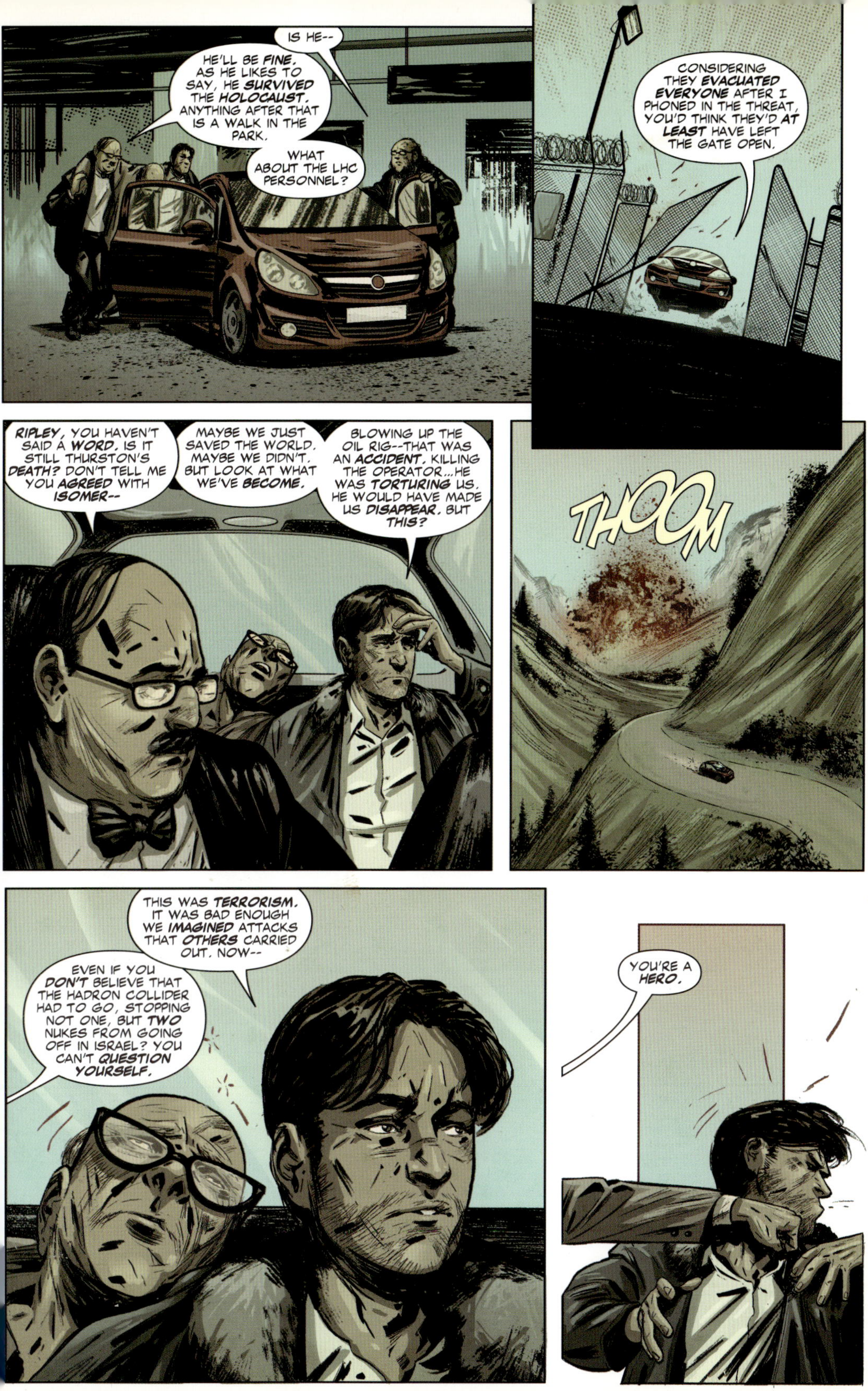
IS HE--
HE'LL BE FINE. AS HE LIKES TO SAY, HE SURVIVED THE HOLOCAUST. ANYTHING AFTER THAT IS A WALK IN THE PARK.
WHAT ABOUT THE LHC PERSONNEL?
CONSIDERING THEY EVACUATED EVERYONE AFTER I PHONED IN THE THREAT, YOU'D THINK THEY'D AT LEAST HAVE LEFT THE GATE OPEN.
RIPLEY, YOU HAVEN'T SAID A WORD. IS IT STILL THURSTON'S DEATH? DON'T TELL ME YOU AGREED WITH ISOMER--
MAYBE WE JUST SAVED THE WORLD. MAYBE WE DIDN'T. BUT LOOK AT WHAT WE'VE BECOME.
BLOWING UP THE OIL RIG--THAT WAS AN ACCIDENT. KILLING THE OPERATOR...HE WAS TORTURING US. HE WOULD HAVE MADE US DISAPPEAR. BUT THIS?
THOOM
THIS WAS TERRORISM. IT WAS BAD ENOUGH WE IMAGINED ATTACKS THAT OTHERS CARRIED OUT. NOW--
EVEN IF YOU DON'T BELIEVE THAT THE HADRON COLLIDER HAD TO GO, STOPPING NOT ONE, BUT TWO NUKES FROM GOING OFF IN ISRAEL? YOU CAN'T QUESTION YOURSELF.
YOU'RE A HERO.

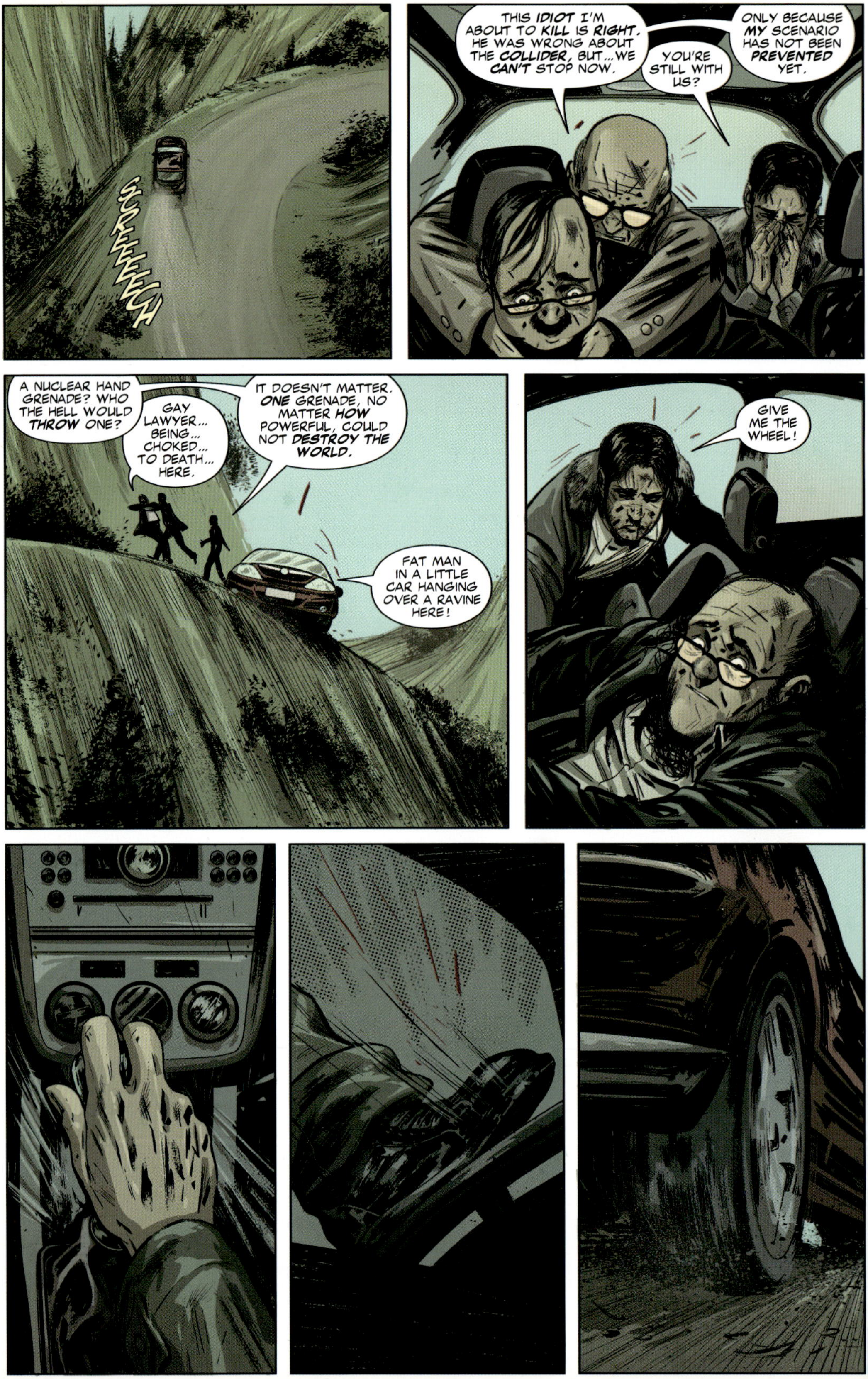
SCREEEEECH
THIS IDIOT I'M ABOUT TO KILL IS RIGHT. HE WAS WRONG ABOUT THE COLLIDER, BUT...WE CAN'T STOP NOW.
YOU'RE STILL WITH US?
ONLY BECAUSE MY SCENARIO HAS NOT BEEN PREVENTED YET.
A NUCLEAR HAND GRENADE? WHO THE HELL WOULD THROW ONE?
GAY LAWYER... BEING... CHOKED... TO DEATH... HERE.
IT DOESN'T MATTER. ONE GRENADE, NO MATTER HOW POWERFUL, COULD NOT DESTROY THE WORLD.
FAT MAN IN A LITTLE CAR HANGING OVER A RAVINE HERE!
GIVE ME THE WHEEL!

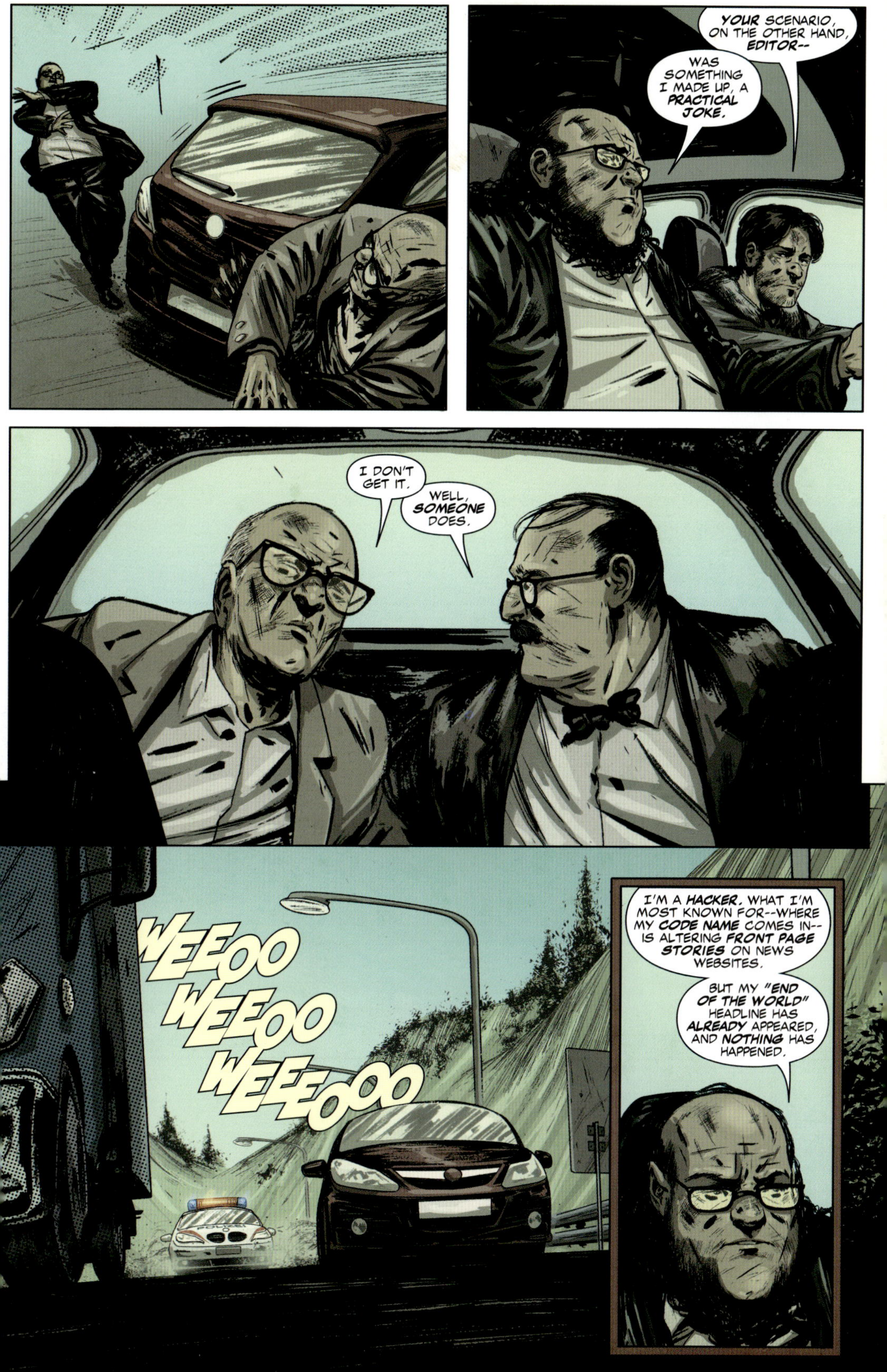

YOUR SCENARIO, ON THE OTHER HAND, EDITOR--
WAS SOMETHING I MADE UP, A PRACTICAL JOKE.
I DON'T GET IT.
WELL, SOMEONE DOES.
WEEOO WEEOO WEEEOOO
I'M A HACKER. WHAT I'M MOST KNOWN FOR--WHERE MY CODE NAME COMES IN--IS ALTERING FRONT PAGE STORIES ON NEWS WEBSITES.
BUT MY "END OF THE WORLD" HEADLINE HAS ALREADY APPEARED, AND NOTHING HAS HAPPENED.

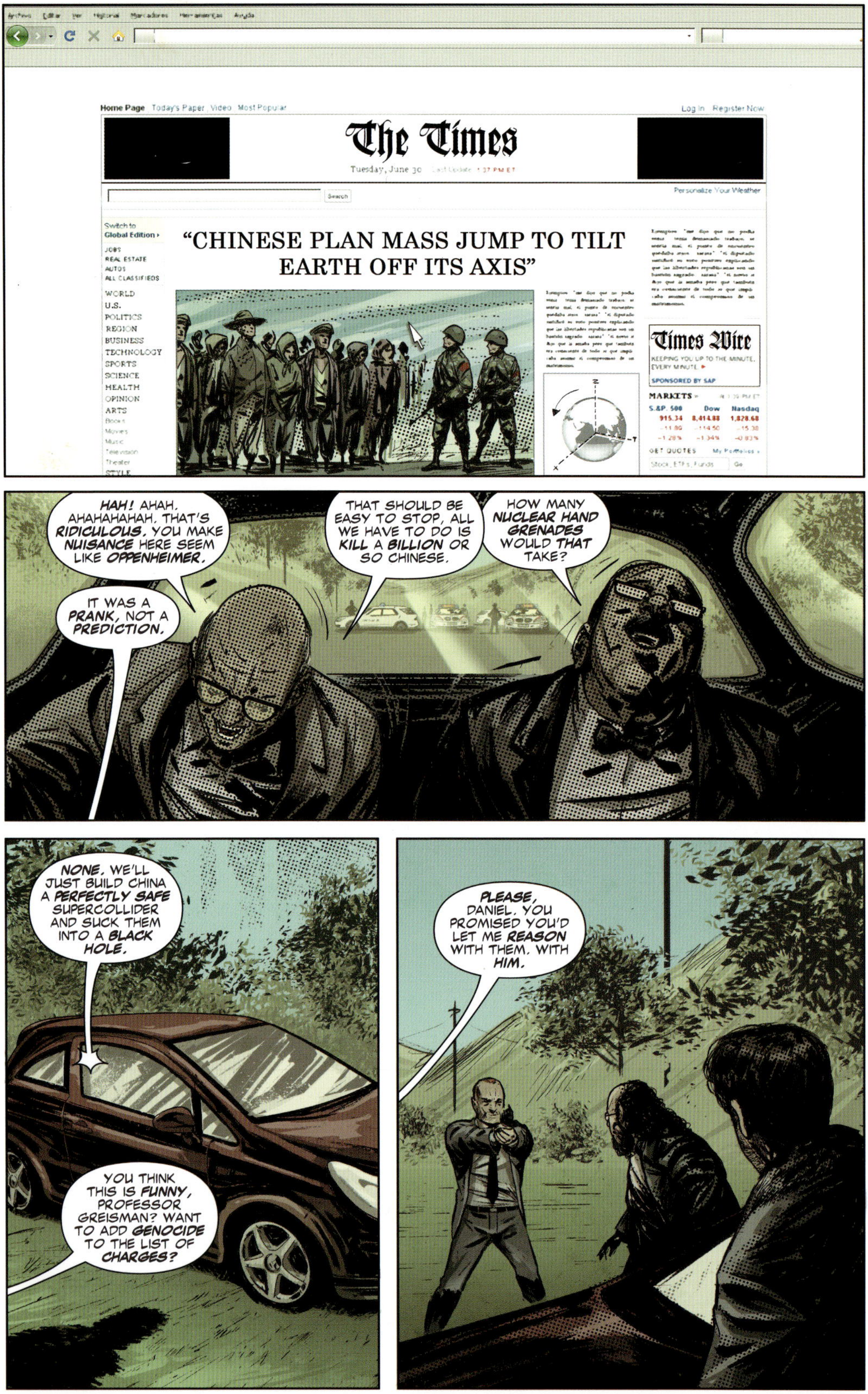

Home Page Today's Paper Video Most Popular
Log In Register Now
The Times
Tuesday, June 30
Search
Personalize Your Weather
Switch to Global Edition
JOBS
REAL ESTATE
AUTOS
ALL CLASSIFIEDS
WORLD
U.S.
POLITICS
REGION
BUSINESS
TECHNOLOGY
SPORTS
SCIENCE
HEALTH
OPINION
ARTS
STYLE
"CHINESE PLAN MASS JUMP TO TILT EARTH OFF ITS AXIS"
Times Wire
KEEPING YOU UP TO THE MINUTE, EVERY MINUTE
SPONSORED BY SAP
MARKETS
S.&P. 500
Dow
Nasdaq
GET QUOTES
My Portfolios
HAH! AHAH. AHAHAHAHAH. THAT'S RIDICULOUS. YOU MAKE NUISANCE HERE SEEM LIKE OPPENHEIMER.
IT WAS A PRANK, NOT A PREDICTION.
THAT SHOULD BE EASY TO STOP, ALL WE HAVE TO DO IS KILL A BILLION OR SO CHINESE.
HOW MANY NUCLEAR HAND GRENADES WOULD THAT TAKE?
NONE. WE'LL JUST BUILD CHINA A PERFECTLY SAFE SUPERCOLLIDER AND SUCK THEM INTO A BLACK HOLE.
YOU THINK THIS IS FUNNY, PROFESSOR GREISMAN? WANT TO ADD GENOCIDE TO THE LIST OF CHARGES?
PLEASE, DANIEL. YOU PROMISED YOU'D LET ME REASON WITH THEM. WITH HIM.

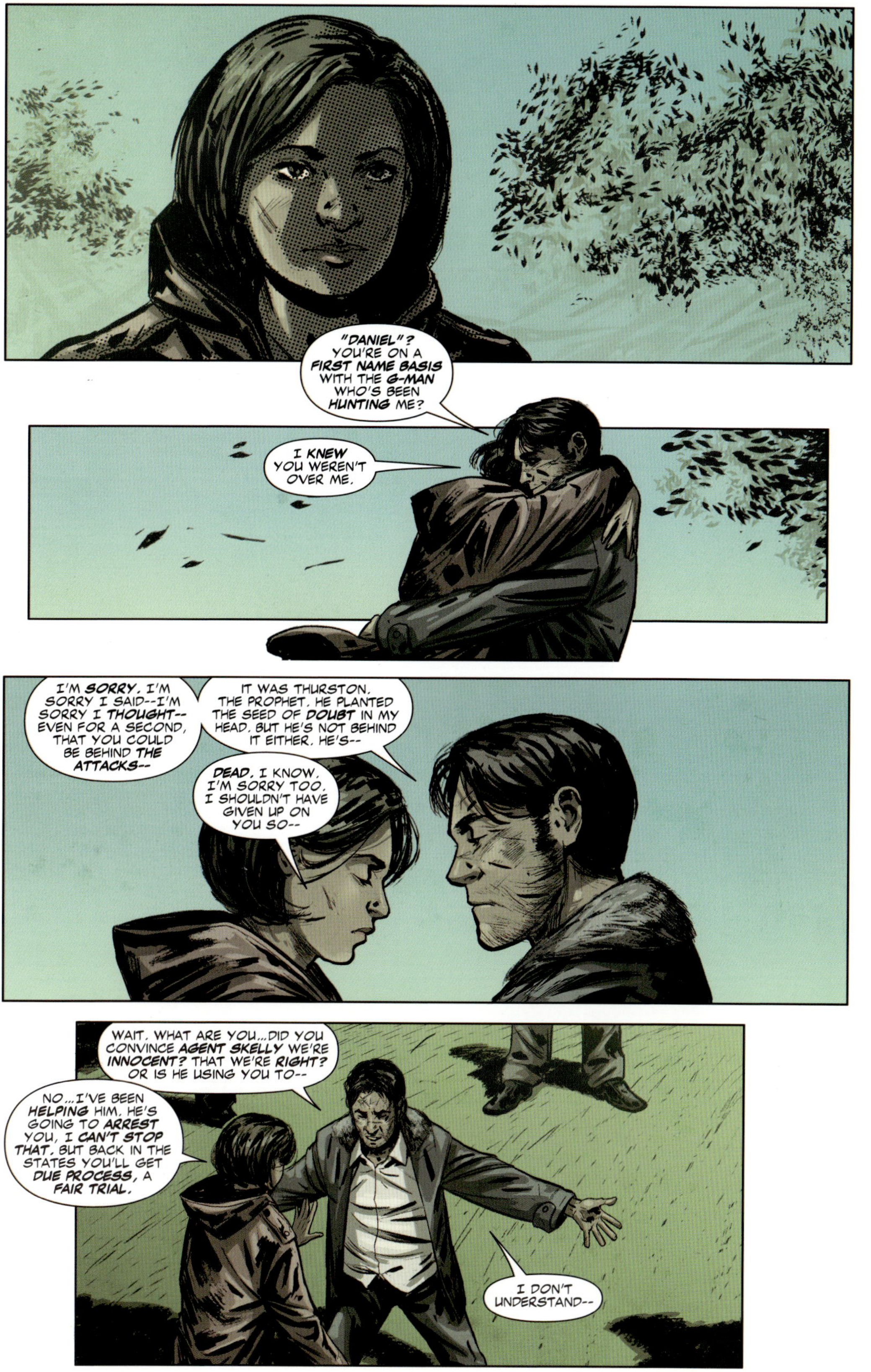
"DANIEL"? YOU'RE ON A FIRST NAME BASIS WITH THE G-MAN WHO'S BEEN HUNTING ME?
I KNEW YOU WEREN'T OVER ME.
I'M SORRY. I'M SORRY I SAID--I'M SORRY I THOUGHT-- EVEN FOR A SECOND, THAT YOU COULD BE BEHIND THE ATTACKS--
IT WAS THURSTON. THE PROPHET. HE PLANTED THE SEED OF DOUBT IN MY HEAD. BUT HE'S NOT BEHIND IT EITHER. HE'S--
DEAD. I KNOW. I'M SORRY TOO. I SHOULDN'T HAVE GIVEN UP ON YOU SO--
WAIT. WHAT ARE YOU...DID YOU CONVINCE AGENT SKELLY WE'RE INNOCENT? THAT WE'RE RIGHT? OR IS HE USING YOU TO--
NO...I'VE BEEN HELPING HIM. HE'S GOING TO ARREST YOU, I CAN'T STOP THAT. BUT BACK IN THE STATES YOU'LL GET DUE PROCESS, A FAIR TRIAL.
I DON'T UNDERSTAND--

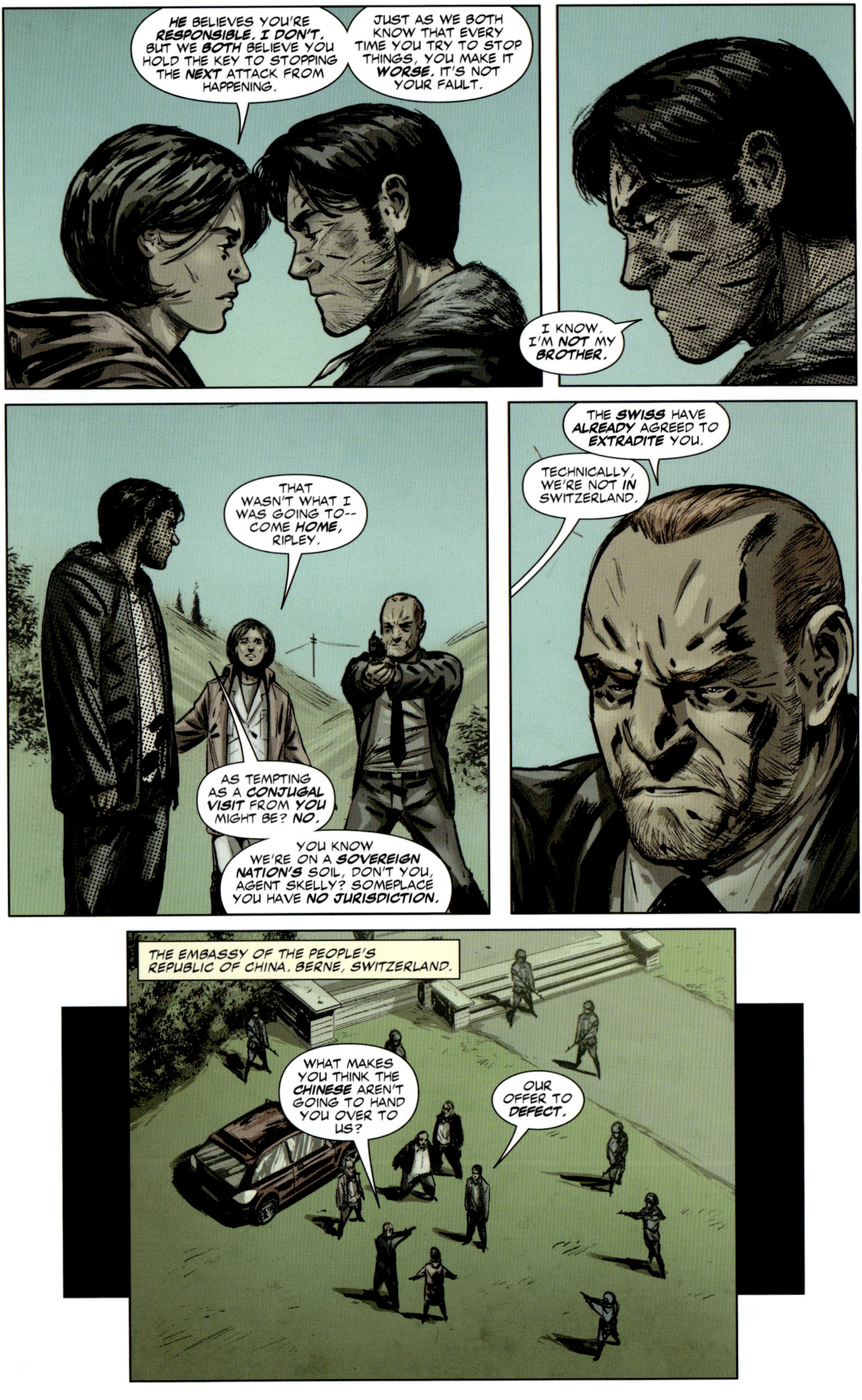
HE BELIEVES YOU'RE RESPONSIBLE. I DON'T. BUT WE BOTH BELIEVE YOU HOLD THE KEY TO STOPPING THE NEXT ATTACK FROM HAPPENING.
JUST AS WE BOTH KNOW THAT EVERY TIME YOU TRY TO STOP THINGS, YOU MAKE IT WORSE. IT'S NOT YOUR FAULT.
I KNOW. I'M NOT MY BROTHER.
THAT WASN'T WHAT I WAS GOING TO-- COME HOME, RIPLEY.
AS TEMPTING AS A CONJUGAL VISIT FROM YOU MIGHT BE? NO.
YOU KNOW WE'RE ON A SOVEREIGN NATION'S SOIL, DON'T YOU, AGENT SKELLY? SOMEPLACE YOU HAVE NO JURISDICTION.
THE SWISS HAVE ALREADY AGREED TO EXTRADITE YOU.
TECHNICALLY, WE'RE NOT IN SWITZERLAND.
THE EMBASSY OF THE PEOPLE'S REPUBLIC OF CHINA. BERNE, SWITZERLAND.
WHAT MAKES YOU THINK THE CHINESE AREN'T GOING TO HAND YOU OVER TO US?
OUR OFFER TO DEFECT.

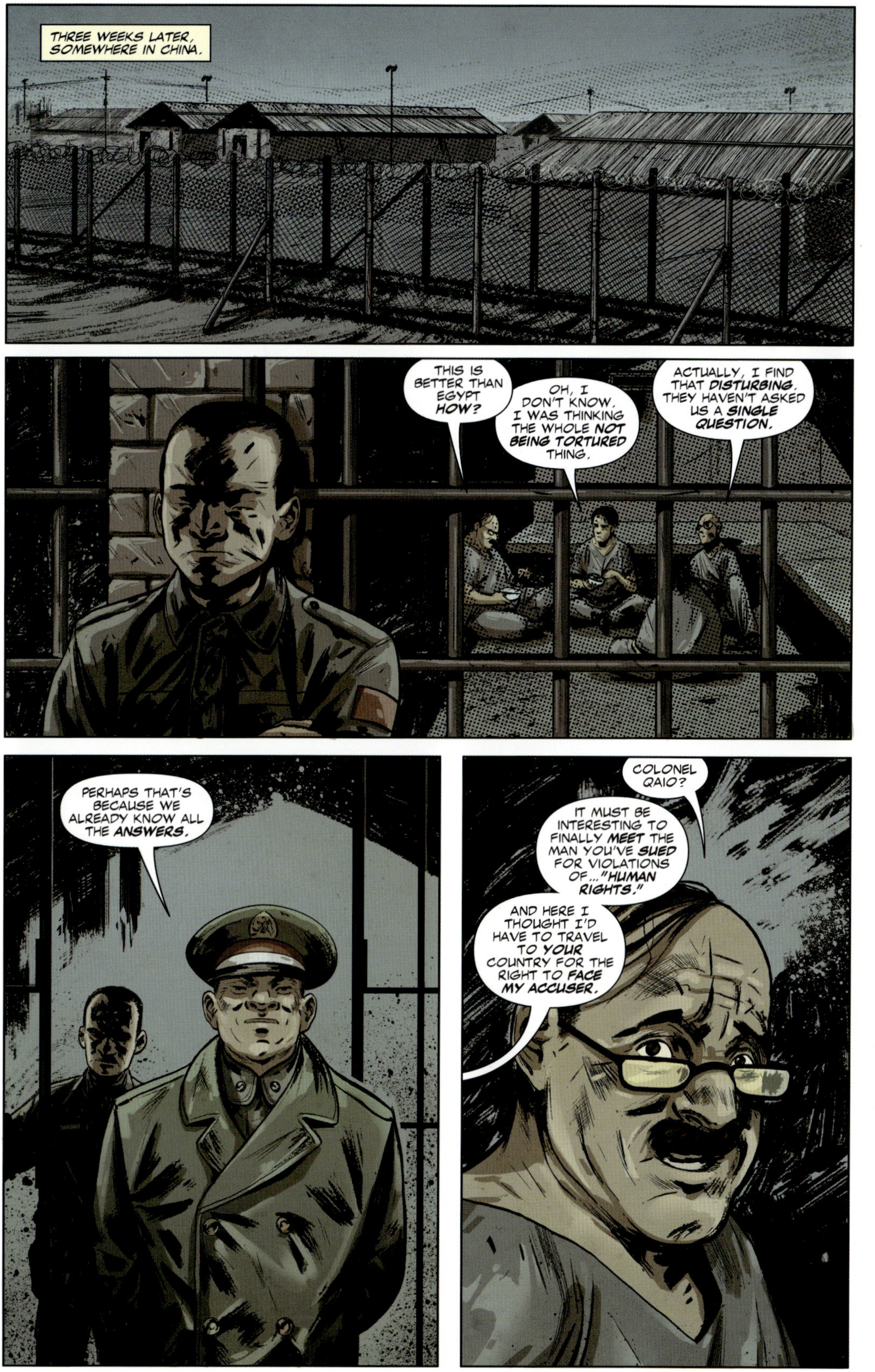
THREE WEEKS LATER, SOMEWHERE IN CHINA.
THIS IS BETTER THAN EGYPT HOW?
OH, I DON'T KNOW. I WAS THINKING THE WHOLE NOT BEING TORTURED THING.
ACTUALLY, I FIND THAT DISTURBING. THEY HAVEN'T ASKED US A SINGLE QUESTION.
PERHAPS THAT'S BECAUSE WE ALREADY KNOW ALL THE ANSWERS.
COLONEL QAIO?
IT MUST BE INTERESTING TO FINALLY MEET THE MAN YOU'VE SUED FOR VIOLATIONS OF..."HUMAN RIGHTS."
AND HERE I THOUGHT I'D HAVE TO TRAVEL TO YOUR COUNTRY FOR THE RIGHT TO FACE MY ACCUSER.

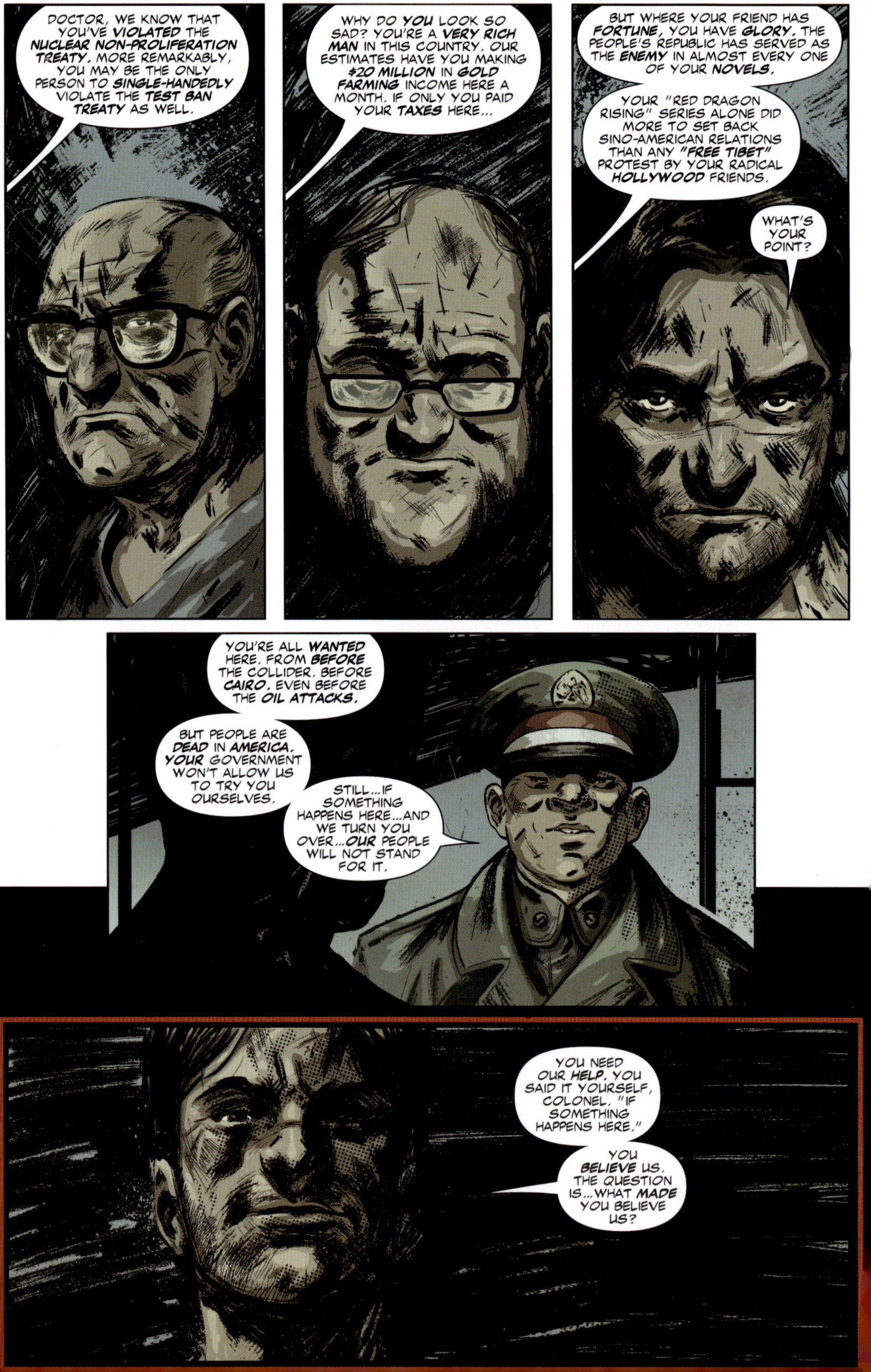
DOCTOR, WE KNOW THAT YOU'VE VIOLATED THE NUCLEAR NON-PROLIFERATION TREATY. MORE REMARKABLY, YOU MAY BE THE ONLY PERSON TO SINGLE-HANDEDLY VIOLATE THE TEST BAN TREATY AS WELL.
WHY DO YOU LOOK SO SAD? YOU'RE A VERY RICH MAN IN THIS COUNTRY. OUR ESTIMATES HAVE YOU MAKING $20 MILLION IN GOLD FARMING INCOME HERE A MONTH. IF ONLY YOU PAID YOUR TAXES HERE...
BUT WHERE YOUR FRIEND HAS FORTUNE, YOU HAVE GLORY. THE PEOPLE'S REPUBLIC HAS SERVED AS THE ENEMY IN ALMOST EVERY ONE OF YOUR NOVELS.
YOUR "RED DRAGON RISING" SERIES ALONE DID MORE TO SET BACK SINO-AMERICAN RELATIONS THAN ANY "FREE TIBET" PROTEST BY YOUR RADICAL HOLLYWOOD FRIENDS.
WHAT'S YOUR POINT?
YOU'RE ALL WANTED HERE. FROM BEFORE THE COLLIDER. BEFORE CAIRO. EVEN BEFORE THE OIL ATTACKS.
BUT PEOPLE ARE DEAD IN AMERICA. YOUR GOVERNMENT WON'T ALLOW US TO TRY YOU OURSELVES.
STILL...IF SOMETHING HAPPENS HERE...AND WE TURN YOU OVER...OUR PEOPLE WILL NOT STAND FOR IT.
YOU NEED OUR HELP. YOU SAID IT YOURSELF, COLONEL. "IF SOMETHING HAPPENS HERE."
YOU BELIEVE US. THE QUESTION IS...WHAT MADE YOU BELIEVE US?

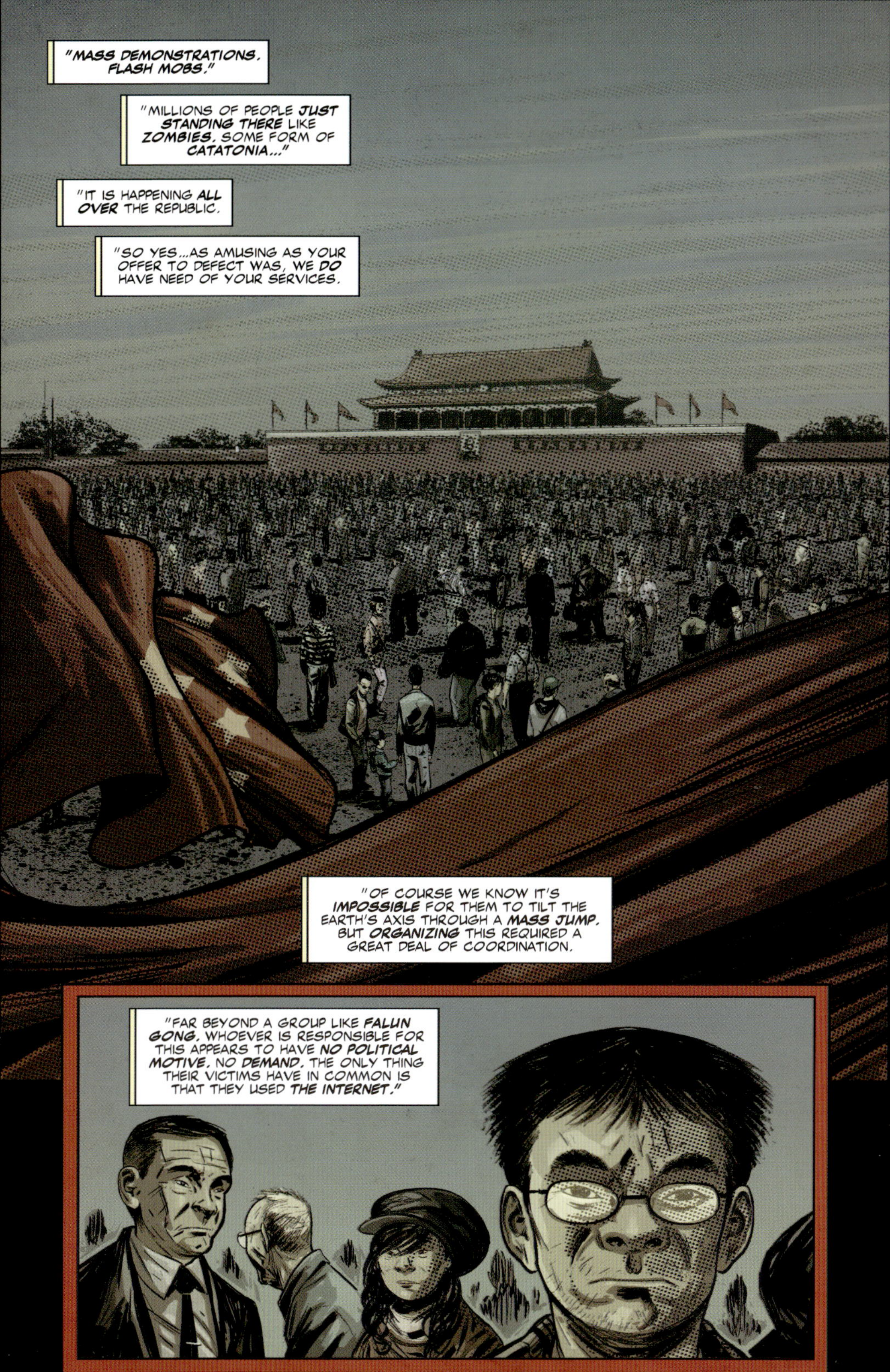
"MASS DEMONSTRATIONS. FLASH MOBS."
"MILLIONS OF PEOPLE JUST STANDING THERE LIKE ZOMBIES. SOME FORM OF CATATONIA..."
"IT IS HAPPENING ALL OVER THE REPUBLIC.
"SO YES...AS AMUSING AS YOUR OFFER TO DEFECT WAS, WE DO HAVE NEED OF YOUR SERVICES.
"OF COURSE WE KNOW IT'S IMPOSSIBLE FOR THEM TO TILT THE EARTH'S AXIS THROUGH A MASS JUMP, BUT ORGANIZING THIS REQUIRED A GREAT DEAL OF COORDINATION.
"FAR BEYOND A GROUP LIKE FALUN GONG. WHOEVER IS RESPONSIBLE FOR THIS APPEARS TO HAVE NO POLITICAL MOTIVE, NO DEMAND. THE ONLY THING THEIR VICTIMS HAVE IN COMMON IS THAT THEY USED THE INTERNET."

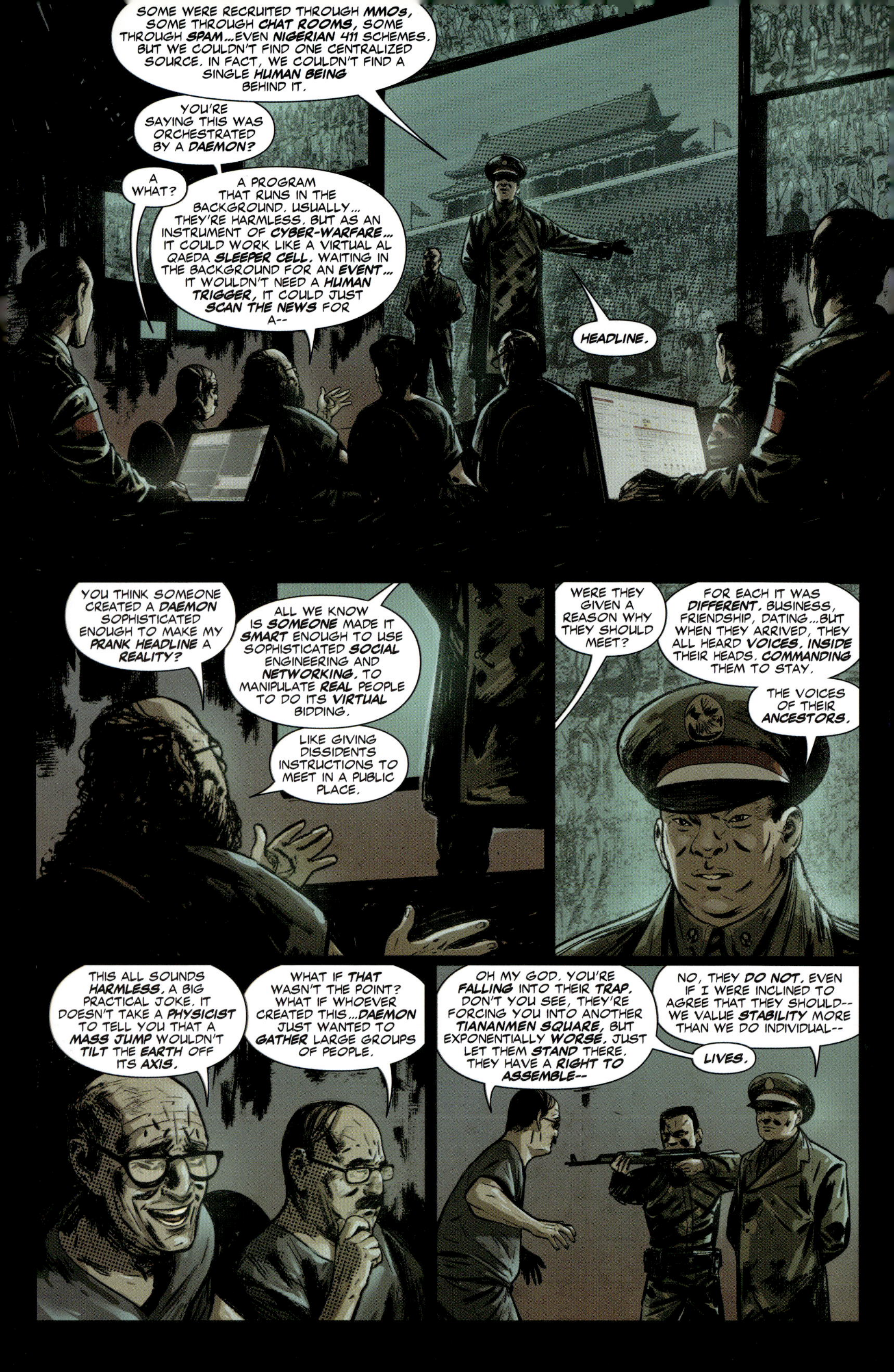
SOME WERE RECRUITED THROUGH MMOs, SOME THROUGH CHAT ROOMS, SOME THROUGH SPAM...EVEN NIGERIAN 411 SCHEMES. BUT WE COULDN'T FIND ONE CENTRALIZED SOURCE. IN FACT, WE COULDN'T FIND A SINGLE HUMAN BEING BEHIND IT.
YOU'RE SAYING THIS WAS ORCHESTRATED BY A DAEMON?
A WHAT?
A PROGRAM THAT RUNS IN THE BACKGROUND. USUALLY... THEY'RE HARMLESS. BUT AS AN INSTRUMENT OF CYBER-WARFARE... IT COULD WORK LIKE A VIRTUAL AL QAEDA SLEEPER CELL. WAITING IN THE BACKGROUND FOR AN EVENT... IT WOULDN'T NEED A HUMAN TRIGGER, IT COULD JUST SCAN THE NEWS FOR A--
HEADLINE.
YOU THINK SOMEONE CREATED A DAEMON SOPHISTICATED ENOUGH TO MAKE MY PRANK HEADLINE A REALITY?
ALL WE KNOW IS SOMEONE MADE IT SMART ENOUGH TO USE SOPHISTICATED SOCIAL ENGINEERING AND NETWORKING, TO MANIPULATE REAL PEOPLE TO DO ITS VIRTUAL BIDDING.
LIKE GIVING DISSIDENTS INSTRUCTIONS TO MEET IN A PUBLIC PLACE.
WERE THEY GIVEN A REASON WHY THEY SHOULD MEET?
FOR EACH IT WAS DIFFERENT. BUSINESS, FRIENDSHIP, DATING...BUT WHEN THEY ARRIVED, THEY ALL HEARD VOICES. INSIDE THEIR HEADS. COMMANDING THEM TO STAY.
THE VOICES OF THEIR ANCESTORS.
THIS ALL SOUNDS HARMLESS. A BIG PRACTICAL JOKE. IT DOESN'T TAKE A PHYSICIST TO TELL YOU THAT A MASS JUMP WOULDN'T TILT THE EARTH OFF ITS AXIS.
WHAT IF THAT WASN'T THE POINT? WHAT IF WHOEVER CREATED THIS...DAEMON JUST WANTED TO GATHER LARGE GROUPS OF PEOPLE.
OH MY GOD. YOU'RE FALLING INTO THEIR TRAP. DON'T YOU SEE, THEY'RE FORCING YOU INTO ANOTHER TIANANMEN SQUARE, BUT EXPONENTIALLY WORSE. JUST LET THEM STAND THERE. THEY HAVE A RIGHT TO ASSEMBLE--
NO, THEY DO NOT. EVEN IF I WERE INCLINED TO AGREE THAT THEY SHOULD-- WE VALUE STABILITY MORE THAN WE DO INDIVIDUAL--
LIVES.

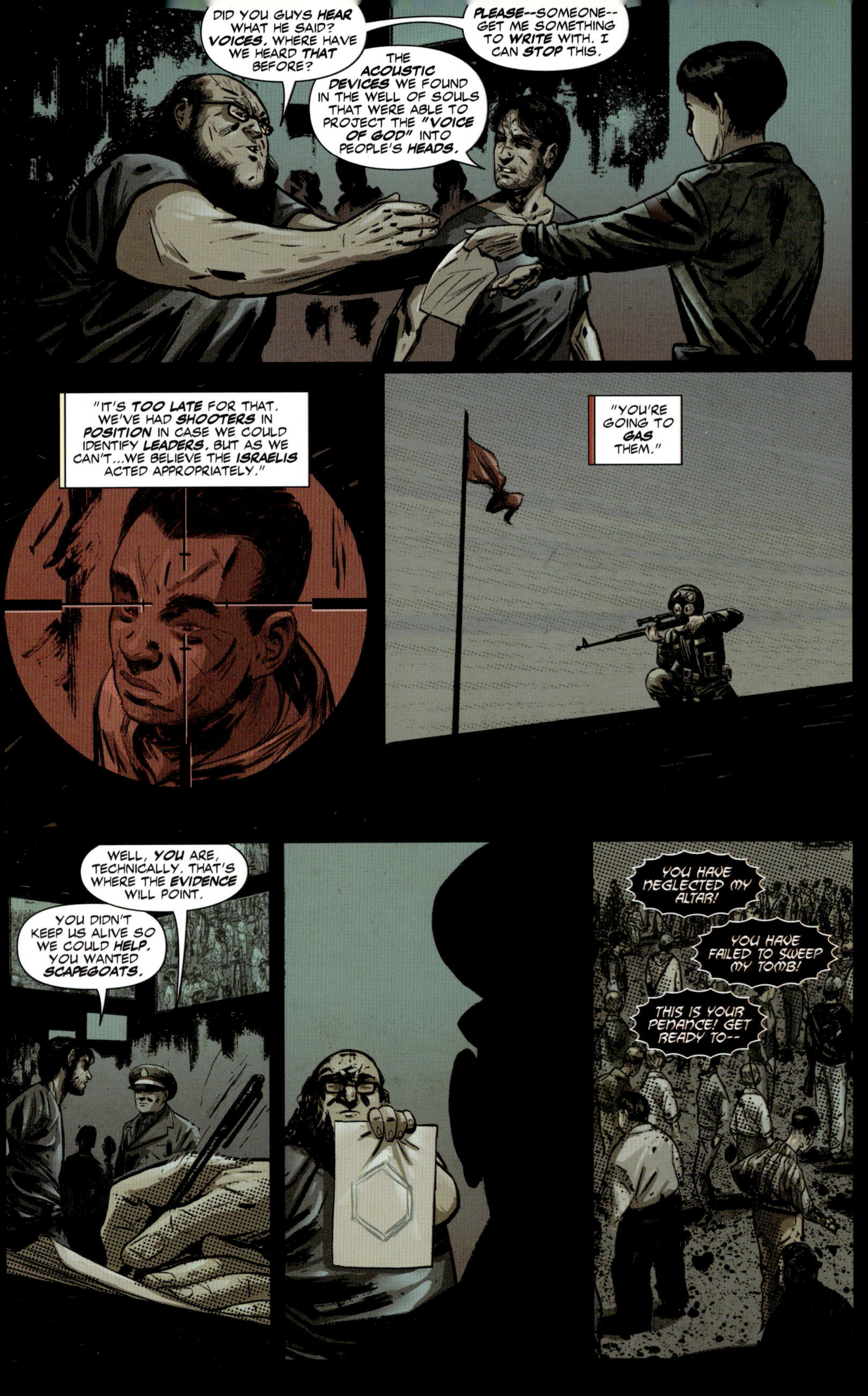

DID YOU GUYS HEAR WHAT HE SAID? VOICES. WHERE HAVE WE HEARD THAT BEFORE?
PLEASE--SOMEONE--GET ME SOMETHING TO WRITE WITH. I CAN STOP THIS.
THE ACOUSTIC DEVICES WE FOUND IN THE WELL OF SOULS THAT WERE ABLE TO PROJECT THE "VOICE OF GOD" INTO PEOPLE'S HEADS.
"IT'S TOO LATE FOR THAT. WE'VE HAD SHOOTERS IN POSITION IN CASE WE COULD IDENTIFY LEADERS. BUT AS WE CAN'T... WE BELIEVE THE ISRAELIS ACTED APPROPRIATELY."
"YOU'RE GOING TO GAS THEM."
WELL, YOU ARE, TECHNICALLY. THAT'S WHERE THE EVIDENCE WILL POINT.
YOU DIDN'T KEEP US ALIVE SO WE COULD HELP. YOU WANTED SCAPEGOATS.
YOU HAVE NEGLECTED MY ALTAR!
YOU HAVE FAILED TO SWEEP MY TOMB!
THIS IS YOUR PENANCE! GET READY TO--

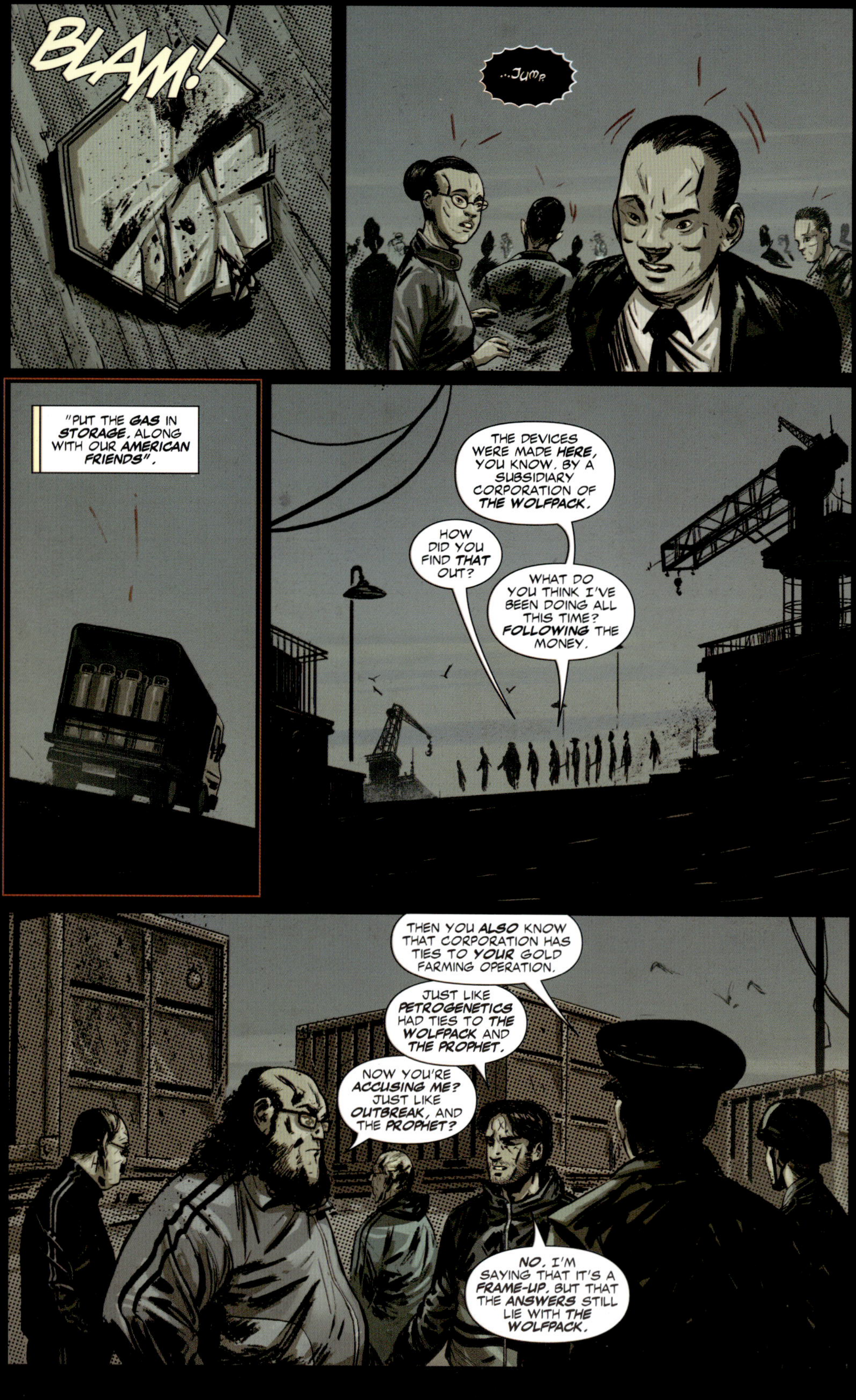
BLAM!
...JUMP.
"PUT THE GAS IN STORAGE. ALONG WITH OUR AMERICAN FRIENDS".
THE DEVICES WERE MADE HERE, YOU KNOW. BY A SUBSIDIARY CORPORATION OF THE WOLFPACK.
HOW DID YOU FIND THAT OUT?
WHAT DO YOU THINK I'VE BEEN DOING ALL THIS TIME? FOLLOWING THE MONEY.
THEN YOU ALSO KNOW THAT CORPORATION HAS TIES TO YOUR GOLD FARMING OPERATION.
JUST LIKE PETROGENETICS HAD TIES TO THE WOLFPACK AND THE PROPHET.
NOW YOU'RE ACCUSING ME? JUST LIKE OUTBREAK, AND THE PROPHET?
NO. I'M SAYING THAT IT'S A FRAME-UP. BUT THAT THE ANSWERS STILL LIE WITH THE WOLFPACK.

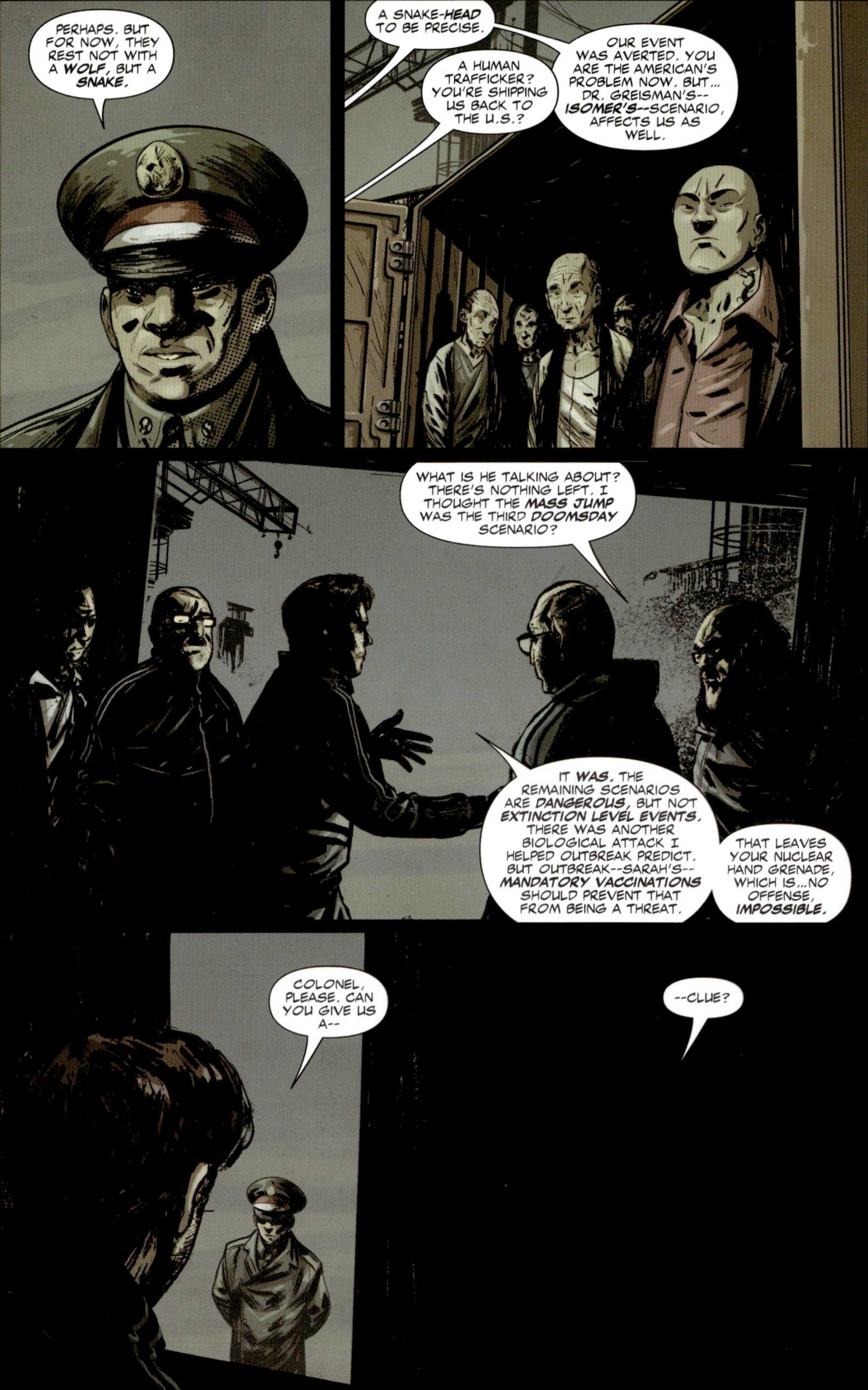
PERHAPS. BUT FOR NOW, THEY REST NOT WITH A WOLF, BUT A SNAKE.
A SNAKE-HEAD TO BE PRECISE.
A HUMAN TRAFFICKER? YOU'RE SHIPPING US BACK TO THE U.S.?
OUR EVENT WAS AVERTED. YOU ARE THE AMERICAN'S PROBLEM NOW. BUT... DR. GREISMAN'S--ISOMER'S--SCENARIO, AFFECTS US AS WELL.
WHAT IS HE TALKING ABOUT? THERE'S NOTHING LEFT. I THOUGHT THE MASS JUMP WAS THE THIRD DOOMSDAY SCENARIO?
IT WAS. THE REMAINING SCENARIOS ARE DANGEROUS, BUT NOT EXTINCTION LEVEL EVENTS. THERE WAS ANOTHER BIOLOGICAL ATTACK I HELPED OUTBREAK PREDICT. BUT OUTBREAK--SARAH'S--MANDATORY VACCINATIONS SHOULD PREVENT THAT FROM BEING A THREAT.
THAT LEAVES YOUR NUCLEAR HAND GRENADE, WHICH IS...NO OFFENSE, IMPOSSIBLE.
COLONEL, PLEASE. CAN YOU GIVE US A--
--CLUE?

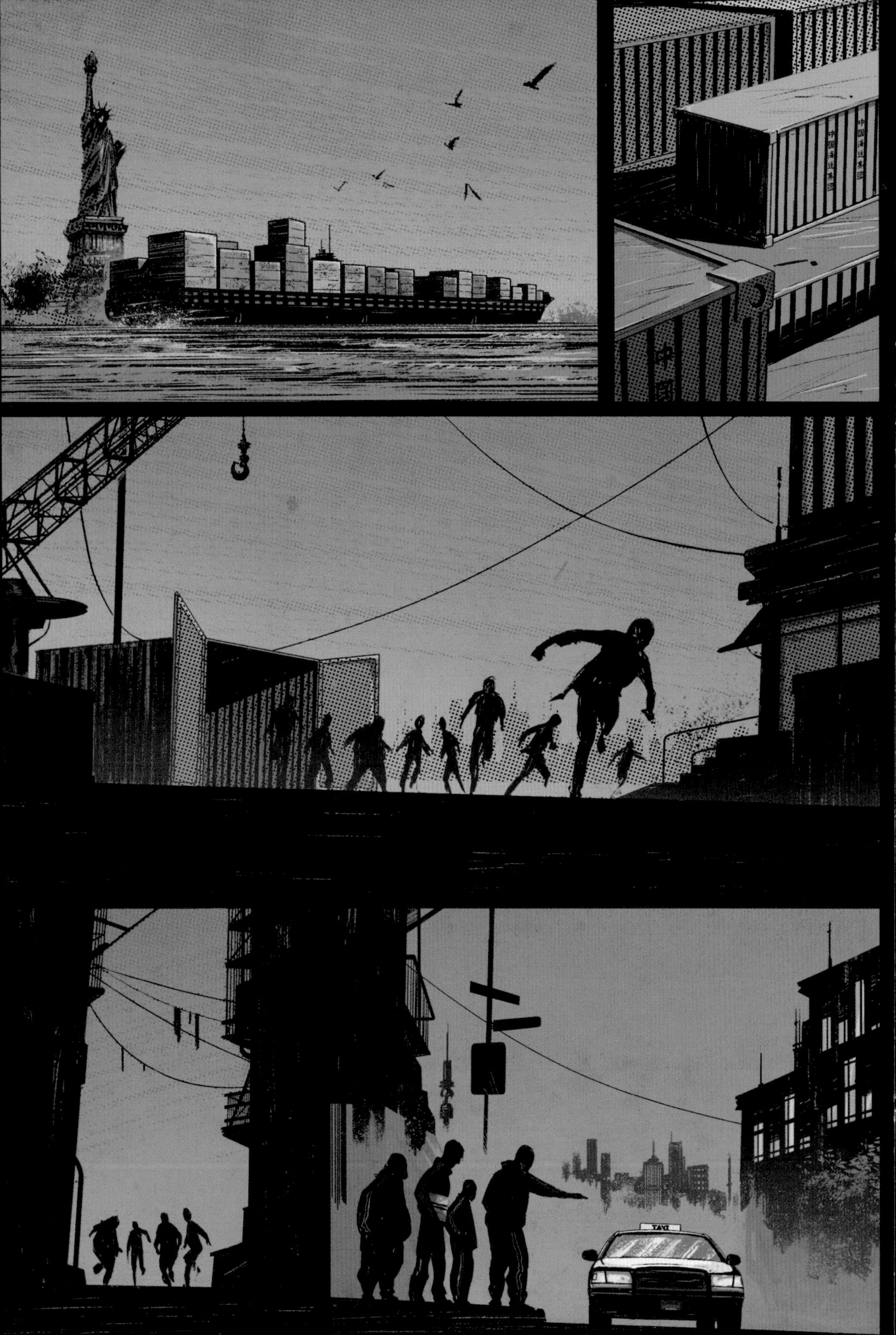

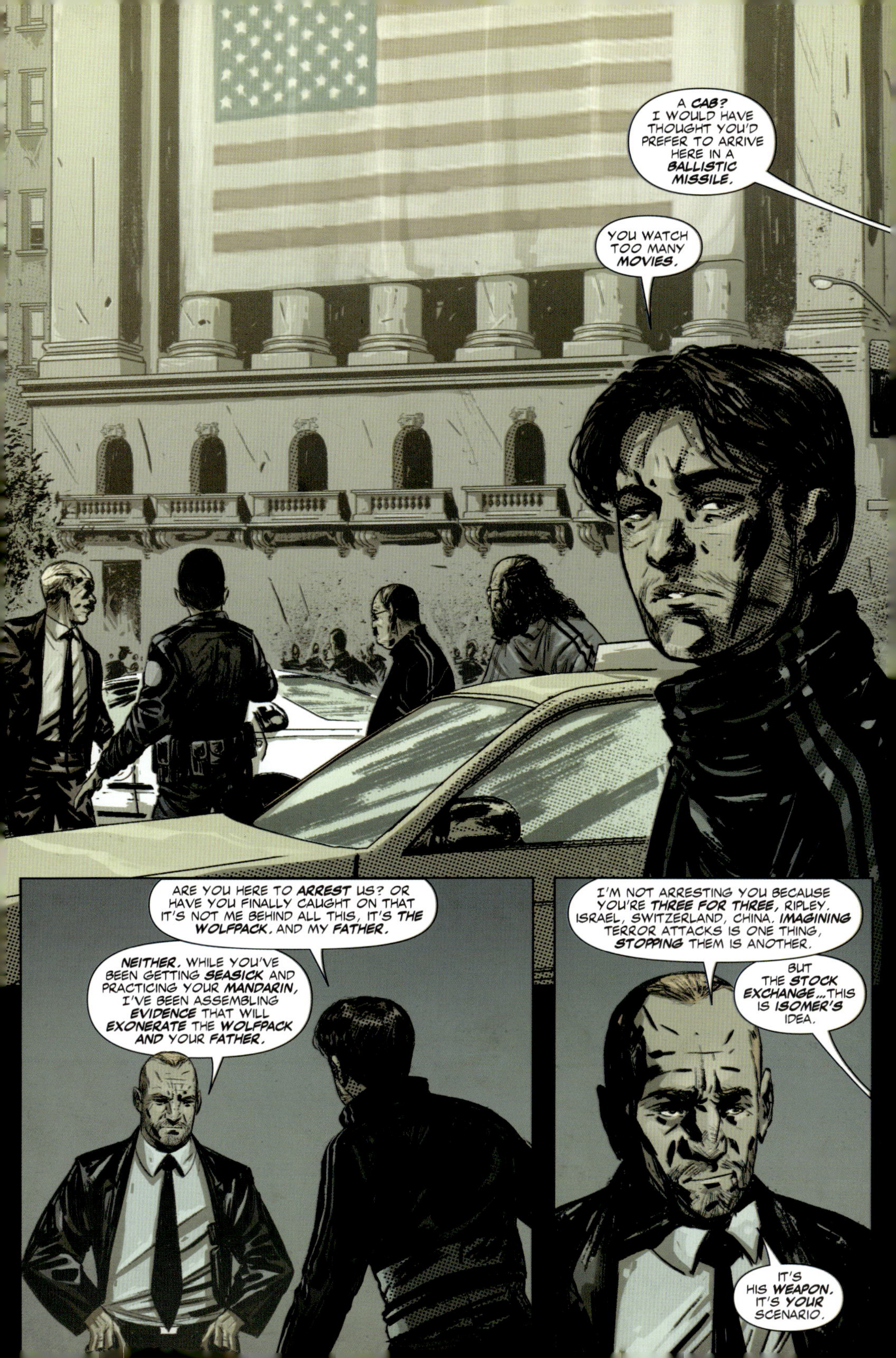
A CAB? I WOULD HAVE THOUGHT YOU'D PREFER TO ARRIVE HERE IN A BALLISTIC MISSILE.
YOU WATCH TOO MANY MOVIES.
ARE YOU HERE TO ARREST US? OR HAVE YOU FINALLY CAUGHT ON THAT IT'S NOT ME BEHIND ALL THIS, IT'S THE WOLFPACK. AND MY FATHER.
NEITHER. WHILE YOU'VE BEEN GETTING SEASICK AND PRACTICING YOUR MANDARIN, I'VE BEEN ASSEMBLING EVIDENCE THAT WILL EXONERATE THE WOLFPACK AND YOUR FATHER.
I'M NOT ARRESTING YOU BECAUSE YOU'RE THREE FOR THREE, RIPLEY. ISRAEL, SWITZERLAND, CHINA. IMAGINING TERROR ATTACKS IS ONE THING, STOPPING THEM IS ANOTHER.
BUT THE STOCK EXCHANGE... THIS IS ISOMER'S IDEA.
IT'S HIS WEAPON. IT'S YOUR SCENARIO.

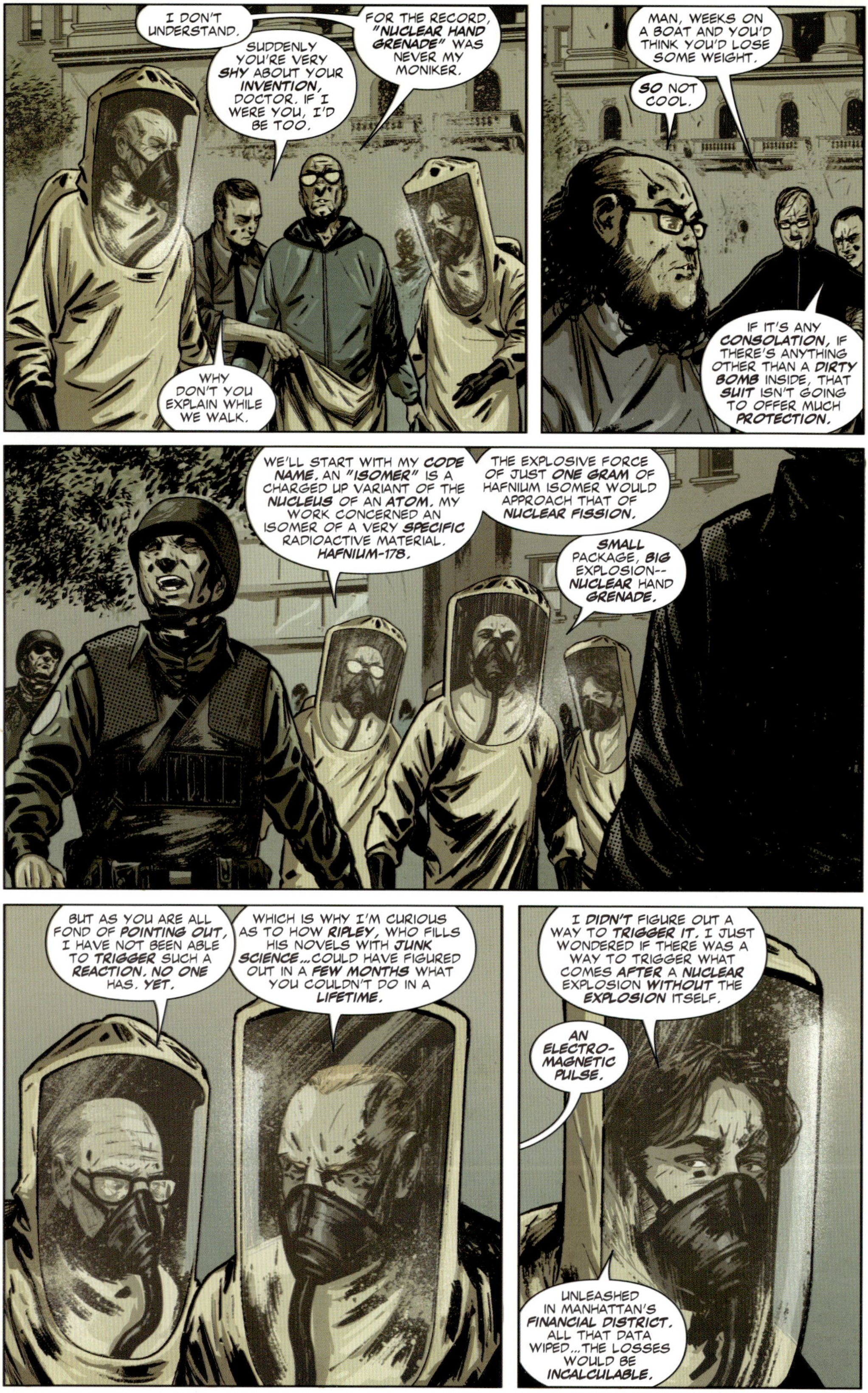
I DON'T UNDERSTAND.
FOR THE RECORD, **"NUCLEAR HAND GRENADE"** WAS NEVER MY MONIKER.
SUDDENLY YOU'RE VERY **SHY** ABOUT YOUR **INVENTION**, DOCTOR. IF I WERE YOU, I'D BE TOO.
WHY DON'T YOU EXPLAIN WHILE WE WALK.
MAN, WEEKS ON A BOAT AND YOU'D THINK YOU'D LOSE SOME WEIGHT.
SO NOT COOL.
IF IT'S ANY **CONSOLATION**, IF THERE'S ANYTHING OTHER THAN A **DIRTY BOMB** INSIDE, THAT **SUIT** ISN'T GOING TO OFFER MUCH **PROTECTION**.
WE'LL START WITH MY **CODE NAME**. AN **"ISOMER"** IS A CHARGED UP VARIANT OF THE **NUCLEUS** OF AN **ATOM**. MY WORK CONCERNED AN ISOMER OF A VERY **SPECIFIC** RADIOACTIVE MATERIAL. **HAFNIUM-178.**
THE EXPLOSIVE FORCE OF JUST **ONE GRAM** OF HAFNIUM ISOMER WOULD APPROACH THAT OF **NUCLEAR FISSION.**
SMALL PACKAGE, **BIG** EXPLOSION-- **NUCLEAR** HAND **GRENADE.**
BUT AS YOU ARE ALL FOND OF **POINTING OUT**, I HAVE NOT BEEN ABLE TO **TRIGGER** SUCH A **REACTION**. **NO ONE** HAS. **YET.**
WHICH IS WHY I'M CURIOUS AS TO HOW **RIPLEY**, WHO FILLS HIS NOVELS WITH **JUNK SCIENCE**...COULD HAVE FIGURED OUT IN A **FEW MONTHS** WHAT YOU COULDN'T DO IN A **LIFETIME.**
I **DIDN'T** FIGURE OUT A WAY TO **TRIGGER IT**. I JUST WONDERED IF THERE WAS A WAY TO TRIGGER WHAT COMES **AFTER** A **NUCLEAR** EXPLOSION **WITHOUT** THE **EXPLOSION** ITSELF.
AN ELECTRO-MAGNETIC PULSE.
UNLEASHED IN MANHATTAN'S **FINANCIAL DISTRICT**. ALL THAT DATA WIPED...THE LOSSES WOULD BE **INCALCULABLE.**

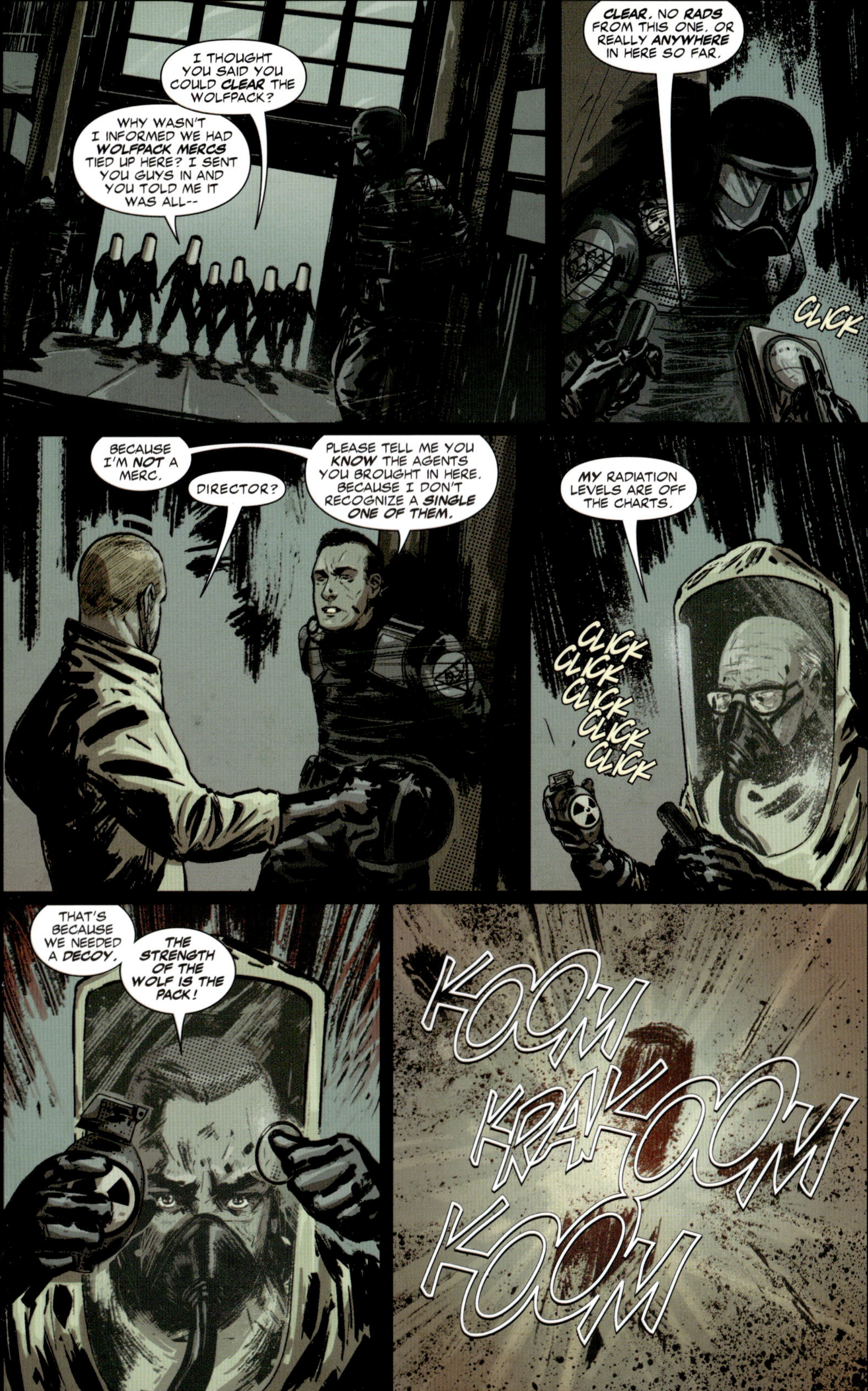
I THOUGHT YOU SAID YOU COULD CLEAR THE WOLFPACK?
WHY WASN'T I INFORMED WE HAD WOLFPACK MERCS TIED UP HERE? I SENT YOU GUYS IN AND YOU TOLD ME IT WAS ALL--
CLEAR. NO RADS FROM THIS ONE. OR REALLY ANYWHERE IN HERE SO FAR.
CLICK
BECAUSE I'M NOT A MERC.
DIRECTOR?
PLEASE TELL ME YOU KNOW THE AGENTS YOU BROUGHT IN HERE. BECAUSE I DON'T RECOGNIZE A SINGLE ONE OF THEM.
MY RADIATION LEVELS ARE OFF THE CHARTS.
CLICK CLICK CLICK CLICK CLICK
THAT'S BECAUSE WE NEEDED A DECOY.
THE STRENGTH OF THE WOLF IS THE PACK!
KOOM
KRAKOOM
KOOM

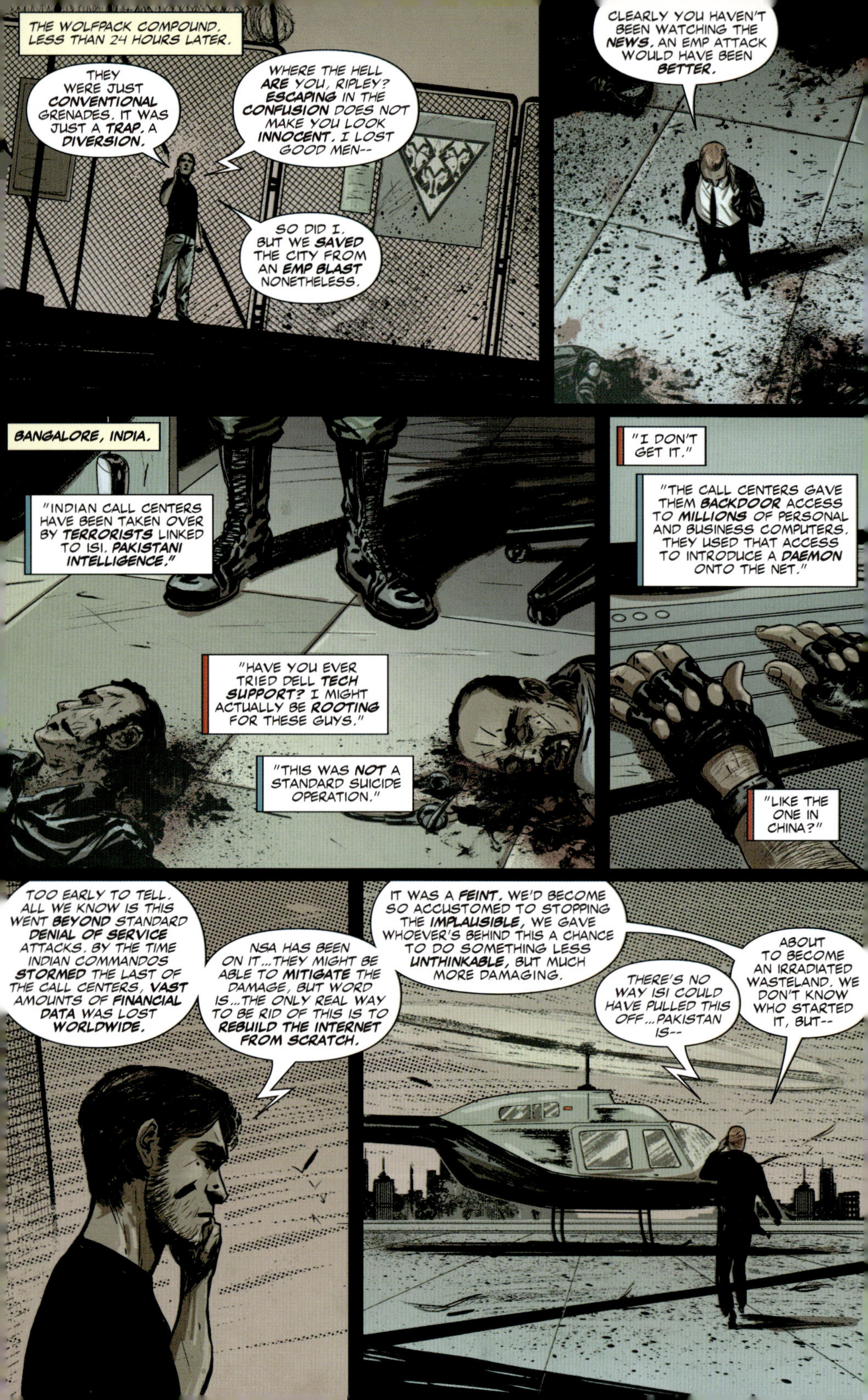

THE WOLFPACK COMPOUND. LESS THAN 24 HOURS LATER.
THEY WERE JUST CONVENTIONAL GRENADES. IT WAS JUST A TRAP. A DIVERSION.
WHERE THE HELL ARE YOU, RIPLEY? ESCAPING IN THE CONFUSION DOES NOT MAKE YOU LOOK INNOCENT. I LOST GOOD MEN--
SO DID I. BUT WE SAVED THE CITY FROM AN EMP BLAST NONETHELESS.
CLEARLY YOU HAVEN'T BEEN WATCHING THE NEWS. AN EMP ATTACK WOULD HAVE BEEN BETTER.
BANGALORE, INDIA.
"INDIAN CALL CENTERS HAVE BEEN TAKEN OVER BY TERRORISTS LINKED TO ISI. PAKISTANI INTELLIGENCE."
"HAVE YOU EVER TRIED DELL TECH SUPPORT? I MIGHT ACTUALLY BE ROOTING FOR THESE GUYS."
"THIS WAS NOT A STANDARD SUICIDE OPERATION."
"I DON'T GET IT."
"THE CALL CENTERS GAVE THEM BACKDOOR ACCESS TO MILLIONS OF PERSONAL AND BUSINESS COMPUTERS. THEY USED THAT ACCESS TO INTRODUCE A DAEMON ONTO THE NET."
"LIKE THE ONE IN CHINA?"
TOO EARLY TO TELL. ALL WE KNOW IS THIS WENT BEYOND STANDARD DENIAL OF SERVICE ATTACKS. BY THE TIME INDIAN COMMANDOS STORMED THE LAST OF THE CALL CENTERS, VAST AMOUNTS OF FINANCIAL DATA WAS LOST WORLDWIDE.
NSA HAS BEEN ON IT...THEY MIGHT BE ABLE TO MITIGATE THE DAMAGE, BUT WORD IS...THE ONLY REAL WAY TO BE RID OF THIS IS TO REBUILD THE INTERNET FROM SCRATCH.
IT WAS A FEINT. WE'D BECOME SO ACCUSTOMED TO STOPPING THE IMPLAUSIBLE, WE GAVE WHOEVER'S BEHIND THIS A CHANCE TO DO SOMETHING LESS UNTHINKABLE, BUT MUCH MORE DAMAGING.
THERE'S NO WAY ISI COULD HAVE PULLED THIS OFF...PAKISTAN IS--
ABOUT TO BECOME AN IRRADIATED WASTELAND. WE DON'T KNOW WHO STARTED IT, BUT--

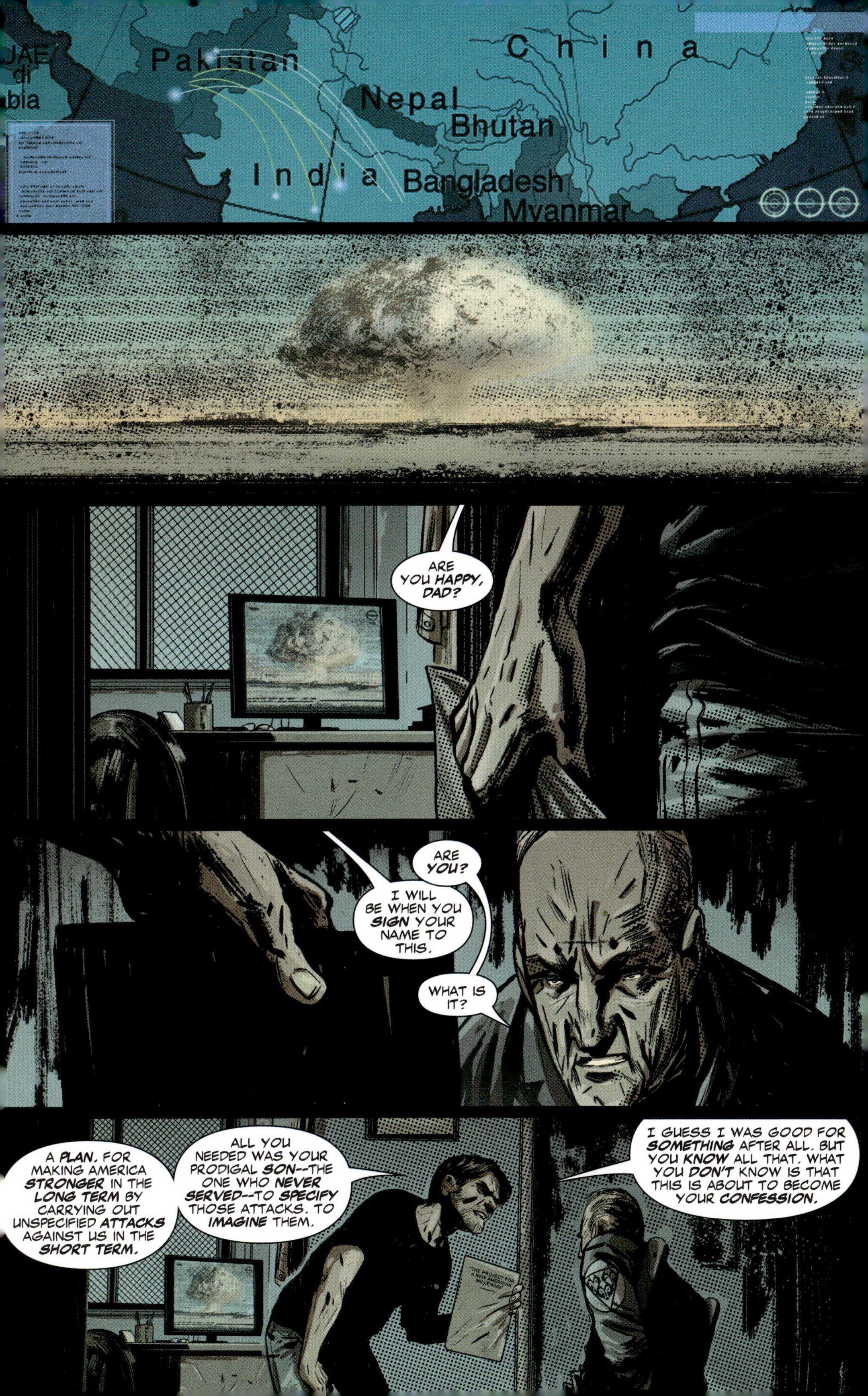
Pakistan
China
Nepal
Bhutan
India
Bangladesh
Myanmar
ARE YOU HAPPY, DAD?
ARE YOU?
I WILL BE WHEN YOU SIGN YOUR NAME TO THIS.
WHAT IS IT?
A PLAN. FOR MAKING AMERICA STRONGER IN THE LONG TERM BY CARRYING OUT UNSPECIFIED ATTACKS AGAINST US IN THE SHORT TERM.
ALL YOU NEEDED WAS YOUR PRODIGAL SON--THE ONE WHO NEVER SERVED--TO SPECIFY THOSE ATTACKS. TO IMAGINE THEM.
I GUESS I WAS GOOD FOR SOMETHING AFTER ALL. BUT YOU KNOW ALL THAT. WHAT YOU DON'T KNOW IS THAT THIS IS ABOUT TO BECOME YOUR CONFESSION.

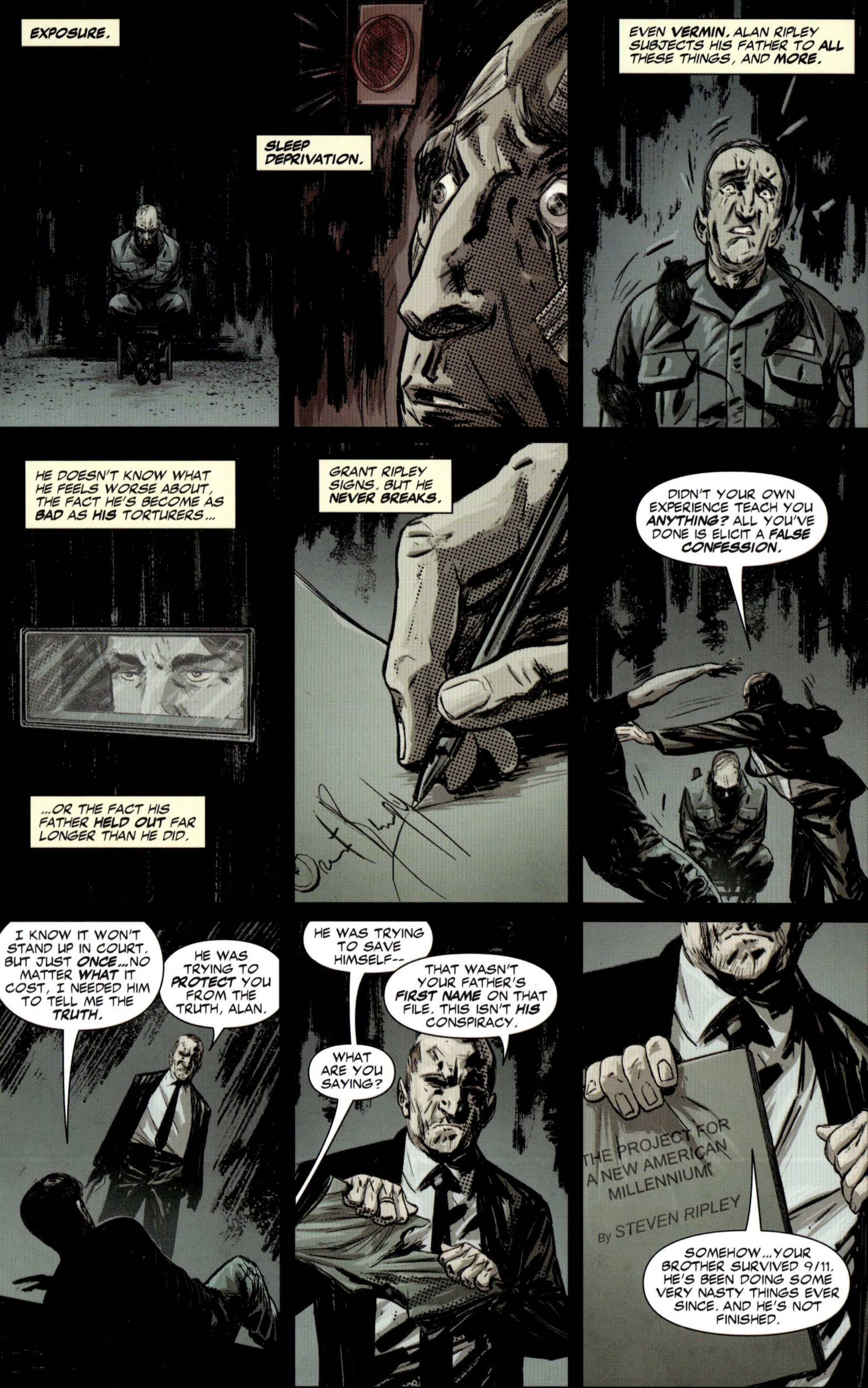
EXPOSURE.
SLEEP DEPRIVATION.
EVEN VERMIN. ALAN RIPLEY SUBJECTS HIS FATHER TO ALL THESE THINGS, AND MORE.
HE DOESN'T KNOW WHAT HE FEELS WORSE ABOUT, THE FACT HE'S BECOME AS BAD AS HIS TORTURERS...
...OR THE FACT HIS FATHER HELD OUT FAR LONGER THAN HE DID.
GRANT RIPLEY SIGNS, BUT HE NEVER BREAKS.
DIDN'T YOUR OWN EXPERIENCE TEACH YOU ANYTHING? ALL YOU'VE DONE IS ELICIT A FALSE CONFESSION.
I KNOW IT WON'T STAND UP IN COURT, BUT JUST ONCE...NO MATTER WHAT IT COST, I NEEDED HIM TO TELL ME THE TRUTH.
HE WAS TRYING TO PROTECT YOU FROM THE TRUTH, ALAN.
HE WAS TRYING TO SAVE HIMSELF--
THAT WASN'T YOUR FATHER'S FIRST NAME ON THAT FILE. THIS ISN'T HIS CONSPIRACY.
WHAT ARE YOU SAYING?
THE PROJECT FOR A NEW AMERICAN MILLENNIUM
By STEVEN RIPLEY
SOMEHOW...YOUR BROTHER SURVIVED 9/11. HE'S BEEN DOING SOME VERY NASTY THINGS EVER SINCE, AND HE'S NOT FINISHED.

CHAPTER FIVE

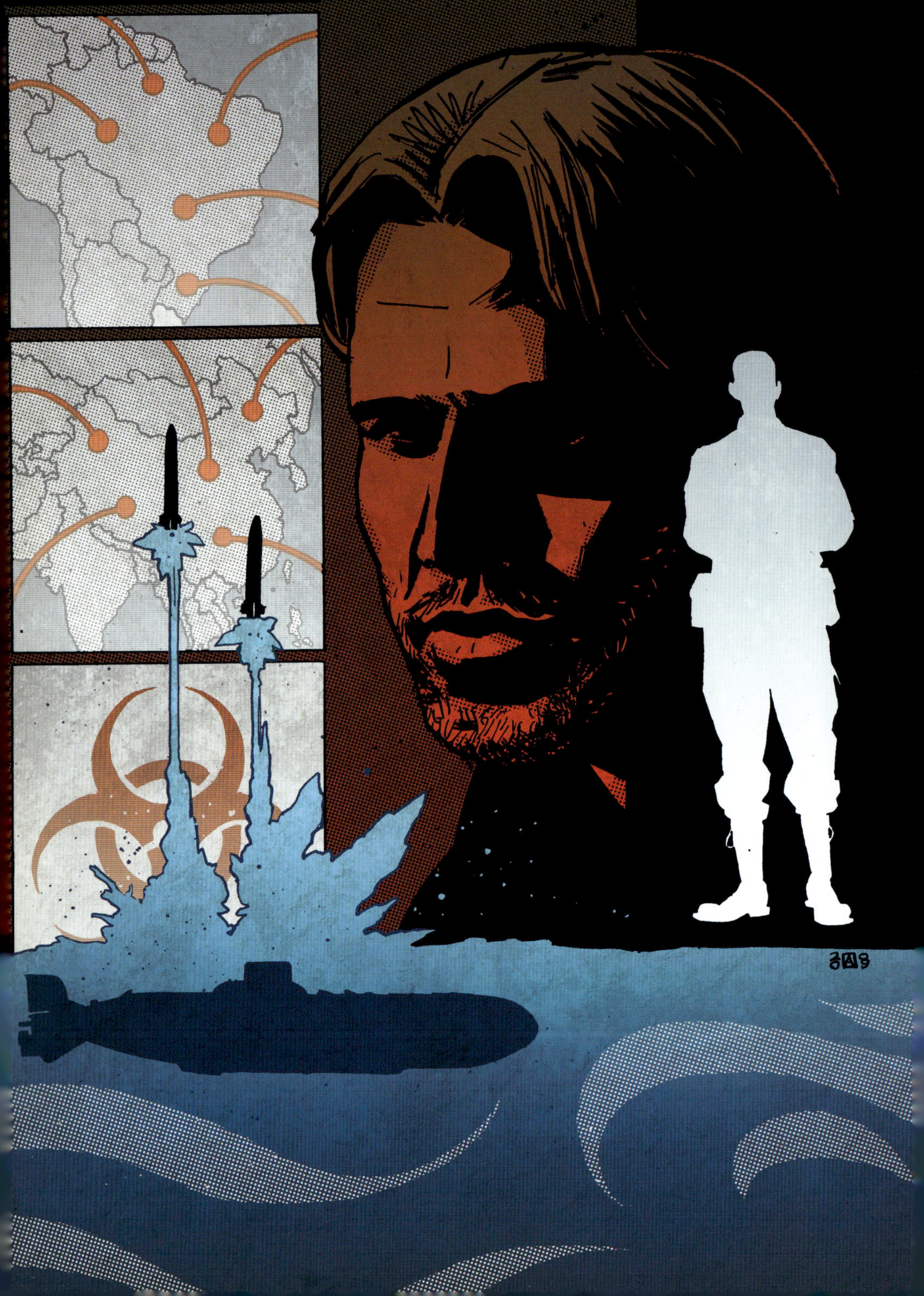

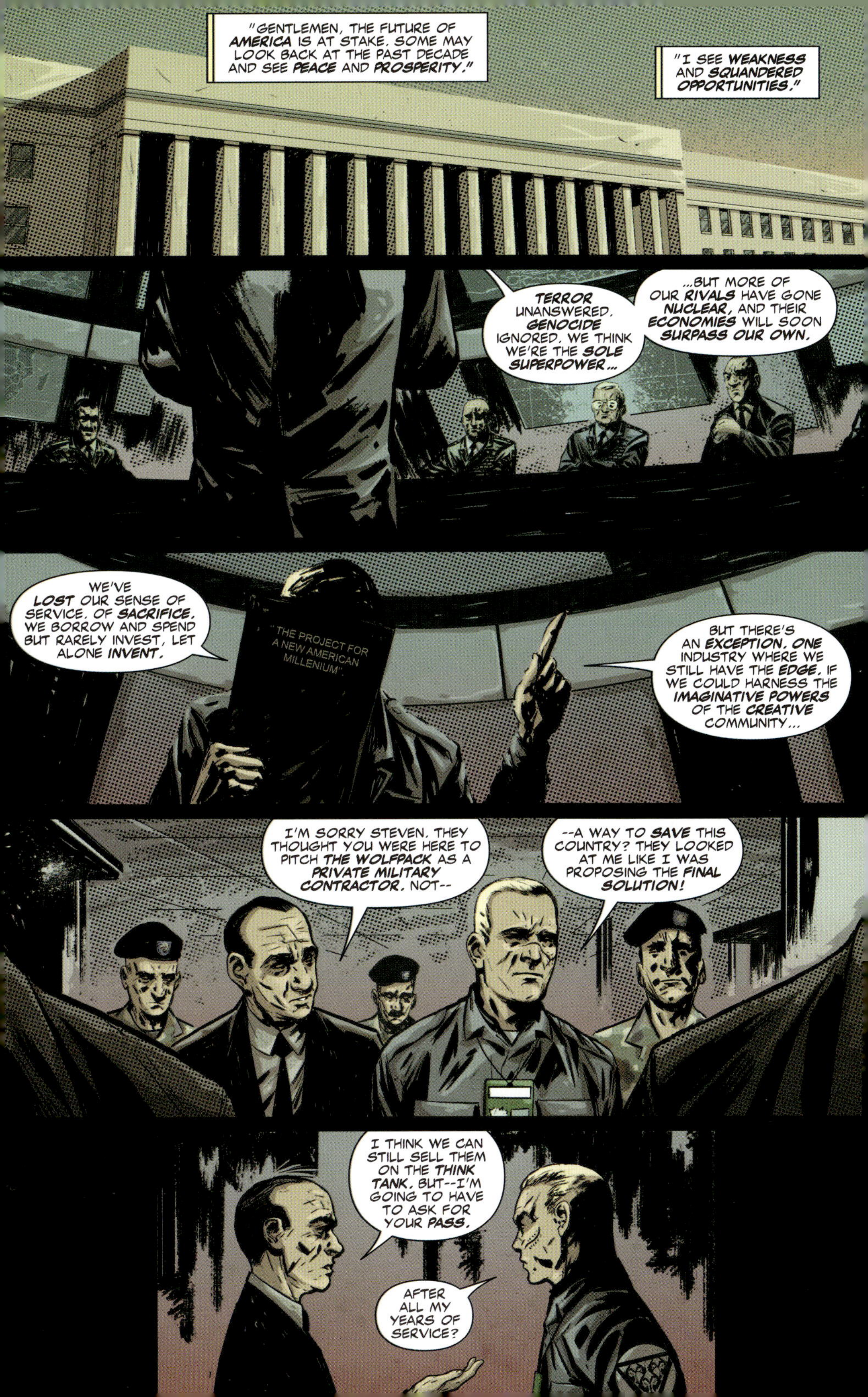
"GENTLEMEN, THE FUTURE OF AMERICA IS AT STAKE. SOME MAY LOOK BACK AT THE PAST DECADE AND SEE PEACE AND PROSPERITY."
"I SEE WEAKNESS AND SQUANDERED OPPORTUNITIES."
TERROR UNANSWERED. GENOCIDE IGNORED. WE THINK WE'RE THE SOLE SUPERPOWER...
...BUT MORE OF OUR RIVALS HAVE GONE NUCLEAR, AND THEIR ECONOMIES WILL SOON SURPASS OUR OWN.
WE'VE LOST OUR SENSE OF SERVICE. OF SACRIFICE. WE BORROW AND SPEND BUT RARELY INVEST, LET ALONE INVENT.
"THE PROJECT FOR A NEW AMERICAN MILLENIUM"
BUT THERE'S AN EXCEPTION. ONE INDUSTRY WHERE WE STILL HAVE THE EDGE. IF WE COULD HARNESS THE IMAGINATIVE POWERS OF THE CREATIVE COMMUNITY...
I'M SORRY STEVEN. THEY THOUGHT YOU WERE HERE TO PITCH THE WOLFPACK AS A PRIVATE MILITARY CONTRACTOR. NOT--
--A WAY TO SAVE THIS COUNTRY? THEY LOOKED AT ME LIKE I WAS PROPOSING THE FINAL SOLUTION!
I THINK WE CAN STILL SELL THEM ON THE THINK TANK. BUT--I'M GOING TO HAVE TO ASK FOR YOUR PASS.
AFTER ALL MY YEARS OF SERVICE?

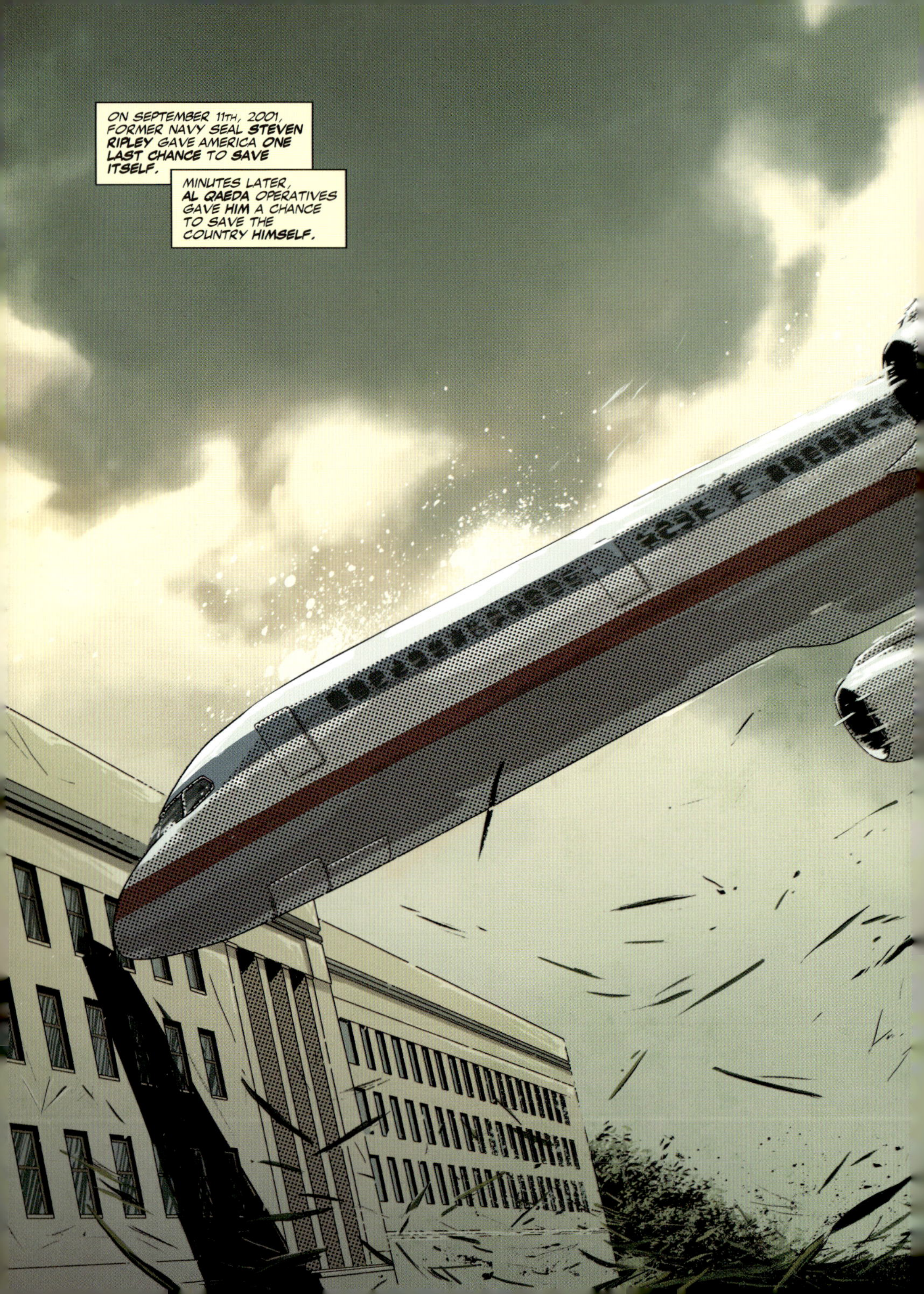
ON SEPTEMBER 11TH, 2001, FORMER NAVY SEAL STEVEN RIPLEY GAVE AMERICA ONE LAST CHANCE TO SAVE ITSELF.
MINUTES LATER, AL QAEDA OPERATIVES GAVE HIM A CHANCE TO SAVE THE COUNTRY HIMSELF.

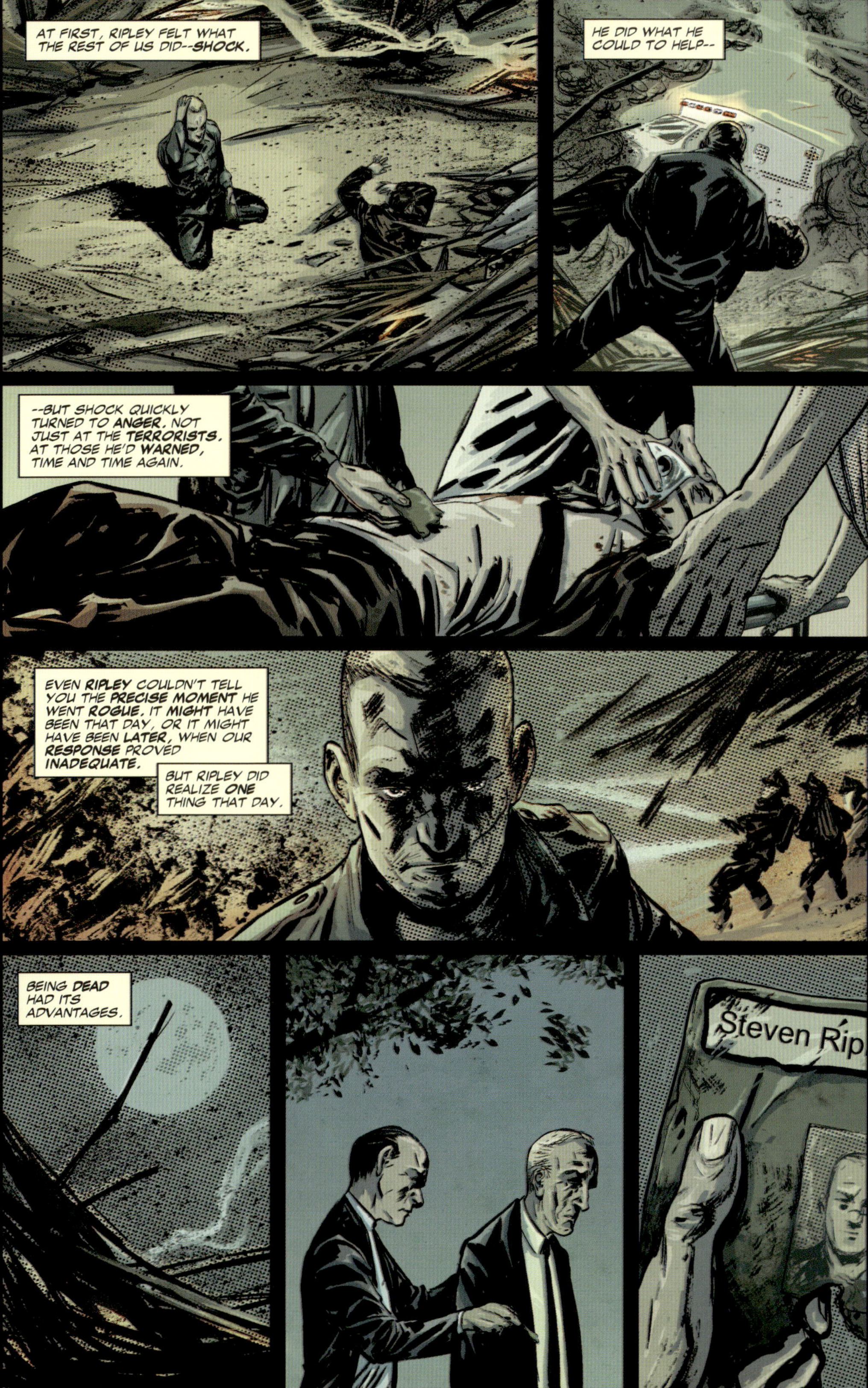
AT FIRST, RIPLEY FELT WHAT THE REST OF US DID--SHOCK.
HE DID WHAT HE COULD TO HELP--
--BUT SHOCK QUICKLY TURNED TO ANGER. NOT JUST AT THE TERRORISTS. AT THOSE HE'D WARNED, TIME AND TIME AGAIN.
EVEN RIPLEY COULDN'T TELL YOU THE PRECISE MOMENT HE WENT ROGUE. IT MIGHT HAVE BEEN THAT DAY, OR IT MIGHT HAVE BEEN LATER, WHEN OUR RESPONSE PROVED INADEQUATE.
BUT RIPLEY DID REALIZE ONE THING THAT DAY.
BEING DEAD HAD ITS ADVANTAGES.
Steven Rip

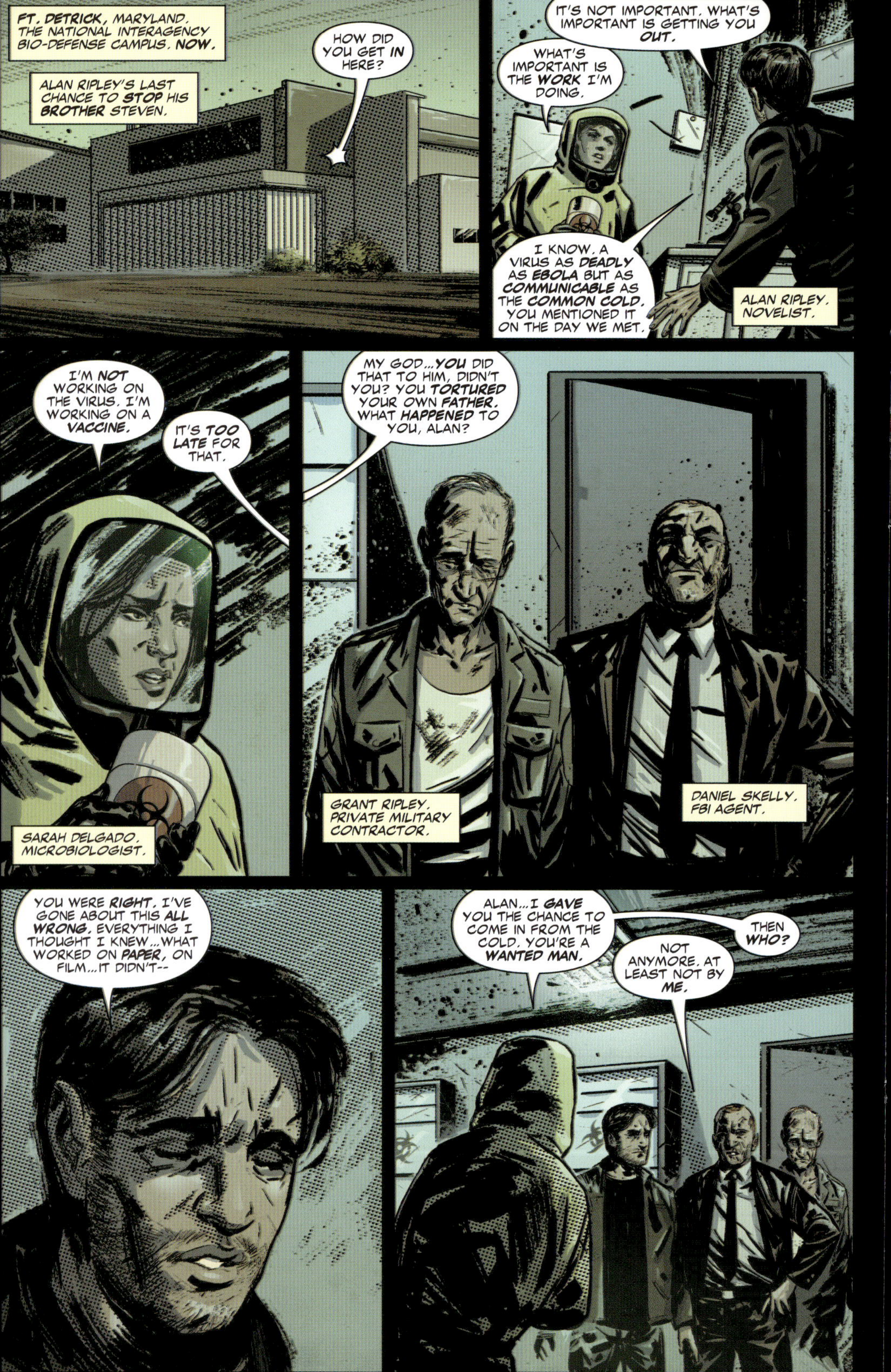

FT. DETRICK, MARYLAND. THE NATIONAL INTERAGENCY BIO-DEFENSE CAMPUS. NOW.
ALAN RIPLEY'S LAST CHANCE TO STOP HIS BROTHER STEVEN.
HOW DID YOU GET IN HERE?
IT'S NOT IMPORTANT. WHAT'S IMPORTANT IS GETTING YOU OUT.
WHAT'S IMPORTANT IS THE WORK I'M DOING.
I KNOW. A VIRUS AS DEADLY AS EBOLA BUT AS COMMUNICABLE AS THE COMMON COLD. YOU MENTIONED IT ON THE DAY WE MET.
ALAN RIPLEY. NOVELIST.
I'M NOT WORKING ON THE VIRUS. I'M WORKING ON A VACCINE.
IT'S TOO LATE FOR THAT.
SARAH DELGADO. MICROBIOLOGIST.
MY GOD...YOU DID THAT TO HIM, DIDN'T YOU? YOU TORTURED YOUR OWN FATHER. WHAT HAPPENED TO YOU, ALAN?
GRANT RIPLEY. PRIVATE MILITARY CONTRACTOR.
DANIEL SKELLY. FBI AGENT.
YOU WERE RIGHT. I'VE GONE ABOUT THIS ALL WRONG. EVERYTHING I THOUGHT I KNEW...WHAT WORKED ON PAPER, ON FILM...IT DIDN'T--
ALAN...I GAVE YOU THE CHANCE TO COME IN FROM THE COLD. YOU'RE A WANTED MAN.
THEN WHO?
NOT ANYMORE. AT LEAST NOT BY ME.

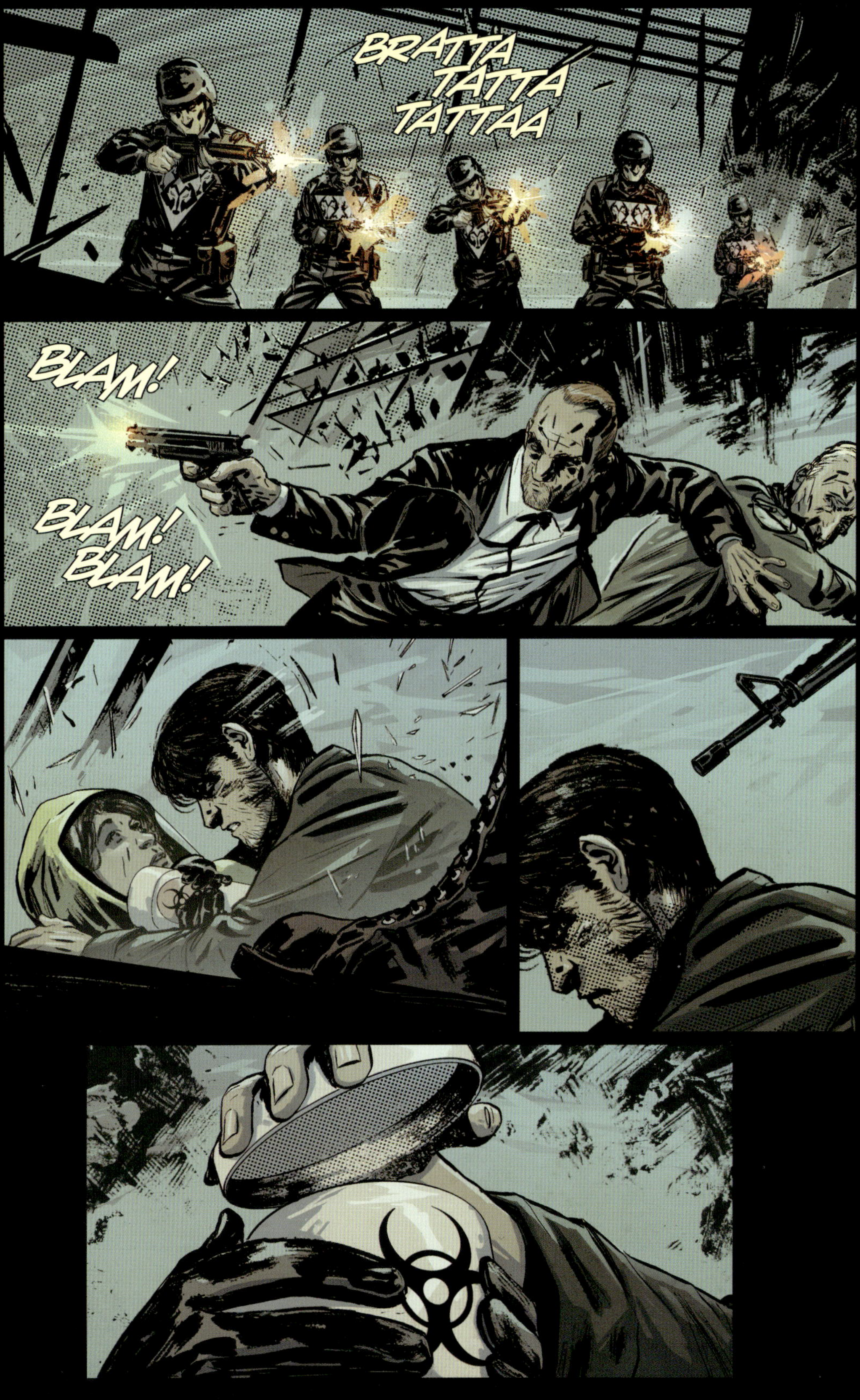
BRATTA TATTA TATTAA
BLAM!
BLAM! BLAM!

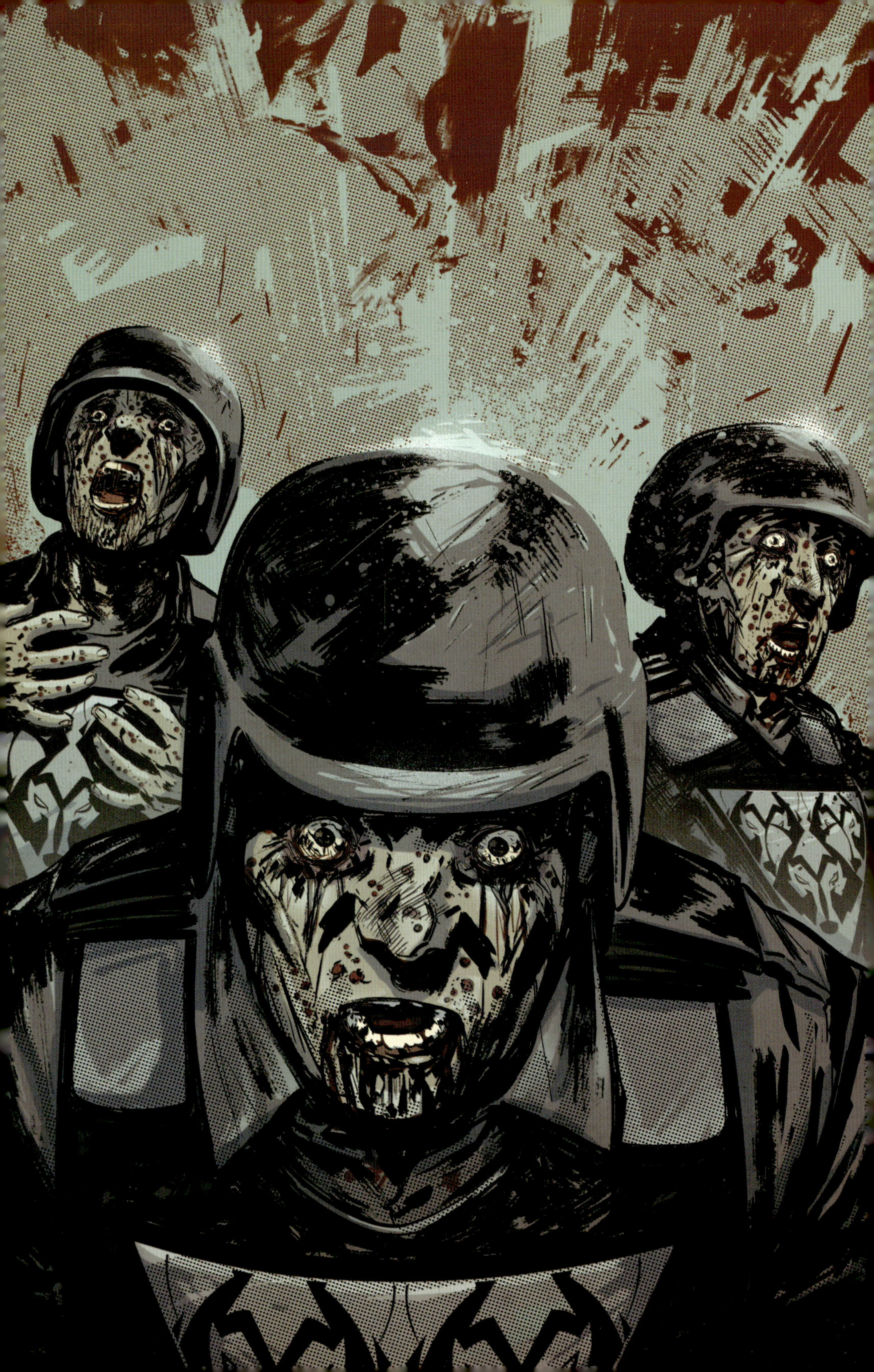

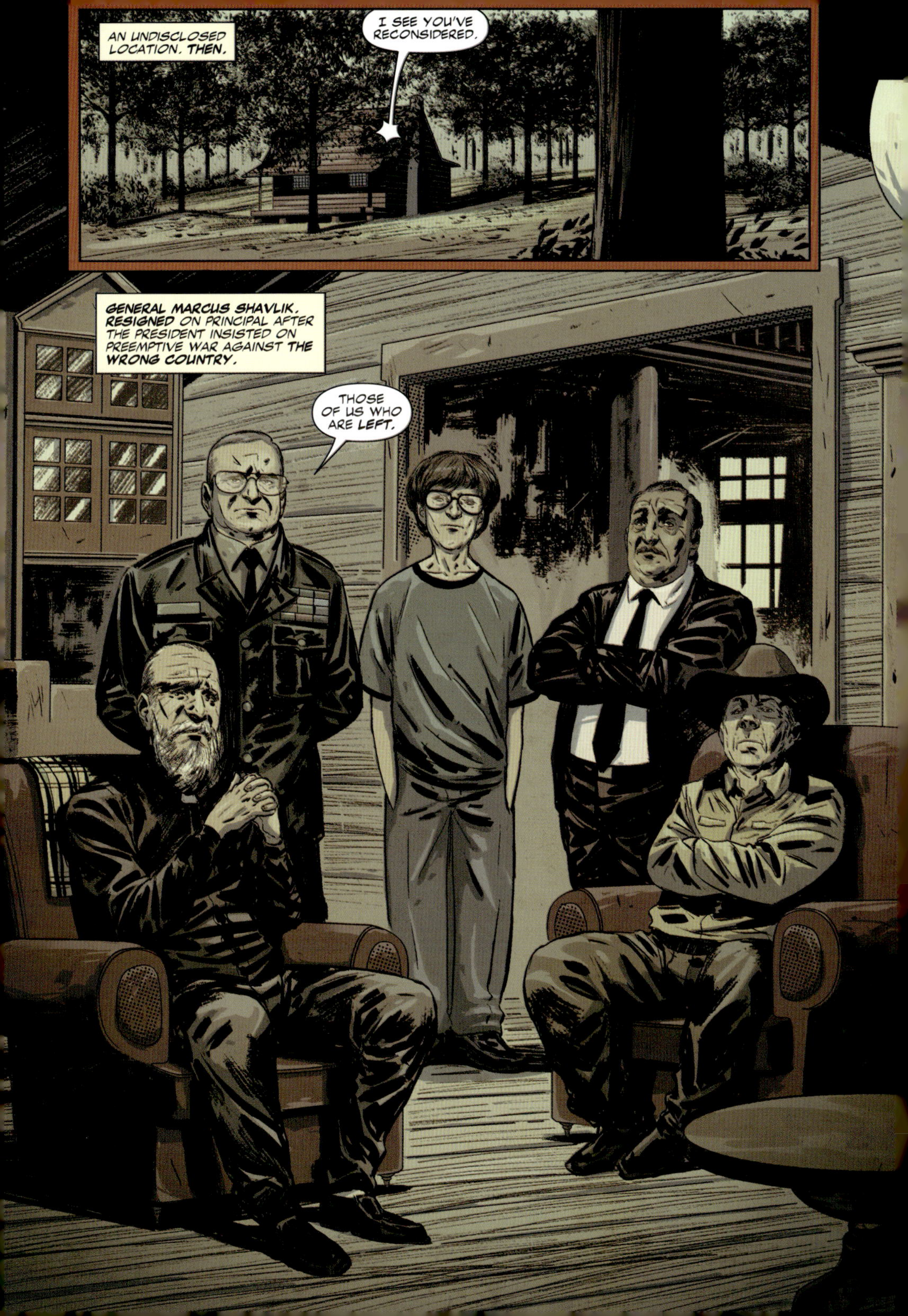
AN UNDISCLOSED LOCATION. THEN.
I SEE YOU'VE RECONSIDERED.
GENERAL MARCUS SHAVLIK. RESIGNED ON PRINCIPAL AFTER THE PRESIDENT INSISTED ON PREEMPTIVE WAR AGAINST THE WRONG COUNTRY.
THOSE OF US WHO ARE LEFT.

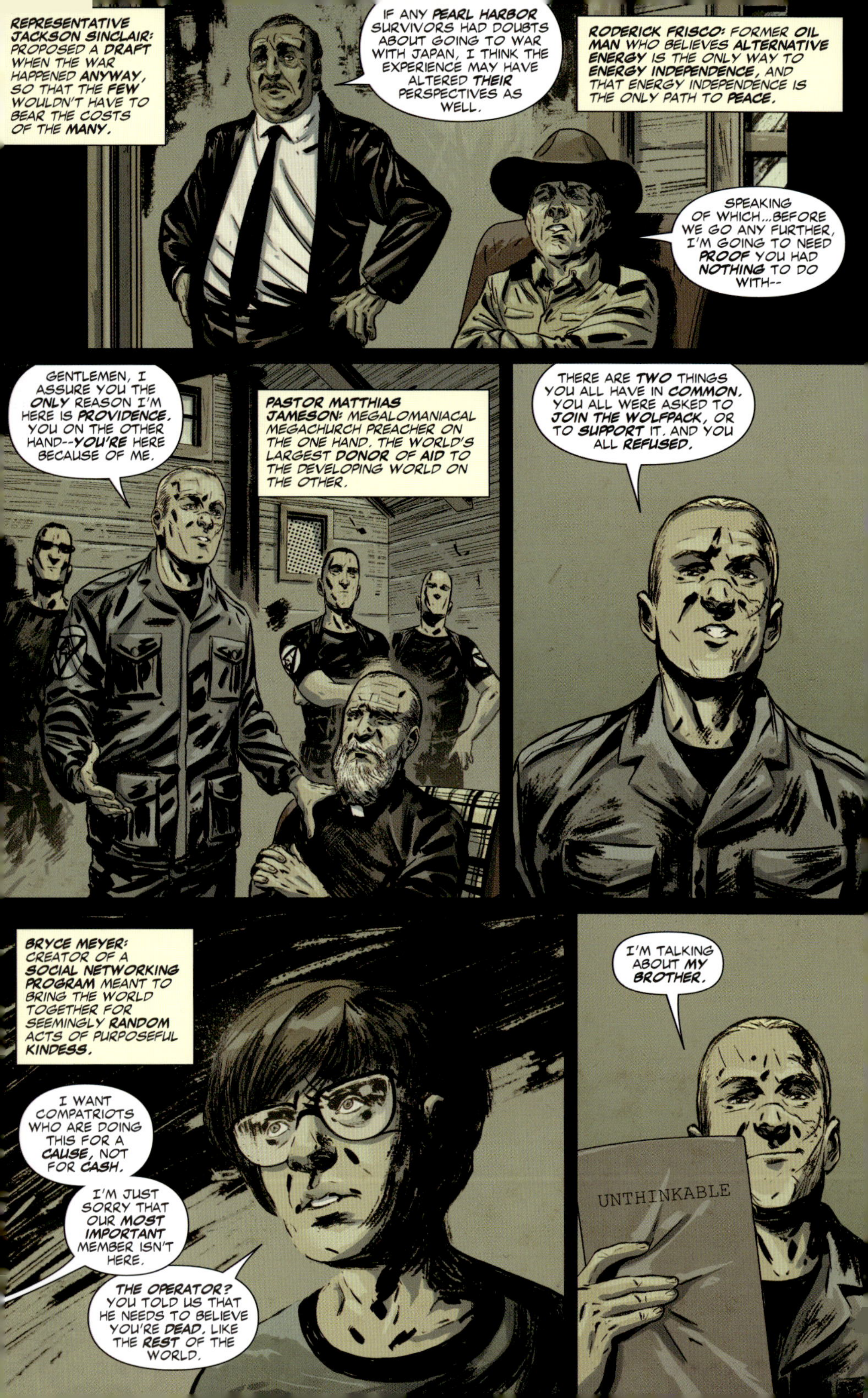

REPRESENTATIVE JACKSON SINCLAIR: PROPOSED A DRAFT WHEN THE WAR HAPPENED ANYWAY, SO THAT THE FEW WOULDN'T HAVE TO BEAR THE COSTS OF THE MANY.
IF ANY PEARL HARBOR SURVIVORS HAD DOUBTS ABOUT GOING TO WAR WITH JAPAN, I THINK THE EXPERIENCE MAY HAVE ALTERED THEIR PERSPECTIVES AS WELL.
RODERICK FRISCO: FORMER OIL MAN WHO BELIEVES ALTERNATIVE ENERGY IS THE ONLY WAY TO ENERGY INDEPENDENCE, AND THAT ENERGY INDEPENDENCE IS THE ONLY PATH TO PEACE.
SPEAKING OF WHICH...BEFORE WE GO ANY FURTHER, I'M GOING TO NEED PROOF YOU HAD NOTHING TO DO WITH--
GENTLEMEN, I ASSURE YOU THE ONLY REASON I'M HERE IS PROVIDENCE. YOU ON THE OTHER HAND--YOU'RE HERE BECAUSE OF ME.
PASTOR MATTHIAS JAMESON: MEGALOMANIACAL MEGACHURCH PREACHER ON THE ONE HAND. THE WORLD'S LARGEST DONOR OF AID TO THE DEVELOPING WORLD ON THE OTHER.
THERE ARE TWO THINGS YOU ALL HAVE IN COMMON. YOU ALL WERE ASKED TO JOIN THE WOLFPACK, OR TO SUPPORT IT. AND YOU ALL REFUSED.
BRYCE MEYER: CREATOR OF A SOCIAL NETWORKING PROGRAM MEANT TO BRING THE WORLD TOGETHER FOR SEEMINGLY RANDOM ACTS OF PURPOSEFUL KINDESS.
I WANT COMPATRIOTS WHO ARE DOING THIS FOR A CAUSE, NOT FOR CASH.
I'M JUST SORRY THAT OUR MOST IMPORTANT MEMBER ISN'T HERE.
THE OPERATOR? YOU TOLD US THAT HE NEEDS TO BELIEVE YOU'RE DEAD. LIKE THE REST OF THE WORLD.
I'M TALKING ABOUT MY BROTHER.
UNTHINKABLE

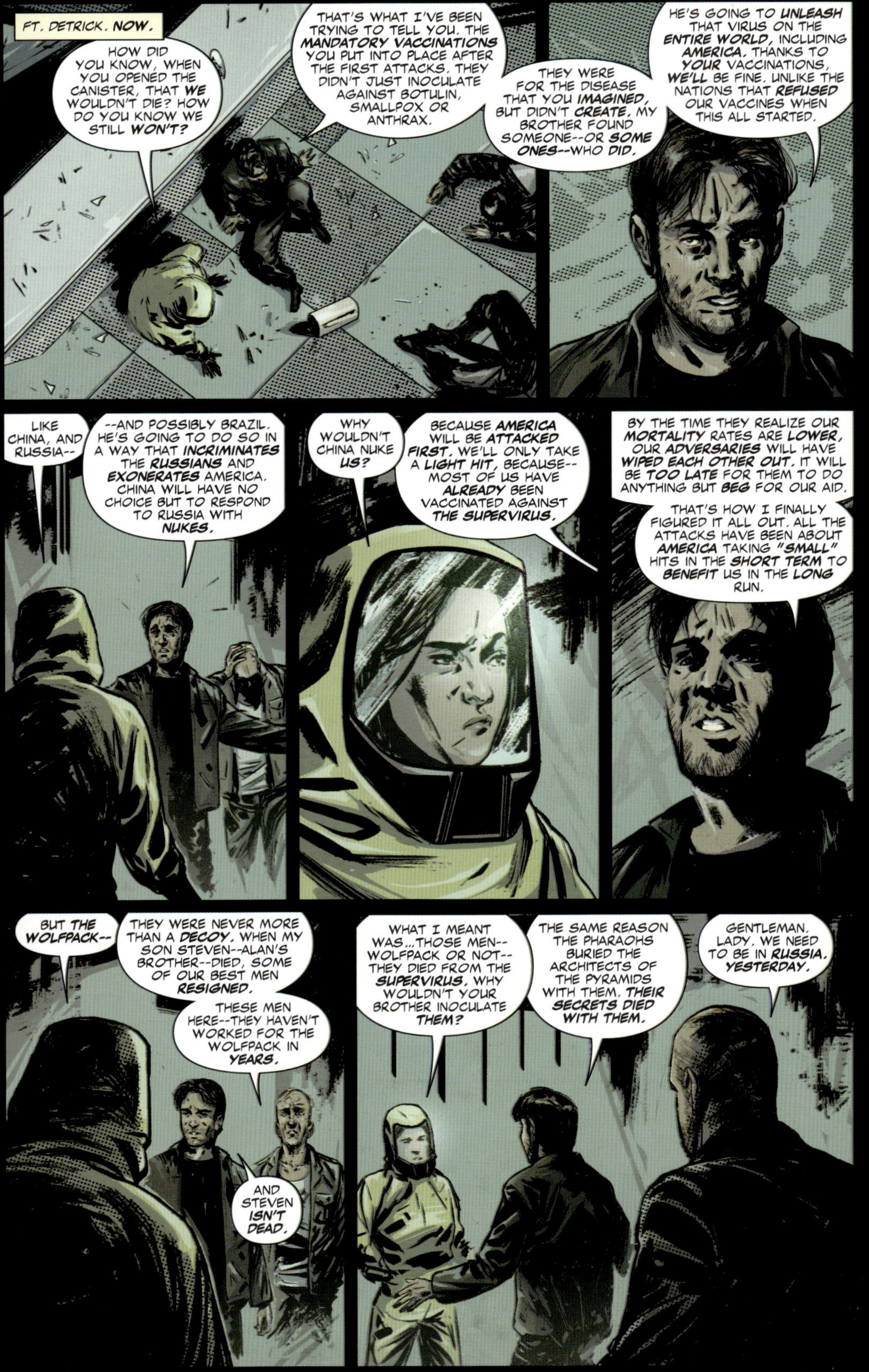
FT. DETRICK. NOW.
HOW DID YOU KNOW, WHEN YOU OPENED THE CANISTER, THAT WE WOULDN'T DIE? HOW DO YOU KNOW WE STILL WON'T?
THAT'S WHAT I'VE BEEN TRYING TO TELL YOU. THE MANDATORY VACCINATIONS YOU PUT INTO PLACE AFTER THE FIRST ATTACKS. THEY DIDN'T JUST INOCULATE AGAINST BOTULIN, SMALLPOX OR ANTHRAX.
THEY WERE FOR THE DISEASE THAT YOU IMAGINED, BUT DIDN'T CREATE. MY BROTHER FOUND SOMEONE--OR SOME ONES--WHO DID.
HE'S GOING TO UNLEASH THAT VIRUS ON THE ENTIRE WORLD, INCLUDING AMERICA. THANKS TO YOUR VACCINATIONS, WE'LL BE FINE. UNLIKE THE NATIONS THAT REFUSED OUR VACCINES WHEN THIS ALL STARTED.
LIKE CHINA, AND RUSSIA--
--AND POSSIBLY BRAZIL. HE'S GOING TO DO SO IN A WAY THAT INCRIMINATES THE RUSSIANS AND EXONERATES AMERICA. CHINA WILL HAVE NO CHOICE BUT TO RESPOND TO RUSSIA WITH NUKES.
WHY WOULDN'T CHINA NUKE US?
BECAUSE AMERICA WILL BE ATTACKED FIRST. WE'LL ONLY TAKE A LIGHT HIT, BECAUSE--MOST OF US HAVE ALREADY BEEN VACCINATED AGAINST THE SUPERVIRUS.
BY THE TIME THEY REALIZE OUR MORTALITY RATES ARE LOWER, OUR ADVERSARIES WILL HAVE WIPED EACH OTHER OUT. IT WILL BE TOO LATE FOR THEM TO DO ANYTHING BUT BEG FOR OUR AID.
THAT'S HOW I FINALLY FIGURED IT ALL OUT. ALL THE ATTACKS HAVE BEEN ABOUT AMERICA TAKING "SMALL" HITS IN THE SHORT TERM TO BENEFIT US IN THE LONG RUN.
BUT THE WOLFPACK--
THEY WERE NEVER MORE THAN A DECOY. WHEN MY SON STEVEN--ALAN'S BROTHER--DIED, SOME OF OUR BEST MEN RESIGNED.
THESE MEN HERE--THEY HAVEN'T WORKED FOR THE WOLFPACK IN YEARS.
AND STEVEN ISN'T DEAD.
WHAT I MEANT WAS... THOSE MEN--WOLFPACK OR NOT--THEY DIED FROM THE SUPERVIRUS. WHY WOULDN'T YOUR BROTHER INOCULATE THEM?
THE SAME REASON THE PHARAOHS BURIED THE ARCHITECTS OF THE PYRAMIDS WITH THEM. THEIR SECRETS DIED WITH THEM.
GENTLEMAN. LADY. WE NEED TO BE IN RUSSIA. YESTERDAY.

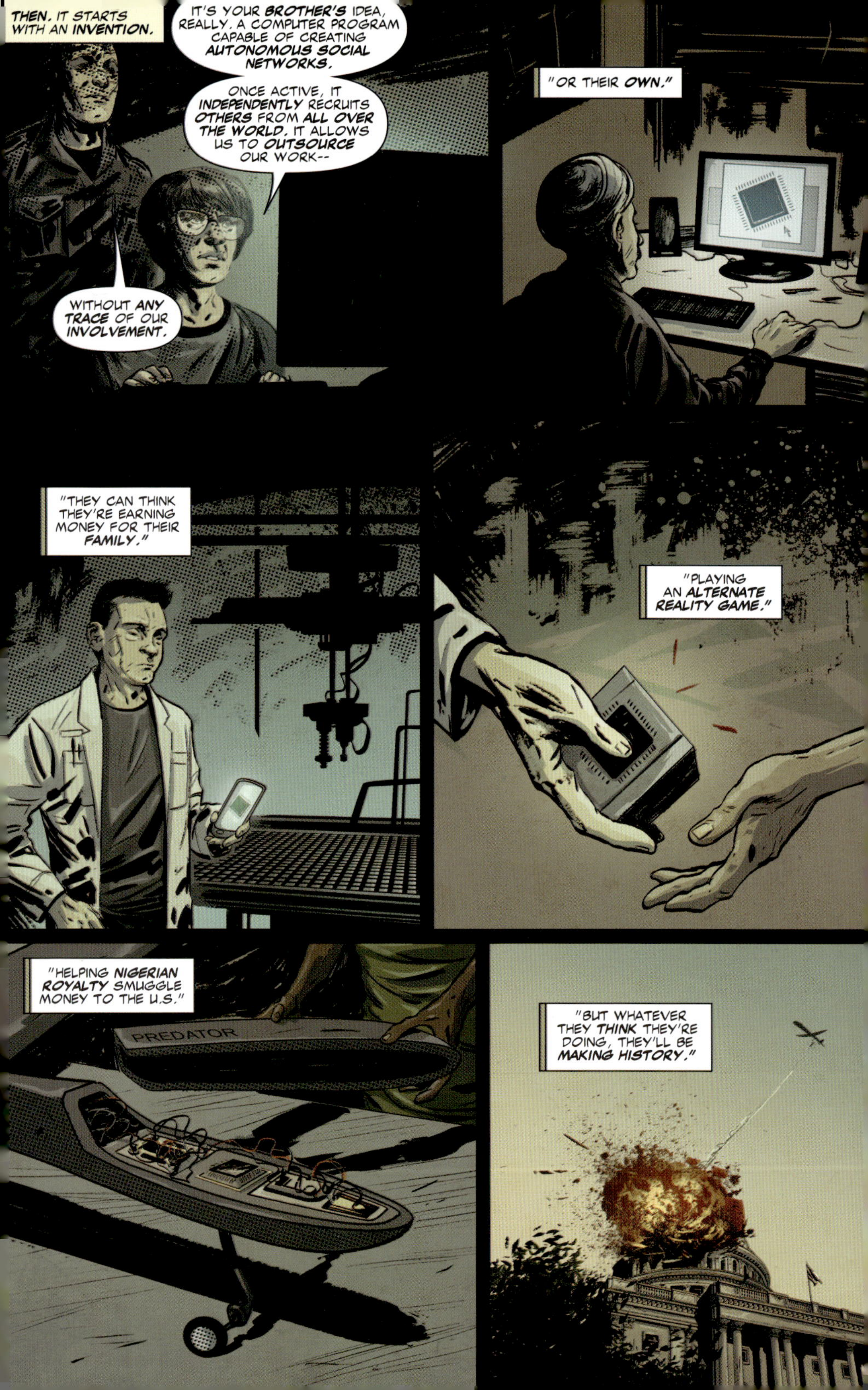
THEN, IT STARTS WITH AN INVENTION.
IT'S YOUR BROTHER'S IDEA, REALLY. A COMPUTER PROGRAM CAPABLE OF CREATING AUTONOMOUS SOCIAL NETWORKS.
ONCE ACTIVE, IT INDEPENDENTLY RECRUITS OTHERS FROM ALL OVER THE WORLD. IT ALLOWS US TO OUTSOURCE OUR WORK--
WITHOUT ANY TRACE OF OUR INVOLVEMENT.
"OR THEIR OWN."
"THEY CAN THINK THEY'RE EARNING MONEY FOR THEIR FAMILY."
"PLAYING AN ALTERNATE REALITY GAME."
"HELPING NIGERIAN ROYALTY SMUGGLE MONEY TO THE U.S."
PREDATOR
"BUT WHATEVER THEY THINK THEY'RE DOING, THEY'LL BE MAKING HISTORY."

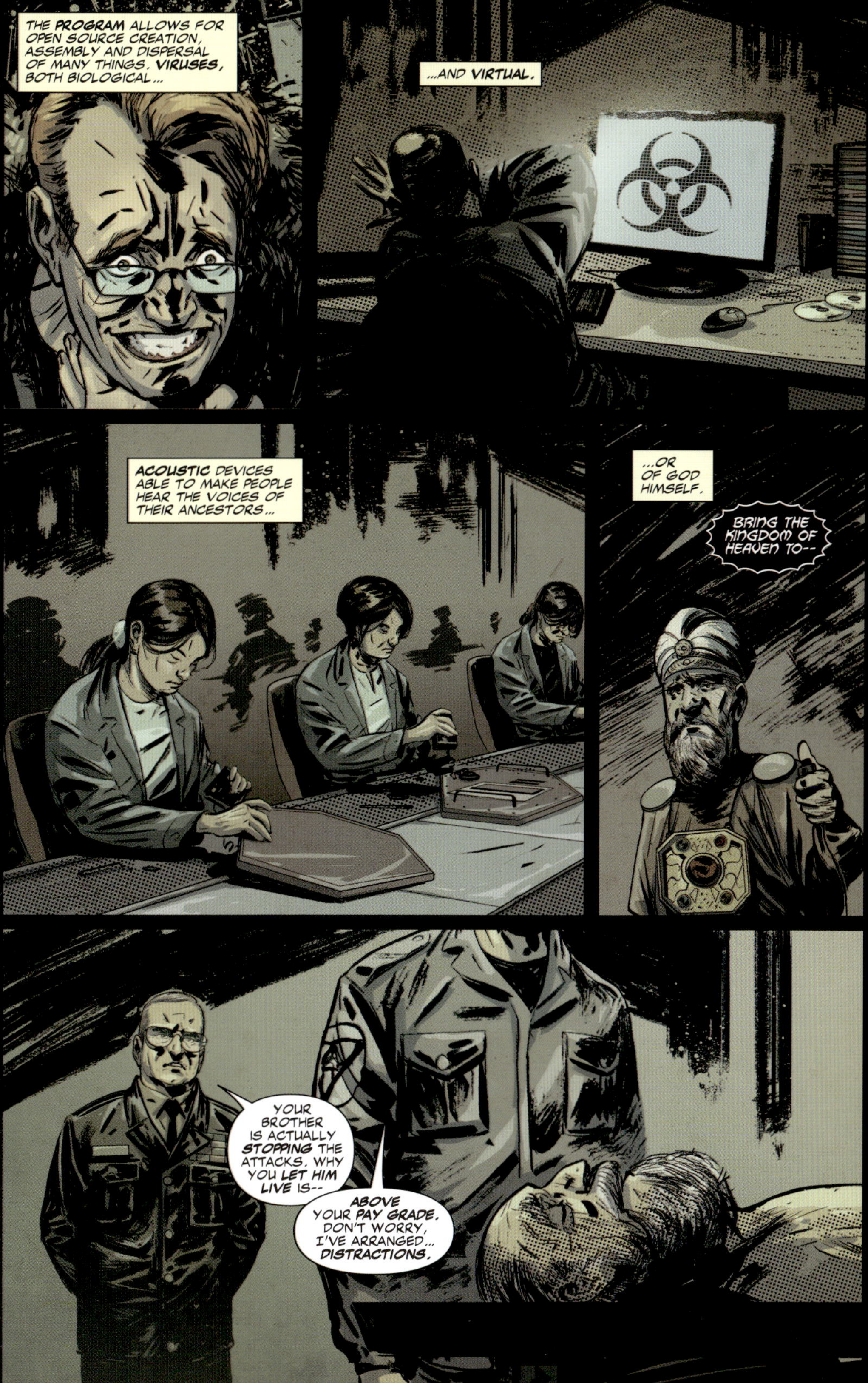

THE PROGRAM ALLOWS FOR OPEN SOURCE CREATION, ASSEMBLY AND DISPERSAL OF MANY THINGS. VIRUSES, BOTH BIOLOGICAL...
...AND VIRTUAL.
ACOUSTIC DEVICES ABLE TO MAKE PEOPLE HEAR THE VOICES OF THEIR ANCESTORS...
...OR OF GOD HIMSELF.
BRING THE KINGDOM OF HEAVEN TO--
YOUR BROTHER IS ACTUALLY STOPPING THE ATTACKS. WHY YOU LET HIM LIVE IS--
ABOVE YOUR PAY GRADE. DON'T WORRY, I'VE ARRANGED... DISTRACTIONS.

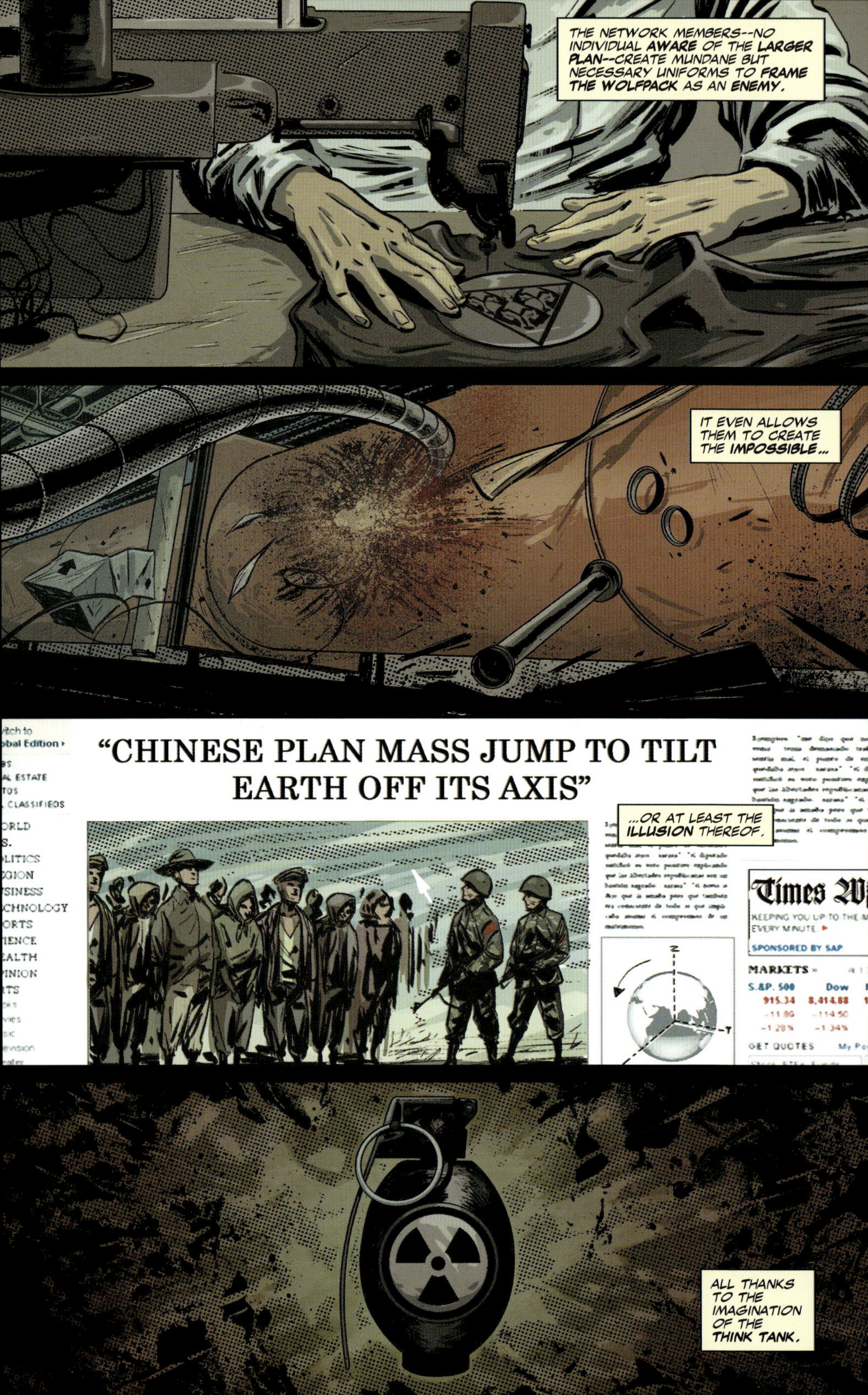
THE NETWORK MEMBERS--NO INDIVIDUAL AWARE OF THE LARGER PLAN--CREATE MUNDANE BUT NECESSARY UNIFORMS TO FRAME THE WOLFPACK AS AN ENEMY.
IT EVEN ALLOWS THEM TO CREATE THE IMPOSSIBLE...
"CHINESE PLAN MASS JUMP TO TILT EARTH OFF ITS AXIS"
...OR AT LEAST THE ILLUSION THEREOF.
EVERY MINUTE
SPONSORED BY SAP
MARKETS
S.&P. 500
Dow
915.34
8,414.88
-11.86
-114.50
-1.28%
-1.34%
GET QUOTES
ALL THANKS TO THE IMAGINATION OF THE THINK TANK.

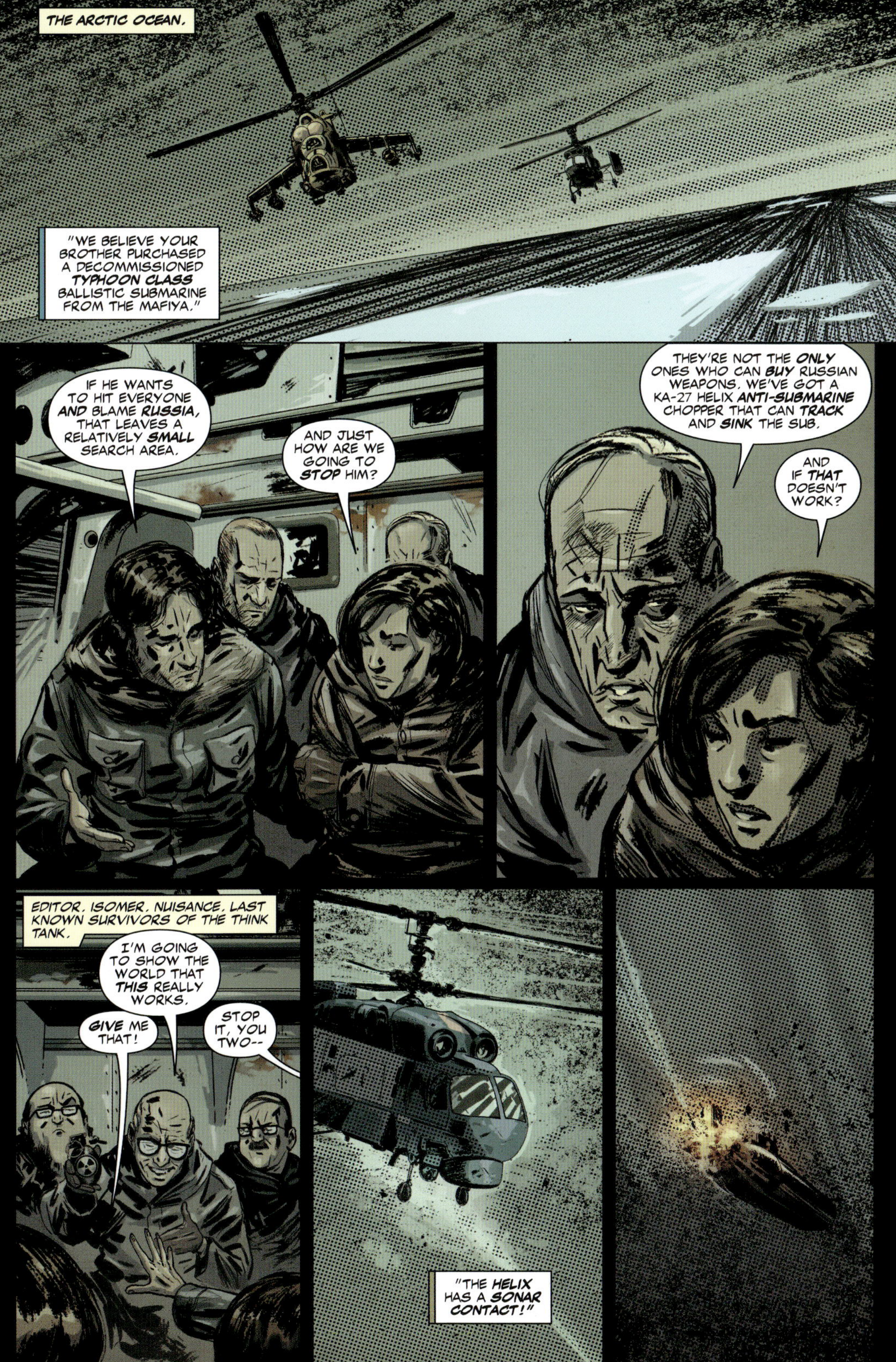
THE ARCTIC OCEAN.
"WE BELIEVE YOUR BROTHER PURCHASED A DECOMMISSIONED TYPHOON CLASS BALLISTIC SUBMARINE FROM THE MAFIYA."
IF HE WANTS TO HIT EVERYONE AND BLAME RUSSIA, THAT LEAVES A RELATIVELY SMALL SEARCH AREA.
AND JUST HOW ARE WE GOING TO STOP HIM?
THEY'RE NOT THE ONLY ONES WHO CAN BUY RUSSIAN WEAPONS. WE'VE GOT A KA-27 HELIX ANTI-SUBMARINE CHOPPER THAT CAN TRACK AND SINK THE SUB.
AND IF THAT DOESN'T WORK?
EDITOR. ISOMER. NUISANCE. LAST KNOWN SURVIVORS OF THE THINK TANK.
I'M GOING TO SHOW THE WORLD THAT THIS REALLY WORKS.
GIVE ME THAT!
STOP IT, YOU TWO--
"THE HELIX HAS A SONAR CONTACT!"

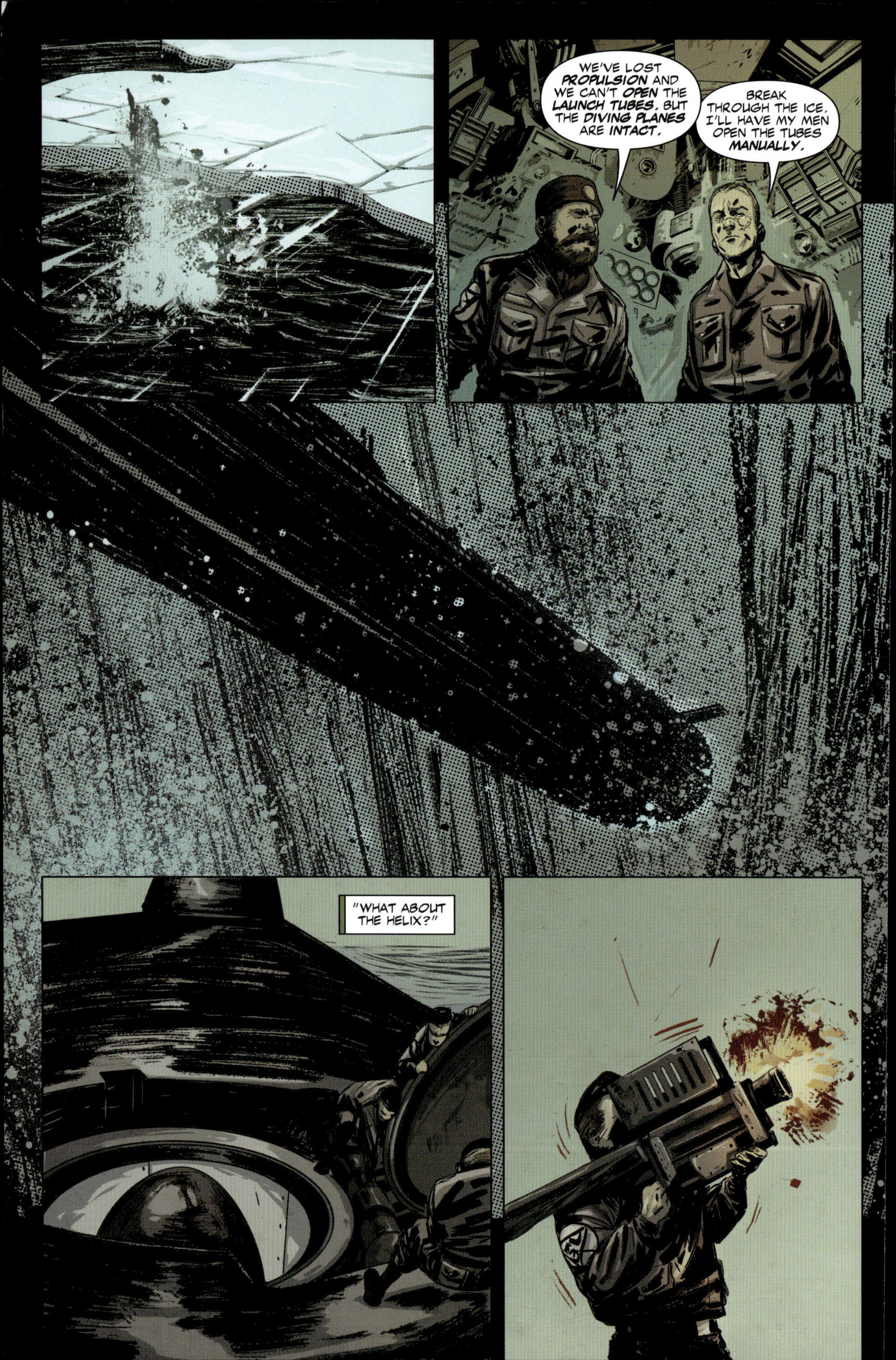
WE'VE LOST PROPULSION AND WE CAN'T OPEN THE LAUNCH TUBES, BUT THE DIVING PLANES ARE INTACT.
BREAK THROUGH THE ICE. I'LL HAVE MY MEN OPEN THE TUBES MANUALLY.
"WHAT ABOUT THE HELIX?"

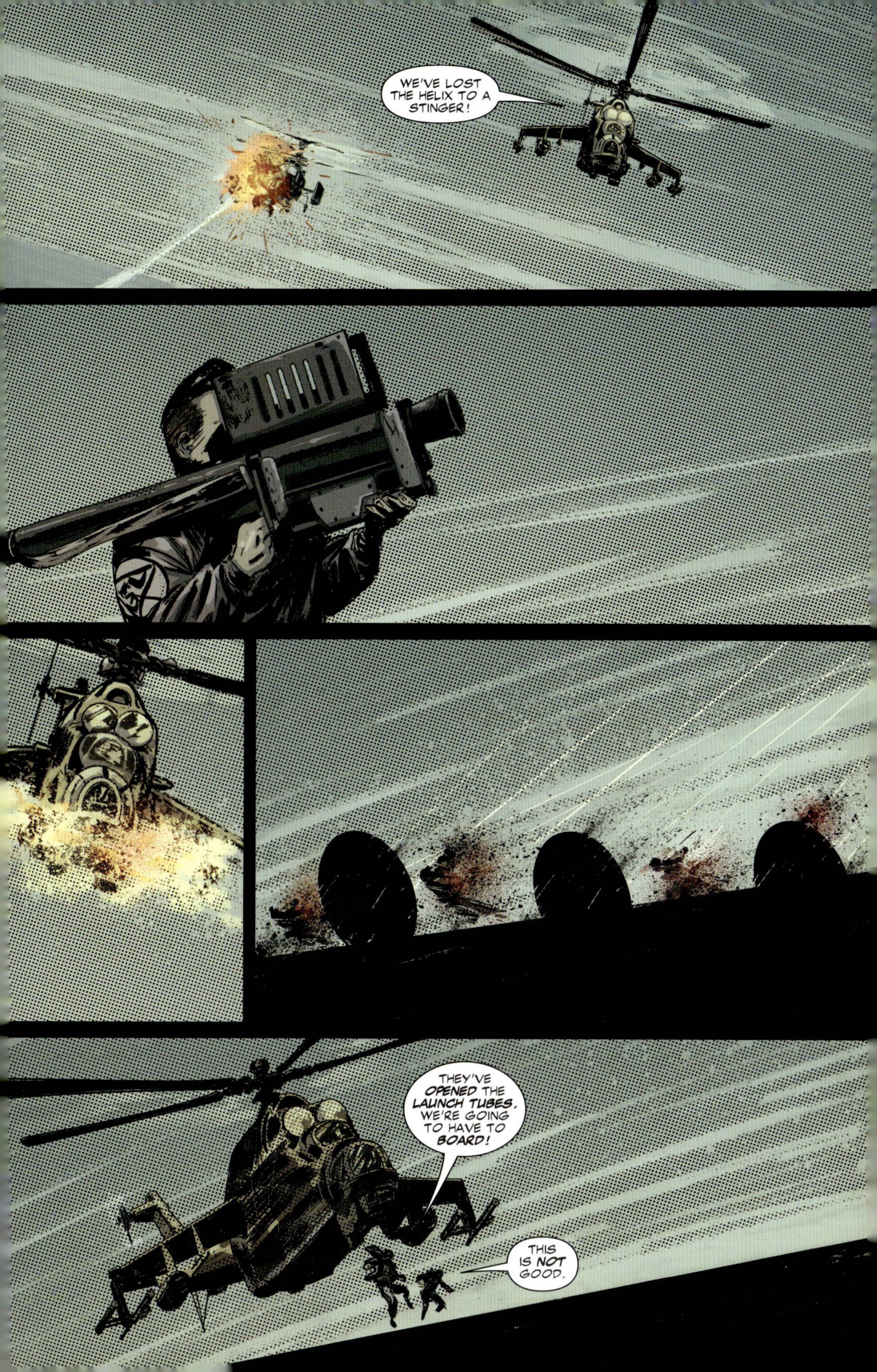
WE'VE LOST THE HELIX TO A STINGER!
THEY'VE OPENED THE LAUNCH TUBES. WE'RE GOING TO HAVE TO BOARD!
THIS IS NOT GOOD.

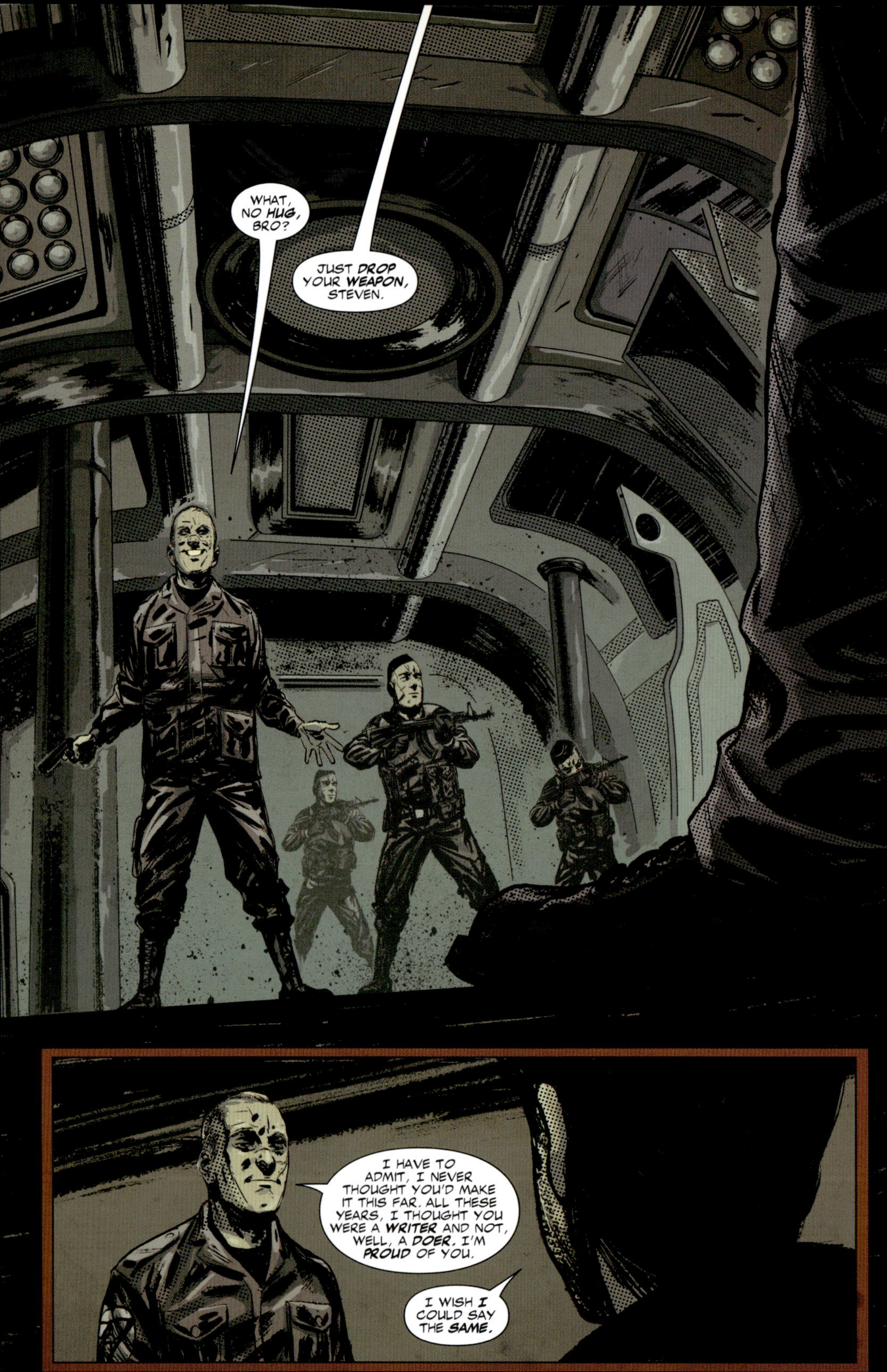
WHAT, NO HUG, BRO?
JUST DROP YOUR WEAPON, STEVEN.
I HAVE TO ADMIT, I NEVER THOUGHT YOU'D MAKE IT THIS FAR. ALL THESE YEARS, I THOUGHT YOU WERE A WRITER AND NOT, WELL, A DOER. I'M PROUD OF YOU.
I WISH I COULD SAY THE SAME.

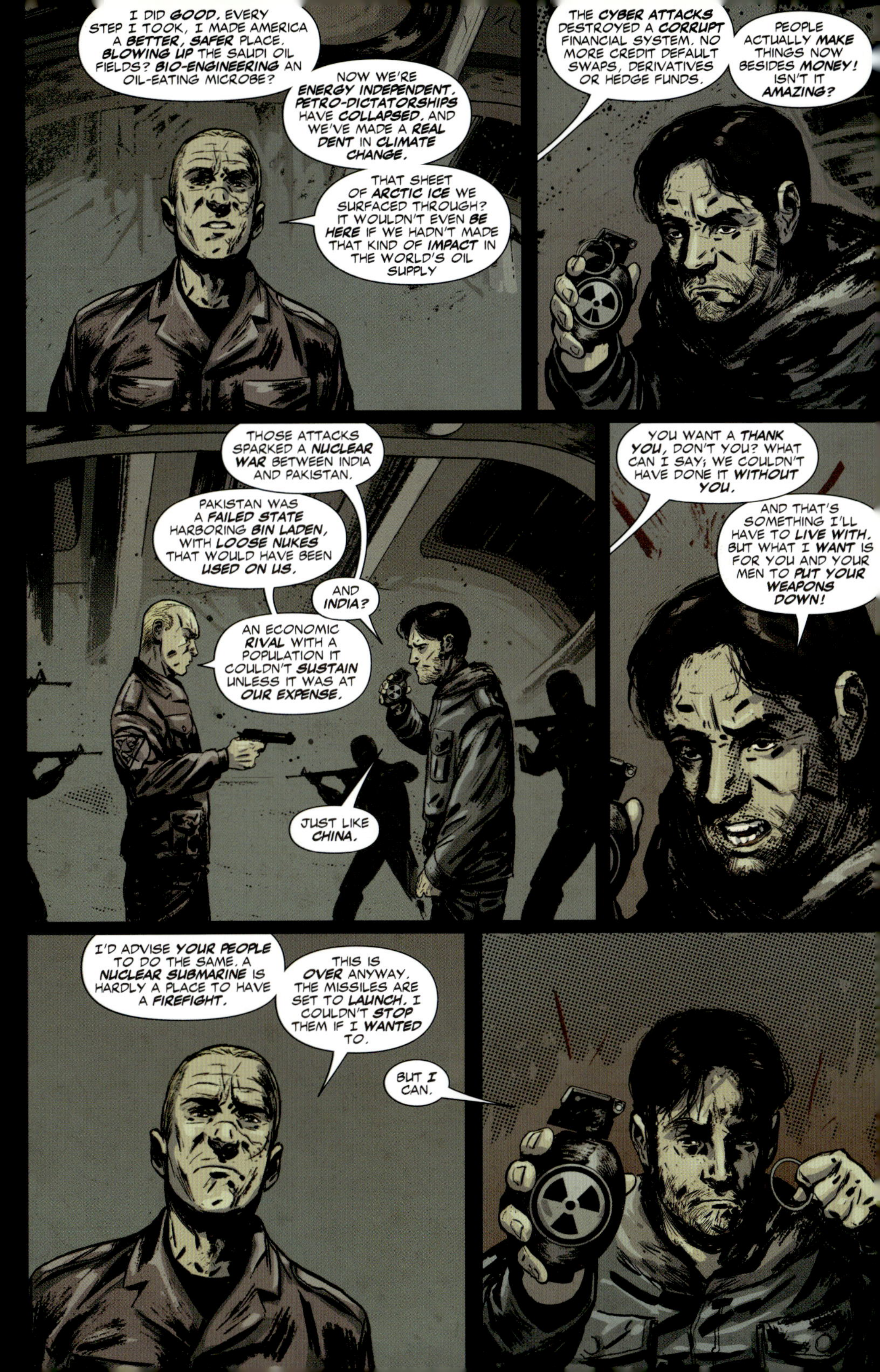
I DID GOOD. EVERY STEP I TOOK, I MADE AMERICA A BETTER, SAFER PLACE. BLOWING UP THE SAUDI OIL FIELDS? BIO-ENGINEERING AN OIL-EATING MICROBE?
NOW WE'RE ENERGY INDEPENDENT. PETRO-DICTATORSHIPS HAVE COLLAPSED, AND WE'VE MADE A REAL DENT IN CLIMATE CHANGE.
THAT SHEET OF ARCTIC ICE WE SURFACED THROUGH? IT WOULDN'T EVEN BE HERE IF WE HADN'T MADE THAT KIND OF IMPACT IN THE WORLD'S OIL SUPPLY
THE CYBER ATTACKS DESTROYED A CORRUPT FINANCIAL SYSTEM. NO MORE CREDIT DEFAULT SWAPS, DERIVATIVES OR HEDGE FUNDS.
PEOPLE ACTUALLY MAKE THINGS NOW BESIDES MONEY! ISN'T IT AMAZING?
THOSE ATTACKS SPARKED A NUCLEAR WAR BETWEEN INDIA AND PAKISTAN.
PAKISTAN WAS A FAILED STATE HARBORING BIN LADEN, WITH LOOSE NUKES THAT WOULD HAVE BEEN USED ON US.
AND INDIA?
AN ECONOMIC RIVAL WITH A POPULATION IT COULDN'T SUSTAIN UNLESS IT WAS AT OUR EXPENSE.
JUST LIKE CHINA.
YOU WANT A THANK YOU, DON'T YOU? WHAT CAN I SAY; WE COULDN'T HAVE DONE IT WITHOUT YOU.
AND THAT'S SOMETHING I'LL HAVE TO LIVE WITH. BUT WHAT I WANT IS FOR YOU AND YOUR MEN TO PUT YOUR WEAPONS DOWN!
I'D ADVISE YOUR PEOPLE TO DO THE SAME. A NUCLEAR SUBMARINE IS HARDLY A PLACE TO HAVE A FIREFIGHT.
THIS IS OVER ANYWAY. THE MISSILES ARE SET TO LAUNCH. I COULDN'T STOP THEM IF I WANTED TO.
BUT I CAN.

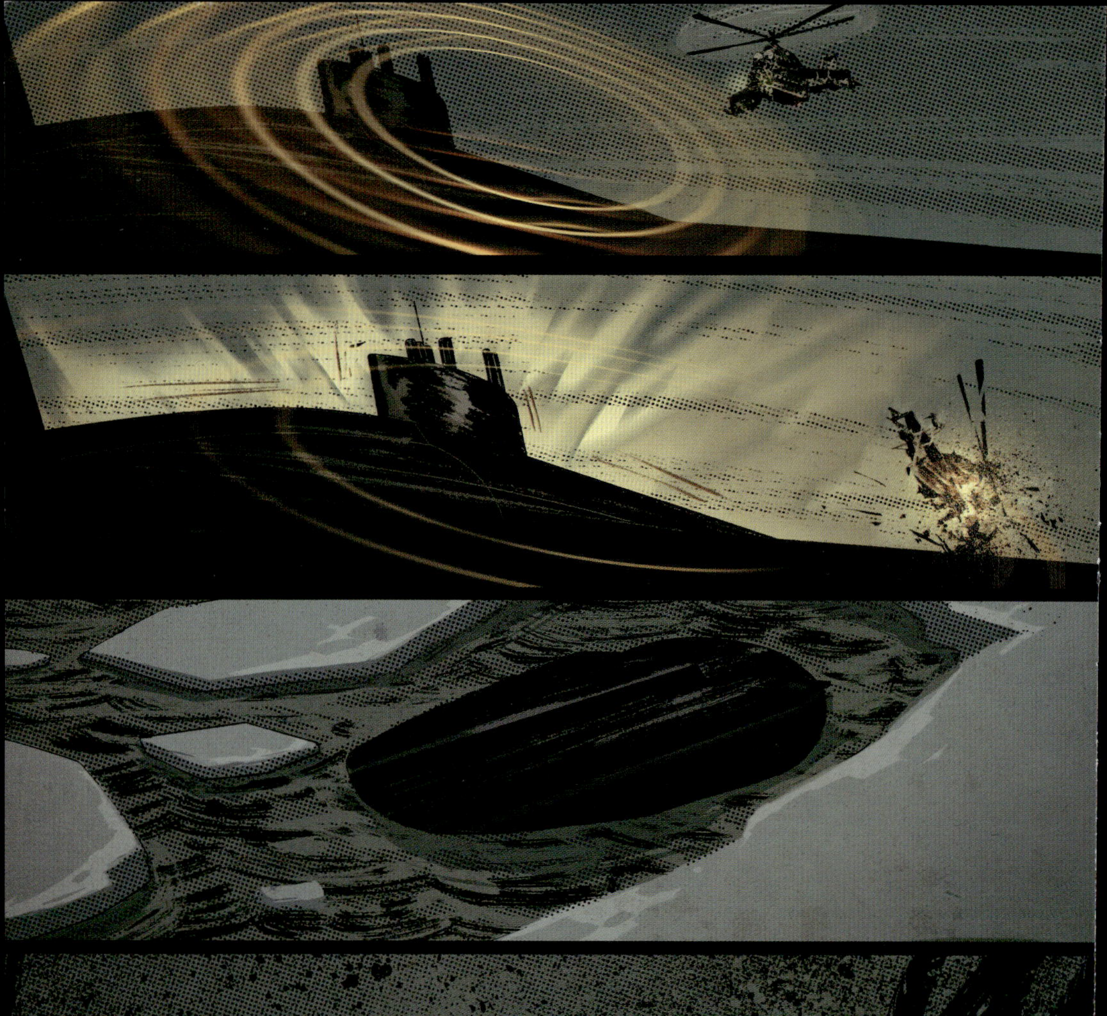

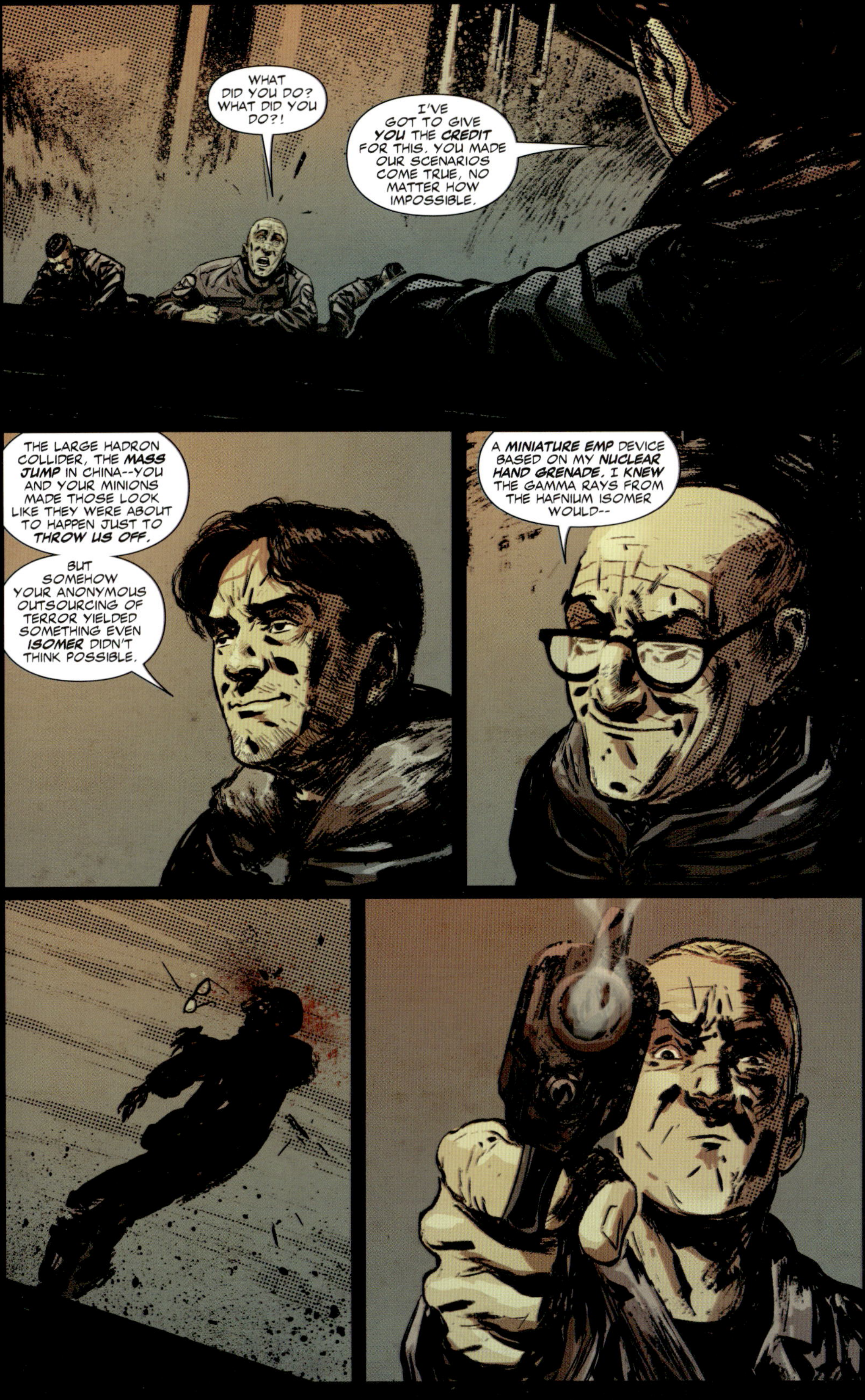
WHAT DID YOU DO? WHAT DID YOU DO?!
I'VE GOT TO GIVE YOU THE CREDIT FOR THIS. YOU MADE OUR SCENARIOS COME TRUE, NO MATTER HOW IMPOSSIBLE.
THE LARGE HADRON COLLIDER, THE MASS JUMP IN CHINA--YOU AND YOUR MINIONS MADE THOSE LOOK LIKE THEY WERE ABOUT TO HAPPEN JUST TO THROW US OFF.
BUT SOMEHOW YOUR ANONYMOUS OUTSOURCING OF TERROR YIELDED SOMETHING EVEN ISOMER DIDN'T THINK POSSIBLE.
A MINIATURE EMP DEVICE BASED ON MY NUCLEAR HAND GRENADE. I KNEW THE GAMMA RAYS FROM THE HAFNIUM ISOMER WOULD--

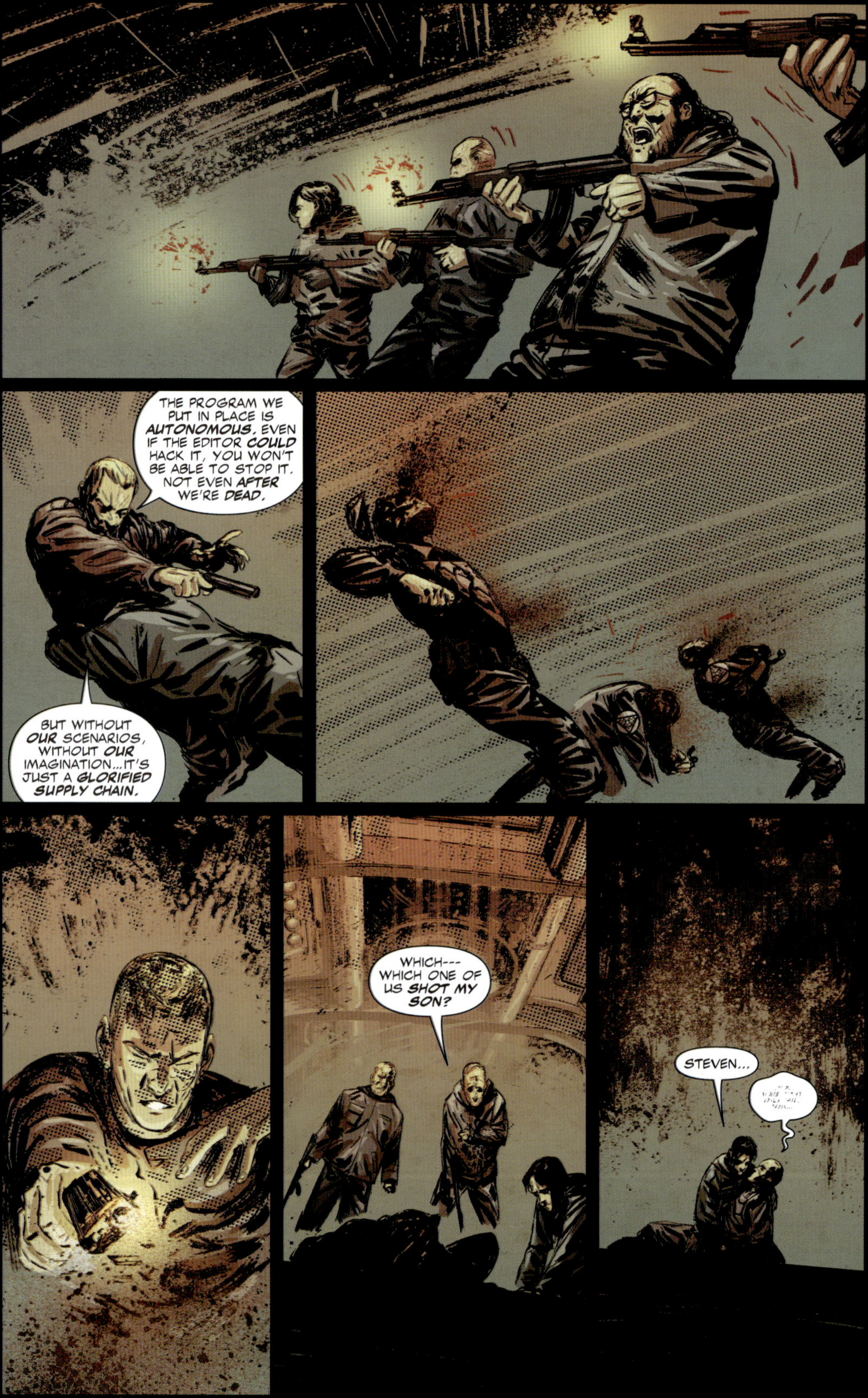
THE PROGRAM WE PUT IN PLACE IS AUTONOMOUS. EVEN IF THE EDITOR COULD HACK IT, YOU WON'T BE ABLE TO STOP IT. NOT EVEN AFTER WE'RE DEAD.
BUT WITHOUT OUR SCENARIOS, WITHOUT OUR IMAGINATION...IT'S JUST A GLORIFIED SUPPLY CHAIN.
WHICH--- WHICH ONE OF US SHOT MY SON?
STEVEN...

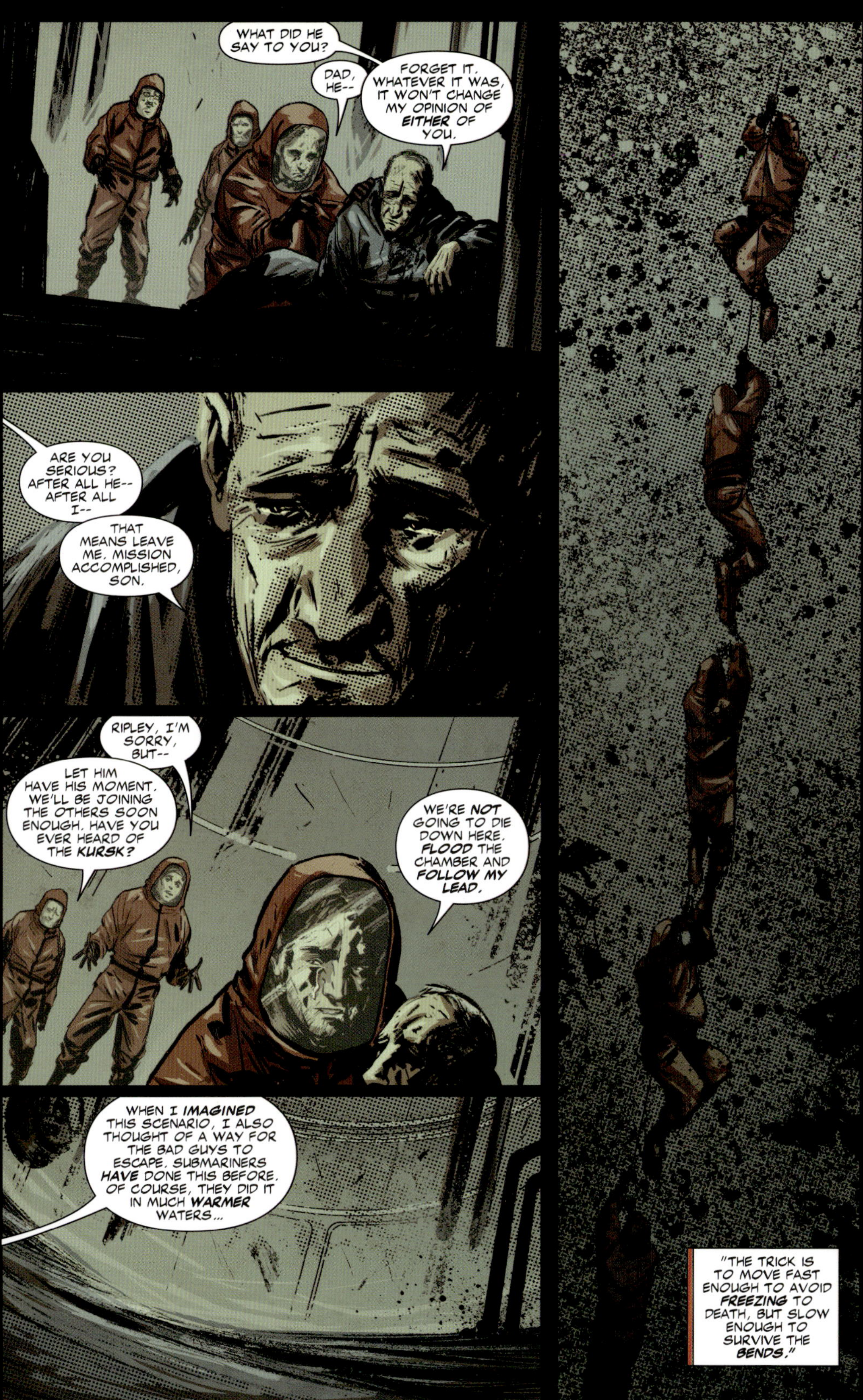
WHAT DID HE SAY TO YOU?
DAD, HE--
FORGET IT. WHATEVER IT WAS, IT WON'T CHANGE MY OPINION OF EITHER OF YOU.
ARE YOU SERIOUS? AFTER ALL HE-- AFTER ALL I--
THAT MEANS LEAVE ME. MISSION ACCOMPLISHED, SON.
RIPLEY, I'M SORRY, BUT--
LET HIM HAVE HIS MOMENT. WE'LL BE JOINING THE OTHERS SOON ENOUGH. HAVE YOU EVER HEARD OF THE KURSK?
WE'RE NOT GOING TO DIE DOWN HERE. FLOOD THE CHAMBER AND FOLLOW MY LEAD.
WHEN I IMAGINED THIS SCENARIO, I ALSO THOUGHT OF A WAY FOR THE BAD GUYS TO ESCAPE. SUBMARINERS HAVE DONE THIS BEFORE. OF COURSE, THEY DID IT IN MUCH WARMER WATERS...
"THE TRICK IS TO MOVE FAST ENOUGH TO AVOID FREEZING TO DEATH, BUT SLOW ENOUGH TO SURVIVE THE BENDS."

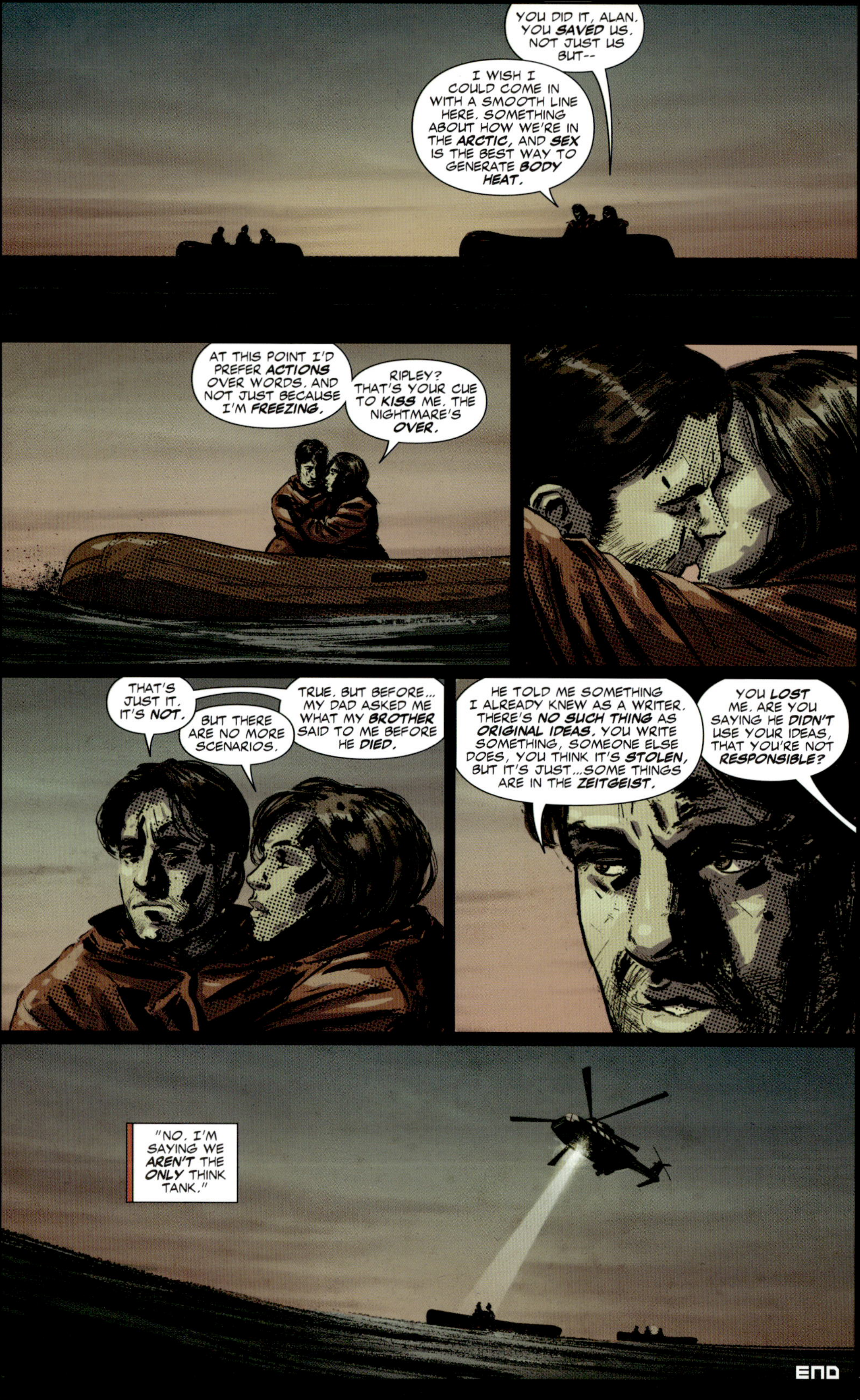
YOU DID IT, ALAN. YOU SAVED US. NOT JUST US BUT--
I WISH I COULD COME IN WITH A SMOOTH LINE HERE. SOMETHING ABOUT HOW WE'RE IN THE ARCTIC, AND SEX IS THE BEST WAY TO GENERATE BODY HEAT.
AT THIS POINT I'D PREFER ACTIONS OVER WORDS. AND NOT JUST BECAUSE I'M FREEZING.
RIPLEY? THAT'S YOUR CUE TO KISS ME. THE NIGHTMARE'S OVER.
THAT'S JUST IT. IT'S NOT.
BUT THERE ARE NO MORE SCENARIOS.
TRUE. BUT BEFORE... MY DAD ASKED ME WHAT MY BROTHER SAID TO ME BEFORE HE DIED.
HE TOLD ME SOMETHING I ALREADY KNEW AS A WRITER. THERE'S NO SUCH THING AS ORIGINAL IDEAS. YOU WRITE SOMETHING, SOMEONE ELSE DOES, YOU THINK IT'S STOLEN, BUT IT'S JUST...SOME THINGS ARE IN THE ZEITGEIST.
YOU LOST ME. ARE YOU SAYING HE DIDN'T USE YOUR IDEAS, THAT YOU'RE NOT RESPONSIBLE?
"NO. I'M SAYING WE AREN'T THE ONLY THINK TANK."
END

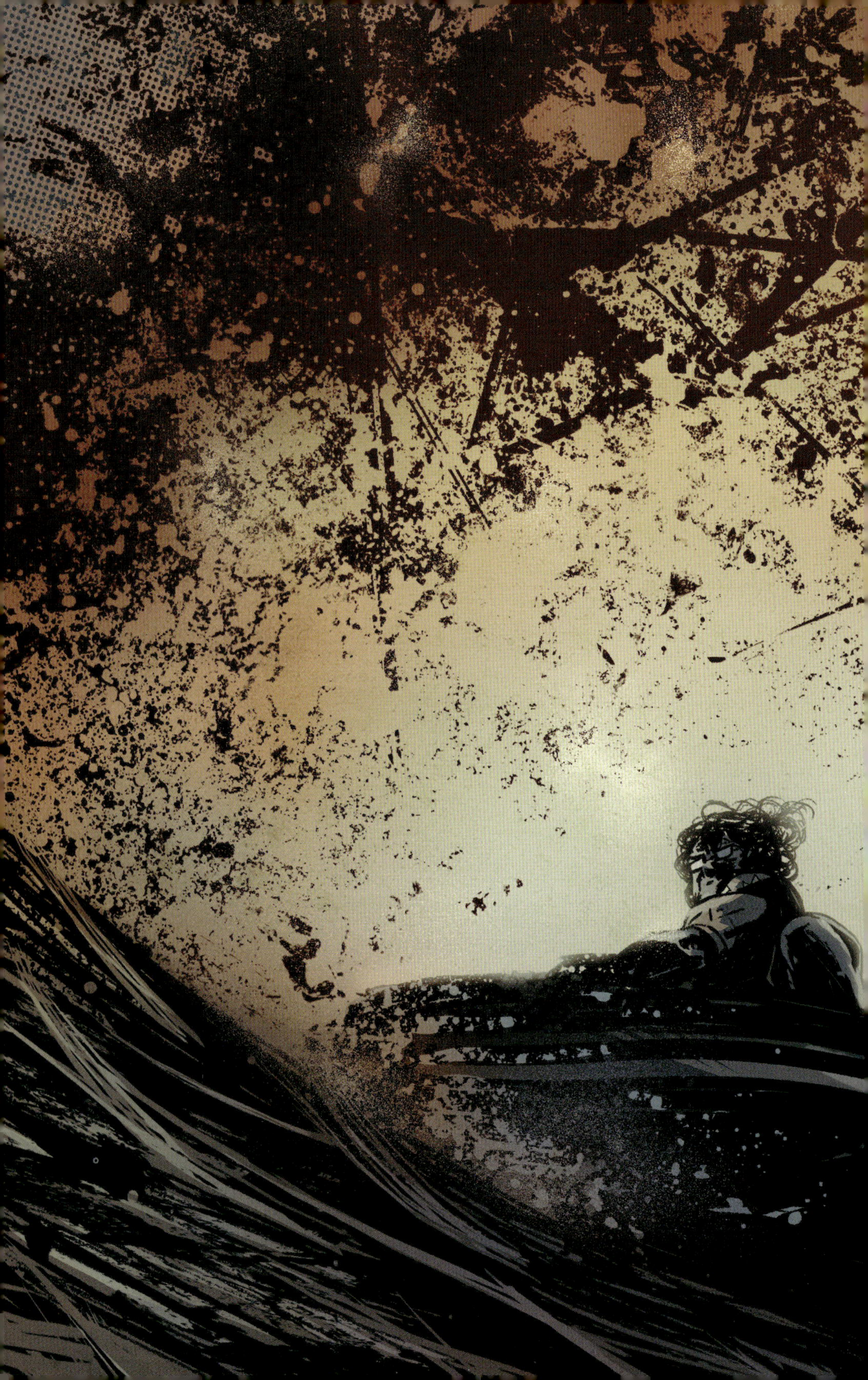

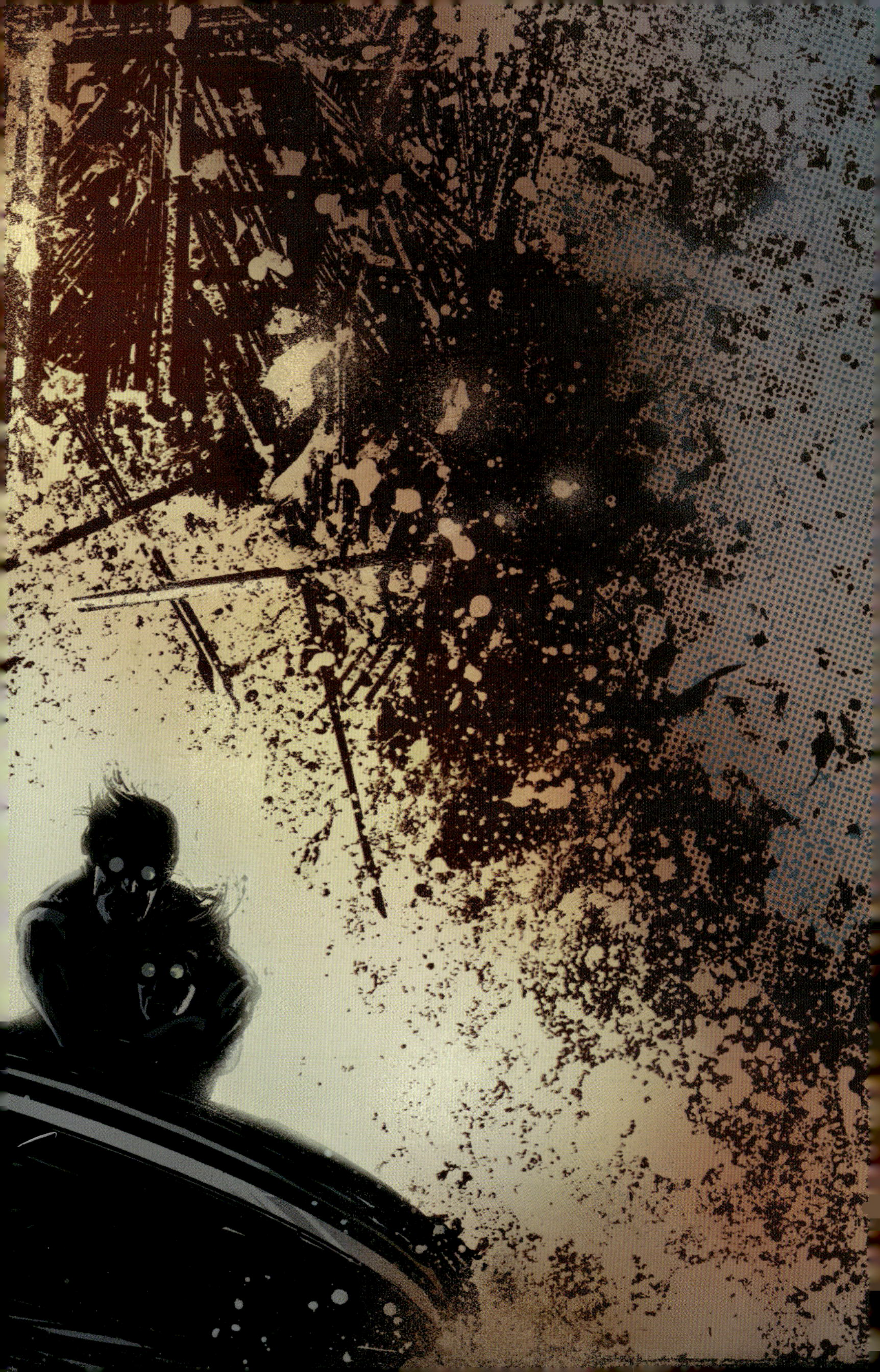

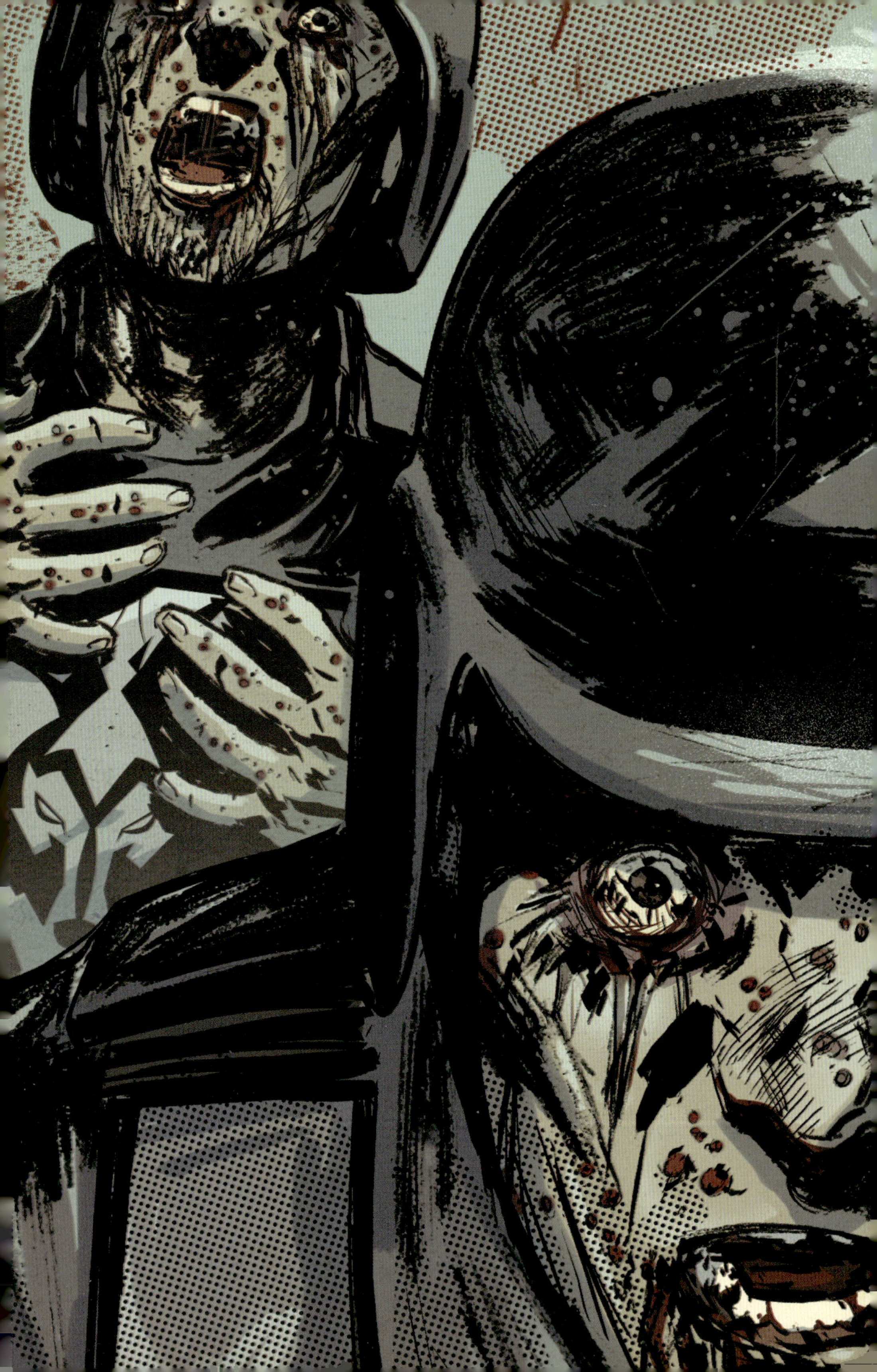